Smuggle

JUI

CU00855398

www.j

www.smuggleddiamonds.com

SYNOPSIS

Holidaying on the beautiful island of Majorca with his parents and 13-year old sister Becky, 11-year old Steve Parker accepts an invitation from 12-year old Majorcan Maria to go to see the massive Black vultures nesting in the cliffs. And becomes swiftly embroiled with a dangerous gang of diamond smugglers with links to international terrorism and corruption in high places.

Published by:

VAN MIERS
PRODUCTION$

First published 2013 by Van Miers Productions
Re-Printed June 2013
Third Floor, 207 Regent Street London W1B 3HH
www.vanmiersproductions.com

ISBN 978-0-9576751-0-0

Visit: www.juliahands.com for further details of new releases etc.

ACKNOWLEDGEMENTS

With thanks to the Warden at Dalkeith Country Park,
The Harbour Master at Leith and the taxi driver
who answered my questions.

Illustrations by: Peter Wilks

SMUGGLED DIAMONDS

PART ONE: MAJORCA

CHAPTER ONE
The Festival

In mid-July, in the still, increasingly hot mid-morning on the Spanish island of Majorca, Maria Munos, a pretty twelve-year-old Majorcan girl, was waiting to join in the main pageant of a very old fishing festival. This year they were starting the festival in the morning instead of the evening, so it would be easier for younger children and people with disabilities to take part. Although fish stocks around the island were dwindling and people didn't do so much fishing as they used to from Puerto Pollensa, the old fishing port on the northern edge of the island where she lived, they still held the festival in honour of the patron saint of seafarers and fishermen.

Unlike the fish, tourists were in plentiful supply. They lined the main square where she was waiting with a group of traditional Majorcan dancers, and thronged the streets, decorated with bunting, leading off it. Maria's brother Pablo, who'd just joined the local police force, was helping to direct the traffic. He was medium height, with a very upright bearing and wavy, dark auburn-brown hair.

Maria was wearing her traditional Majorcan costume - a brightly coloured tiered skirt with flounced edges, and a fringed white lace shawl made by her grandmother across her embroidered blouse. The girls all wore large trumpet-shaped hibiscus flowers in their hair – the other girls had pink ones but her grandmother had selected a white flower for her long, thick black hair, so they could spot her in the procession. Maria was trying to refasten the pin of the old brooch which pinned her shawl at the shoulder. She couldn't refasten it, but any minute now the band of traditional old Majorcan instruments - including one like the Scottish bagpipes - would strike up a tune in front of her group of dancers and she'd have to start processing through the narrow streets of the old port. The brooch was a big, old silver traditional one - in the form of three fan-shaped leaves tied together with a ribbon - belonging to her mother, and before that, to <u>her</u> mother. The strong pin kept coming loose from its clasp because it was very old, and there was a lot of material to take up in the shawl; perhaps also, Maria realised, her great-grandmother hadn't pinned it for her at the right angle, with her arthritic hands, in the first place. Her mother hadn't had time to help her dress today, as she was very busy working in their shop which was a favourite with tourists.

As the tambourinist and the pipes player - the last musicians to take up their positions in the band - started to stroll over to the procession from the other side of the square, Maria still hadn't managed to fasten her brooch. The crowd lining the sides of the square was becoming excited, leaning – and moving - forwards. On the left hand side, she recognised her brother Pablo directing some youths, who were standing in the street, back onto the pavement. Maria decided there was time to ask him to refasten the brooch for her, and breaking out of the line of the procession, ran over quickly to him. "Trust my kid sister to be making a fuss!" Pablo laughed as he refastened the brooch for her. "There! Hurry back or they'll start without you. I can keep my eye on you with that white flower in your hair! And I've a good mind to direct your part of the procession down into the sea with the boats!" he teased, before turning back to face the crowds. Several old fishing boats, highly decorated for the festival, were being paraded behind the band and the dancers. The people nearby were laughing and smiling, but as Maria also turned to go back to her place in the procession she heard, and saw, someone towards the front of the crowd threaten her brother under his breath.

She noticed the man because he was scowling, yet not because he had the sun in his eyes – he was wearing very dark sunglasses. Very slim, in his thirties, medium height, and wearing a white shirt, he had blond hair and a lean, tanned face with quite a long, thin pale pink scar running down one cheek. When he hissed through his teeth: "Not here, police-boy!" in Spanish to Pablo, she shivered, even in the intensifying heat of the morning. Her brother ignored the threat, and hadn't noticed who'd made it anyway. The band struck up the first few notes of a lively tune and the voice of the crowd surged up, then died down again to a murmur as they listened, and Maria hurried back to begin the procession.

The threat from the blond man had unnerved her. She looked nervously about her instead of smiling directly at the crowds of people as she walked across the main square, where Steve Parker, who was holidaying with his parents and sister Becky, was sitting out on the largest café terrace. Several parasols had already been put up to give some shade. From here you could get a really good view of the procession as it passed through the square.

Steve was eleven, with soft brown eyes and hair; slim-faced with a reasonably ordinary nose and a jawline which could sometimes become quite square when he was feeling determined about something. He tanned with less difficulty in the strong Spanish sunshine than his thirteen-year-old sister, but was wearing long navy shorts and a short-sleeved cream cotton shirt nevertheless. He had a lively interest in natural history and conservation, which his sister teased as being over-enthusiastic. But he could be very determined. Like his father, who tanned fairly easily and was also enjoying the sunshine, he'd pushed his sunglasses up over his forehead under the shade of the parasol.

Becky's blue eyes were staring at him stubbornly under her white sun hat (which she was wearing to stop her face getting any pinker, anticipating the midday sun). Through her sunglasses. "But who wants to go and wait about while you stare through the binoculars for ages at some silly seabirds?" she was insisting, tucking her straight blond hair behind her ears. They were discussing what they could do after the processions had passed by. She wanted to watch the folk dances the whole afternoon. Everything he wanted to do she had vetoed so far, giving some excuse like "*I'm* too old for that", or, "How silly!"

"They're <u>not</u> silly seabirds," replied Steve, trying to reply airily and not let his annoyance show: "they're black vultures, and they're <u>very</u> rare." He'd been reminded by his mother not to reply to Becky that she was boring. (But his jaw was beginning to square off.)

"There are hundreds of species of vultures, daddy told me", Becky cited her father's authority with a smug smile and nod of the head. "Who cares if some of them are black!" And she took a sip of her iced lemonade through her drinking straw.

Steve felt like reaching over and pulling her hair hard, but instead started swinging his leg under the table to relieve his irritation. His jaw stayed just as it was. He added: "Apparently they've started nesting on the cliffs here. They've got a three metre wingspan, massive beaks and those big ruffles of feathers round their necks. They look really good spiralling up on a current of hot air in the sky - they hardly need to flap their wings!"

Becky was oblivious. He wished one would swoop down and snatch the sausage off her plate. She'd been quick to announce that she didn't like the taste, but she wasn't going to offer hers to <u>him</u>, even though he'd finished his very quickly and really enjoyed it.

Their father Chris Parker joined in. He was a businessman taking a break from work, still in the process of mentally unwinding on holiday. He was already enjoying not being at the beck and call of lots of people on the phone, and had decided to keep his mobile switched off for most of the time. Wearing a short-sleeved blue shirt and white trousers, he had a broad face, light brown hair and fairly round blue eyes. He'd tried to book a holiday for the spring when the bird watching groups were organised, but hadn't managed to get enough time off work until July. By now, the weather was very hot and he didn't want his holiday spoiled by disputes between his son and daughter. "There aren't many black vultures in the world, you know, Becky," he negotiated, running his hand through his hair and smiling at her hopefully with a frank expression.

"And only one person as idiotic as Steve," she said.

Their mother Pat was sitting next to Steve, diagonally opposite Becky. She rarely wore a hat when she was outdoors back in England, but now sported a sunhat. She looked at both of them with her blue eyes appealing over the rims of her sunglasses, deciding to intercede. "Let's discuss it later," she suggested, leaning forward elegantly on an elbow, with her hand holding her chin in a calm, wise gesture, "but we should certainly stay and watch the first few dances. They're quite spectacular – especially the flamenco dancers!"

Steve was getting a closer look at the men's shirts, which had rows of big ruffles on the sleeves to accentuate their dance movements, made with their arms up in the air. "Sure," he said, sarcastically, "<u>aren't</u> they? In red and orange <u>frilly blouses</u>??!!" - catching Maria's eye as she walked past and making her grin. (She was a spirited girl and couldn't stay intimidated by the blond man's threat for very long.) She rescued her sudden grin by calmly blinking with big, black eyelashes: it turned into a more decorous smile. Steve grinned back.

"And the men look really dramatic in their black trousers and hats," his mother insisted, to stop him saying anything else rude when the '*oferta*' - as the traditional religious Majorcan dancers are called – came round.

Steve was laughing now and had lost the momentum of his argument in favour of seeing the black vultures. He'd realised Maria had understood his remark, and was wondering who else in the procession might have done. But the old, white-haired Majorcan couple who'd come and sat down at the table adjacent to them seemed to be the only others. The sprightly old Majorcan man had lots of lines on his face and generous laughter crinkles around his faded brown eyes. He'd been listening to Steve as he'd remarked on the men's "blouses", and suddenly began laughing as he was drinking his glass of wine, and nearly started spluttering. In fact, he was Maria's great-grandfather. When he was younger he had run their shop, much frequented by English tourists; selling clothes, amongst other things … and he understood English perfectly. (He and his wife, who wore her hair in a small bun and was wearing her shawl for the festival, had just given directions to some American tourists, in quite good English.)

Steve decided he could remain in this congenial atmosphere; until, after an hour or so, the main pageantry of the procession round the old part of town, the flamenco dancing and the *oferta* dances, were all over. He now tried to commandeer a renewed debate about the vultures with Becky, which was <u>nearly</u> breaking into an argument. "But I <u>must</u> see them," he was contending, just as Maria approached the adjacent table, with two other Majorcan girls in traditional costume. Her great-grandparents had been reserving places for them at their table. Becky hadn't seen the costumes close up and instead of replying to her brother, turned round to look at them.

The Majorcan girls exchanged greetings with Maria's great-grandparents and Steve decided that the traditional Majorcan costume looked rather better on girls than it did on boys. Then Maria's great-grandfather politely asked Mr Parker in English if he'd mind taking a photograph of them all at the table, suddenly producing an old camera. Mr Parker, keen to show off the Spanish he'd learned at their evening classes, replied *"De nada"* - not exactly the right words for "not at all" on the island of Majorca, where they speak Mallorqui and Catalan, but Spanish all right and perfectly understood. After he'd taken the photo, Maria's great-grandfather thanked him and said: "Please allow me to introduce us to you. I am Josep Munos and this is my wife Anna-Maria; and my great- granddaughter Maria; her friends Manolita and Luisa." Maria and Manolita, a fairly plump girl with wavy chestnut hair and blue eyes, gave bright smiles, while Luisa, slim with long straight hair, nodded crisply and said: *"Bon dia!"*, Majorcan for "Good day!" Mr Parker then introduced himself, Chris; his wife Pat and children Steve and Becky.

They were all in a very good humour, except for Becky - who still wasn't sure whether she was going to be 'dragged off' to watch the vultures, and looked a little reticent. Mr Parker, deciding to try out a mixture of Spanish and Catalan, said: *"Hay muy bien el festa"*, "I like the festival very much", hoping this would be understood by the Mallorquin-speaking islanders. He had to raise his voice a little for Maria's great-grandfather, who was a little deaf.

Marias's great-grandmother, Senora Anna-Maria Munos, replied carefully in English: "It's an old festival. Apart from the day of the boat procession, it's not so religious any more." Mr Parker was smiling broadly as he ensured his daughter's sausage wasn't left to waste, by eating it himself. The old lady leaned towards him: "But we still pray to the saint," she said in a distinct Majorcan accent. "I understand", said Mrs Parker in Catalan.

The old lady then asked Steve: *"Hace mucho el festa?"* ("Do you like the festival?").

She had a kind face. Unfortunately, Steve hadn't bothered to learn his Catalan and Spanish phrases, and could only reply *"Lo siento, no entiendo Espanol"* (I'm sorry, I don't understand Spanish"). Before his father could translate for him, Maria helped Steve: "That means, 'Are you enjoying the festival?'" she said in a very good English accent, and smiled at him. He wished he'd learned his phrases now, and replied slowly in English: "Yes."

"Yes?" Maria repeated and paused politely.

"And now I want to see the birds on the cliffs - the black vultures".

Because her parents spent a lot of time in the shop giving directions and discussing the local sights with tourists, Maria, who often helped them, had learned lots of English phrases. *"Ah, si,"* she said enthusiastically, *"los voltors!"* - as they called the black vultures locally.

"But I don't know where exactly they are on the coast," pursued Steve fervently as his sister's face started to fall. "It's a long coastline." The Parkers had only been in the resort two days and hadn't yet made any enquiries about the environmentally protected vultures.

"They're just along the coast, on the cliffs on the other side of the peninsula." Maria pointed across the square, beyond the sandy beach with its rows of modern hotels, to a promenade with a path leading off it up the side of the headland. There were a few similar rugged grey cliffs on this side of the peninsula, and Steve could picture them on the other side. "You can walk to them from here," she added.

"Oh really!" he was delighted.

"We can show them to you," Maria offered smilingly, to the Parkers.

"But I'm not interested!" Becky protested to her parents. She was sulking a little in the presence of the Majorcan girls, who were wearing such pretty dresses and flowers in their hair, whilst she had a sunburned face.

Maria went quiet, and then said to Steve: "We can take you to see them now, if you like!"

Mr Parker realised it might be a good idea to get his son's interest in the vultures satisfied while there was the opportunity of doing so, without forcing Becky on an excursion she wasn't interested in. He and his wife Pat could afford to give seeing them a miss, if it stopped the children squabbling. Anyway, they could go to see the rare vultures themselves later on, if they could find something else for Steve and Becky to do together. So he suggested that Steve accompany Maria there after lunch at the café, "…if someone else goes with them too." Maria's great-grandparents agreed this was a good idea, and stayed on at the café too, to discuss it, while her friends Manolita and Luisa had to go home to get changed.

Maria's great-grandmother now suggested, in English: "I think it's a good idea, if my husband - he walks behind them, to the cliffs, to er……make sure they are all right. There are no hotels there…..not many people."

The Parkers agreed. The old lady added: "There is a balustrade - rails, yes?"

"Railings?" helped Mrs Parker.

"*Si*, railings." She pronounced it with emphasis. "They must walk …..*detras de?*" she asked her husband for the word, which he supplied: "behind the railings - only. *Solamente*." She emphasized this with a quick sideways cutting motion of her old hand. "Behind the railings..."

"And from there, you can see the vultures," added her husband, "but don't approach them!"

"And they should return within an hour", said the old lady. "We will all stay here."

"No talking to strangers," completed Mrs Parker.

"Brilliant," said Steve.

Becky was pleased as well. They had got rid of Steve for a while.

Maria and Steve set off, not too fast as they were being followed by Great-Granpa Munos, who had a slight limp after a wound he'd received at the end of the Spanish Civil War. Once out of the main square, they still found crowds everywhere – choking the streets of the port and congregating around the marina, looking at a few old fishing boats moored there which weren't being taken out to sea. But gradually, as the youngsters made their way along the promenade towards the promontory, the numbers of people – Majorcans and tourists – decreased. There weren't so many people on the beaches that day because of the festival, and fewer mopeds buzzing about.

As they came to the dry, stony path which began at the foot of the headland, Maria turned to wave to her great-grandfather, who was a little way behind. He waved back. They started the ascent up the gentle, lowest part of the slopes, where the grass, dotted with bushes of pink-flowered heather, was becoming very dry.   "I hope you won't spoil your festival dress on the ground," Steve said to Maria, pointing to where it was dipping onto the grass. "It doesn't matter," she said, "it will be washed… anyway because of the …" (she searched for the word, waving her hand in the air) "…dust. There's a lot of dust from the procession!" Steve recalled that there <u>had</u> been a lot of dust thrown up from the procession in the square. Now the sky was a lovely clear turquoise colour and the sea a dazzling deep blue. He took a deep breath. It was very pleasant to be able to go exploring without being constrained by his family, fond as he was of all of them, he thought.

Once they were well away from anyone else, Maria explained: "The black vultures used to nest in the pine trees by the cliff tops. But now, they are nesting right on the front of the cliffs –"

"On the cliff face," Steve supplied. "The part of the cliffs going down to the sea, we call the cliff face." He pointed to a rock ledge, and along it left to right. "On the ledges of the cliffs, not in the trees."

"We don't know why," she said.

As they carried on up the gently winding path, higher up the side of the headland, Steve could see the huge mountain ranges beyond, of a bluey-purple colour and misty at the tops. The wildflowers were proliferating on the steeper slopes - yellow, pink and white rockroses, and rosemary plants with blue flowers, which Maria pointed out to him: "You use it for cooking lamb," she explained, and he recognised the smell when he trod on their leaves and they released a pungent aroma.   As they moved on, a white goat came over and started nibbling the plants. A few seconds later, Steve gasped as a little, golden-brown lizard slithered away from his feet and under a rock, but Maria had seen them many times. It was getting hotter further into the afternoon.

Once they gained the top of the promontory, they were looking down into a beautiful little valley, the Boquer Valley, in the Peninsula de Formentor. Along its sides, there were gorges edged with pine trees and orange and lemon groves - Steve could smell the sweetness of the fruit drifting up towards him. He could also hear the very high-pitched, musical twitterings of songbirds: some were fluttering about the bright-yellow-flowering broom bushes nearby, while others were soaring up high into the sky. In the distance was an old farm, with zigzagging old dry stone walls separating the almond trees from the terraces of ancient olive groves, with their silvery grey foliage and gnarled, twisted trunks.

"My family were farmers here before we had a shop…" said Maria, pointing out the almond trees. "These are very pretty in January and February - they have pink and white flowers."

Steve was glad Becky wasn't there to spoil it by complaining about something.

They made their way down the slope, descending into the valley, having to push carefully past some dwarf palms with sharp, sword-like leaves. Steve held these aside for Maria so they wouldn't catch on her dress. The deeper, cooing notes of wood pigeons could be heard further down. Steve saw the biggest daisies he'd ever seen, and orchids, which he knew were rare plants in Majorca too because his mother had told him. A gorgeous swallowtail butterfly was floating about on the island breeze, and several small blue ones were fluttering from flower to flower. "This is the most beautiful place I've ever been to," he declared.

"I love it very much too," said Maria. "Do you see these trees?" and she pointed to one of the tall, dark evergreen Holm Oak trees that were growing there. "They stay alive for hundreds of years. The trees give very hard wood for burning. What do you call the black wood, when it is…has burned, please?"

"Charcoal," said Steve, grateful that he could help her with some words, since she was trying so hard speaking in English and he was speaking no Catalan, not even any Spanish.

"Charcoal," she repeated. "And also, they give these," she picked up a twig from the ground which had just fallen from the trees, with an early, tiny green acorn on it: "for pigs to eat, in the winter." Then she pulled off a loose strip of bark from the tree. "And this bark was used in the process of making clothes of leather."

Steve was fascinated. But they mustn't forget old Senor Munos. He turned round and looked back up the slope, and saw the old man picking his way past the dwarf palm trees. "Let's wait here for your great-grandfather." he said.

Maria turned round as well and beckoned her great-grandfather on in a big gesture. "*Venga, venga!*" she was saying, 'Come on!' "It's not now far to the cliffs, Steve, you can see."

And she pointed up the far slope of the valley and through a little grove of deciduous trees to some pine trees, growing right along the cliff edge, where the black vultures had usually nested.

When old Senor Munos caught up with them at the top of the far slope, he needed to rest. It was very hot, so they walked on a little into the shade of the deciduous grove. He sat down on a log and wiped his forehead with a handkerchief, remembering the days when as young men they would leave their farming tools lying in the grass while they took a break. Then he said in English to both youngsters: "There's the cliff top – all along, where the pine trees are...." and pointed to it. "Stay behind the railings. I will watch you from here. And stay away from the vultures: they are very... fierce now, aggressive, when they protect their chicks!" Then he added again, in Mallorqui to Maria, "You go on ahead to the cliffs. Don't forget to stay behind the railings! I'll stay here and think about the old times!"

Steve and Maria walked on, and emerging from the little grove of trees, came to a flat, dry stretch of grass with pine trees. In one or two of the pine trees, there were the signs of nest-building which had been started, then abandoned, in its early stages. Maria pointed up to the clusters of very large twigs and small branches. "You see where the Vultures were <u>usually</u> building their nests…" They walked over towards the huge set of cliffs. Along the edge of them, was a thin black railing.

The grass growing up to the edge of the cliffs was sparse, disappearing into crevices and fissures in the hard grey rock which jutted into the sea with waves churning a hundred metres or so below around its base. Steve and Maria walked towards the railings and, leaning carefully over them to look down over the edge, noticed the iron was starting to rust at the joints, and that these had been loosened a little in their concrete setting. Neither of them trusted the railings not to give way and they both withdrew their weight from them. (Maria's great-grandparents hadn't been there since last year, when the railings had seemed strong enough.) "Be careful!" said Maria.

Starting off with thirty or so new steps at the top of the cliff, a rather narrow, sandy path, quite steep in places, led down to a cove with a little shingle beach. She noticed some sturdy new railings had been added very recently, to follow the line of the path down as far as the steps. At the top of the path was a turnstile gate set in the old railings, and around it grew several broom bushes.

They both noticed five men with two motorboats, pulled up on the shore of the cove: one quite old, painted white and yellow with a lot of standing room; the other a large, expensive-looking bright red speedboat. Two of the men were sitting in the old boat listening to the other three – who were standing around discussing something, as one of them pulled out his mobile to answer it. None of the men's features were discernible from that distance, but one stood out as he was very large, fat, and wearing black; another was quite tall. One of the men sitting in the old boat, stockily built, was now shaking his head. Out to sea on the western, Puerto Pollensa side of the promontory there was a little flotilla of decorated fishing boats and some pleasure boats, assembled for games to take place later on, as part of the festival. All around this the sea was speckled with yachts.

Although the water in the little cove was sparkling in the hot sun and clear enough for swimming, there was a fair amount of debris on the beach and there was no-one else there… just the five men with the two motorboats, whom Steve assumed were going to take part in the games.

Steve pointed down at the cliff face. "There are lots of big white splashes down the rock!" (Maria called it 'guano'.) "And look! Look at those old nests!" There were several vast, disused nests made of dry vegetation and small tree branches on ledges in the cliff face. They were too large for any other type of bird but vultures.

"Yes," said Maria, "this is where the black vultures are nesting – if you listen you can hear the nests further along do have baby vultures... they'll start crying when this one comes back, look!" And she pointed to a black vulture returning to its nest, coming up behind them in the distance.

It was a little cooler right on the coast and a breeze was picking up, ruffling the feathers around the vulture's neck as it circled now only a few metres away from them, lowering huge talons as it gradually came down to the nest. It was the most colossal bird Steve had ever seen, with a huge wingspan; a big, thick, vicious-looking bill just visible from that distance, and broad wings, black as night, curving to the 'fingered' tips. It looked very sinister against the bright sky as it planed down. "Look, Maria!" he then shouted, pointing in tremendous excitement at some more vultures, several metres above the cliff tops. They'd been following in from further inland, and now started wheeling down in ever tighter circles, fairly warily - they could obviously see the youngsters by the railings.

Then the first vulture started to fly a little out to sea, spiralling upwards again. "They don't like us being so near their nests," explained Maria. The birds would probably have preferred a deserted beach and cliff top, but were gradually getting used to the presence of conservationists. "The rest may come here in a small... crowd?.....you know..."

"Flock," supplied Steve.

"Yes - when they're feeding their chicks. We have to go now!"

Old Senor Munos had also sighted the vultures in the distance. Confident that Maria and Steve would stay behind the cliff top railings as they'd been warned, he decided to take his eyes off them for a while and reach in his pockets for his pipe and tobacco: to reminisce for ten minutes or so on farming in the old days.

Steve considered it was still 'within the letter of the law' of his parents' instruction not to go beyond the railings along the cliff tops, if he went down the path steps with the <u>new</u> railings, to take a closer look at the nests.

"Don't go further down," Maria said, as he started to go through the turnstile, "the path is dangerous. And the birds might attack you if you touch their nests!"

"Just to the end of the rails, the bottom of the steps," insisted Steve, pointing to them. "I want to see if there are any unhatched eggs in the <u>old</u> nests!" He thought there might be some old, unhatched eggs left from last year in one of the nests nearest to the path, deserted by the vultures disturbed by people going up and down the path.

The five men on the beach, he could see more clearly now, were still there with their speedboats. He went down to the end of the steps. He was right. On the right hand side, he could just see the curved surface of a vulture's egg above the rim of a massive, deserted nest, which was mainly hidden from view by vegetation growing from the cliff-face, at the end of a ledge about 4 metres long. Knowing that black vultures usually lay just one egg, Steve wanted to take a closer look. The ledge of rock was about a metre and a half wide, with a sheer drop beneath it. He could walk along the ledge and get a really good look inside the nest. It didn't look like the sort of rock that would easily crumble into the sea, so he stepped out onto the ledge, his jaw squared as he tensed up, concentrating on keeping his balance. Keeping to the rock face, he walked a few paces along towards the nest.

"Steve, it's dangerous!" warned Maria.

He called back to her: "It's all right; I'm just going to <u>look</u> at the egg, not take it!"

She watched him anxiously. "Come back onto the path!" she cried, and followed him down the steps, hitching up her festival dress as she did so to avoid tripping on the hem.

Gripping with the fingers of both hands into the crevices of the rock, Steve leaned over to look into the nest. There was an enormous white egg - he could only just have held it in the palm of his hand. As he tightened his finger grips in the crevices, he suddenly touched what felt like plastic with his right hand fingers. He turned his head back round to see what it was, and what he was doing, and had to grip deeper into the crevice to keep his balance. He couldn't help taking hold of more of the plastic, until it started to give way and he had to return to a more upright position quickly to avoid losing his grip and slipping. It was quite a strong, transparent plastic bag which had been wedged into a crevice in the rock: now most of it was sticking out. It was taped up at the top and Steve pulled it out to look at it. Inside was what looked like transparent, shining white crystals. Peering at the crevice he saw that there were more plastic bags stuffed into it.

Meanwhile, old Senor Munos, sitting on the log in the deciduous grove, started searching in his pockets for his pipe and tobacco. Staring down frowning in concentration at the long grass growing abundantly around the log, he noticed a rusting old farming implement lying in it, in the shade just under the log. He managed to find his pipe and tobacco. He filled and lit the pipe, and sat looking at the old tool lying in the grass for a moment. He found it easier this way to recall the words of an old Majorcan folk song which he hadn't sung for years. Gradually his memory came back and he lifted his head up again and started singing the song, slowly and quietly at first, then a little louder as his confidence grew.

He could still see Steve and Maria on the top of the cliff… But his stiff leg was becoming uncomfortable so he shifted round to ease it, until he couldn't keep an eye on them anymore by looking straight ahead: he had to look sideways. He was now sitting facing a nearby strawberry tree. Admiring its pink bark and bright fruits which were turning from bright green to yellow and would be scarlet by winter, he remembered having tried to eat one as a boy - they tasted horrible. He took a few sucks on his pipe, drawing in some of the lines on his face in a co-operative cluster. It was just then that Steve and Maria had gone down the cliff path steps.

Steve carried the bag of gleaming crystals which he'd dislodged from the cliff-face back along the ledge – trembling with excitement - to the bottom of the path steps, where Maria had been waiting, worried. "Look what I've found," he said, puzzled, and handed it to her. "There are lots more in the cliff."

The men on the beach had stopped talking with one another. One of them, medium height and very slim with blond hair, in a white shirt and blue jeans, who'd been watching Steve while talking intermittently into his mobile, suddenly interrupted his mobile discussion to alert all of them. He could now see what the boy was carrying. He pointed up at Steve, and cried out in a harsh voice: "*Ordenes de Senor C.: Detengale!*" ("Order from Senor C.: <u>Stop him</u>!", which Steve didn't understand,) then started running up the path towards the youngsters.

Maria was looking at the plastic bag and the crystals it contained. She realised at once that these were secret caches of diamonds. She'd been told by her brother Pablo that the police were on the look-out for a gang of criminals they suspected of smuggling diamonds into the country, from Africa. Steve was just standing there with no sense of alarm. He didn't know the white crystals were real diamonds, traded by some of the most dangerous criminals. He thought the men were interested in looking at the vultures, and might also be warning him not to get too close to their nests. Perhaps they'd become so excited because they were conservationists and thought he'd been interfering with a fresh nest to steal some eggs. He thought Maria would be able to explain to them that he'd only taken a look at a deserted nest, not a new one.

Maria had forgotten her English momentarily in her panic. As the blond man approached at a very fast sprint up the path, she recognised him as the man who'd been scowling at her from the crowd when she was taking part in the festival procession. His face was growing red with exertion and the long pale pink scar on his cheek stood out. "!*Venga rapido!*" ("Come quickly!") he was shouting, and beckoning the others to follow him.

Two more diamond smugglers, the tall one and the stocky one, ran up the path. The big, hefty man, dressed in a black shirt stretched taut over a big beer stomach and black jeans, decided to join in the pursuit a few seconds later. Then Maria managed to say to Steve in English: "They are criminals, these are diamonds! Follow me!" and picking up her long full skirts a little she started to run as fast as she could back up the steep steps, with Steve, who now understood what a dangerous situation they were in, close behind, still clutching the packet. But she tripped and fell over on the steps, cutting herself badly on one knee and Steve stopped to help her up.

The last diamond smuggler to remain on the beach now began to run up the path. The blond man leading them recognised her as the sister of the policeman in the square at Puerto Pollensa, from the white hibiscus flower which was in her hair. "The girl's brother's in the police!", he was shouting in Spanish: "*Su hermano es policia!*"

Steve only understood the word '*policia*': the thought occurred to him that these men just might be plain clothes detectives who believed he and Maria were young criminals come to collect the diamonds. But both he and Maria were at first too breathless and confused either for him to ask her what the man had just said, or for her to reply in English. So after he'd helped Maria to her feet, and she carried on running up the steps as fast as she could, he turned to look round again.

The tall one following the blond man had short brown hair, blue eyes and an anxious expression. Steve certainly didn't like the look of the big heavy man, who had a swarthy complexion with a low forehead, heavy black eyebrows, down-turned mouth and a basically cruel expression. Seeing him and the thuggishly animated face of the stocky man convinced Steve they were all definitely criminals. He dropped the package and started to run again.

But the blond man had gained a lot of ground, and hurled himself up the steps, grabbing hold of Steve and dragging him down to the ground. Maria screamed and Steve shouted for help, but their cries were drowned by the volley of distress rockets that was suddenly let off by the flotilla of little boats out to sea, to start one of the festival boat races. The criminal following behind the blond one, tall with long legs, was also a fast runner. He snatched up and pocketed the diamond packet, then caught Maria just as she was about to reach the top of the steps, putting his hand over her mouth so she couldn't scream any more.

Meanwhile, the mildly deaf old Senor Munos, still sitting on the fallen log and singing to himself, puffing on his pipe between verses, had glanced again at the cliff edge and noticed that Steve and Maria were no longer by the railings. Perhaps they'd walked a little further along the cliff edge. He knew that if they had, they'd be temporarily obscured by the clump of broom bushes by the turnstile gate. But because he couldn't see them from where he was, he decided to get up and move to where he could see them.

Stretching, Great-Granpa Munos stood up and started to stroll through the little copse, still carrying his pipe, to look for them and take a closer look at the vultures himself. Then he thought he heard a boy shouting - it seemed to be coming from the cliff path. He quickened his pace, his war wound making him wince a little.

Steve and Maria had been quickly gagged and were being frog-marched roughly and fast down the path towards the speedboats by the criminals. By the time old Great-Granpa Munos was out of the copse, he could see along the coastline from right to left for a long way, but the youngsters were nowhere to be seen. They weren't by the broom bushes – he checked. He called out their names, cupping his hands to his mouth, and ran to the railings.

The little beach below was deserted. He saw two motorboats, one white and yellow and the other a bright red, already quite far out to sea to the east of the flotilla, the red one rushing away over the water at very high speed, leaving a large wake behind it.

A pair of black vultures had started to wheel in towards the cliffs again, and following behind them was a tattered-looking, undisciplined formation of a few of their comrades, coming from further along the coast. Great-Granpa Munos knew that, despite their gigantic, intimidating size, they only fed off dead and very badly wounded animals (or people). So provided he didn't trip and fall so badly that he couldn't get up, or go too near their nests, they wouldn't attack him. But this was now only a small concern compared to the safety of his beloved great-grandchild Maria and the friendly English boy.

He made his way carefully down the first few steps of the cliff path, holding onto the rail, until he could see most of the cove. Unless they were hiding behind some rocks, they definitely weren't there. He couldn't venture down any further with his stiff leg. He shouted again, first in Mallorqui to Maria: " Where are you?" asking her to come back and not to play any silly games as it was too dangerous. He heard nothing except in the far distance a man using a megaphone, introducing some feature of the festivities. With his poor hearing, he wasn't even sure what was being announced. Then he shouted at the top of his cracked old voice in English, to reassure Steve. "Steve! Please come back here! Don't walk too far...." Again he heard nothing.

A vulture called out once, in a harsh, but almost inaudible sound. They were usually silent birds, though on landing, they would make a clattering noise with their wings.

"Steve! Maria!" he shouted as loudly as he could, with all the force of his lungs, in all four directions. He ended up coughing.

But <u>where</u> were they? Had they gone off, in one of those two motorboats he'd just seen, with someone - after all that Maria had been warned <u>never</u> to accept lifts from strangers? Had some friends of hers offered them a trip round the coast? Great-Granpa Munos believed he knew most of Maria's friends. Some belonged to fishing families, but none of them owned a speedboat. One of Pablo's friends had a blue speedboat, which could conceivably have been very recently repainted......... but no: Maria would surely have told him first if she'd just been offered a ride in it............... neither she nor Pablo's friend would be as rude or thoughtless as to leave Great-Granpa Munos waiting for them, and worrying like that.

He called out their names again; frustrated that he couldn't venture down the steep cliff path with his stiff leg. There was no time to lose. Great-Granpa went back up the steps. The pine trees where the black vultures had nested before stretched parallel to the cliffs for some way, bent and stunted by the buffeting of winter winds. Perhaps the youngsters had run and slipped back amongst these - further along the cliffs - while he'd briefly been turned away from them. "Stop hiding!" he was calling now. He made his way, first east along the cliff top for nearly a mile; then west back towards Puerto Pollensa, always shouting for the children as clearly as he could in Mallorqui and English. Had one or both of them been abducted? If so, they might be in one of those motorboats. His heart was pounding. But why would anyone kidnap Maria? He could think of several nasty reasons. He fretted, continuing to ask himself *"Por que? Por que?"* ('Why? Why?') He loved her dearly. And he just could never believe that Steve - even though they <u>had</u> only just met - wished her harm; and anyway, even if he <u>had</u> wished her harm, he wouldn't have dared try to harm her when her great-grandfather was so near.

Great-Granpa Munos decided to look quickly around the little copse before returning to the others at the terrace cafe. As he searched, several pigeons clattered up out of the trees, and little birds fluttered among the branches; but otherwise the copse was still. "Please!" he entreated in Mallorqui: *"Por favor!"*

The first black vultures had begun to arrive, gliding and swooping down. They flapped around the cliff tops, springing about on the rock and dry grass, squabbling amongst each other over some sandwiches left by a tourist near their nests. Great-Granpa Munos saw this, and decided to go back again to the cliff top railings to finally satisfy himself that the youngsters weren't playing a prank on him. If they'd been hiding, they'd probably return to watch these tremendous birds of prey at closer quarters.

But there was still no sign of them. He checked the broom bushes by the turnstile again and scanned the ocean for any boats. The festival flotilla was moving southwards from Puerto Pollensa, not eastwards towards the cove. It would have been an uplifting sight normally, but as no boats were heading back in the direction of the cove, he had an instinctive feeling that something very bad had happened. Fear gripped his chest and his eyes filled with tears as he called their names in frustration for a final time: "Steve! Mar- i - a!". The faint echoes of his voice blended ominously with some more subdued, harsh cries from the normally quiet black vultures. He suddenly felt intimidated by their cruel, grotesque, movements. Then he started to make his way back to the cafe terrace as fast as he could, wishing for the first time in his life that he'd had a mobile phone on him.

CHAPTER THREE
What Next?

As the blond man pulled him back up off the ground, Steve was kicking out at him and trying to punch him, but the man had his arms locked round him in a vice. Then with one hand over his mouth, the criminal started to drag him down the cliff path. Steve instinctively tried to find his feet on the path rather than continue to kick out at his captor, because it was such a dangerous slope. The stockily-built man he'd first seen shaking his head asked Steve sarcastically "May I assist you?" in Spanish before quickly gagging him with a big handkerchief, then he grabbed him and helped his accomplice frogmarch him down the path. Steve didn't understand the dry joke, but Maria wondered if perhaps this man was used to serving in a shop.

Maria was also forced to walk down the path, though she was struggling as hard as she could, by the tall man with long legs, who kept his hand over her mouth. The big fat one wearing black preceded him down the slope and would have cushioned their fall if they'd slipped. "We'll have to dispose of them!" he was shouting in Spanish, " They've seen too much!" Before they reached the beach, he turned back and ensured Maria was also gagged, tightly with his neck cloth, to stifle any screaming.

"What are we going to do with them?" demanded the last diamond smuggler, who had run only a little way up the path. He was young with typically Spanish features, dark wavy hair and dark eyes behind his sunglasses. He had, to Steve and Maria's terror, produced a pistol from inside a leather waistcoat which he was wearing over a tee-shirt and faded black jeans.

"Put that away, Manuel!" said the very tall man anxiously.

"I don't take orders from you, Alto!" he replied.

"Don't use it here!" commanded the blond man. He was the ring leader. "The most important thing is to get off this beach as soon as we can. Someone might see us!"

The young dark man put his pistol away, looking at Steve and Maria, with a frighteningly desperate expression. All the others had hard faces which showed no compassion. Maria felt faint. She tried to kick out at the tall man who was holding her but he was holding her hard from behind.

"I'll take the kids to the island with Manuel and 'Alto' in my boat," said the blond man - " the others can follow. We must stay together till we decide what's to be done. But we'll decide that on the island. It's safer. We don't want bloodstains on the boats and they might be difficult to shoot in the water!" he added very quietly to Manuel, which Maria couldn't hear. He let go of Steve and got into his red speedboat.

Before Steve could resume struggling against his remaining assailant, Manuel had pushed him into the red speedboat, onto the floor, and started to tie his ankles together with some rope that was coiled up in the bottom of it, while the stocky man held his arms fast. The tall criminal, 'Alto', dragged Maria into this boat as well, on the opposite side to Steve, and began to look about for something to tie her up with. "Here, use this!" shouted the swarthy fat one, as he produced another piece of rope from the yellow and white motorboat. "An old fishing rope of mine!" Within a few seconds the youngsters had been bound at their ankles and wrists, with ankles and wrists tied up together as well, then positioned facing each other on the floor of the red speedboat. The swarthy fat criminal, with the help of the short stocky one, who was equally very strong, pushed them out into the sea. The blond ring leader started the engine, and with their necks aching as their heads were made to bow down towards their feet, Steve and Maria were taken away at high speed, bumping hard across the waves, with the yellow and white motorboat following a short way behind.

Steve, by craning his neck up as high as he could in that awkward position, lifting his eyebrows high with the strain and looking to the left, could see past the shoulder of the ring leader as he steered the speedboat. They were heading towards a small island which lay a long way out to sea, to the east of the promontory. He'd understood nothing of the exchanges in Spanish between the criminals. But realised that, because he and Maria had discovered the bags of diamonds, and could give a good description of the men to the police, this wasn't likely to be a kidnapping: it was very likely that the criminals would try to kill them, to silence them forever.

However had he allowed these men to tie him up? he thought in desperation. If only they'd take the gag from his mouth, he could try to reason with them in English - if, that is, they understood his language. He looked across at Maria but she had dropped her eyes: she was so terrified that she was unable to look at the criminals. Then he looked to the left at 'Alto', who was sitting in the passenger seat looking out to sea, shifting his long drawn-up limbs in and out like a half-opened pocketknife; then right at Manuel, who was staring ahead to the island, his jaws clenching and unclenching as he thought through possible ways of disposing of the youngsters. He was sitting with his arms folded loosely across his chest, as if ready to take his gun out again. Steve's feet were within only a few centimetres of Maria's, and he nudged one of her feet with his, to make her look up at him. He wanted so much to apologise for going along the precipice to take a closer look at the black vultures' egg - feeling very strongly that this was his entire fault.

Maria looked up at him, and as her big dark eyes met his, he winked instinctively, so as to say "Don't worry, I'll get us out of this" - although he didn't even have a penknife on him. Suddenly he felt very brave and that these men were cowards to be doing this. He would beg them to let him and Maria go free......he would say Maria's brother was in the police force – no! ....(he thought frantically)..... he would insist neither he nor Maria would tell anyone about what they'd seen: because then they'd have to admit to their parents they'd strayed from the cliff paths - and then they'd <u>never</u> be allowed to do anything by themselves again. Yes - this was a good bargaining tool, Steve decided. But first, he'd have to get the criminals to ungag him - and Maria to interpret for him, unless one of them knew English very well. <u>How</u> ?? As the speedboat bumped over the waves, closer and closer to the island, Steve felt sick to his stomach with fear.

Maria had already wondered if Steve might have a penknife in his shorts pocket which they could use to cut the ropes binding their wrists and ankles, if the criminals just left them on the island to die. She imagined they might leave them both tied up in a cleft in the rock, unseen by anyone who might pass by in a boat. Perhaps the vultures would find them and eat them alive. But she'd also understood that the men were considering shooting them and now started thinking through all her prayers. Occasionally forgetting the words, she kept wondering, "How could <u>anyone</u> do this?"

Suddenly they were in the shallow, light turquoise waters around the far side of the island. It was rugged and grey, made of the same rock as the cliffs which they'd just left; a big, intense flock of seagulls was flying around and nesting on it. "Now!" shouted the ring leader, turning round to 'Alto' and back to Manuel. His scarred face was looking even harder than it had previously. "Let's wait for the others to catch up before we agree what to do! Just get the kids onto the sandy bit!" There was a very large cleft in the rock which seemed to go back some way, taller and wider than a man, and in front of it, a very small patch of sand. He tied the speedboat up to a mooring in the shallows behind some huge boulders, where it wasn't obvious to passing boats. Then the three criminals between them picked up Steve and Maria in turn, still tied up with ropes, and put them on the sand. The ring leader returned to the speedboat and dragged a big grey tarpaulin over it. "We don't want to be seen from the air," he said.

"So what are we going to do, Rodrigo?" asked Manuel impatiently. "These kids could get us locked away for years!"

"Wait for the others!" Rodrigo insisted, holding his hand up in a swift 'Halt!' gesture. Manuel was obviously a hot-head.

Steve tried to get them to ungag him by making lots of noise, which came out as an anxious mumble through the handkerchief; but the criminals weren't interested in anything he had to say by this stage and after a few seconds of his muffled protest, he was ordered to "Shut up!" by Manuel, who gestured angrily with his finger to his lips. Steve and Maria could only wait for the other criminals to arrive. Soon they were hauling the large yellow and white speedboat up the sandy strip, pulling it alongside the two youngsters. "I say kill them, now!" shouted Manuel, and took his pistol out again, menacingly.

"Why not?" consented the very heavy man in black.

"We could bury them in this sand," added the stocky older one, "if we dig deep enough."

"What with?" demanded their ring leader. "If we used makeshift tools, it would be hard enough digging deep – but there's nothing to dig with here anyway!"

Maria began to cry. 'Alto' felt a twinge of guilt - he had a daughter of the same age. "But they're only kids," he said, "we can't just kill them."

"I didn't want this either," snapped Rodrigo, " but we've got to - otherwise we're all going to lose our freedom."

"We'll stay in prison for life – or death - if we kill them and we're found out!" 'Alto' argued, swinging a long arm out in a sweeping gesture.

"We must kill them now!" shouted Manuel and raised his gun to point it at Maria, who was now so alarmed she suddenly drew in a huge breath and stopped crying. "You know what they still say - 'Women and children first'!" He used this phrase - usually used as an order in an emergency – with heavy irony.

"NO!" 'Alto' insisted: "I won't be an accomplice."

"We'll get bloodstains on our clothing!" put in the stocky one.

"Let's strangle them, then," said Manuel.

"But where can we dump the bodies?" asked Rodrigo. "There are no big loose rocks around this island to tie to them to make them sink..." he gestured about.

A few seconds of intense argument ensued, still all in Spanish, which terrified both youngsters, until Rodrigo came up with an idea. "I tell you what - if we leave them tied up in the cave, with the grille door shut, we can ungag them and give them time to say their prayers before they die. No-one but God will hear them in there above the noise of the seagulls. We can let the incoming tide do the work for us. We can return when they've drowned and the tide's gone down again, and dump the bodies out to sea at night when there aren't so many people sailing out there to see us." (He still held some religious beliefs and, astonishingly, hoped that allowing the children to say prayers might atone for the terrible deed of killing them.)

"I wouldn't even risk <u>that</u>!" insisted Manuel. "Shoot them in the cave straightaway!"

"Rodrigo's right," said 'Alto', appearing persuaded by the others that the youngsters shouldn't be released, but feeling very guilty, "let's give them a fair chance! Leave them in the cave to drown, and if someone rescues them, it really <u>would</u> be a miracle - God's will!"

"They're celebrating the Patron Saint of Fishing today in Puerto Pollensa," said Rodrigo, "<u>everyone</u>'s at the festival today - and no-one's out fishing….huh! unless <u>He</u> is! How long does it take for the tide to come up, Antonio?" he then asked the heavy man dressed in black, who was well acquainted with the movements of tides in the area.

"Two, maybe three hours," he replied, "no more."

"OK," said Rodrigo. "If we're all agreed....." and he glanced at Manuel, who was shaking his head, reluctantly, but putting his gun away. "Antonio and Julio can take them to the cave." Julio, the stocky man, said "Certainly – as you wish!" like a waiter or a shop assistant again, while Antonio nodded. Rodrigo added to Manuel: "Here's the key. You, Manuel, can watch them. It'll teach you not to be so impetuous."

Antonio and Julio each picked up one of the youngsters, who resumed struggling, and followed Manuel; who, having put away his gun took the key from Rodrigo and walked into the big cleft in the rock. The sandy floor sloped downwards slightly. The cleft narrowed for quite a few paces, then opened out to about two metres. Across this opening was a heavy metal grille door fastened with a big, heavy padlock, which Manuel opened grimly with the key he'd been given.

Beyond it was a cave, which very few people knew the existence of, and which the criminals sometimes used to store their packets of diamonds. It was quite a large natural cavern, about the size of Steve's living room at home, but there the similarities ended. The sandy floor was damp and the air smelled of drying algae and the decaying corpses of dozens of little crabs and molluscs which lay about. A fissure high up in the rocky ceiling let in the few shafts of sunlight; fixed on a bracket on the wall of rock was an underwater lamp which the criminals lit when they were operating at night time. Large straggling clumps of green seaweed trailed down the cave walls, showing an unmistakable tide mark about seven feet high all around.

After Steve and Maria had been put down on the floor of the cave, Julio untied the strong ropes binding each one's wrists and ankles up together, then untied their hands and quickly retied them behind their backs, leaving their wrists and ankles tied up separately.

"So you can pray, but not eat the crabs!" Antonio told Maria in Spanish, as Julio removed the gags from their mouths: first Steve's, then Maria's. Steve, even in his terror, immediately started to reason with Julio by saying they wouldn't tell anyone about what they'd witnessed; but it was to no avail, as Julio had as much knowledge of English as Steve had of Spanish. Antonio, an ex-fisherman, had never had much to do with tourists and knew no English either - he turned and walked hastily out of the cave back up the sloping cleft in the rock to the small patch of sand outside. As Maria was pleading with them: "Let us go!" Steve exhorted her: "Translate for me! Tell them we won't talk!"

But Julio was already following Antonio out, saying to Maria in Spanish as he turned round, just beyond the grille door, for a final time: "Just say your prayers. Do you see the tide mark?" and he pointed to it with a thick finger. As Julio exited back up the rock cleft, Manuel swung the grille door shut behind them with a dull clang which resonated horribly in the cavern, then turned the key in the padlock. Steve continued to shout at Julio and Manuel *"Por favor!* ", some of the only words he could remember of Spanish, but saw from this man's face that he had made a very firm decision. Steve added in English: "We won't talk!" while Maria was also still pleading with them in Spanish. Manuel followed Julio out. Then Antonio returned, his figure looming large in the dim light of the rock cleft, to leer gloatingly through the bars at them and take a photo of them with his mobile: *"No hay escapada!"* ('There's no escape!') he said. Then his big black bulk disappeared in the gloom, back through the crevice after the others. He was the last to leave.

Steve immediately told Maria: "I'm very sorry! I haven't got my penknife on me! But perhaps we could cut our ropes on a jagged rock...." He glanced around the gloomy cavern with his jaw squaring up, straining to pull his wrists up from his ankles, which they were still tied to.

"Use the rocks to cut our ropes: yes!" she said, then asked doubtfully, looking up at it: "And climb right up...to the...ceiling?" The walls were slippery and sheer, with a lot of overhanging towards the top where the light came filtering through.

After a few seconds the youngsters heard the roar of the yellow and white motorboat as all four men left the island on it. Steve shouted at them in English, knowing they couldn't hear: "You evil men! You won't get away with this!" Just as he was shouting, Rodrigo adjusted the throttle on the motorboat and the pitch of the engine altered. Blending with the keening cries of the seagulls, it sounded to the youngsters as if the red speedboat were being driven away as well.

G reat-Granpa Munos was quite breathless by the time he returned to the café terrace and the table where his wife and the Parkers were waiting. He wasn't any later than they'd expected, but everyone was surprised that he'd returned alone. Before Mrs Parker could ask " Where are the children?", he had gasped out in Mallorqui to his wife: "The children – haven't come back yet!" Mrs Parker, who understood Spanish better, couldn't understand what he'd said. Great-Granma Munos repeated it slowly in quiet dismay, in English for the Parkers' benefit: "They haven't come back yet?" Then the old lady gave a look to her husband which confirmed that no-one at the table had seen either Steve or Maria since they'd left with him to see the vultures. She could tell by her husband's breathlessness, and the tone of his voice, that all was not going well.

Mr Parker, however, who'd just drunk a glass of wine, hadn't realised. He just smiled expansively and said with an air of genial satisfaction, "Oh, all right!" (He thought Great-Granma Munos's flat tone sounded calm, not dismayed; he assumed her husband was about to explain that Steve and Maria were following a little way behind, or that they'd been left watching one of the festival diversions in a nearby street. And he supposed that Great-Grandpa Munos usually got short of breath after a fairly long walk.)

"That suits me," said Becky, "Steve's so boring!"

Great-Granpa Munos was still very out of breath, but added as soon as he could to Great-Granma, again in Mallorqui: "They're missing! I ran all the way back!", just as Mrs Parker, beginning to understand the situation, was asking him in English: "Where are they?"

(Great-Granma Munos had already realised that he didn't know.) He turned to Mrs Parker first, and then the others, with his hands clasped together in a gesture of begging for forgiveness, and said in English: "I don't know. I don't know where they are.....*no se.*"

"Oh, no!" said Becky. "Trust Steve to get lost!" and she raised her eyes upwards in an expression which meant: 'Typical!'.

"How could...did you lose them?" asked Mr Parker, worried, yet retaining considerable sympathy for Great-Granpa Munos, and not cross with him. He knew Steve could be headstrong at times.

"I lose them......" began Great-Granpa Munos in imperfect English because he was upset, "...I lose them I don't know how, one minute they are on the cliffs and they are watching the black vultures. And the next minute, they are gone!" He leaned on his hands on the back of his wife's chair.

"Have you looked for them?" asked Great-Granma Munos anxiously in English.

"Yes, all along the cliffs," he replied in Mallorqui. "But I couldn't see them." Which Great-Granma Munos quickly told the Parkers in English. It was more serious that they had disappeared from the cliffs.

Mrs Parker, already perturbed, took a short, sharp intake of breath, and then sighed with a frown. "Perhaps they decided to come back into the town and look around for a while... and thought that you were still following them, Senor Munos."

"I sat down with my pipe to smoke," he confessed, " while they were on the cliffs - and I was not always watching them.....because I had to change the way I was sitting because of my leg."

"Sit down, sit down," Mr Parker encouraged him in a calming gesture. He wasn't yet suspecting the worst as the old man was; feeling fairly sure, like his wife Pat, that Steve and Maria had returned to the town thinking that Great-Granpa Munos was following them. "Have something to drink," he insisted, "you mustn't worry like this - it's bad for you."

"....not every second, I was not watching them every second...."

Great-Granpa did need to quench his thirst and get his breath back. At the same time he managed to convince everyone that Steve and Maria could only have given him the slip and returned to the town by running very fast - and undercover for most of the way. They would have had to have done so almost as soon as they'd reached the black vultures' nesting place on the cliffs - which was very unlikely, given their enthusiasm for watching the birds.

"Then this could be a kidnap," suggested Mr Parker.

Great-Granpa Munos looked at him in a way which showed he believed this to be the case, then described the two motorboats he'd seen going out to sea: "...It's possible, I'm afraid. We must tell the police."

Mrs Parker asked: "Shall I stay here with Becky and Senora Munos in case they come back here, while my husband and Mr Munos" (she couldn't bring herself to call Maria's great-grandparents Josep and Anna-Maria as she was getting rather cross and anxious) "go to the police station? All right, darling?" she asked her husband, who after a pause nodded, adding: "Then we can take our turn waiting here at the table while you and Becky go and look for them around the town - it's not a large place."

"Good" she concluded. "OK", he affirmed. Everyone agreed, even Becky, although she only agreed to the action they should take and still didn't believe that anything untoward had happened to her brother. "He's probably looking around the shops with Maria, she hasn't realised how boring he is!" she said, feeling that her parents had overreacted. And that, yet again her brother had claimed all their attention – this time, just by his absence.

Great-Granpa Munos led Mr Parker to the nearby local police station, where his grandson Pablo was based - right then Pablo was still out on the streets policing the land part of the festival while the fishing procession boats were in the sea. Mr Parker found the Majorcan police station had a different atmosphere from a provincial English one. The regular uniforms were blue and white, rather like the British black and white ones, but the two policemen who were standing up talking when they walked in, also wore shoulder holsters with pistols.

Behind the counter was an older policeman, with light brown hair and a big walrus moustache, who wasn't carrying a gun. Mr Parker and Great-Granpa Munos went up to him as he completed some paper work. He looked up and instantly recognised Great-Granpa Munos. "Josep Munos! What, turning yourself in?" he jested in Spanish. "What have you done?"

"I'm here on very serious business, I'm afraid, Jose" said Great-Granpa in their native Mallorqui, and explained everything to him.

Jose's expression grew increasingly serious, until even his moustache drooped. He asked Great-Granpa a great many questions, in Mallorqui, and occasionally asked Mr Parker a question in English. These included: "May I see proof of your identity?", "How old is your son?" and " Would he have any reason to run away?". Then he took down all the details about Steve, such as his height, build, hair and eye colour, also about the clothes he was wearing - long navy shorts and a short-sleeved cream cotton shirt. All the while, Jose sighed and made 'tusk, tusk' noises of sympathy. He took the name, address and phone number of the Parkers' hotel; the names and ages of Becky and Mrs Parker, and finally said to Mr Parker in English (his English was fortunately very good): "We know Maria - because she's the sister of one of our officers, Pablo Munos: he's on patrol now, looking after the fishing festival. What we will do for you is no more than we would do for anyone; but it really helps that we already know Maria and what she looks like. Also, she's wearing traditional Majorcan costume...

"We must act as soon as possible to search for them," continued Jose in English, "even if it's the case that right now they're just sitting in a cafe eating ice creams! We'll use all our powers to find your children for you. Several of our policemen are patrolling the festival events today – I'll give them a full description of the children by mobile. And I myself will go out with a loudhailer in the car and ask anyone who has seen them in the last hour - since they've been missing - to report to the police station. Also, for anyone who was in a yellow and white motorboat or a red speedboat in the area of the Pollensa cliffs when Steve and Maria disappeared, to come forward. We'll also ask the sea patrol to search the bay for them: they may have gone down the cliff steps to the cove. And we'll let you know as soon as we hear anything. Now....do either of you have any questions for me?"

"Yes," said Mr Parker, "can any of your policemen come with me and Senor Munos to the cliff tops to search again for the children?" He trusted that Great-Granpa Munos had made a thorough search, but wanted to satisfy himself that everything possible had been done.

"Of course…" replied Jose, breaking off to gesture to one of the other policemen to come to relieve him at desk duty, just as two English people, who looked very obviously like tourists, walked in – they'd just had their pockets picked. "…I was myself about to suggest a search of the cliffs," he continued to Mr Parker and Great-Granpa Munos. "We can alert Maria's brother first. It should be him who helps search, if we can get someone to replace him on patrol duty. Haven't you seen him yet, Josep?" he asked Great-Granpa Munos. (He would have asked him in Mallorqui, but to be fair to Mr Parker he still spoke in English.)

"No", replied Great-Granpa Munos, "I didn't see Pablo on my way back through the crowds and I came back to the Parkers first - 'a priori ' " - he used a Latin phrase as he couldn't recall the English for 'as a priority'. Then he spoke again in Mallorqui to Jose. They discussed how to tell Maria's parents, who would be busy in their shop, about her disappearance. Jose suggested that Great-Granpa Munos phone them from the police station, and get them to look out a photo of Maria for a 'MISSING' poster, and he would get an insert in the last edition of the local paper – as quickly as possible. Then the younger Snr. Munos – Maria's father Ramon – could meet with Pablo and Mr Parker to search the cliffs along the path the youngsters took there, which Great-Granpa Munos could describe to them as exactly as possible, if they all met at the police station; while Jose added this to his notes. "Then take some rest," the policeman advised, "and let the younger men take over the search."

Jose turned again to Mr Parker and said in English: "If Maria and Steve aren't found in the next two hours we will put up 'MISSING' posters of them in the town, so everyone will recognise them if they see them. Do you have any recent photographs, or one in your camera that we can enlarge as soon as possible?" Mr Parker had taken a photo of Steve eating one of the sausages at the cafe table, but wasn't sure if it would make a suitable poster - just when <u>had</u> he clicked the camera? They'd been laughing at that point. Anyway, the picture could, if necessary, be trimmed for the purpose. "Yes, I do, " he replied, "I took one of him just now sitting at the table. I'll go back and get my camera - thank you."

"Maybe there will still be time to put them into the late edition of the local evening paper as well," added Jose. As Mr Parker was about to leave straightaway, to return to the cafe table to get their camera, Jose continued: "Just a moment. It's quite likely that the children have been abducted. If either of you receives any communication from anyone who says they have seen either of them, or knows of their whereabouts, you will of course ask them their names and contact details and be in touch with us immediately?" Great-Granpa Munos said "*Si,*" and Mr Parker nodded his assent: "And I'll keep my mobile switched on day and night, till we find them!"

Mr Parker returned to the cafe table and told the others of the arrangements. He took his camera back to the police station where the photo of Steve was enlarged from their computer urgently for a 'MISSING' poster. Another copy was sent to the offices of the local evening paper, so a 'MISSING' insert for the paper could be quickly printed.

Arriving back at the police station, he found Maria's father, Senor Ramon Munos, waiting. He looked a little like her great-grandfather. He had wavy dark brown hair and a patient, determined expression. They shook hands. "I'm sorry this has happened!" said Senor Munos. "Me too," replied Mr Parker. Maria's father explained he had left his wife Isabel waiting at home in case there was any news to receive of their daughter. Pablo had already been contacted by Jose and been told what had happened. He'd replied that he would wait for them at the top end of the main street and then go with them to the cliffs to search.

Soon, the four men - Pablo, the youngsters' fathers and Great-Granpa Munos who insisted on joining them - were searching the area where they'd disappeared. All the police who were already on the streets had been advised that Steve and Maria had gone missing and were keeping an eye out for them. Jose crawled through crowds of tourists in a police car driven by another policeman, leaning out of the window with a loudhailer (his moustache now bristling with determination, not drooping with dismay) asking people who'd seen either of the youngsters, the motorboats or anything suspicious, to report it to the police. He gave out descriptions in English and Mallorqui.

By 4.00 pm - having found no sign of Steve or Maria because the criminals had kicked over their footprints on the little cove beach at the foot of the cliffs, concealing all traces - the four searchers returned to Mrs Parker and Becky at the café table. Pablo, controlling his emotions, explained to them in good English, that it had been a very painstaking search, even looking through the debris on the beach: flotsam and jetsam and general rubbish which should have been thrown into waste bins. Meanwhile they'd been liaising with the sea-patrol, who couldn't see any sign of Steve or Maria – although someone had reported seeing a big red speedboat approach the festival boat games and then drive off, without being able to get a good look at the drivers.

Maria's father Senor Munos was insistent that it was very unlike his daughter to go missing: she was always very responsibly behaved. As she knew the locality very well, she and Steve couldn't possibly have just lost their way.

Even Becky was beginning to worry. While her father stayed on at the café table with Senor Munos, and Pablo went home with Great-Granpa Munos, she went walking through the streets with her mother. Mrs Parker stopped to ask the festival stallholders and shopkeepers if they'd seen an English boy and a Majorcan girl in traditional costume, explaining who they were. The apologetic response of 'lo siento' was building up like a refrain to a lament sung by Mrs Parker. At least it wasn't as hot as it had been at lunchtime. "What time did we agree to return to the cafe table, again?" Becky asked her, because she couldn't remember. "Five o'clock," replied Mrs Parker.

"I'll bet he'll come back for five o'clock," suggested Becky. "We'll soon be able to tell if he's <u>really</u> had an accident or been kidnapped: if he doesn't come back for <u>tea-time</u>." She often criticised Steve for being predictable.

Steve and Maria were getting into deep trouble indeed. They first saw the tide as a few thin, silver threads trickling under the lower bar of the grille door in the cave fissure. It had quickly increased to a fast-moving little cascade of water which surged through the bottom of the grille, forming a growing, very shallow pool of water as the cave widened out from the fissure, which was moving nearer and nearer to them. The thugs had left them sitting back to back, but separately tied up, in the middle of the cave; Steve had managed to shuffle up, with his wrists tied behind his back, to the nearest rock to try to cut through his ropes with the roughest edge he could find along the bottom of it. But all the rock edges were fairly smooth, and he could see it wasn't going to work. "It's no use!" he said, "The rock isn't sharp enough!"

Maria started shuffling back towards the rear wall, tossing her head back to it. "Get back over here!"

He followed suit and they now both sat facing the approaching water.

Soon, the very gradually rising tide was touching their feet, and then the water started to swirl about them. Both had been trying to be brave and not say anything, maintaining a noble silence in the face of death. "How could anyone <u>do</u> this?" was all Maria could think at first. Steve was thinking so hard of a means of escape that he hadn't even thought of blaming Becky for not wanting to come along to see the vultures, with their parents.

The gentle, hushing, rhythmical sound started, of tiny waves as they came into the cave. It actually had a calming effect on Maria - who knew that as they rose up, at least the creepy little dead crab shells couldn't stay clinging to her lovely dress. She tried to remember the words of a hymn, to stay very calm. But suddenly she screamed as she saw the large, flattened globe of a deadly stinging Portuguese man-of-war, looking like and often called a jellyfish, slip under the grille door. The poisonous siphonophore floated towards them a little, borne along by the incoming tide. It was about the size of a dinner plate. Its pale pink tentacles were several metres long, and its translucent, nearly transparent flesh, like rubbery pink jelly, a little violet around the edges, pulsed slightly. It was alive. "A Portuguese man-of-war!" she cried to Steve. "They are <u>very</u> poisonous! *Sante Maria!* It will sting us! What shall we do?" she begged.

Then Steve had a brilliant idea. He could lift the shawl off Maria's shoulders with his teeth, and drop it onto the Portuguese man-of-war to disable it: so it couldn't move, or see them. (Incidentally, where *were* its eyes? he wondered.) He told Maria. "OK!" she agreed, and then shouted: "No, wait! First: take the big silver brooch on my shawl! The pin is …baggy…loose! You can hold the brooch in your teeth, to cut our ropes – with the pin! Be careful!" she warned, "it's already loose! Take care it doesn't fall into the water!"

Steve craned his neck out and positioned his mouth at the old silver brooch at Maria's shoulder. Maria thanked God she was wearing her mother's traditional old brooch, which had belonged to her grandmother, rather than a modern one from her parents' shop. Its heavy, fairly sharp pin was easier to dislodge from the clasp in this way than a lighter, modern pin, which would have been impossible to undo from its clasp.

Steve hoped the pin wouldn't dislodge from its socket suddenly, and spring out, as he felt for it between his teeth and waggled his lower jaw forwards and backwards to loosen it from the shawl. After an infuriating fifteen seconds, the pin sprang from its notch, and the folds of the shawl slackened. The brooch now lay at a new angle on the shawl, with its pin half-way through the material. "Well done, Steve!" exclaimed Maria. "But the jellyfish!……" she added, quickly drawing her legs in.

"Siphonophore!" he corrected, to keep steady.

The Portuguese man-of-war was now deliberately starting to approach them with a slight increase in its pulsing movement, which contracted and then relaxed the head-like main blob, its tentacles streaming out behind as it did so. "Hurry, Steve!" Maria cried.

Steve took the whole brooch in his teeth, drawing the pin out of the shawl. He manoeuvred it so that he was holding the pin out straight from his mouth (again, it helped that the pin was on an old, flexible hinge), then Maria turned her back to him and raised her hands, tied behind her, as high as she could. Steve lowered his head and started to grate away with the brooch pin at the threads of the rope binding her wrists. This was a real emergency. His own hands, of course, being tied behind his back, made it quite a strain on his neck and back muscles. The strands of the rope were tightly packed together and the brooch pin wasn't particularly sharp, so at first he didn't think he was going to succeed at cutting through them. But then the first few strands frayed, and some minutes later he had severed one of the three twists making up the rope.

The water was by now up to the calves of their legs. Although the heat had started to build up in the sea by mid-afternoon, the sand it ran over in the cave was cold, and it felt quite cool. Maria was shivering. The poisonous Portuguese man-of-war was swimming nearer and nearer to her. It was now fewer than two metres away. She no longer felt able to encourage Steve in English. Her knees felt weak and she wanted to start screaming in Mallorqui: for her parents and to God for help. Even once their arms and legs were free, how would they escape? Would there be enough air for them to breathe if they floated right up to the ceiling on the rising tide?

Steve was wondering about these things too. And he wanted to free them both in time to deal with the Portuguese man-of-war first, before it could sting them. His frantic efforts at freeing the ropes around Maria's wrists finally paid off: the last strands snapped apart. She immediately drew her hands round in front of her to rub her wrists where her blood circulation had been constricted. Steve dropped the old brooch from his mouth in relief, gasping "Thank God!" It quickly sank beneath the surface of the water, which was surging round their knees. "Quick!" he shouted: "Now untie mine!"

"Sure!" Maria needed no prompting. His hands were only just above the water.

Once Steve's wrists were free from the ropes (which didn't take long, though it

40

was a tough knot) they both untied their own ankles, lifting them up just above the water, and could finally stand up straight. Steve took Maria's shawl from her shoulders and threw it over the Portuguese man-of-war which was now only an arm's length away. Its tentacles became entangled in the fringe and it would be quite some time before it could free itself, if at all.

Now it felt even more frustrating, however: they could move about, but they were still trapped in the cave. With the tide rising. Steve and Maria looked at each other. "How about if you stood on my shoulders - could you reach the ceiling?" he asked her: "And look to see if there's enough room to get out?" But they decided the ceiling was too high for that, and anyway it looked as if the opening where the light came through was <u>very</u> narrow, a fissure of only about fifteen or so centimetres wide. The only way out, they realised with absolute certainty, was through that locked grille door. Steve looked at it. *Through the grille door*, he thought. Then he went up to it and measured himself against its bars, standing sideways. *Or - through its bars…. Through its bars!!!* He realised, and started laughing. "Oh no," whispered Maria to herself in Mallorqui, "he's having hysterics."

Festival revellers, and the more placid onlookers, were still milling about the streets of Puerto Pollensa by 5.50 pm in the late afternoon, after the boat games had finished and the festival was over. A sinking sun cast a pink, then carmine glow on the white buildings and white dresses of the girls who had taken part in the traditional dances. People were eating spicy sausages – *sobasada* - on sticks and wrapped up in serviettes, walking about and looking in the shops, which were still open. Some members of the festival procession band were reluctantly packing away their instruments after a final, spontaneous reprise of the best song, while several others had stopped for a drink at a bar.

Steve wasn't back by tea-time. Becky had returned to her parents' hotel room with them and been told to stay in the hotel while they went out again for a final search in the town. She was given strict instructions to stay in the hotel; and not to go out with anyone, no matter what they said. If she went out of her parents' room, to the lobby or the games room, for example, she was to lock their door with the key they were giving her. And she must under no circumstances give the key to anyone else. In the meantime Mr and Mrs Parker would walk around the streets searching for any clues as to the whereabouts of Steve and Maria.

Becky now realised what grown-ups felt like when they complained about being worried. This was serious. She caught sight of herself in the big gilt mirror and noticed she had a new frown line on her sunburnt forehead. Did he have to do this? She sat down with her father's deck of playing cards, and tried to think constructively about her brother.

After she'd played one or two games of cards designed for one person, she took out a piece of paper and a pen and wrote down a list of all Steve's good points. He was a good brother: he had always looked after her and stopped her getting into trouble even though he was younger; he didn't swear... The list went on, until Becky had written down a lot of good points about Steve which she'd previously taken for granted and never bothered to draw anyone's attention to. Having finally noted down, as afterthoughts, that Steve had stopped a boy called Simon bullying her once; that he took the most responsibility for Rex, their dog, and that he'd once let her play with his favourite computer games when she was getting over a nasty cold, she felt satisfied she should feel very guilty indeed. About refusing to go along to see the rare black vultures with him.

Yes, Becky felt guilty. It was probably her fault that Steve had gone missing. If she had consented to going to see the black vultures as well, the whole family would have gone. She resolved to be very kind to her brother in future, and not call him predictable or argue with him - about anything. If he came back.

Making sure to lock her parents' hotel room door, Becky went down to the hotel foyer to watch the fish in the aquarium there. They looked calmly indifferent to what was going on around them in the hotel. She wondered if Steve and Maria had gone down to the beach for a swim and drowned. Then she speculated again about their being kidnapped.

Suddenly everyone she saw seemed to appear suspicious. One of the English hotel guests, a man about her father's age, was sitting in the foyer and said "Hello" to her in quite a friendly manner. The Parkers had sat and chatted to him each morning so far at breakfast and he'd talked quite a lot to Steve about speedboats, she remembered. Becky wondered if he might have been involved in her brother's disappearance and decided to ask him if he'd seen Steve later that morning.

"No, I'm afraid I haven't seen him since breakfast," came the reply.

"He went missing after he went up to the cliffs to see the black vultures with a Majorcan girl called Maria Munos," she persisted, searching his face for any sign he was lying. And so it was with all the other English guests she questioned in the hotel.

Mr Parker had told the receptionists at the desk about Steve's mysterious disappearance with Maria. As requested by him, they were asking all the guests, in various languages, whether they'd seen the youngsters since, or heard anything suspicious in connection with them. Becky now went up to them and asked if they had any news. "No, we're sorry," they said.

Meanwhile, dusk was drawing on, much of the heat and light had faded away and Mrs Parker wore a cardigan round her slim shoulders with the sleeves knotted at the front. She and her husband still looked like the other tourists who were strolling about the town, except for the expressions on their faces: both of them were very, very worried. They had searched down every street, as the noise of the day gradually died down. Only a few members of the procession band remained drinking at the outdoor cafes. The sound of scooters' accelerating up the streets was heard less frequently, and the processioners who were still milling about with their friends were beginning to get tired. They looked different in their festival costumes now, more incongruous.

The couple decided to take one last check down a long street they had already searched. Suddenly two girls, who'd been in Maria's procession, still wearing their tiered white dresses and fringed shawls, rounded the corner at the end of it. One of them at first looked like Maria......"Could it be?" wondered Mrs Parker; but no....this girl was wearing a pink, not a white, hibiscus flower. And as the Parkers walked towards them, they could see she only bore a passing resemblance to Maria. It had been Mrs Parker's wishful thinking. Mr Parker asked the girls in English if they knew anything about Maria's disappearance, but remained disappointed when they replied: "No, we're sorry!" Mrs Parker watched the two costumed girls disappear from view. They looked eerie, like ghosts, in the swiftly gathering dusk.

There was a general feeling of relief amongst the dispersing crowds, of having had an enjoyable day with plenty of excitement and entertainment. Most of the tourists who had heard the police alert during the celebrations, assumed the two youngsters were bound to turn up later on – they had probably gone off exploring somewhere.

On a newsstand, a young delivery boy dropped a bundle of the latest edition of the local evening paper. Mr Parker, depressed, went to pick one up. As he opened it, an insert fell out. This usually annoyed him, but now he was relatively pleased to see that it was a poster using the photo he'd taken of Steve, alongside one of Maria, alerting the public to their disappearance. It said in English and Spanish: '**MISSING:** Steve Parker aged 11 and Maria Munos aged 12, last seen at 14:30

hours on festival day, Saturday 16 July at the Pollensa cliffs. Please notify police immediately if you can help them with their enquiries.'

Becky also saw one of these posters in a copy of the newspaper at their hotel. It showed a regular, pleasant photo of Maria, and one of Steve laughing (his open mouth in fact also awaiting insertion of a festival sausage, which had been cropped out of the photograph). It made her smile despite all the worry of wondering where he was: he looked so highly irresponsible on the poster. Yes, her brother certainly did seem to be able to grab all the attention, even by his absence. And she was missing him!

CHAPTER SEVEN
Deliverance

Maria was standing up, but feeling faint with panic, just behind Steve as he stood laughing at the grille door. (His expression was like the one on his 'MISSING' poster photo, now being displayed across Puerto Pollensa and the neighbouring districts.) Then he turned round and said "Don't you see I could squeeze through those bars?" Maria didn't understand. She had heard of the word 'squeeze' in the phrase 'freshly-squeezed orange juice" from the English menus in the hotels, but didn't understand its meaning in <u>this</u> context. She knew he wasn't strong enough to bend them. *"Non comprendo!"* she said to Steve - "I don't understand!" So Steve explained carefully. "The bars are too wide apart! I can go - pass - <u>through</u> them! Look!" and he turned his head sideways and just managed to ease himself through the grille bars. As he did so, the thick steel felt cold on his face. Maria followed suit.

Wading out through the fissure in the rock onto the tiny beach, which was now under the sea, they climbed up the island a little way - the moored speedboat was just out of their sight, down behind a rocky outcrop, as they looked about. Passing a few seagulls' nests, they worked their way round to the Puerto Pollensa side, to look back to the mainland. They had escaped the worst of their ordeal. Both were elated and much more confident, and Maria laughed in triumph. Antonio, the big fat criminal wearing black, had clearly been mistaken when he'd said *"no hay escapada"*.

They climbed up to very near the top of the island, then sat down for a while to decide how best to get back to Puerto Pollensa alive. "How's your knee?" Steve asked Maria.

"OK, thanks" she replied, showing the big graze on it: "it stopped bleeding. And the salt in the seawater is ....."

"Healing?" he supplied, "Makes it better?"

"Yes!"

During the speedboat ride Steve's face, though he'd applied a sunblock cream to it earlier, had been finely sprayed with salty seawater spume, and it now started to sting slightly in the fierce heat. But he was determined not to complain. His jaw squared up as he looked out to sea, all the way around. There were no boats anywhere near enough to call to for help, although there were two or three yachts just visible far out on the western horizon. "Can you swim?" he asked Maria. "Yes," she replied. "But it's a long way back."

After five minutes debating whether it would be safe to swim back, they decided there were probably various species of sharks which didn't care what time of year they were supposed to be swimming around the north coast of Majorca. Or when it was that they were most likely to attack humans. So they waited for two hours, still hoping for a friendly-looking boat to pass by. Their wet clothes dried out on them in the late afternoon sun; yet nothing sailed by the uninhabited islet (which was too small to be a tourist attraction like the ones to the South of Majorca.) The sea-patrol exploring the bay was working from north to south and they were too far out east to be noticed until it widened its search.

They looked out across the huge, fairly calm expanse of sparkling sea, knowing the sun set very fast at this time of year. "The police search helicopter....they might see us here, where we are, from the air!" suggested Maria, although they couldn't see one.

Then Steve, crying: "I know! Follow me!" started clambering back round to the far side of the island where the little beach had been.

"What are you going to do?" asked Maria, taking him up.

"See if I can get some seagull eggs to eat," he said. "At least we won't starve while we're waiting for it! They might be a long time yet. Let's see if they'll fry on the rock in this heat! And anyway, they're over populating around this area, the seagulls!"

Making his way down the rock from the easiest point to get to an unguarded nest with eggs in it, Steve suddenly saw the speedboat covered with its tarpaulin as he looked down over his shoulder. "Hey! There's a boat down there!" he shouted.

"Where?" called Maria, looking out across the sea.

"Down there!" He pointed. "Covered with a tarpaulin – it's moored by the rocks near the cave entrance!"

"It might belong to the criminals!" she shouted back, following him down.

"Let's see if there are any distress flares in it we can let off to signal for help!"

"I don't understand," she said.

"Like fireworks. To ask for help…"

"Oh, *si, si*."

"Someone ought to see them!"

"What if it's only the criminals?"

"That's a risk we'll have to take!" urged Steve: "We must take a risk!"

"I understand – 'At your own risk', OK!" Maria had seen this phrase on notices.

He waded into the water and went over to the rocks where Rodrigo had moored the red speedboat which had taken them to the island. He had to start swimming, swam round the speedboat, then hauled himself up onto it and pulled back the grey tarpaulin halfway over the powerful red hull. "If only we could drive back in this!" he said. "It's like the one they took us here in…oh no!… they haven't come back, have they?"

"No!" reassured Maria. "They must have all left in the other one. Anyway, the police helicopter will see us when it comes," she added: "it will come – with a big light if it's dark."

"A searchlight," Steve supplied. Then he decided. " No - it's already getting too late…," he pointed out. "We can't wait for that….the thugs might come back anyway to make sure we drown!" He got into the boat to look around for flares. And just had to take a look at the controls. They were very impressive….complicated. It was a brand new, expensive speedboat. And then, to his great relief, he saw a small bunch of keys dangling from the ignition!

This speedboat was used for most of the diamond-smuggling runs from larger ocean-going vessels, and the criminals didn't want it noticed at the Puerto Pollensa yacht club; so they usually left it moored near the rock fissure, camouflaged by the tarpaulin, amongst the large grey rocks just off the island. Any one of several smugglers might suddenly be ordered to use it at short notice, so the keys were usually left in the ignition ready for any of them whenever they needed it. (Rodrigo had only been using it around the coast area in the daytime during the last few days, because he knew it wouldn't be so conspicuous during the boat festival.)

All Steve had to do now was untie the boat's mooring and head back for Puerto Pollensa.

"They've left the keys in the ignition!"

"Let's go back in it!" Maria, who'd been out in a speedboat before with her brother, felt sure she could steer her way back to Puerto Pollensa. Pablo had taken her out recently in a speedboat owned by a friend of his, who'd described how to operate the controls. And Steve had been dying to drive one since his breakfast conversations with the English guest at the hotel. Maria swam out to the speedboat, which was pointing back towards the island with the incoming tide. First of all they decided to have a proper look for any flares or distress rockets, because it would still be a good idea to let them off before they set out. But there weren't any.

Between them they managed to untie it from its moorings – the rope was now mainly underwater. "I'll drive!" insisted Maria, "I know the way back!" and she stood at the helm with her hands on the steering wheel, her saturated skirt clinging to her like a statue's. Steve leant over her and turned the keys in the ignition. He turned them once, twice and the powerful engine surged up. It was very noisy, and they sped away across the brilliant turquoise-blue waves, this time in control of things.

Maria let Steve take over the steering as they approached the shore. But between them and the harbour were the boat festival games. There were dozens of gaily decorated fishing vessels, all engaged in various activities and races, as well as lots of boats and yachts being sailed by onlookers – stretching across the sea where they needed to pass through. The sun was just beginning to slip down the sky and was casting a peach glow on the waves. It was still quite warm.

No-one took much notice of them as they were all preoccupied with the boat festival activities. Steve decided he was going to make a detour, suddenly slowed the speedboat right down and turned it around 180 degrees, inadvertently sending a smart arc of water over an old fishing boat as he did so, this just splashed the people in it. "Sorry!" he shouted, as the engine surged up again and he and Maria roared off fast northwards up the bay before they could get much of a look at either of them.

Some participants in the boat games had received a police alert, by mobile, to be on the look-out for the missing youngsters and the two suspicious motorboats Great-Granpa Munos had reported. They'd passed this on to the others, yet no-one involved in the boat activities had time to notice who was in the red speedboat. Someone phoned the Puerto Pollensa police to let them know they'd just seen it heading off north; but there were several red speedboats out that day along the coast being watched by the police sea patrol and it would be some time before this sighting could be followed up.

Meanwhile, as Steve was racing up the coast with Maria, she asked him: "Why didn't you just ask to pass through the fishing boats?"

"I didn't like to interrupt," he said: "it's a religious festival, after all…"

"Oh. Well, if we keep on going, we'll come to the northern tip of Majorca! Let's stop!"

"Sure, OK! I was just about to ask you where else we could disembark…but we may as well sit and dry our clothes off a bit before we go back." Steve hoped she was understanding what he was saying.

They cruised to a halt, quite far off the coast, and switched the engine off. The new quiet was nearly humming in their ears, and the nearest yachts were little specks on the horizon. While Maria sat spreading the flounces of her dress to dry, she and Steve discussed the likelihood of being spotted by the criminals.

"There aren't many people sailing out here .....I wonder where they are?" Steve frowned, trying not to shiver in the gradually diminishing heat of the sun. He scanned round the horizon. "We'd see them coming if they were in their yellow and white motorboat...."

"We'd better stay away from the shore, in case they recognise this one," said Maria.

"All right....in fact, why don't we stay out here until it gets dark, then we can get back safely straight to Puerto Pollensa without them noticing us?"

"It would be good to get back as soon as possible....." began Maria.

"Yes, but we don't want to be spotted by those pirates!.....They might still be hanging about."

So they waited out there through a brief, resplendent sunset of glowing pinks with vermilion banding, until the sky became deep indigo over the darkening sea, a few stars started appearing and a large, golden moon rose up. The sea patrol boat, further down south along the coast, still hadn't found them. Then Steve, who was driving back, started the powerful engine up again. Maria had pointed out the switch for the lights, but they'd agreed not to put them on driving back until they reached Puerto Pollensa harbour, in case the criminals were still around to see them.

Looking back once to the menacing silhouette of the island, Maria noticed several dark shark fins scything through the moonlit water. They'd been right not to try swimming back! Steve grinned.

As they approached the harbour, the lights of the Puerto Pollensa yacht club had started to come out and Maria could see their way in easily. They became elated as the twinkling white points gradually grew nearer.

Steve's parents had meanwhile walked the length and breadth of the town, and eventually been joined by Senor Ramon and Senorina Isabel Munos - who had dark auburn brown hair like Pablo - to look for them. The Parkers said goodbye to the Majorcan couple at the harbour, after it had been agreed the Snrs. Munos were going to make enquiries in the nearby villages. (Pablo had gone back on duty and was back in the police station, arranging for a sea-search helicopter from police headquarters to search around the coastline with a strong searchlight.) Now Mr and Mrs Parker stayed to look at all the various sailing vessels. A few old fishing boats with peeling paintwork - decorative vestiges for the festival, mainly - bobbed alongside smart, new white yachts. Had Steve and Maria gone away in someone's boat?

Pat Parker was looking out to sea with tears in her eyes as her husband was holding her hand. Suddenly she noticed a faint humming sound in the background. Then a large, noisy red speedboat came into view, approaching the harbour; its lights suddenly came on, and two small figures, one standing at the wheel, one sitting, could be seen in the dark. It was Steve and Maria! Mr Parker jumped for joy on the harbour wall as he recognised his son, who was now slowing the speed: "It's them, Pat! They're safe!" - while his wife clung to him laughing and crying at the same time. Then they both started shouting at Steve to stop the speedboat in plenty of time to avoid colliding with the harbour wall or the other boats.

He and Maria were both out of breath again as they came to a 'safe' stop, just short of the harbour wall. They'd been shouting to each other over the noise of the engine. Mr Parker shouted at them to throw him the mooring rope, which he tied round a post. The youngsters had to clamber over some other boats to reach the nearest steps up the harbour wall. As he helped them ashore, Mr Parker anxiously demanded "Where've you <u>been</u>? The police have been out searching for you!"

Steve did the explaining, with Maria making only a few interjections. He started off by saying: "We found some diamonds in the cliffs."

"<u>Diamonds</u>!!??" exclaimed his mother.

"Yes, loads and loads - in bags. And a gang of criminals spotted us - they grabbed us and took us away to an island cave..."

"In this speedboat!" added Maria.

"… and tied us up……."

"The tide came in and we nearly drowned!" said Maria.

"But we escaped in their speedboat back here!" Steve put in quickly, anticipating his father's reaction.

"And you expect me to <u>believe</u> this?" demanded Mr Parker, becoming angry after his initial relief at getting them back alive. "This is just a far-fetched story to cover up the fact you've been joy-riding!" and he took Steve by the arm and stared intently into his face. "Did or did you not take this speedboat without the owner's permission?" he asked him.

"No!" insisted Steve. "We'll show you where we found the diamonds in the cliffs!"

Maria didn't understand everything Mr Parker said next, but she realised he didn't believe his son. So she showed him and Mrs Parker the red marks on her wrists and ankles. (Steve's had more or less disappeared under his socks and the wristwatch round his left wrist had prevented much of a mark there.) "Look!" she said, "They tied us with ropes - they used ropes to tie together our hands and feet! Please, it's true! Steve used my brooch pin to cut the ropes!" Still the Parkers could hardly take in what had happened. They took them to the police station.

There, Jose, Great-Granpa Munos' old friend, was still manning the main reception. He jumped up out of his seat with pleasure when the two youngsters walked through the doors with the Parkers. The ends of his moustache practically turned up at the ends with delight. "So you're back!" he said in Mallorqui to Maria. Then, "What happened?" he asked Steve in English, more formally. It took a long time for Steve and Maria to explain what had happened to them, but they eventually told the Majorcan police sergeant the full story, including how they halted the advance of the Portuguese man-of-war with Maria's shawl. His expression became more severe. Mr Parker gradually began to believe them as they explained that there had been two motorboats and the criminals had all left in the yellow and white one.

Jose made lots of notes, then said to the Parkers: "From the descriptions given by Steve and Maria of the criminals, and the names they heard - Antonio, Julio, Manuel and Rodrigo - it seems we already know most of them. But 'Alto' must be a nickname: we haven't heard that one before. They're Spanish, they don't live in Majorca - and are suspected to be involved in diamond smuggling. We can investigate the ownership of the speedboat you've left in the harbour, and take it away for a forensic check. And check out the wall lamp in the cave the same way. I'll send an officer over immediately." He made a quick phone call. "Tomorrow, first thing, we'll search the cliffs where the children say they found the diamonds. If we find anything, we can wait to see who comes to collect them. Then we can go out to the island cave and look for clues to catch the criminals…" and he looked at Steve and Maria: "perhaps the handkerchiefs and necktie they used to gag you are still floating about, and maybe we can get some DNA samples. We might even find the old silver brooch for Maria to keep as a souvenir of her experience, if we're lucky!"

Steve and Maria didn't emerge from the police station until well after dark. Snr and Senorina Munos had been phoned, and came to collect Maria. They too were tremendously relieved that nothing worse had happened to their daughter. They didn't blame Steve for going beyond the cliff top railings, and of course no-one blamed poor old Great-Granpa Munos, who was at Maria's home and delighted to hear the youngsters were safe and sound. Senorina Munos, a friendly, bubbly person, suggested the two families go out for a meal to celebrate their children's safe return, the next day. And the Parkers agreed this was a good idea.

Becky was overjoyed – she even pretended to say so sarcastically - when her parents came back to the hotel in the evening with Steve. They were just in time for dinner there at eight o'clock. Steve talked all through the meal about the ordeal which he and Maria had been through. Becky could hardly believe it, finding it hard to swallow each mouthful of food as she stared at him with her eyes very wide. "But it is true!" said Steve when she said she didn't believe there was a deadly stinging siphonophore in the cave. Neither he nor his parents mentioned to her that the police were going back very early in the morning, undercover, to investigate the cache of diamonds hidden in the cliffs. Jose had briefed them to say nothing - to protect these undercover officers who'd be posing as tourists and photographers near the cliffs, hoping to observe the criminals if they returned. The police didn't think these men would risk returning to the cliffs in the dark, it would look highly suspicious - and it was very dangerous. They'd be more likely to quickly get onto the vulture's ledge in daylight to collect the diamonds while they thought no-one could see them.

CHAPTER EIGHT

Closing In…

Very early next morning, the smugglers' leader Rodrigo Gonzalez was arrested by two policemen as he went to pick up the diamonds - which he'd decided to leave in the cliff crevice overnight and pick up himself, to ensure there were no blunders. The national police had been watching him from the nearby copse with binoculars. He fitted Steve and Maria's description perfectly: a slim-built blond man with a long, thin scar running down his left cheek. The two officers ran to arrest him with their guns drawn for self-protection, just as he was packing the packets of diamonds into his large back-pack; he was going back to his car, parked in the town. The police were pleased they'd caught one of the criminals red-handed.

Yet it was doubtful they would catch the others so easily. A local couple out walking had seen Rodrigo Gonzalez's arrest.   Once the news of it broke, his accomplices might flee that part of Spain - and the police had no proof yet of their activities.

When the Munos and Parker families met for lunch to celebrate their children's safe return, Pablo, finally off duty, knew it was safe by now to relate the progress made by the police to everyone. Because this news would already be travelling fast all over the island. He and Maria, Snr and Senorina, Great-Granma and Great-Granpa Munos; Steve, Becky and Mr and Mrs Parker - were all sitting round a large table. When Steve had finished describing the cave, they continued talking (in English.) It was a long and happy lunch and eventually Mr Parker settled the bill. (He felt responsible that it had been Steve's straying from the path - literally - which had precipitated their entanglement with such dangerous people.)

Steve and Maria had agreed to meet again for some beach games and they all strolled, relaxed and happy, out of the restaurant. It was another afternoon filled with very brilliant light and Steve put on his sunglasses straightaway, even though the street they were in enjoyed some shade. Then, as they were going down some steps to the main street, where there were market stalls extending from the market in the main square, Steve suddenly couldn't believe his eyes.

Ambling a few metres away from them down the main street was the unmistakeable, bulky figure of one of the criminals, the ex-fisherman Antonio, who now worked part-time in the kitchens at a little café run by Rodrigo in Madrid, Spain. He was dressed in his black jeans as before, an outsize black tee-shirt stretched tightly across his stomach. Although Antonio was unshaven and wearing sunspecs, Steve immediately recognised him by his swarthy complexion, low forehead, those heavy black eyebrows and the cruel, down-turned mouth. Antonio turned to say something to his companion - who was no other than Manuel. Manuel was also wearing the clothes he was wearing yesterday - faded black jeans and a leather waistcoat, with a clean tee-shirt. Steve wondered whether he was carrying his gun.

Both criminals were stopping to look at a display of vegetables on one of the market stalls. They'd arrived a little early in Puerto Pollensa for their rendezvous with Rodrigo Gonzalez, not knowing he'd been arrested by the police that morning. Their own 'WANTED' descriptions weren't out in the local newspapers yet; neither of them knew anyone in the town and they'd heard nothing of the youngsters' escape from the cave, because they'd both got up very late after drinking heavily. They'd assumed Steve and Maria had drowned.

Steve turned to Pablo who was coming down the steps close behind him, and shouted in his excitement when he should have whispered: "There are two of the criminals! Look! Those two men looking at the vegetables!" And he pointed. He'd shouted in English, so Antonio and Manuel, now standing with their backs to him, hadn't understood. Two English people, who <u>did</u> understand, now stood rooted to the spot in the street. Most of the crowd went on moving about. Antonio, like a few people, turned round and stared at Steve, but failed to recognise him in his sunglasses. Then the crook saw Maria, recognised her, and so realised who Steve was. They had escaped!

At the same moment, Pablo ran through the crowd of shoppers towards the criminals, shouting in Mallorqui: "Police! Let me through!" But it was very crowded and by the time people had made way for him, Antonio and Manuel had pushed two or three others roughly out of the way and started running down a side street. What they hadn't realised, was that this street also had stalls set up in it and was effectively much narrower than they'd anticipated. So there were people in their way there, too. However, Antonio was so heavy that no-one felt confident enough to try to stand in his path as he bulldozed his way along, Manuel following.

Pablo came after them, with Steve and Maria running behind and their parents and Becky a little way behind that. Pablo was gaining ground on the two men, when Antonio decided to try to make his way down another side street. The entrance to this was flanked by stalls on either side, making it even narrower than the other one. Antonio drew in his breath and attempted to squeeze his bulk through the first two stalls. One of them was bedecked with jars of pasta, and the other displayed a choice of cakes. He became wedged in between them. He couldn't shift them further apart because the stallholders behind them didn't want to be squashed up against the walls - so pushed back against him as hard as they could. Manuel tried pushing him forwards as they both started to panic, but it was no use. Antonio was stuck.

Pablo reached them with Steve just behind him. "You're under citizen's arrest!" he told them in Spanish. One of the stallholders had phoned the police, and two or three of the men amongst the crowd moved protectively up behind Pablo. "Wait here, or you could also be charged with resisting arrest!" he added. The two criminals realised they'd be prevented from running away again – now that they'd been stopped - by the local shoppers, half of whom had guessed they'd abducted the young English lad and the Munos' daughter.

"*No hay escapada!*" Steve couldn't resist saying to Antonio - 'There's no escape!' - which were the last words Antonio had said to him after they'd closed the grille door of the cave. They were the only new words he'd picked up in Spanish and understood. (He already knew that '*no hay*' meant 'there is/are no' and had guessed what '*escapada*' meant, and checked this with Pablo over lunch). Antonio stayed where he was, sandwiched between the two stalls, looking very uncomfortable indeed.

Steve and Maria's parents came up and put their hands on their children's shoulders, staring at the two men who had tried to kill them and saying nothing. Steve and Maria also were silent, whilst people in the crowd were discussing whether these were the men who'd abducted them. It only took a few minutes for four armed, uniformed police officers to arrive. They got out of two cars and greeted Pablo. Pablo quickly explained to them that Steve had identified the men as two of the criminals in the diamond-smuggling gang - and they swiftly handcuffed Antonio and Manuel.

"Two more!" exclaimed one of the police officers in Spanish. "Just how did you manage it?" he asked Steve, with Pablo translating for him.

"I'd recognise them again anywhere," asserted Steve.

The two criminals were driven off to the police station and the crowds started to move about their business again.

Mrs Parker was delighted. "I feel like another celebration!" she said, to which Becky responded: " I just couldn't *stand* hearing Steve's bragging all over again!"

Mr Parker was shaking hands with Snr Munos: "We've caught half of the criminals!" he was saying.

"Well done, Steve!" Maria congratulated him.

Pablo had had to accompany the officers back to the police station, so couldn't rejoin the two families now they'd decided to take a cup of tea in another cafe, before finally parting. This latest development had given them more to discuss. Senor Ramon Munos observed: "Steve and Maria may have to participate in Court by videoconferencing to describe what happened to them."

His wife Isabel added: "Or perhaps, if Steve goes home to England before the ..." (searching for the word which Pablo often had to use) "...trial, he can just give a statement to the police."

The two families continued talking about bringing the criminals to justice and how to catch the other two Maria had described: the very tall one nicknamed 'Alto', whose real name they hadn't discovered; and the stocky one called Julio, who she remembered feeling may have been a shopkeeper, because of the sarcastic way he'd first accosted Steve and the mocking counter assistant style he adopted as they took them into the cave. Chris Parker said: "We must make sure that the two criminals who're still free never harm our children again."

Ramon Munos agreed. "But," he said, "I don't think they'll return to this town when they hear of the arrest of their friends." Everyone felt he was right.

Nevertheless, a few days later - when Steve and Maria met up on the beach for the game of volleyball they'd agreed on with some other young people - their parents, with Becky, sat nearby to watch them. "We don't want you having another adventure like that," Pat Parker had warned. "Not yet, anyway," Becky teased Steve, "but I expect you'll be back to your boring old self again soon!" He was having a great time with Maria.

By the time the Parkers' holiday finally came to an end, Steve had given another statement to the police - and he and Maria had identified Rodrigo, Manuel and Antonio from photographs of them taken at Palma Police Station. Steve and Becky gave their home telephone number, address and e-mail address to Pablo and Maria, who reciprocated, promising to write first.

O n the morning of his arrest, two people had just been arrested in Puerto
Pollensa for pick-pocketing, so Rodrigo, instead of being taken to the
nearest local police station, was driven straight to the main police station
at Palma. He was locked in a cell for an hour. It was already very hot and in the
still, humid air he felt sticky and uncomfortable. Then, by late morning, he was
let out to have his photograph taken and for questioning in the interview room.
Two policemen were sitting at a table, with notepads and recording equipment.
The senior of the two officers was just finishing a telephone conversation as he
entered. The junior officer invited him to sit on the chair facing them. Lots of filing
cabinets around the room suggested to Rodrigo that everything he was about to
say would be recorded - and kept for a long time. There was an electric fan on top
of one of the filing cabinets, cooling down the room.

He had to verify his name as Rodrigo Gonzalez - he was already known to the
police. But he carefully gave as many vague, evasive replies as possible to the
other questions put to him by the senior police officer.

"What were you going to do with the packets of diamonds which had been left in
the cliffs?"

*"I didn't know what they were. I wondered if some ecologists were leaving minerals
– or ice cubes or something - there to see if the black vultures would take them to
eat. They don't usually nest there. I took some for myself to look at once I got back
onto the cliff top, intending to return them."*

"But you stuffed them into your rucksack."

"I was going to sit down nearby, on a bench if I could find one, and look at them."

"You've been named by two youngsters – Steve Parker and Maria Munos - as one
of the people who abducted them yesterday afternoon and left them tied up in the
island cave off Puerto Pollensa. They could have drowned. Do you admit this?"

"No. Some friends I'd just made that day and I offered to take the kids on an excursion in our speedboats! out to the island, because Steve expressed interest in mine. It was fishing festival day, after all, and everyone was in an outgoing, friendly mood."

"Then why did you tie them up and leave them to drown?"

"We didn't," Rodrigo replied, *"when we were on the island the kids suddenly jumped into my speedboat and took it for a joy ride – I'd left the keys in the ignition."*

"What time was that, about?"

"I don't know – but we had to stay out there for a long time waiting for them to bring it back, and in the end we all drove back in the other speedboat because they <u>didn't</u> come back. They must have been out in it for ages – there was enough fuel in the tank."

"What were the names of your new friends?"

"Oh, Manuel and ….I can't remember right now, perhaps they'll come to me in a bit…"

"Were they the ones in a yellow and white motorboat?"

"No – it was a black speedboat, actually," he lied yet again.

After a while, Rodrigo asked permission to smoke a cigarette.

"Don't you know they're very bad for you health?" asked the junior officer, while the senior police officer nodded his assent to the detainee's request. Rodrigo didn't reply to this last question, but slowly and deliberately retrieved a packet of cigarettes from a pocket while the junior policeman went to fetch some matches for him (they'd confiscated his cigarette lighter when he arrived). Rodrigo took a cigarette and put it in his mouth, listening to the junior officer talking to another policeman just outside the door of the interview room.

The junior officer's voice was deep and quite distinct: "It's time we arranged an investigation of the island cave at Puerto Pollensa. The police there are overstretched and haven't had time yet. We've just phoned them and the nearest sea patrol's too busy helping tourists out of difficulties. We'd better move fast - the tide's due in again soon."

The officer he was talking to spoke in a lighter pitch, which Rodrigo could just hear: "Yes, there may be some evidence there. The English lad was talking about a waterproof lamp that was fixed high up on the wall – it may have fingerprints on it – especially on the inside!"

"You've seen a copy of the kids' statements!"

"Yes. What an escape!" said the other officer admiringly in a low voice barely audible to Rodrigo.

The first junior officer flicked his head backwards indicating Rodrigo sitting at the interview table and lowered his own voice: "If you can believe them…." he said, meaning that he wasn't corroborating what the youngsters had told the police.

Rodrigo thought fast. It was only a question of time before his smuggling boss, Senor C., would get to hear of his arrest. Then he'd probably order someone to try to remove any evidence from the cave while the tide was out, provided the police weren't in the area.

That included the waterproof lamp, which Senor C. had provided for the cave as a temporary fitting - they were always changing their pick-up points to avoid detection. Senor C.'s own fingerprints might still be on it, as he'd checked it was working properly, and the police might be able to trace him by checking on where he'd bought it. And he wouldn't want any of his gang convicted by the fingerprints on the outside of it, either, if he could help it. Rodrigo didn't even know the real name of his boss, but he was known as 'Senor C.', and apparently had an old criminal record.

Taking the cigarette out of his mouth again, Rodrigo asked the senior officer sitting at the table: "Do you mind if I assist you in your investigations, with some more helpful information?"

The senior officer raised his eyebrows disbelievingly. "What's this, then, Rodrigo? Are you going to confess?"

"I don't mind offering some <u>more</u> helpful information - in return for decent treatment," he insisted.

"Go ahead."

"I just heard what you were discussing. Well, judging by my watch and that barometer on the wall, you're just a bit too late now to check out the cave while the tide's out. I know the barometric tide times as well as the astronomical ones."

"Oh yes – what's the difference?"

"Well, I expect the sea patrol uses the astronomical tide charts. But I'll bet they don't know there's a little mini-tide – they're called rip-tides - that comes in and goes out again, quite fast, around the island, about now if it's very hot, without affecting the main beach." Rodrigo was bluffing. There was never a rip-tide there. "It's just a minor cross-current running over the rocky bottom around the island. But it's irregular and it's too small to be put into the main charts: it's affected by the barometer, not the moon, or the sun."

"Really?"

"Yes," Rodrigo smiled at the junior police officer, who'd returned with some matches and now listened in, interested. "If you go out to the cave now in the next hour or so, with the build-up of this stifling heat," he continued, coolly availing himself of the lighted match being held out for him, "you'll find it flooded!" He took the first drag on his cigarette and looked directly at each of the officers. "But if you wait another couple of hours it'll be far easier to investigate. The tide will be suddenly out again."

The two officers considered this, exchanging looks. "Look, we do have some paperwork urgently needing completing," the senior one pointed out to his colleague. "I think it's best if we call a halt to this questioning for a while, take heed of what Rodrigo's been saying and get the sea patrol nearest Puerto Pollensa to investigate the cave just a bit later on. They probably won't be freed up till then anyway. What time exactly would you suggest then, Rodrigo?"

"About 4.00 to 4.30pm."

"Fine. So, you can go back to your cell and wait, while I have a word with the relevant sea patrol. Then we can see if what you've said is sound advice……or whether perhaps you've been telling us lies since we started talking to you." And the senior officer gave him a hard look. "Is there anything else you want to add in relation to what you've told us so far?"

Rodrigo shook his head.

They returned him to his hot cell down the corridor. Shortly after lunchtime, he was surprised to hear the voices of Antonio and Manuel as they were being ushered into an adjacent cell. Finding there were already two men being held in the adjacent one, the officers who'd just taken charge of the cells decided instead to lock the new arrivals in the same cell as Rodrigo. "They can all wait here while I get someone to stand guard," one of the officers told a colleague, "then we can try to get them into separate cells."

He went to see if someone was free to stand guard.

Rodrigo greeted his two accomplices: "So they caught you too?"

"Yes," Antonio began, about to describe the chase through the vegetable market, but he was cut short by his ring leader: "Listen, before the guard comes back: we've got to make sure they believe what I've just told them. Then we might get lighter sentences."

"What have you just told them?" asked Manuel suspiciously.

Rodrigo managed to explain hastily, just before the first guard returned to their cell with another policeman who was to stand guard outside.

"We're waiting before we send the sea patrol out to the cave," the first guard said to the three men in the cell, "so you'd better be right about the rip-tide, Rodrigo!"

"The rip-tide?" Manuel joined in, carefully and supportively.

"Believe me, there's a rip-tide mid-afternoon at this time of year - it comes up very fast and then goes away almost as soon as it's up," persisted Rodrigo.

"That odd surprise tide that comes up round the island?" Antonio took up. "Sure there's a rip-tide….oh yes, trust me, I'm a fisherman! It's a barometric tide you get around the Puerto Pollensa bay - but not on the beach - when the water's a certain temperature. It's not in the tide charts." And he pressed his face persuasively, enthusiastically, to the grille in the door. The guard turned his back on him.

The senior police officer was liasing on the phone again with the police at Puerto Pollensa. "What a stroke of luck! So now we have three of the diamond smuggling suspects here. We can question them individually to see if their stories add up."

He was speaking this time with Jose, who was still resisting the smugglers' suggestion that a rip-tide would have prevented them from searching the cave at an earlier time than they'd just arranged. "I'm not at all convinced by this rip-tide yarn," said Jose, his moustache drooping: "I haven't heard of it and I've lived here all my life…..But anyway, it won't matter if there aren't any footprints in the cave, which there probably won't be, or even if we can't get the wall lamp the youngsters described to us. The forensic evidence isn't vital in this case, because we've got the kids as witnesses! Maria and her English friend Steve both give exactly the same story. And they'll both be able to identify all three men from their photographs, if it was them! We can do that with videoconferencing as well, can't we?"

"Yes; anyway, there's no need for the kids to be present at an identity parade," assured his Palma colleague.

"Steve Parker's returning to England shortly," said Jose, "he can do it from there."

CHAPTER TEN

Tide Work

That morning, Alto was still on the run, hiding out in a holiday villa which was being decorated by local builders for rental; they'd left off working on it for a couple of weeks, and the smugglers had an illegally cut key to it. On the way back from the cave the gang had dropped him off on the coast near Alcudia, the next big bay going south from Puerto Pollensa. From there he'd made his way to a small, pretty village some way inland, and let himself in.

There was only the old carpeting, a few paint pots left about and not much furniture in the villa, and there was no phone installed yet; but there was a television. He'd missed the news bulletins the previous evening and the morning bulletins for two days because of getting up late after a poor night's sleep. So he hadn't heard of the youngsters' escape or of Rodrigo's arrest.

The smugglers hadn't been sure whether they'd be able to return to the cave unseen, to dispose of the kids' bodies, or whether they'd have to leave them there until they became skeletons. And he still hadn't heard from them – one of the reasons why he'd been unable to sleep easily. The smugglers <u>had</u> decided, however, that as he was the only one of them not recognisable to the police, because he didn't have a criminal record, he should be the one to stay in the general area nearest Puerto Pollensa. From there, he could set up a new, safe route for the next consignments of diamonds to come in, after they'd all lain low for a long time, keeping an eye out for police activity. It had been agreed he wouldn't try to contact anyone else in the gang by mobile for a couple of days, as a precautionary measure, just in case they were being monitored by the police.

A little before lunchtime, Alto went out. It was another hot day, with a brilliant, cloudless blue sky. Buying two newspapers, one local and one national, from the village shop, he walked on to an outdoor café. Nearby, on his left across the little square were the old grey stone walls of a church. Up the slope, on his right, were the brilliant white walls of new holiday villas. He sat down at a table at the far side of the café terrace from the only other occupied table, where a couple was sitting, so that the man's back was turned to him. The waiter wasn't about yet.

Alto scanned the national newspaper. There was nothing mentioned of the youngsters' escape, which would go into the next day's paper. Then he opened out the front page of the local weekly newspaper, which had just been printed overnight, and discovered that the youngsters had escaped. He felt his face flush as he read on. The police had their description of him, and his nickname, to go by in catching the criminals. They were described as a group of very dangerous men who shouldn't be approached by members of the public under any circumstances. He was now very wary of staying anywhere near the Puerto Pollensa area.

Alto had already been contemplating giving up his recent involvement with the diamond smugglers. His conscience was weighing on him hard enough anyway - and he didn't like the fact that he'd now suddenly had to help with the attempt to dispose of the nosey kids - even if it hadn't worked. He knew he'd nearly become a murderer as well. He desperately needed money – but he couldn't live like this! There were other less dangerous ways of making money, and even if they were more difficult, he would try them again. He was in serious trouble.

He decided to risk staying at the café table for lunch. Suddenly he received a call on his mobile from another man involved with the diamond smuggling, Miguel, whom he'd never met. Rodrigo had primed him to expect a call from this man. Miguel gave the special password used by the larger cartel of diamond smugglers, confirming that this wasn't a call from an undercover police officer. Then he told him about the arrest of Rodrigo at the cliffs, and then Manuel and Antonio at the Puerto Pollensa market, saying: "Alto, there's a reward for you if you do us a favour and go back to the Pollensa cave with me."

"What for?" Alto, already taken aback, asked him in a low voice so the couple sitting a little way away from him couldn't listen in to what he was saying.

"To collect the waterproof lamp from the wall, and anything else incriminating which may have been left there."

"There won't be much!"

"Yes, but someone might have left some fibres from their clothes, or their hair – it's what they can do with DNA tests these days! We'd better search the place meticulously….and you and I are the men to do it: the police don't know <u>my</u> face; and all they'll have to go on for you will be a stupid photo fit…."

"Still, that's quite a risk – they must be going there any time now," Alto said emphatically, then hunched his shoulders down and drew his long legs in under his table as the man at the table across the terrace heard him and turned round to look at him.

"Yes," returned Miguel urgently, "but that's why you're being paid to do this. And we can make sure they're nowhere around the cave first. And we'll take a hired yacht there so they won't be able to trace us easily – we'll just look like sports fishermen. Tourists."

Alto felt like closing the conversation: this was so risky. But instead - partly because the couple nearby were now giving their orders to the waiter, and definitely weren't listening in to him, or taking any notice of him - he stayed talking to Miguel. "What's the reward?"

"A small percentage of the profits from the next diamonds consignment…"

Alto kept one hand cupped round the receiver of his mobile as he said carefully and quietly: "Rodrigo's already let me keep a few packets of diamonds as compensation now I'm a suspect in an attempted murder investigation. Which I never expected. But going <u>back</u> there!"

"….And promotion," Miguel declared the bonus on offer tentatively. "How would you like to get involved in our diamond operations in Western Europe?   It's cleaner….."

"And pays better, I suppose."

"You drive a hard bargain."

"I'm just not sure I want to stay involved with these operations at all. The kids have given my description to the police!" Alto hissed desperately, still with his hand cupped round the mobile's receiver.

"But if that's the case, you can best avoid being detected now by coming out North-West with us. Then maybe you can return in a few years when it's safe: even richer…."

Miguel was experienced in this game of persuasion, and Alto was now definitely tempted by his offer of a small percentage of the diamonds racketeering profits just for removing the evidence from the cave. "Are you in this with me?" pressed Miguel.

"OK!…I'll do the cave for 15% of the next consignment, if it's as big as the last one." "It should be…" Miguel had to rely on Alto to do it as soon as possible, so gave in: "OK."

"But I'll decide about the international opportunity after I've done this job. I'll have to wipe away my own fingerprints last - I wouldn't want to take all the blame…." Alto suggested suspiciously. Furtively keeping his head down and his voice low, he flicked his eyes across at the waiter, then the couple at the far table on the terrace, still worrying in case they recognised him. Secretly, the newest member of the smuggling gang was still hoping he'd be able to get an ordinary job after this and draw a line under all his criminal activity. He thought: *'Let's first wait and see if they pay what they've just offered me for returning to the cave.'*

"The police may have gone to investigate the cave already anyway," said Miguel, "but just in case they haven't, we'll go just as the tide's coming in, so we don't leave any footprints. We've got to move fast. If we're lucky we can get the waterproof lamp and clean up anything else that's been left there."

They agreed to meet up at Port d'Alcudia. "I'll sail up to Pollensa with you in the small fishing motorboat I've already hired from further down the coast," promised Miguel. "Now what do you look like, so we recognise each other?"

"Well, I'm quite tall – two metres or so; slim; blue eyes and short brown hair, in case you haven't seen the photo fit 'WANTED' poster of me," Alto said wryly, "and I'm wearing dark blue jeans and a white T-shirt. Oh, and I'm growing a small beard!"

Miguel gave his own description: "I'm medium height, brown eyes and brown hair, wearing mid-blue jeans and a dark green short-sleeved shirt. Wait for me at the café by the very tall palm trees, by the main port walkway."

Alto took the bus from the village to Alcudia. He got off outside the old fourteenth century walls of the ancient city – Majorca's oldest - deciding not to wait with all the tourists for another bus to take him to the port. With his long legs he could easily walk the couple of kilometres - and probably get there faster than if he'd waited for the bus. He made his way through the shady maze of narrow, Arabic streets, crowded with the smells of leather goods, baking and perfumes, and bought a new pale blue T-shirt in one of the shops; then he kept in one direction until he came out to a wide modern road leading to the port. Nearby were the columns of an old Roman ruin: just one of numerous remains of several civilizations which had come and gone there. The sky was building up into deep purple thunderclouds behind the ruin's columns as the heavy July heat built up, threatening to break down into rain soon.

People have been moving from one place to another down the centuries, Alto thought: *perhaps I should consider joining the diamond smuggling in North-western Europe, if it pays well, and try being a bit more daring - for my daughter's sake.* But he knew she wouldn't want to learn that her father was a criminal: she thought he was an honest carpenter. Perhaps he could find better, legal work opportunities out there - maybe he could even get his family to join him out there somewhere, if he managed to disengage himself from all this criminal activity. He would take the opportunity if Miguel offered it him again, so he had a chance of escaping the Spanish police – but then look around for honest work straightaway, he decided.

There was a thunder crack and a flash of lightening as Alto made his way swiftly along the road to the port. After a few minutes he was caught in a brief downpour of very heavy rain, and had to take shelter at a petrol station shop. He bought another local newspaper and read it there quickly to see if there were any articles about his gang, but there weren't any.

After a while the rain stopped and the sky quickly cleared. It was cooler but the heat would begin to build up again, slowly and relentlessly. Alto left the garage shop and strode on, drying off the white T-shirt he was wearing in the light breeze and saving the new pale blue one to change into after he'd been to the cave.

Port d'Alcudia harbour was packed with lots of small sailing and motor boats. The sea sparkled in the new afternoon sunshine and the dazzling white beach was attracting lots of tourists now that the weather had brightened again. Alto walked along the main walkway. The leaves of the very tall palm trees along it were fluttering gently in the lessening sea breeze. As soon as he approached the outdoor café they'd agreed to meet at, he recognised Miguel from his description. A man with wavy brown hair in jeans and a dark green short-sleeved shirt was sitting at a table with two glasses and a bottle of mineral water on it, watching everyone go by. He removed his sunglasses when he saw Alto. He had a slightly pugnacious-looking face but wore an intelligent expression: his large, rather hang-dog brown eyes were unfathomable. As he gestured for him to sit down while looking about them, he showed an aquiline nose and a passionate, slightly down-turned mouth a bit like a fish's. Alto decided he wouldn't like to get on the wrong side of Miguel: somehow he looked dedicated to leading his life in the underworld.

After quickly quenching his thirst with a drink of mineral water, Alto set off with him in a small hired motor boat north up the coast to the cave off Pollensa.

"I wish you'd all just fled the area as soon as you saw the kids interfering with the diamonds in the cliffs," said Miguel, looking ahead as he steered the boat.

"Why <u>didn't</u> we do that?" agreed Alto.

"Because they probably would have got you all caught by the police straight away! They must have suspected it was you when they saw you in the cove. At least you were giving yourselves a chance to escape." He turned to look at him.

"Anyway, we'd better not be sailing into a trap now," Alto said.

"Don't worry," replied Miguel, "we'll keep our eyes open."

It was very hot again by the time they reached the small uninhabited island, at about 3.30pm. There were one or two boats sailing about near it. Alto and Miguel took a careful look at them through binoculars before stopping and mooring theirs. One boat, some way out off the seaward side of the island where the cave was, was obviously being sailed by a tourist family.

Miguel wasn't so sure about the people in the other two boats off the island's coastal side, but eventually decided they weren't plain clothes police officers by their appearance. "They look too relaxed," agreed Alto.

The tide was just beginning to trickle into the cave as Miguel moored the hired boat. Taking the key to the grille door, he gave it to Alto and told him to go in and bring back anything incriminating he could find, "While I keep watch here! Be quick about it – that tide comes in fast, but not so fast as the police come up on you!"

Alto opened the grille door and switched on the waterproof lamp which was still on its hook on the bracket on the cave wall, realising that the police couldn't have searched the cave yet. The next thing he saw was the old silver brooch. It was in a crack in a small rock near the entrance. Splashing about in the water, he went over to retrieve it. He'd read in the local newspaper how Steve and Maria had managed to escape by cutting their ropes with it.

Trying to extricate it from the rock, he realised the surge of the outgoing tide had wedged it tightly in the crack as it rushed out around it. As he at last got it out, he accidentally bent the ends of two of its three fan-shaped leaves. Alto examined it, intrigued: three fan-shaped leaves bound by a ribbon around the stalks. Now it resembled a starfish, or a melting snowflake, he mused, thinking about the diamond smuggling in Western Europe. He decided to keep it himself for good luck and put it in his pocket.

Then he quickly looked about the cave for anything else remaining. The ropes were gone, washed out to sea; there were no frayed ends or fibres lingering, either, as far as he could see. He took a thorough check, looking carefully at the sandy floor and the rocks on it, and sweeping hanging sheets of seaweed aside. Stuck against a rock, was the dead body of a Portuguese man-of-war, entangled in Maria's hand-made shawl. The criminals hadn't yet heard how Steve had used Maria's shawl to disable the deadly creature. Alto shuddered and left the shawl there, wrapped around the lifeless blob of jelly. He was really after the handkerchief and the neck scarf they'd used to gag the youngsters with, which they hadn't put back in their pockets. These must have drifted out to sea.

The gentle murmur of the waves as they started coming into the cave gave him an eerie feeling. He switched off the waterproof lamp, removed it from its bracket, wiping it with his handkerchief to remove any fingerprints, and quickly plashed back out through the grille door. He locked it with a grimace then wiped all the bars and the lock with his handkerchief before wading through the big cleft to the waiting boat. "That'll keep the police forensics department out of work," he said to Miguel as he handed over the waterproof lamp to him, wrapped in the handkerchief. He wondered if the forensics team would want to deal with Maria's shawl now that it had come into contact with the stinging tentacles of the Portuguese man-of-war. The kids had had to get in the sea to escape, which would probably have washed out any clues from their clothes, hair and faces.

"Now let's get out of here!" said Miguel. Alto was surprised at the cool countenance prevailing over his piscine features.

As they set off from the island in the hired motorboat back down the coast to Alcudia, Miguel asked him: "So: would you like to be dropped back at Alcudia? Or are you interested in joining our North Sea Operations? If you're interested in joining us, I can take you onto our yacht now for discussions with the boss…"

Alto was quickly changing into the new pale blue T-shirt he'd bought in Alcudia on his way over to meet him. He was very worried about being detected by the police, turning round to see if the boats they'd been looking at through binoculars were still by the island. "I'll accept the offer of an interview," he said, "and anyway I'd like first-hand confirmation from your boss that I'm getting a 15% profit share from the next diamonds consignment for doing this latest job."

"We get them cut and polished in Scotland," Miguel told him as he suddenly steered right out towards the horizon. "I'll drop you off at our yacht and then get back with you once I've returned this hire boat."

After a while they caught up with a very large, luxurious white cruiser yacht, the *Carisma*. Alto had never been on one that large before. Miguel gave a call and a young Spanish man dressed in white shorts, shirt and a navy yachting cap came over from the other side of the big main deck to greet them. He had dark curly hair, a slight beard and a small gold earring in one ear; his eyebrows came low down over his deep-set blue eyes and their thick curving lashes as he smiled keenly. "Alto, this is Jaime," Miguel introduced him: "he'll advise you what to do." Alto climbed up on board by a ladder on the side as Miguel drove away in the hired motorboat. They'd pick him up later.

PART TWO: SCOTLAND

CHAPTER ELEVEN
Let's Go.........

Back at the Parkers' home in Surrey, autumn set in with a strong glow. While the light was becoming softer and mellow, there'd been a long spell of dry weather without any frosts, until the colours of the leaves, as they hung crisping up on the trees in the cool air, were particularly rich. On the estate of large, mature modern houses where the Parkers lived, most of the leaves were a bright, intense gold; interspersed with a few brilliant scarlet cherries and maples, and deep blood-red ivy creepers. There weren't many butterflies left in the gardens, and everyone had put away their summer clothes. The evenings had become dark again.

In the middle of a Saturday morning, Chris and Pat Parker were sitting indoors discussing the next family holiday, which they'd been doing for the last two weekends. Steve sat a little apart from them near the patio windows giving onto the back garden, looking wistfully at a newspaper cutting in his scrapbook. It was a large article from their local newspaper, headed: 'International Diamond Smuggling Busted!' with a photo of him, captioned '*Steve Parker, heroic catcher of diamond smugglers.*' It described his adventure in Majorca in fullest, accurate detail.

When it had come out in August, he'd enjoyed quite a lot of acclaim in his local area. This had increased to adulation at the start of the school term: everyone wanted to hear his story and was asking him about how he'd managed to escape. But now, after the initial excitement of beginning a new year, school was becoming routine again; and to Steve, gazing out through the patio windows as a few leaves were falling gently onto the lawn, the adventure in Majorca seemed a long way off. He'd sent a long e-mail to Pablo and Maria a week ago, but hadn't heard back from them yet. He closed the scrapbook to join in the family discussion.

"Let's go on a properly organised bird-watching holiday this time," Chris was saying, "and why not nearer home?" he suggested. (He was determined to steer the discussion his own way as much as possible, while carefully taking on board everyone's preferences.)

"Yes," agreed his wife, "Majorca was too hot for me: especially in July….."

"…..How about the UK?"

"England might <u>do</u>," she responded.

"At least we could all understand the language," put in Steve compliantly before they started discussing when to go. He wanted the final say on that.

Becky had started her new senior school and still teased him: "Yes, it's a pity you can't talk about your diamond smuggling escapade in Spanish, Steve: it <u>would</u> make a change – for <u>everyone</u>!"

Chris took the opportunity to say "Britain it is, then!" before any confrontation developed between brother and sister, then took them with him to their high street travel agent to get several brochures offering holidays in the UK.

Later on that morning, they still hadn't reached any agreement about whereabouts in the UK they wanted to holiday. But they <u>were</u> concurring about going away in late spring, which Steve had suggested as a great time for watching various bird species nesting. Everyone was listening to Becky, who was insisting on reading out again enthusiastically about holidays in Wales, where you could go pony trekking, when the clattering letterbox heralded the arrival of the postman. Rex, their dog, rushed barking to the front door to greet him. Steve and Becky got up and raced into the hall, to see a letter from Maria fall onto the doormat amongst one or two bills in brown envelopes. It was a pale blue airmail envelope with bright little stamps with birds on, postmarked 'Majorca' and addressed to both of them. They were both very excited.

Steve reached it first and opened it, reading it walking back into the living room. Maria wrote very good English. "She says, sorry she didn't reply to the e-mail earlier but she's been very busy at school…" he began.

Becky (who'd been holding Rex by the collar and calming him) now snatched the letter from her brother and started reading from it aloud. "She says: '*Since our escape from the crooks, I've been interested in joining the police, following in my brother's footprints…*'!! she means 'footsteps' !! And then she says…..but behind-the-scenes would suit her more…she's interested in becoming a forensics expert!" Becky read on to herself, then quoted: "'*They found tiny pieces of forensic evidence in the red speedboat which might be useful if they ever catch Julio and Alto*' – those are the other criminals, aren't they? Then she says, '*and the police got my lovely lace shawl back from the cave, it got stuck against a rock with the Portuguese man-of-war, which died! There was no DNA evidence on my shawl by the time they'd safely washed it to get rid of the venom from the Portuguese man-of-war. My mother sewed up a small hole in it where it got caught on the rock.*' Then she says, by the way, it's a pity but they never recovered her mother's silver brooch….."

Steve was reading over Becky's shoulder. He suddenly exclaimed at something further down the page: "Hey look! She says she's coming to the UK in spring!" He snatched the letter back and read aloud: '*I'm going to Edinburgh, Scotland in the spring (February 16 – 23) on a school trip to an international archaeological site. It should be fun. We're also visiting the Dynamic Earth Centre where they explain natural phenomena like earthquakes and tsunamis….unfortunately it's too far away to visit you, but thank-you for saying I could. Do you have a mobile? I do, now….*'

"She's given us her mobile number. Oh Dad," Steve observed, "that's a shame: Maria's coming all the way over to Scotland in February and we were thinking of going away in March or April…why don't we fix our holiday earlier - and go up to Edinburgh? On the East Coast, isn't it? And then we can meet up again?"

"It's a very cold time of year to be going," remarked his mother: "especially on an archaeological dig. I expect it's cheaper then, though…..Still, there'd be some interesting cultural things to see and do there!"

Chris was going out with Steve anyway that afternoon, to take a quick look in a shop which sold mobile phones. Steve had been asking for a new one for his forthcoming Christmas present. So he agreed to go back to the travel agent, this time just with Steve, to look out all the brochures on Scotland.

There were quite a few of them and when they brought them home, everyone decided to have a tea break with biscuits. Although Steve had been prepared to sacrifice seeing the birds' nesting activities to meet up with Maria in February, they discovered that, in winter, Edinburgh is warmer than the more popular Western Scotland. "Great!" he realised. "So maybe the birds will have just started nesting there in February!"

Becky was very keen on the fact of less rain falling there in February than in summer. "Look!" she pointed at a temperature graph. "February's one of the two driest months of the year there – it must be sunny!"

And then, Pat, picking up one of the brochures on Edinburgh, noticed that the bird tours are run in mid-February on Scotland's East Coast – as luck would have it.

Steve realised from his brochure that he'd be able to look out for the White-tailed eagle, recently re-introduced to the East Coast from Norway. His sister, from hers, pointed out to everyone that the magnificent Golden Eagle, which isn't just confined to the West Coast, starts breeding in February: "So the East Coast will do fine, then!" (Steve had already made up his mind.) "But you'll <u>never</u> get me on a special trip to watch those," insisted Becky, "They're <u>very</u> elusive. It'd be <u>so</u> boring; you'd be hanging around waiting for ages. I can go shopping instead...."

"I bet they're <u>not</u> difficult to spot," returned Steve, who loved a challenge. "And who'd ask <u>you</u> to come along anyway? You'd frighten them away."

"Let's think about this for a while and decide in a few days' time," said Chris.

Steve made a long-distance phone call to Maria on her mobile in the evening to tell her (in English) that his family, by coincidence, had been planning for a Spring holiday in the UK when her letter arrived. And that they were now keen on opting for Edinburgh. "We think we may be able to make it for the same time <u>you'll</u> be going there – so we can all meet up again. What do you think?"

Maria was delighted with this. Becky took the phone over from Steve, saying:

"Hello, Maria – it's Becky! What Steve's just said: why not? Isn't it a great idea?"

They agreed to exchange all the details of their travel and accommodation arrangements when they came through, and Maria said she'd send an e-mail this time.

The Parkers duly agreed on, and booked, a two-week holiday for around the English schools' half-term break in February. Arriving a little before and leaving a few days after Maria, staying at a hotel in Edinburgh. Confirmation from the Scottish Tourist Board was due by the end of that week.

The next evening, Sunday, Steve and Becky were in the study on the family computer, watching the promotional film about Edinburgh and the Lothians, provided by the Tourist Board with its brochure. The pony trekking appealed to Becky. Steve was enthused by an indoor conservation centre with quite large foreign spiders roaming freely about it. "You can let them crawl on your arm!" he approved.

"I'm not going in there!" Becky declared; which she reiterated at the end of the film: "Otherwise it all looks really interesting. Now let's watch it again – in Spanish," she said, selecting the language option. "Then you'll be able to reply to Maria in Spanish when she gets over."

"NO….!" Steve gently mouthed a very round negative at her as the film began again in Spanish and Becky started teasing him. But he waited a while before he closed down the programme, removed the disc and went to give it to his parents.

A moment later, he returned with a newspaper article he'd pulled out of the Saturday supplement about a charming little Mediterranean bird like a robin, called the Bluethroat.

There was a very good photograph of it – it was very attractive, with a strong, iridescent red, white and blue breast, and mostly bright blue on the throat. Steve pointed to it. "Look! It's come over to overwinter in Scotland! But it's supposed to be somewhere like Majorca at the moment, having it warm and sunny! That's because the climate's changing. Maybe we'll see one in February. They're rare here."

Becky had been gazing out of the window, thinking of writing an e-mail to a friend. She turned round to see. "It's <u>very</u> cute," she agreed. "Unlike <u>most</u> of the endangered species you're interested in!"

"It says in this article, it has an exceptional ability to imitate other birds' songs – <u>and</u> man-made sounds! <u>That</u> would be a difficult one to track down!" As Becky turned back to the computer, he went to show it to his father.

"Thanks for the film," said his mother. "We're really looking forward to this holiday – we'll be able to go on rugged bird-watching treks <u>and</u> enjoy all the cultural things in the city – like the theatre!"

"And if it <u>does</u> snow heavily," said Chris, "which there's a chance it might do - too heavily for bird-watching – we can always try skiing. Let's hope they manage to confirm the booking…." he added, as Steve passed him the article on the Bluethroat.

Confirmation of the holiday booking came through the next day.

CHAPTER TWELVE
The Carisma

Maria's letter had been opened and read before it arrived at the Parkers' address. One of the casual sorters working in the mail system at Palma, Majorca, was heavily involved in the criminal underworld. His regular, legal mail duty was to check through all the land and air-mail letters to ensure they were being channelled through to the right destinations. And this gave him the opportunity to look at the senders' names and addresses on all the envelopes.

He'd recently been asked by the cartel operating the diamond smuggling to look out for any letters to, or from, Pablo Munos: they might hold clues about any police investigations into their activities. They'd also asked him to intercept letters to or from Pablo's sister Maria. As he sifted through thousands of air-mail letters on his night-shift duty, he wondered whether this was to find out if they could get hold of her when she was away from the protection of her family. It was widely known she'd helped track down several members of the diamond smuggling gang, and described the others. She must be a dangerous witness to them.

When he spotted the airmail letter with Maria's name and address on the back, marked 'sender', he pocketed it and took it home, where he steamed the envelope open by holding it over a saucepan of boiling water. He faxed a copy of it to the man in the diamond smuggling cartel he was in contact with, and then took the original airmail letter back to work with him the next day, putting it back in the system.

The copy of Maria's letter to Becky and Steve soon reached the eyes of a Spanish man who had an old criminal record for petty theft, but wasn't known to be still operating as a criminal to the international police. He sent a text message in Spanish to the *Carisma*, sailing off the West Coast of Scotland. It was headed 'Settling Scores':

'Maria Munos – sister of Pablo Munos in the Majorcan police, and witness to the abortive run to the island cave last July (resulting in the arrest and imprisonment

of three of our men) is travelling around the region of Edinburgh, Scotland, 16-23 February. She will be staying with her school party at a youth hostel in Edinburgh and studying around an international archaeological site just south of Edinburgh. Any further details of this will be relayed as soon as they're obtained. Start dropping the diamond consignments off at the Firth of Forth – speak to Alastair about it next week – and try to ensure **Maria never returns to Majorca**, *without taking any risks. Anyone successfully carrying out this* mission will be substantially rewarded.*

Senor C.'

Then he sent a copy of this instruction in English to his second-in-command in Scotland, Alastair, with a covering note: *'Hope you approve of this strategy...'*

Alastair was sitting in his study when he received it. He was a tall, portly Scotsman with a ruddy face, fair hair and rather watery blue eyes. He quickly printed it out and put it in an unnamed file with a sticker on it with a skull logo, then put that in a lower drawer of his mahogany desk. Lighting a cigar, he sat staring at an old print of a Scottish lighthouse on the wall opposite, until the room filled with cigar smoke.

When the instruction concerning Maria came through to the *Carisma*, all messages were being diverted to the navigational control station. This was fore to the starboard, and the blinds were drawn down its big windows to prevent the low afternoon sunshine obliterating the figures on the computer screens. Miguel was 'showing the ropes' of their smuggling operations to Alto. Fluent in Spanish and English, he'd been acting as deputy for the crew's boss, Eulalia, while she'd been away for several months. She'd only just returned from Spain and was drinking coffee on the top deck. Alto hadn't met her yet, and believed their boss was a man: because for the last three months, ever since he'd been on board, the crew had all jokingly referred to her as 'Eulo', not 'Eulalia', and called her a 'him'. Even when she was on board, they still kept it up when she wasn't about to hear them.

"Working up here makes a change from ordinary crewing," Miguel was saying, "which can take it out of you."

The text message started automatically printing out as it was marked 'URGENT'. He read it then showed it to Alto. "Here. We'd better take this straight through to the boss - when he's back at his desk. I'll introduce you."

A little later he took Alto to the boss' suite, knocking on a polished, panelled wooden door, and then entered with him. The main cabin room was very luxuriously fitted with beige carpeting, big, comfortable cream sofas on two sides, and a bar, stacked with alcoholic drinks, with safety rails on the shelves to stop bottles falling off in rough seas. On the far wall of the cabin a large, state-of-the-art plasma screen was set into the wall above a highly-polished mahogany desk, behind which the back of an executive chair was swivelling round: and to Alto's surprise, a woman was sitting in it.

She was petite, slim and tanned, with blonded hair, very smartly dressed in a nautical-style white trouser-suit with a red-and-white striped top. Miguel introduced Alto to Eulalia Sanchez and she shook his hand. He noticed she wore heavy perfume, several gold rings and a gold bracelet, as well as a delicate gold necklace. She spoke Spanish with a faintly transatlantic accent, and he wondered if Sanchez was really her surname. Then Miguel handed the message to her. While she perused it, Alto gave him an incredulous look, as if to say: "You've been having me on! This is a woman!"

Then Eulalia looked up at Alto and said: "I understand you managed to return to our rendezvous off Puerto Pollensa last July before the police got there." He nodded. "And that you've taken care of any evidence which was left behind." He nodded again.

Miguel put in: "I've got the waterproof lamp on board - with every bit polished! And there shouldn't be anything else anywhere with our fingerprints on....."

Eulalia continued to Alto: "How do you like 'life on the ocean wave' as the British put it?"

"Not bad," he replied, "I didn't have the choice, really. If I'd stayed in Majorca, I'd probably have been arrested – eventually."

"You got a good look at the Majorcan girl, presumably?"

"Yes."

"Her name's Maria Munos. You're aware her family's well associated with the police?"

"Yes, her brother's a police officer."

"Oh, full marks! And is there anything else you know about her that you think we ought to know?" Eulalia raised one of her neat eyebrows.

"I only know what I've read in this text message Miguel's just shown me."

"OK. Well, we've some work opportunities for you; Alto, but we'll discuss them later. You're both free to go. And make sure any messages are put straight through to me from now on, will you? Thanks!"

Eulalia was giving Alto time to consider if he wanted to get involved in another murder attempt on Maria, and was clearly expecting him to confirm that he could do it. His conscience began to take him over again. He realised he couldn't possibly go through with killing Maria. He would avoid it at all costs.

And anyway, he reflected, it would be very difficult to kill her: it wouldn't be easy tracking her down with only the little information they had about her location and movements; and even if they found out more about these, she'd still be in the protection of her school party. For that reason, Alto decided that he could square it with his conscience if he just pointed out which of the girls on the school trip was Maria - if they managed to track her down - leaving it for someone else to attempt the lousy deed. They probably wouldn't get the opportunity to carry it out.

He was definitely going to try going straight now. But he was very worried that this gang might turn against him as well - for knowing too much about them - if he dropped out of its activities too abruptly. He would have to be very, very careful.

It was lunchtime by now, and he and Miguel went along to the crew's mess, which was the breakfasting space adjoining the galley. There drinking variously watered-down glasses of whisky were Mick and Alex - two Scotsmen - and Jaime.

Jaime spoke a limited amount of English, and was being encouraged by Alex, a stocky, florid, bearded red-head with a strong accent and a ribald sense of humour, to practise it. Mick had cropped fair hair and was of a slighter build. He also spoke with a strong Scottish accent, but didn't attempt to talk more slowly so Jaime could easily understand what he was saying. The whisky, he knew, would slow his speech down anyway.

They'd just been listening to the news on the radio and were now talking intently about football; Alto and Miguel were acknowledged with friendly nods when they came in, as they resumed their discussion.

Alto had never asked Miguel why the diamonds were smuggled over to Scotland, so he took the opportunity, as they helped themselves to sandwiches, to ask him. Miguel explained in Spanish that there were no diamond mines in Scotland, so no-one would suspect they were operating there. It was an ideal place, as there were people there with experience in cutting and polishing local crystal, who could be persuaded to transfer to working on the rough diamonds delivered from Majorca. "The greater the geographical distance between each stage of the operation, the less detectable it is," he said, as he sat down at the table with Alto, who carefully avoided bumping his own long legs against anyone else's.

Alex had broken off his football discussion with Mick and Jaime to listen to Miguel. Gathering what he was talking about, the burly Scot then added that the diamonds were cut and polished in the Lothians area. Miguel didn't tell him yet that that was where they were now heading for, cutting out one of the stages along the way. Instead, he instinctively started translating what Alex was describing into Spanish for Alto's benefit, as he was still unused to the Scottish accent.

Alex was saying, running a hand through his thick red hair while he reminisced: "Plenty of people there used to work in the old, small crystal works before they closed down and they were made redundant. A few of them were retrained by the diamond runners to cut the rough diamonds. That's what I am - a rough diamond! I was on that side of things for a while. Just continuing working in the family tradition, so to speak..." He took another sip of whisky. "They look just like pieces of broken frosted glass. It's pretty well the hardest substance known to man. And it takes an expert to cleave them into pieces you can polish. You end up with only about half the weight of the original rough diamond. Then you cut facets into them."

"So they have all the colours of the rainbow" said Alto in English. He'd been learning his weather vocabulary and hoped they'd be impressed. Just at that point, the *Carisma* turned around and started heading for the East Coast of Scotland. He felt the change in the undulating motion of the yacht from his head down to his stomach.

"We're dropping anchor around the Firth of Forth," Miguel now explained to Jaime, Alex and Mick, in English.

"First I've heard of it!" Alex protested.

"We're cutting out the land run from the West Coast." Miguel gazed at him insistently.

"What for?"

"There's a kid who knows too much about our operations... we're expecting her to turn up there – the Forth area - in February – a Majorcan girl. The one who wouldn't drown in the cave! She's coming over on a school archaeological trip, just outside Edinburgh."

Alto said in Spanish: "Our boss' boss wants her dead.....and I believe they want me to do it." Miguel translated this into English.

"Can you?" asked Mick, challengingly.

"I'm the only person her who'd recognise her.....but no, I can't!" he replied in English.

"Mick's done a murder," Alex pointed out casually, in Spanish this time, as if to indicate his friend's versatility.

Alto at first didn't know how to reply to this, but Mick put in quickly and quietly, assisted by Miguel's translation: "I shot someone – a member of the public - close range in a bank raid….it was quick and painless – he died instantly." Alto said nothing and Mick continued, by way of explanation: "I'd already been to prison. Some come out prepared to murder when they only went in prepared to steal!"

Alto finally decided he would only point Maria out in the daytime. There'd be little chance then of anyone being able to immediately move in, unnoticed, to attack her. He said: "I'm prepared to point out who Maria Munos is, but I'm not prepared to dispose of her myself. Someone else will have to do that." He felt sorry for her and this would at least give her a good chance of escaping them altogether. He was determined to get out of diamond smuggling - onto the 'straight and narrow' for the rest of his life, for his daughter's sake. But he had to appear convincingly committed to going along with the business of murder: "Apparently there's going to be a considerable reward for whoever carries it out. Would anyone be in with me if I point her out?" Jaime shook his head immediately. Alto waited while Miguel translated what he'd just said.

Alex shook his head reservedly, but Mick dared: "For the reward? Yes, I would."

"Split 50/50?"

"Make it 80% of the reward," returned Mick.

"How's it usually paid?" Alto asked.

Miguel put in guardedly: "That depends. You'll have to discuss it with Eulalia!"

Mick insisted there was no point in discussing it any further - they'd deal with the situation when it arose, if it did; then he finished off his glass of whisky, accompanying himself with an old traditional Scottish song 'The Boatmen o' the Firth'.

Alex advised Miguel, who also translated for Jaime and Alto: "That song's all about how girls used to sell oysters in baskets from door to door around the Firth of Forth. Nowadays you have to watch the pollution levels in shellfish…….". All three Spaniards had strained to make out the words of the song but could only guess at one or two in the first verse:

'When winter winds howl, and the sea, rolling high,

Our boatmen sae brave all dangers defy;

Their last haul on board, they steer for the shore,

Their live cargo landed is soon at our door.'

CHAPTER THIRTEEN
.........To Edinburgh

By early February, it was very cold in Surrey, but it still hadn't snowed. Up until then the winter had been mild; there'd been plenty of rain, and some frosts; outside, while green shoots speared up from the bulbs, only a few tiny, brown buds were appearing on the tree twigs, which were all still dark except for a few catkins.

One evening, Steve had just finished a call on his mobile to David, his friend from school. They'd both had new mobiles for Christmas and had been regularly contacting each other with them. Becky was finishing looking at the fashion pages in their weekend newspaper magazine, opining to her mother that her hair was losing its summer highlights.

"Who cares?" Steve, staring out of the patio windows at a gleaming sunset, had had his birthday in January and could now claim to be only a year younger than she was. He added: "As long as the <u>evenings</u> are getting lighter again?"

He was about to check up with the Met Office website - on the family computer to get large diagrams - to see if it was likely to be snowing in the Scottish Lothians during their holiday.

"I don't know," went on Becky, "I'd rather be going away on holiday somewhere warm and sunny now…"

"But I thought you were keen on coming to Scotland!" coaxed her father as he switched on the lamps.

"…It's just that, Christmas seems all over such a long time ago already…it didn't snow <u>then</u>, when it should have."

"It's only just getting cold enough to start!" protested Steve. "<u>Do</u> lighten up!" he teased.

"OK, then! Let's look at your horoscope for February, Steve!" she retaliated. "Here we go: '**Capricorn**. *'People born under this sign are influenced by Mars. They* *can be single-minded, tenacious, and are often very ambitious. On the negative side of their personality, they can often be selfish to achieve what they want…"* Becky looked around conclusively.

"That's not <u>all</u> it says. Come on, what about the rest?"

"You probably wouldn't like me to read it <u>all</u> out," she taunted, mysteriously. "And do you know what?" she enlarged, looking up: "This is going to be a <u>winter</u> holiday. I've realised. It's not really spring in February – especially up in Scotland. It'll be <u>freezing</u>."

Her mother encouraged: "There'll be two weeks of sunshine if we've judged it right… and anyway, I bet you'd really enjoy skiing – if it snows…"

"And we're all <u>dying</u> to see you snow-board! Come on, read the rest out!" Steve pressed his sister, flexing his jaw muscles, and reaching for a tangerine from a bowl. She raised her eyebrows with an evasive, sinister look, so he announced he was going to his room to check up on the Met Office website for the long-term weather forecast, anyway.

"Look, we've all agreed we're going," insisted Chris.

Becky, demanding to check out the Met Office forecast with Steve, got up too: "I want to see if it can predict the weather accurately down here in Surrey that far in advance, first! <u>Then</u> we'll know what to expect in Scotland."

As they looked up the Met Office website, Steve asked his sister: "Did you know Britain's the world capital for tornadoes?"

"<u>Tornadoes</u>? How d'you mean?"

"Only mini ones – of course! We get more than any other country."

"Really?"

"Yes."

"No, I didn't!"

"They usually occur inland. There was one in Essex last year while we were away on holiday in Majorca. David told me."

The home page website came up on the computer screen. Becky insisted: "Hang on, wait. Let's just check out the Surrey forecast first." Steve duly brought up the chart for Surrey. "Oh look, there's the 'five-day weather forecast'.

"The next five days..." Steve printed it out as she started reading out rapidly from the symbols: "Sunny, cloudy, rain, cloudy, sunny....OK ...and getting colder. Oh no! I see <u>that</u> includes the night-time weather. OK, so for the daytime, it's: fine, rain, fine, fine, **snow!** "...

Next they had a quick look at the 5-day weather forecast for Edinburgh, which was a few degrees colder, cloudier and damper than usual for February. "It's bound to change again before we get there, though" said Steve. "There <u>is</u> one sure way to check for certain if it's going to snow, but we'll have to wait for five days before the trip. In three days' time."

"What's that?"

"Come on, what did the rest of my horoscope say?" he bargained.

"It said you'll run up against someone from your past you thought you wouldn't see again - unexpectedly, in unfamiliar territory, which could land you in deep water if you allow yourself to get involved."

"I'll have to watch out, then! In fact, I'm going to write that down in the back of my natural history notebook. And check to see if it's happened by the end of February." Steve got his sister to carefully dictate what she'd remembered of his horoscope to him as he noted it down in the back of his natural history notepad, which he tended to take everywhere with him. "<u>Then</u> we'll see." He sat staring for a while at what he'd written, with his eyebrows raised.

"I know, doesn't it sound foreboding! So how do you predict snow, then?"

He looked up, delighted to be asked. "You look at the Mean Sea Level Pressure map, with dashed lines which are all numbered. They show how heavy the cold air is. And there's a special line numbered 500 and something. If that one's even two hundred miles away from the coast you get snow on the northern hills! And if it's actually over Britain, there's snowfall everywhere, even on the low ground."

"OK, let's check it out and see if they've put the 500 and something line over Britain for when it's going to snow here on Friday."

They found the Mean Sea Level Pressure map and the relevant barometric pressure charts for Friday. There was a dashed line with the approximate 500 number on it, just snaking over northern Scotland and back up over the North Sea again. "Hmm, if it's just come in over Scotland that may well mean snow's coming over most of Britain – but how low-lying?" Steve assessed it, guessing it would probably mean snow for Surrey as well, although it was fairly low-lying.

But that Friday, it only snowed on the downs south of Surrey - not where they lived. Becky wouldn't trust the long-term weather prediction after that. "You couldn't even predict the next Ice Age!" she teased him.

"You can make quite a precise forecast based on that line if you know what you're doing!" Steve insisted. Two days before their holiday, he checked it again, and announced it would snow in Edinburgh for the first three days.

They were still debating this on the train going up there, facing each other across the table in a First Class compartment. On the way from Peterborough to Grantham, Becky had inadvertently reopened the debate by saying she could already feel it getting colder. She asked for a cup of tea with their parents as the refreshments trolley came by.

"And it's going to snow in Edinburgh," Steve insisted, "by the way!"

"Look, it didn't snow in Surrey when they said it would!"

They had to break off as one of the railway staff, standing, very carefully poured out hot tea into the cups, which were precariously positioned, on saucers, on the table - not quite sliding about with the jolting of the train over the track. As Steve concentrated on slowly raising his tea cup he resumed carefully: "They ended up saying on the Thursday evening TV forecast there was a <u>slim</u> <u>chance</u> it might......" Becky, now reaching for one of the packets of thick shortbread biscuits offered with the tea, considered whether her brother was teasing her about her weight. "...they can predict it quite accurately," he went on.

"Not <u>five</u> days ahead! It said on the website it <u>would</u> snow in Surrey on Friday! But it didn't!"

"Yes, but on the website, that weather sign of a snowflake just means it's 'likely', you know: that there's a good chance."

"So you <u>can't</u> say it's going to snow in Edinburgh!"

"You haven't seen the Mean Sea Level pressure charts! The 500-odd line was all over the UK!"

"You <u>can't</u> tell from that!"

*   *   *

On the way from Doncaster to York, after Becky, deciding to have another cup of tea, said again: "It's definitely going to be cold up there!" Steve reiterated that it would be snowing as well: "For the next three days!"

His sister insisted she wasn't going to take the five day weather forecast as gospel, "Not even from the Met Office!"

"Then how come you take the Month Ahead horoscope prediction in the newspaper so seriously?" he demanded.

"Oh, I believe <u>that</u>!" she said infuriatingly.

"Well! Say!"

"It's traditional – it wouldn't have survived thousands of years unless it had been proved accurate – again and again!" Becky delighted in her brother's accusatory expression as a train heading south suddenly shot past them very close, at high speed. It was very noisy for a while. She didn't ask him to repeat what he'd just said in reply, but waited for it to finish going past.

He continued, sighing impatiently: "OK, let's test this one out. What did your horoscope say for this month? I mean the rest of it? We've <u>had</u> half of it."

"The rest of this month? Oh, I can't remember it all….it said I'd stumble across a fortune in the second half of the month….."

"'*A fortune*'?! I **know**!" he said cynically. "And a tall dark stranger will walk into your life! <u>Don't</u> tell me!"

"That's a cliché – but yes, it <u>was</u> something like that, actually!" Steve's sarcasm had helped her remember some of it. "A fortune…..but it wouldn't help my financial situation ….."

"That's too vague for words! And you really do <u>believe</u> that?" he said derisively: "D'you know how many people were born under the sign of Aries?!"

"<u>Yours</u> made you think!"

They didn't talk about it again for a while, but as the train passed through Middlesborough, Durham and Newcastle, Steve remained convinced it would be snowing in Edinburgh when they arrived. At Dunbar, Becky told him there was one piece of Met Office information which she <u>could</u> believe. It was, that historically, if Southern and Central England experienced a mild winter, then parts of Scotland (and Northern Ireland) experienced a harsh one – and vice versa. "I believe that - because it's easy to remember, like folk lore."

Steve was interested. "Did you find out whether Edinburgh was one of those 'parts of Scotland'?"

"They didn't say."

He raised his eyes to the ceiling in exasperation with her. Then decided to send a text message to his friend David, to see if the triangulation tracking on his mobile was still working up in that part of the country - it was, sending David a graphic of Steve showing his position on the map.

The scenery far up north was different from any of the British coastal scenery they'd seen before. They saw two long spits of headland reaching out to each other, with an island in the middle, to form a lagoon; one or two small castle ruins, and hills with horizontal ridges running along them, where sheep nibbled at the grass protected from any buffeting winds.

"Anyway," said Steve, looking at the sheep, "what does 'winter' mean? All the seasons are running into each other these days. You can't really decide where autumn stops and winter starts; or where winter stops and spring starts…"

Becky, who was playing with her hair, said experimentally, "You could call <u>that</u> season 'sprinter'…"

"Yes – wintry spring. That's when you feel all excited, like getting up and moving…"

"And you <u>have</u> to move vigorously anyway, to stop feeling freezing!" agreed Becky. "We could call it an 'inter-season', said Steve, "that's a word anyway. They'd be useful to describe the climate. You could have 'wintum'….for the wintry, end part of autumn; and 'autter'….'oughta be snowing'" he punned "…for the boring, autumnal bit of winter, like December is usually."

"How about 'sprummer'?" Becky laughed. "For when it's muddy, cool and dull - and the rain's splatting and drumming on the windows, but it ought to be sunny! That would do for May, when it's more like spring than summer." She paused. "It's like when some people are born on the cusp of one star sign: that means they're born just within one star sign, early or late, nearly falling under another one. So their horoscope isn't always that accurate. Do you think I'd look good if I cut my hair short, now the blonde highlights have grown out?" she then asked.

"You'd look like a sprinter sprite!"

Suddenly he saw small, intermittent snowflakes falling, gently floating about in the soft breeze, as if they might suddenly peter out again. "Great!" he shouted. "It's snowing! I <u>told</u> you it would be!"

They had a fair idea of what winter really <u>felt</u> like, though, when they got off the train at Waverley Station in Edinburgh. It was bitterly cold. The train had been heated and all of them shivered as they stepped down onto the platform with their suitcases, their mother and father carrying two each. They walked past a waiting area - above it was a large domed glass roof feature decorated with scrolling white wrought ironwork. As Steve looked up, briefly he thought he could make out snowflakes falling onto it outside. Public announcements were being given out over the tannoy system; they echoed, addled yet noisy, around the station. Some travellers tried heeding them but no-one could make out what they were. As another train departed noisily from the station, Pat Parker , while she was pointing about her, had spotted the taxi rank and was making her way over to it, knowing her family was following her.

Outside, it <u>was</u> continuing snowing, with slightly larger, faster-falling flakes - although it didn't look as if it would settle. Steve was delighted. It was late afternoon and the sun was just beginning to go down. A long line of slowly moving black taxis waited for queuing travellers to step out for them. The Parkers didn't have to wait long for one. Becky took her woolly gloves from out of her coat pockets and put them on, while the others handed the luggage to the taxi driver. He put it all in the boot and drove them south to their hotel.

Nearby, they saw the sixty-metre-high, pinnacled gothic spire built in honour of Sir Walter Scott, housing his seated statue. And away behind that, the dark, dominant, heavy square of the grim-looking Edinburgh Castle, set high up on a strategic mound on the flank of the huge extinct volcano – called Arthur's Seat – which overpowered the city's skyline on the other side. Driving over the North Bridge linking the New town with the Old, they caught a glimpse of the long straight road called the Royal Mile, packed with lots of small shops. There were a few large stores too. Edinburgh was hilly – built on seven hills, like Rome, Chris pointed out – and many of the streets were on an incline, even the Royal Mile. "We'll never get up and down these streets if the snow settles!" Pat remarked, but the taxi driver assured them that if it did settle, and ice formed, they'd be gritted. "They've had blizzards in the surrounding highlands," he added. "But we don't usually get all that much snow here."

Their hotel, the Garden Hotel, was on a main road heading South East out of Edinburgh, on the outskirts of the city. It was medium-sized and built out of sand-coloured stone around about 1900. There were steps up to the entrance and two wings on either side with little round, slated turrets on the end – like lots of the older buildings in Edinburgh.

It was warm and cosy inside, attractively furnished in an old-fashioned style. But it had a new small indoor swimming pool added on at the side. The staff was all very helpful and polite; one or two of them were Europeans. Steve was well pleased with his room on the second floor – it had a good view towards Salisbury crags, on the volcano's south side. Becky's room looked down onto the garden and had a distant view of the castle.

That evening, they'd seen from the big arrows on the TV weather maps that an icy wind was blowing down from the North Sea. They all decided - over a large dinner in the hotel's dining room, that they'd better spend the first few days sightseeing around the museums, shops and exhibitions, until it stopped snowing. There was no point yet in going on any bird-watching trips, or even skiing. When Becky complained that it was atrociously cold and that she couldn't possibly take a pony out trekking in that weather, snowing or not, her father again suggested they could go skiing in Glencoe for a couple of days, once it stopped – if they didn't mind a journey. This cheered her up. "Be patient," he said.

So for the next two days they went sightseeing round the city, well muffled with scarves, woolly hats and mittens, while it snowed on and off. Some snow settled for a while, but no more than one or two centimetres deep. Overnight it was very cold, and ice started to form on some of the pavements, although the main ones were gritted. But the wintry mornings soon changed into warmer afternoons, as the sweeter, balmy air of very early spring started mingling with the frosty air until it lost its sharp tingle.

They visited the Tourist Information Centre and the Museum of Scotland; saw round Holyrood Palace and split up to go shopping along the Royal Mile. When they all met back up at a tea shop, Pat had bought a tartan rug. They stopped for a while to watch a piper in full Highland dress playing the bagpipes on a cobbled street corner. Steve had learned in Majorca not to make fun of national costumes, and just refrained from doing so on this occasion; so after returning to the hotel, they went out again to listen to live traditional Scottish folk music in the evening.

Because Becky was complaining she couldn't warm up, they also visited Deep Sea World, Scotland's National Aquarium, with an underwater tunnel to observe the marine life through. Steve, who wanted to be a marine biologist, asked if he could see it again before the end of the holiday. And there was still plenty to do. "And if you <u>still</u> can't warm up, Becky" he said, "we can always go to that tropical wildlife place where they have really big spiders, just freely walking about. I'd love to handle one!"

"And I can always make my own way home!" she resisted, trying not to shiver. They could see their breath in the very cold air until mid-afternoon.

That evening, they sent a text message from Steve's mobile to Maria to let her know that it had been snowing for their first two days, and that it was still settling on the higher ground outside Edinburgh.

CHAPTER FOURTEEN
Warming Up

Eventually, on the fourth day, it stopped snowing; the wind changed direction to the more usual south-westerly, and the forecast gave warmer, sunnier weather for the next week: just what they'd hoped for. Steve and Becky were relieved to know that although the recent snowfalls had settled on the surrounding highlands, Maria wouldn't be prevented from going on her archaeological dig when she arrived: the site, which was nearby, was low-lying - and they still hoped to meet up with her there. In the meantime, the three of them were definitely going to have lunch together at the Dynamic Earth Centre on the second day of her stay, as planned.

That morning, the Parkers went round the National Gallery of Scotland. (They were expecting the weather to improve by the afternoon so they could go and explore the coastal scenery around Boness, to the West of Edinburgh. There were several walks; and small museums and a castle there too.) Steve, wearing a new heavy, padded anorak and jeans, brought the new binoculars with him. He left his mobile in the hotel, as their father was carrying his own and they'd all agreed not to carry too much clutter with them. He needed space in his pockets for handkerchiefs and his natural history notebook. Becky, still dressed up very warmly in trousers, jumper and her heaviest woollen coat, didn't bother with her own mobile but retained her music player, which she was listening to in preference to the taped guided tour given by the gallery. The taped guide recommended visitors take their time looking around the exhibits of European and Scottish paintings, but she didn't find antiques in general very fascinating.

After twenty minutes or so, she was concentrating on listening to one of her favourite music tracks when she heard, then suddenly felt, a distinct rumbling of the ground underneath her feet. "What's <u>that</u>?" she asked, very worried: "An earthquake?" (Steve had only recently explained to her over breakfast about volcanic eruptions, also mentioning the giant tidal wave which had swept over the East Coast of Scotland about two thousand years ago.)

"Just the trains going through the tunnel under the Mound to the station!" he reassured her, with a grin. Then he took the opportunity, as she'd removed her earpiece, to suggest they go out looking across the Firth of Forth with the binoculars that afternoon for something of special interest, which he'd read about in *The Scotsman* newspaper yesterday.

"Oh, what's that?" she was curious.

"The new E/S ship: 'Environmentally Sound'. It's too big to dock at any of the ports along the Forth, so they're sending ships out to service her. They said it would be turning around in the Firth of Forth." His sister looked doubtful. "This afternoon. It really is going to stop snowing today. Go on, how would you like to come along with me to check out the ship of the future, Becky?"

The paintings were exhibited in chronological order and she'd been gazing at works by Canaletto of gondolas in Venice, attracted by the warm, sunny Mediterranean scenes. "The ship of the future?" she wondered.

"The future. Not even state-of-the-art!"

"What a silly remark! Who do you think you are, a time traveller?" She turned back to look at the paintings.

"It's a prototype!" insisted Steve. "The first of its kind!"

"OK," she said and faced him again. "It might be more interesting than looking at all these old paintings for hours on end."

"Everyone knows that's an acquired taste!"

As anticipated, it had only been snowing lightly, and it had stopped when the Parkers completed their tour of the gallery; so they took the opportunity to see some of the scenery west of Edinburgh, and drove out in their hire car along the coast towards Boness. Within half an hour they were on the edge of the Trossachs National Park, with Blackness Castle ahead of them. "Let's stop off and take a look around," suggested Chris. It was turning into a sparklingly clear, bright afternoon.

The fifteenth-century castle, once Scotland's state prison, was a fortification with a courtyard - right on the coast, commanding a vast view of the Forth. As they walked up to look round the outside, Steve kept an eye out for the E/S ship. He wondered if the crew would take her up this far past Leith docks. They'd probably want to do some sightseeing, but whether before or after servicing, and how long that would take, he didn't know. He didn't want to miss it if he could help it.

After exploring a little more around the coastline, Pat suggested a break for tea and cakes in the car, but neither Steve nor Becky was hungry yet. Steve explained to their parents the E/S ship was due to be sailing out in the Firth of Forth sometime early in the afternoon. He persuaded them to let him go out exploring further along the coast with Becky, keeping together and not going beyond a certain point.

Brother and sister set off inland up the firth along the fresh green headland. Becky, who'd exchanged her heavy coat for a padded anorak from the car, was still well muffled up in a woolly hat and scarf, although the temperature was increasing. The well-drained ground was solid enough for it not to be too muddy, just moist. Steve explained that the E/S ship was a tremendously important leap into the future. "It's the first completely zero-emission cargo ship. It doesn't give off any polluting emissions into the sea or the atmosphere. It just doesn't use any fossil fuels."

Before they reached the agreed point of the coastline to stop at, Steve looked back again towards the mouth of the Forth and stopped, putting the binoculars to his eyes. "There it is!" he exclaimed. A very light breeze ruffled his hair as he looked out to sea.

Becky could see the huge vessel in the distance, just beyond the Forth Bridge. "It's gigantic!"

"Three times the length of a jumbo jet, with a cargo deck the size of twelve football pitches. Or is it fourteen? A lot, anyway….It can carry 10,000 cars. Look at it!" his breath was still just visible in puffs around him.

The new binoculars were very powerful. Their father had been hoping to spot a

Golden Eagle with them. Steve handed them carefully to Becky, showing her how to adjust the sights. "It's a pentamaran - with fins like a dolphin's for harnessing wave energy....here, take a look! See the three giant sails covered in solar panels for using sun and wind energy?"

"No…"

"You <u>must</u> do…those three rigid sails! They're not canvas, of course!"

"Oh yes…isn't it different?" Becky was reasonably interested – she'd never seen a ship like it before.

"It'll transform international shipping," Steve continued, taking the binoculars back hastily but as gently as he could and readjusting the sights. His jaw jutted out appreciatively as he gazed at it. "Ships usually take in thousands of tons of seawater for ballast, then dump them somewhere else…..Listening?"

"Have to!"

"So all the bits in the seawater, like plankton and shrimps, get dumped away from their natural habitat and the fish that eat them, and the whole marine ecosystem's upset. It's even worse than the oil slick problem. But <u>this</u> ship doesn't do it. It's beautiful…." He paused, still admiring it. "Great for sustaining the marine habitat!"

They continued taking it in turns watching through the binoculars as it approached up the Forth, until Becky decided she'd seen all she wanted to of it, and started training them onto some other tourists who were also looking around the area.

"If you're just going to do that, let me have them!" Steve warned her.

"Just a minute….over there, there's a 'Traditional Fish Smoking Shed'."

"Where?" Steve looked out to where she was pointing.

Becky started reading off from a menu hanging outside the café next to it. "**Smoked Sea Fish.** Haddock. Herring. *Finan Haddie*' - that's fillet of haddock smoked with peat. *'Firth Smokies'*. That's haddock smoked with oak chips."

"Does it do hamburgers?" asked Steve.

"Hang on….'Organic beer…' I'm quite thirsty, are you?"

"Yes."

"I can't read the rest, it's in smaller writing."

"Go up and have a look, then. Go on, it's not very far away!"

"OK!" She handed the binoculars back to her brother and went over to investigate.

The smoking shed was constructed in the style of the old smoking sheds which used to line the Firth of Forth. It was timber-clad, and you could get a look inside. There were strings of fish - herrings and haddock - smoking over two traditional fires, one using oak wood chips, the other made of peat, with outlets to the open air; and chips being fried in large, modern appliances for safety. Next to it was the café. Becky went in – it was nice and warm. On the walls there were copies of old sepia photographs of the original sheds, and local fishing people plying their trade. Recordings of old sea shanties and folk music were being softly played and the staff were dressed in the long white aprons and starched white caps worn in the early years of the previous century. It was sit down or takeaway.

There was a small queue of tourists, and Becky couldn't quite see behind them to read the rest of the menu, so she gently made her way to the counter and asked a woman who was inserting chips into a cardboard box if they did hamburgers. "Sorry, we only do fish!" was the reply. "Here, would you like a menu?" and she gave her a takeaway menu sheet over the counter. "Thanks!" Becky took it back to show Steve, beginning to relax into her holiday.

Meanwhile Steve, after more rapt gazing at the futuristic prototype eco-vessel, suddenly trained the binoculars on a yacht nearer to him, heading inland up the estuary. Just for comparison, intending to switch them back again to the E/S ship. The yacht was a very large luxury cruiser - sleek, dazzling white and very high-tech. Though not so super-advanced in appearance as the E/S ship, it was impressive enough to hold his attention for a little while yet. When Becky returned and asked him: "I've got enough money in my bag to buy us each smoked haddock and

104

chips, would you like some?" he was still watching the yacht, called the *Carisma*, slowly making its way up the estuary. "Haven't they got any hamburgers?" he tried insisting, as he studied three men on the deck. Two of them were sturdily built; the other was tall and angular.

"No. But haddock and chips would do to keep the cold out! I'm having one..."

"OK, yes please!" he agreed, turning to ask her if she'd like him to help pay. As his sister made her way back to the smoking shed cafe to queue up, saying he could treat her back later, he zoomed the binocular focus in further to take an even closer look at the crew.

Mick and Alex both looked like native British sailors to Steve: the clean-shaven, blond Mick was nearly as ruddy-complexioned in the wind as the bearded, red-headed Alex. They were dressed in jeans, thick Arran sweaters, anoraks and knitted hats, attending briskly to their tasks. But the third man looked unused to the biting cold of a Scottish winter. He was tall with fairly dark brown hair, a small beard and quite a dark complexion under a faded tan. He looked Mediterranean.... Spanish. He was wearing jeans and a thick black crew-necked sweater under a heavy navy duffel-coat with what looked like a big metal clip in place of the top toggle, which had come off. The clip was sparkling brilliantly in the early afternoon winter sunshine. As the man turned his face away to look back out to sea, Steve tested the optimum zoom feature on the binoculars, focusing right in on it.

With these binoculars, he could even see the sharp shadow on the duffel-coat cast by the clip in the bright sunshine. Funny, he thought, it seemed familiar to him. If the points of two of its ends hadn't been.....bent round! ....Yes, it would remind him of Maria's mother's old silver brooch! Three fan-shaped leaves bound by a ribbon...

He zoomed out again; then as the man turned his face back round, Steve zoomed back into highest detail and thought he recognised... **Alto!** Then wondered: "Or is it? I could be wrong - this man has a beard." The more he watched him, however, the more he was convinced this was Alto. He was moving like him, too: the same angular, awkward movements reminded Steve of the tall Spanish man on the Majorcan beach.

Just at that moment, Becky returned from the traditional fish-smoking shed, this time startling her brother. As she handed him a handled cardboard box containing his Firth Smokies, and a small carton of apple juice, from a carrier bag with 'Traditional Smoked Fish' on it, he explained to her in a low voice that he thought he'd just recognised one of the Spanish criminals who'd abducted him and Maria in Majorca. "Where?" she whispered excitedly, realising from his tone that he wasn't kidding, and beginning to remember his horoscope for that month. He immediately put his fish and chips back in her carrier bag, saying "We haven't got time to eat these now!" and pointed towards the *Carisma*: "On board that yacht!"

They both started running inland along the green headland of the estuary, following it.

"Keep cool!" hissed Steve, "They mustn't recognise us!"

"I don't even have to <u>try</u> in <u>this</u> weather!" insisted Becky, who soon started shivering again.

After a hundred metres or so they decided they'd better slow their pace to a very fast walk, otherwise they'd draw attention to themselves. The *Carisma* was continuing slowly up the estuary. Steve couldn't get another look through the binoculars at the man he believed was Alto, because he now had his back turned to him. And if he ran on ahead of the yacht, to turn to look back at him, he'd draw attention to himself and Alto might recognise him.

Becky and Steve were now very close up behind the *Carisma*. If only the man would turn round so they could get a look at him without drawing attention to themselves, they willed. (They could see the faces of the other men; but as Steve whispered to Becky, he'd never seen those two before. Nor had she.) Then Alto, still with his back turned to them, whistled a lively tune. Which Steve immediately recognised as the main folk tune the procession band played at the Majorcan fishing festival. They were playing it when Maria led the procession with the Majorcan dancers in their traditional dress. He couldn't forget it. This <u>must</u> be Alto!

Becky, not so musical as Steve, wasn't so sure at first, but as she listened to the tune, she came round to agreeing with him – it was Majorcan. As she whispered, "What shall we do?" the *Carisma* changed course a little, increasing its knots – now cruising up the middle of the firth, instead of keeping near the shore - faster than they could walk. They realised they couldn't go on following it. "Now what shall we do?" Steve agreed. They'd gone further along the estuary than they'd agreed with their parents. Becky demanded a decision: "Just go straight back to Mum and Dad and tell them we've seen a swish yacht called the *Carisma*, and that you think one of the crew looks like one of the Majorcan crooks who abducted you?"

"Alto, with a beard!" Steve was convinced.

"We could phone the police from the car and give a description of the three men and the name of the yacht," suggested Becky. "I only saw the very tall one with dark hair from behind. If it is Alto, d'you think it's just coincidence that he's here? Or do you think we're being followed?"

"Look, it is Alto, OK? But I don't know if he's following us or if it is just coincidence…"

They went on discussing it walking back to the car park by the castle. Fortunately, the other people nearby were speaking French and Gaelic and the youngsters were fairly sure they weren't listening to what they were saying.

"Whistling a popular Majorcan folk tune doesn't make that man Alto," Becky suggested.

Steve was impatient. "No, it doesn't. But I'm telling you I saw him through the binoculars, and it really looks like Alto with a beard. And he's wearing a brooch on his duffel-coat. Strange, but it looks just like the one I took off Maria's shawl to cut through our ropes with after they'd left us to die….."

"Really?"

"Yes. Only it looks as if it's got a bit bent. He must have been back to the island cave and found it. That's where I dropped it."

Becky stopped to look back for a while at the *Carisma* as it disappeared up the firth. The water was sparkling blue and calm - it was the biggest yacht out there. "Do you think we could follow them in the car?"

"No chance, you couldn't see it from the road. We can't tell <u>where</u> they're going. They might well just turn around in the Forth and sail out to sea again...."

They knew they had to get back to the car in time, and carried on walking. "Perhaps there's quite a lot we can prove, if we can get the *Carisma* searched by the police," said Becky, "but we need Maria to take a look at this Alto, too. Unless she backs you up that it's him, they might think you're imagining things!"

"I know, it's such a coincidence unless he's following us about." Steve considered Alto's motive. "If I went back to Majorca in the near future, there might just be a chance I'd see him there again and recognise him, and get him arrested. And he may have heard Maria's coming over here. She's an even greater risk to him..... But as for me going along on my own with the police to point him out, they probably still wouldn't be able to establish his real identity, because 'Alto''s a nickname, according to her. It wouldn't be on his passport, and he may well have a false passport anyway!" Steve had talked about this with Pablo and Maria before he left Majorca. "If they arrested him, they might not be able to convict him just on the evidence of me pointing him out, and once they released him again for lack of proof, he'd escape – to goodness knows where. And we'd <u>still</u> be in deadly trouble!"

"But if Maria gets out here and supports what you say, and recognises her family brooch he's wearing...."

"That would be <u>two</u> of us recognising him!"

"I can't wait for Maria to get out here. If only we can get another look at him!"

Steve decided to stop at a bench they'd passed, on the way, which faced out over the Forth, to try a few of the Firth Smokies before they got cold. "I'm not going to leave my mobile in the hotel room again. And if I get to see Alto again, I'll film him so we can show it to Maria when she arrives – then she and I can make a joint statement to the police."

Becky was glad to sit down. "It'd be even better if she could actually come with us to wherever the *Carisma* anchors, and get a proper look at him," she suggested, spearing a chip with a plastic fork. "Through the binoculars, of course – just don't go anywhere near him, Steve: he's <u>far</u> too dangerous! Then when you're both sure you've identified him from a distance, call the police in!"

Steve was adamant that the bearded man he'd just seen on the yacht was Alto, so they decided to phone Maria and tell her, as soon as they could. Her school party was due to fly into Edinburgh the next evening. "I can borrow Dad's mobile to phone her as soon as we get back to the car," said Steve. "Now, do we tell him and Mum about this yet or not?"

They couldn't decide on this so readily. Brother and sister considered the possible scenario of telling their parents straightaway. "It'd be <u>another</u> fraught holiday!" Becky warned. "They wouldn't let us go <u>anywhere</u> on our own, knowing a dangerous criminal was after us!"

"<u>If</u> they believed us," speculated Steve. "If I told them I'd just seen one of the Spanish criminals, Mum would ask: 'How can you be so sure it was him if he had a beard?'

Then I'd tell her he was whistling one of the folk tunes we heard at the Puerto Pollensa fishing festival - which you'd corroborate…"

"It <u>is</u> a distinctive tune…."

"But that still doesn't <u>prove</u> anything. And it's no use telling them about the brooch yet, because d' you know what? They might say it was just another, similar one - which made me think that man was Alto, when really he was just Spanish, whistling a Majorcan tune. Dad would say it was probably just one of those mass-produced tourist gifts. And like I said, even if we did go to the police at this stage, and they checked up on him, they'd just be alerting him to the fact he's been recognised, and then have to let him go…."

"We'd both be accused of having an overactive imagination!" Becky concluded.

"Mum would be on edge all holiday…"

"And Dad wouldn't let us out of his <u>sight</u>, just in case!" she agreed with finality. "He'd be explaining all the most boring tourist attractions to us, <u>all</u> the time – to keep us behaving sensibly and stop our imaginations from running riot..."

They wolfed down the rest of the fish and chips in their excitement, and to keep out the cold, still finalising what they agreed could possibly be happening. "The diamond smugglers wouldn't come all the way out to Scotland to try to kill Maria while she's with a school party." Steve was sure on that point. "I wonder if they heard she was just going on a single exchange visit... maybe they got to hear she was going to meet up with us, too."

"She must have told her friends in Majorca we're going to meet up here, anyway," agreed Becky. "Or look, perhaps Alto <u>is</u> just on holiday himself!!"

"Far, far too much of a coincidence!" Steve laughed nervously, and Becky felt too, that Alto had come out to silence whoever of the three youngsters he knew was there. "Just think," he said, "this could have been my last order of fish and chips if I'd met him out here on my own!"

"Don't worry, I'd remember you every time I ordered extra chips with mine," Becky teased, suddenly getting up off the bench. She was beginning to feel freezing again.

The *Carisma* was by now hidden behind a curve in the coastline. When they got back to the car park, depositing the fish and chips cartons in a waste bin, their father asked them: "Did you see the E/S ship?"

Steve replied: "Yes, it suddenly appeared in the firth. It's fantastic! And the binoculars are brilliant - we got a really good look at it!" But instead of describing it, he stayed unusually quiet on the subject. *Becky'd better not say anything about the* 'Carisma', he was thinking, as she also answered "Yes!"

Her cheeks were glowing pink with excitement, so their mother decided she was beginning to take a healthy interest in ecology.

"And we've had some smoked fish and chips from a traditional smoking shed, so we don't need any biscuits, thanks," she added, confirming to her brother with a look that she could be trusted not to talk about the yacht yet.

"OK!" beamed Chris, taking a promising weather check from his mobile, "It'll only be snowing overnight, very lightly, without settling for the next few days. We can go back and book a bird-watching tour for tomorrow if we get a move-on now! I haven't got the company's web address on me."

Steve didn't get the opportunity to phone Maria, so he and Becky waited till they all got back to the hotel later that afternoon. There, everyone agreed that just Steve and his father, the real enthusiasts, would go bird-watching the next morning; while Becky (who was still saying she was freezing) and Pat stayed in at the hotel. Chris now waited in the computer room to make the booking with Steve, after Steve, using his own mobile, had made a call to Maria with Becky.

Maria, busy packing, had her mobile switched off so Steve left a message for her. Speaking slowly and clearly in a secluded corner of the lounge, with Becky, he said he thought he'd recognised the tall criminal, Alto, now bearded, on board a yacht called the *Carisma* which he and Becky saw sailing up the Firth of Forth. "And guess what, Maria? He was wearing what looked like your old silver brooch on his coat. I saw it close-up through the binoculars!" He repeated and rephrased the message, ending by saying: "I hope you can understand this, Maria! Have a safe journey!"

"Phone us as soon as you arrive!" added Becky. "Take care and we'll see you soon!"

As his father would be taking his own mobile, Steve arranged to leave his mobile with his sister while he went on the bird-watching trip: "I'll be carrying the video camera. And I'm not going home until I've checked out the marinas along the way in the direction the *Carisma* was heading! The marshland around the estuary's a very important conservation area. With any luck, if they're still around here, I'll be able to film them!"

CHAPTER FIFTEEN
The Bluethroat

C hris hadn't been surprised when Steve told him in the computer room that, actually, he'd rather not join an organised tour for their bird-watching trip: because he often preferred to investigate the reserves unguided anyway. But he <u>was</u> surprised when his son said he wanted to concentrate on Musselburgh and west along the coastline out to Boness, where they'd explored the day before. He thought that even if Steve wasn't interested in visiting Duddingston Loch, which was just south of Arthur's Seat with the biggest reed-beds in the Lothians, he'd at least want to visit the impressive Seabird Centre at North Berwick. This was out East, on the mouth of the Forth: Eastern Scotland's biggest sea loch. It had giant screens which beamed back live images from cameras on islands in the Forth - Bass Rock and Fidra. It had a telescope deck jutting right out into the sea; a migration tunnel simulating seabird journeys; and future scopes, touch screens and interactive. When Steve didn't respond with his usual enthusiasm, he suggested to him: "It's a very impressive centre, but the seabird numbers have generally picked up recently - I suppose you'd rather be looking out for the rarities!"

Steve agreed with him: "I know what you mean! And a bumpy three-mile trip out there on a small sea-boat wouldn't be so much fun - just to see thriving species!"

Still a little rueful, though, that Steve might be missing out on some of the educational experiences on offer, he offered him the chance to change his mind: "We can still pay a quick visit to the Centre, if you like. The numbers may well decline again soon. At least they think they know the reasons for a decline. And Bass Rock's still got the largest Gannet colony in the world." He paused, with his generous expression – eyebrows raised and eyes open – to accept Steve's final decision.

"Britain's biggest seabird... with a wingspan of nearly two metres!" Steve played along with reconsidering going to see it, but with every intention of investigating the coastline as far west of Edinburgh as he could - where the *Carisma* had been heading.

"You can watch them diving at 70 miles an hour into the Forth…." persisted his father.

"What's that in kilometres?"

"Pretty fast! They're coming back to mate about now, for life, so there'll be a lot of neck-stretching and beak-fencing to watch….. and the Razorbills, they're coming back here to nest this month…." (Steve sniffed but stayed resolute.) "Then the puffins are due back at Fidra in March, so we might see one or two…."

"No – no, it's OK, I'd rather watch out for the rarities," Steve said.

"Well, then, there are some great ducks and swans around Linlithgow Loch - and Musselburgh's the best place in Scotland for Mediterranean gulls."

"And they've seen the Bluethroat in Musselburgh: we don't have to go out to Bass Rock to see one!"

"Have they seen one <u>there</u>?"

"Bass Rock? Sure. They've sighted them in both reserves. Let's keep to Musselburgh and west of it – along the coast."

And Chris finally assented.

The next morning, as they drove to Musselburgh, Steve, though he was very keen to see the coastal birdlife, was more intent on keeping his eyes peeled for the *Carisma*. He knew there were several new marinas along the coastline of the Forth where it may have anchored.

While he watched out for any large yachts, he noticed there was a variety of a coastal and inter-tidal habitat. He was heartened to see this area, where man was actually helping other species to flourish as he developed the coastline for his own purposes. His father had explained that the Musselburgh lagoons at the mouth of the River Esk were a man-made, internationally important conservation site. Created in 1964 by the Electricity Board! After it had built a big concrete sea wall around four large lagoons to dump fly-ash from the nearby power station, a high tide roosting site for waders, gulls and ducks was suddenly formed, so the East

Lothian District Council set up a nature reserve around them.

It was still very cold when they got out of the car at the lagoons, but there were plenty of very enthusiastic birders about. They walked around the seawall, and saw several black and white ducks bobbing about on the sea. They were mainly males: beautiful male Eiders, looking rather plump, with striking black and white plumage; almost entirely black Velvet Scoters; the distinctive Goldeneye males with iridescent green heads, and the Long-tailed ducks, with long streamers at the end of their tail feathers.

Then they checked out the different lagoons. Steve was very impressed by the views from the scrapes and high tide roosts: "It's brilliant here for observing all the species!" They saw a lot of rare species, comparing notes with some of the other birders, and he shot plenty of film with the video camera. They watched the unusual sight of a male Peregrine Falcon chasing some Marsh Harriers, then scouted round the tree area for little warblers.

First they heard the loud yodel of a Golden Oriole, which usually stayed hidden in dense foliage: then they saw one. It was very bright yellow and black. Then Steve saw a Redstart, which he recognised by its constantly twitching tail. A Grasshopper Warbler was trying to keep itself well-hidden as it gave out its fairly monotonous, single tone, but they just got a glimpse of its little olive-brown form in the foliage through the binoculars.

Then Steve, as he listened to the excitable gusto of a long, fast-flowing song which ingeniously mimicked the clicks, chirring and whistles of some of the other bird species, thought he might be close to a Bluethroat. But he was disappointed when the singer, one of the few rare little Sedge Warblers, suddenly showed itself off, flying conspicuously from branch to branch. Not shy, it was a relatively unremarkable shade of buffy brown, with a few streaks in neutral colours.

They had no luck with finding a Bluethroat. Still, apart from that brilliant little migrant - which could imitate human sounds, as well as other birds, and was very rarely seen in February - they'd spotted quite a few on their list of over 90 species which they were looking out for on the trip.

They warmed up in the car driving back through Edinburgh, past Leith and onto Hound Point, where the Firth of Forth narrowed to form the Inner Forth. All the while, Steve was keeping his eyes open for the large white yacht - and keeping up his stock of excuses to suddenly ask if they could stop to do some filming if he saw it.

They saw plenty of spectacular estuary birds at Hound Point, and then Chris suggested they drive to busy Linlithgow town for lunch before heading to the large loch to look at the ducks and swans. "The Linlithgow reserve's completely different from Musselburgh – it's in a very classical-romantic setting, just north of the town, with the ruins of the old palace where Mary Queen of Scots was born, still standing by the loch."

Steve was tempted, but he didn't want to spend any time there, wanting instead to head back up to Boness and West along the coast. "OK, let's go there later with Pat and Becky. They might like it. I'm sure they'd enjoy the Great Crested Grebes' spring courtship rituals anyway. It's great fun, they're very complicated. They dive underwater and resurface with weeds to offer each other! Anyway, we can go right up to Grangemore Park today," said Chris, looking at the map again, "and have something to eat there."

Steve reminded him they might just see Golden Eagles, so along the way – west along the Firth, through Boness, and eventually on past Grangemouth, under the Kincardine Bridge and right up to Dunmore Park where the river was quite narrow - they stopped near wide cliff ledges and old pine trees to look out for them. The north winds of the previous week had ushered in little flocks of bright Firecrests and Chiffchaff, which liked the pine trees.

By mid-afternoon, it had warmed up again and the estuary was sparkling under a bright blue sky. A few small and medium sized yachts were now out on it. But still there was no sign of the *Carisma*. Or a Golden Eagle. Steve was more tense than usual, but his father assumed it was the excitement of looking out for such an enormous bird. On the way back, they filmed some Rock Ptarmigan and Arctic Wharblers, while the sun set and the lobster fishermen hauled up their creels further along towards the mouth of the estuary.

It was dark by the time they returned to the Garden hotel. The sign was illuminated and all the lamps were on in the lounge. They just had time to get changed to go down for dinner. Steve met up with his sister in the lounge before their parents came down. She was wearing a warm winter dress, with her fringed shawl bought on the Majorcan holiday. "Any luck with finding the *Carisma*?" she whispered.

"Nothing," he said, very disappointed. "But let's not tell anyone about it yet. We might just get another opportunity to film them on it. Anyway, we saw some <u>fantastic</u> birds, and I got some great shots of them on film!"

"How about the Bluethroat?" Becky knew he was really keen to see one, because he'd been keeping the page turned down where it featured in his birds' handbook.

"No – I'm afraid that one got away, too," he said despondently. "I guess it's too shy."

"<u>Shy</u>??" she said, triumphantly, "Anything but! I was practically hand-feeding one in the garden this afternoon!"

Steve looked at his sister in disbelief. Then started to get jealous, just as their parents were coming down the staircase to go into dinner. "All right, then, what colouration did it have?" he asked, exasperated, as they all made their way into the dining room.

"It was a male Bluethroat, just like the one in the Saturday magazine article you showed me, and the picture in your Birds handbook," she said. "And guess what?" she added as their parents went on ahead of them, "I <u>think</u> it was whistling the beginning of that Majorcan tune….the one Alto was whistling on the yacht!"

"That's ridiculous!" exclaimed Steve mistrustfully, going the long way round the dining room over to their table. "What was it wearing? Boots, cap and a little scarf round its neck??!...A tam-o'-shanter? …A frilly orange blouse??"

"Just its feathers – it's true, you can listen to it! I made a recording of it on my mobile!" Becky, following him, sidled past another chair and gave him one of her accomplished 'Wait and see!' looks as their parents, already sitting down, started paying them attention, and they had to wait until after dinner to resume talking properly about it. She just mentioned to everyone that she'd filmed the little bird out in the hotel garden, and that she'd show Steve after dinner.

When their parents went back upstairs to their room, they went to a quiet corner of the large lounge to look at it. The walls were decorated with old sketches of Scottish town life and watercolours of the Lothians landscape. Large, deep-cushioned sofas, coffee tables with magazines and side-tables with lamps were arranged in cosy groups. Becky was carrying the new handbag with a tartan lining she'd just bought from a shop along the Royal Mile. She sat down next to Steve under the peach glow of a lamp and took out from it a new, starched white handkerchief embroidered with Scottish heather and her initial, tucking it up her dress sleeve. "I'm still so cold! But I haven't actually <u>caught</u> cold yet…"

Then she took out her mobile and played back to him the high-quality-sound film she'd taken, holding it out at arm's length towards the male Bluethroat she'd seen in the hotel garden early that afternoon. "What do you make of <u>that</u>?" she asked.

A beautiful little specimen with a very bright, iridescent sapphire-blue throat and rings of brilliant scarlet, white and blue round its breast, was perching on a rose bush, swayed slightly by a gentle spring breeze. It was singing a vigorous rendition of….definitely the first few bars of the Majorcan tune, he decided: "That's the festival tune Alto was singing!"

"I thought so. "I was just taking a look around the garden when I saw him! Is it a Bluethroat?"

"Sure!"

"It just flitted off into a shrub after this. I filmed him for a few minutes," Becky added with her voice hushed, increasing the volume while it repeated, distinctly, the notes of the first bar; then the second bar, of the tune.

Steve reflected on this puzzling little performance, astonished. "It's been listening to Alto singing the folk tune! And repeating it!"

"Or it's brought it all the way over from Majorca anyway…. Isn't it fantastic? And would you believe, it was just hopping about here in the hotel garden, taking crumbs from me!"

"Did you feed it?"

"I threw him some shortbread biscuit!"

"Funny – they're described as extremely shy!"

"Perhaps it thinks if it varies its tune all the time, it won't be so easily followed!"

"It's smarter than Alto!" laughed Steve, relieving some of Becky's tension. They knew he might be there to kill them. "Perhaps he's been feeding it," he added. Then he had an idea. "Why don't we check out all the recent local sightings of the male Bluethroat on bird watchers' websites? They might lead us to where Alto's been.....or even where he hangs around."

"Look, be careful!" Becky warned. "He might be out here with the rest of the international smuggling ring. People like that are ruthless!"

"He might even be staying at a hotel round here. And one of the waiters is Spanish. He might be connected with them. Have you thought of that?"

But they'd been served breakfast by this waiter, who was very helpful and friendly: they felt sure he couldn't be connected with the diamond smugglers. He was probably just working in Edinburgh to improve his English, perhaps in a 'gap' year (after school and before going to university).

"Let's ask him questions about where he's from anyway, next time he waits at our table!" decided Becky.

Then Steve suggested: "Alto might be rich enough by now from diamond smuggling to own the Carisma himself!" But somehow, he thought, he hadn't quite seemed to be the owner, as he watched him working with the Scottish crew.

And Becky could tell by the way her brother said it that he didn't think that was likely. "Hey!" she said, "If the owner's British, he might be a member of a yacht club round here. Why don't we phone the nearest one and ask if anyone knows about it?" Steve's friend David had said there were several yacht clubs near Edinburgh.

"That's a good idea. I could say I'd seen it in the Forth, and I wanted to take a picture of it if it was still around….just ask them if it's ever moored in their marina."

Before they turned in for the night, Steve told his parents they were going to look up the local bird sanctuaries on the internet. Then he asked the French receptionist how long he'd been working at the hotel. When he told them he'd been there over a year, Becky asked him: "Have you seen many Spanish visitors in Edinburgh recently?"

"There are always a few at the language schools. Otherwise, not many: but you see some more at the Festival."

"D'you mean the International Festival in August and September?" she queried.

"Yes. May I ask why you're asking?"

Steve said quickly: "We're expecting a Spanish friend over here, and not many of the guidebooks in the bookshops here give a Spanish translation."

"I know some Spanish," the receptionist offered helpfully, " – and one of our waiters is Spanish….there's usually someone around who can translate for you," he added, smiling.

"Thanks!" said Becky. "And - please could you give us the names and phone numbers of the yacht clubs near here? There are quite a few, aren't there? There are quite a few marinas."

"Yacht clubs….." The receptionist was already thumbing through the Edinburgh business directory. "There are a dozen or so near here. Here!" He gave them the names and numbers of two of the nearest ones on a piece of paper, which Steve took from him. "Thanks! That's great. By the way," he asked him, "may we use your internet facility please?"

"Of course! It's along the corridor, turn right, first door on your left. How long do you think you might be?"

"Oh, only about half an hour or so," Becky assured him.

"Thank you, that's fine!" the receptionist smiled again.

"Good night!" Steve knew he'd have to wait until office hours the next day to phone the yacht clubs, and now led the way along to the computer room, to research all the most recent sightings of the Bluethroat.

It should have returned to the Mediterranean in the autumn, but had, particularly unusually, stayed to overwinter on Scotland's East coast, which had been experiencing very mild weather. Steve found the website of a local bird watching group, which listed sightings for various birds in chronological order. "Great! Here we are! '**Bluethroat**'." He ran his finger down the list. "A male one's been seen on a farm last month…..and look! A male's actually been spotted right outside the <u>Visitor Centre</u> at the Hermitage of Braid!" He dropped his jaw open with incredulity. "And there I was, <u>creeping</u> around the reed beds at Musselburgh in case I scared one away! In a freezing sleet shower, for a while! <u>Peeping</u> through the binoculars…And see <u>this</u>!" (He was breathless with indignation, which amused Becky.) "One's even been down to a <u>shopping</u> <u>centre</u>!!"

That one was a female. Becky decided that one of the sites in particular was most likely to have been visited by both the male Bluethroat <u>and</u> Alto, whistling the fishing festival tune: "Newhaven East Pier Lighthouse, at Leith. Look. On the 5th February."

"Let's get there!"

CHAPTER SIXTEEN
News Travelling Fast

That evening, after Maria's flight from Palma Majorca arrived at Edinburgh Airport, her school party made its way by coach to the city hostel where they were all going to be staying, pupils and teaching staff. It was colder than some of the Majorcan youngsters had expected, but everyone enjoyed identifying the landmarks they could make out by the lights of the city under a clear sky. Once they'd arrived at the hostel and all found their rooms (boys and girls were in separate ones, eight to a room) Maria's friends Manolita, a plump, fairly quiet girl, and Luisa went to check out where the TV, dining room and bathrooms were with their room's teacher before they phoned home; while the others started excitedly unpacking, practising their English, and contacting home by mobile.

Maria had found herself a bed at the far end of the room they were in. She needed a quiet moment to catch up with the messages on her mobile. She replayed the voice message sent from Steve the day before, saying he thought he'd recognised Alto, now bearded, sailing in the Firth of Forth on board the *Carisma*. When he said he believed Alto was wearing her mother's old silver brooch on his duffel-coat, she decided he might well have recognised the tall Spaniard. Straightaway she phoned Pablo, who was now living away from the family home, before she phoned her parents. "I've arrived safely," she told him when she got through, "but Steve and Becky have sent me quite a convincing voice message by mobile – they're alerting me about a man they've seen here who they think may be the diamond smuggler called Alto..." she said quietly.

As soon as she'd relayed the information Steve had given her, Pablo told her he'd contact the Scottish police with a description of Alto. He assured her he'd do his best to get someone to keep an eye on the hostel, in case anyone was thinking of hanging around there. And in the meantime, he was taking the next flight into Edinburgh – as soon as he could get his boss's permission. "Look, don't worry if Steve's wrong about this," he said. "I can always make myself useful to the police in Edinburgh, in any of their general on-going investigations while I'm there! It'll help me understand the Scottish accent better for the Majorcan holiday season!

But this <u>could</u> be the man. Just stay calm and with your school group – at all times. Will you do that for me? And don't leave your mobile lying around anywhere, or a stranger can get into its triangulation system and track you down once you pick it back up."

"I know!" Maria was well bolstered by her brother's response. "Of course! Thanks! Let me know as soon as you get here! And could you phone Mum and Dad for me to let them know I'm here and what's going on? I want to phone Steve and Becky back now."

Just then, as Maria was putting on her heavy olive green jumper over her lightweight one, Manolita and Luisa walked back into the coolish room with their teacher, who knew the least English of the teachers in the party. Maria, and another girl sitting at the other end of the room from her, were the two most fluent English-speaking pupils. She just had time to hang up her dark blue anorak and jeans then waited while their teacher explained the hostel's rules and regulations on things like fire and security alarms, which had been translated for her by another teacher. She went on to tell them about the facilities and arrangements for the trip, and then, when she'd finished instructing them, and no-one had any questions to ask, Manolita added in the precious silence: "And haggis is on the menu for tomorrow!"

The Majorcan girls who'd heard about haggis either grimaced or laughed, then they all started talking again. Maria quickly let Manolita know that something unexpected was afoot and she'd tell her about it later. As she dialled Steve's mobile number, her expression was very tense - but it looked to all the other girls as if she was thinking unenthusiastically about the Scottish national dish.

She managed to reach Becky and Steve just as they were about to leave their hotel computer room. All three youngsters were very excited they were about to be reunited, possibly in close proximity to the diamond smugglers again. "I've told Pablo and he's coming over here as soon as he can," said Maria in slow, careful English. "Are you sure the man you saw on the yacht was Alto – the tall one? And do you think he's following us?" she added more rapidly, in a low voice.

Becky was holding her mobile. "We don't know why he should be here in Edinburgh," she said, trying not to speak unnecessarily loudly, "but Steve's convinced it was him because he saw his face through very powerful binoculars."

Steve put in: "He's grown a beard!"

Becky, still holding the mobile, added: "He had his back turned to me by the time I could look through the binoculars – so I didn't see his face - but we both heard him whistle!"

"What does 'wissel' mean?" Maria struggled to understand. Becky explained, and she castigated herself for not recognising the word: "Oh yes! I forgot! I'm so stupid!"

"No, no!" Becky reassured her, "Your English is very good. "He was whistling the Majorcan festival tune you were dancing to. But we didn't hear him speak. So he's probably Majorcan, or at least he knows the fishing festival tune!"

"Alto was definitely Spanish," Maria confirmed, becoming increasingly convinced.

Steve took over holding the mobile: "I know! Perhaps he knows the tune because he used to holiday in Majorca."

"Yes, that's possible, Steve…."

He insisted: "He's whistling it because he's Alto and he's wearing your mother's brooch, which reminds him of the fishing festival!"

Gesturing for Steve to hold her mobile out to her, Becky managed to interject calmly: "Anyway, Maria, we think he may have heard you were coming here and he's after – following - you. But perhaps he doesn't know that you're with your school. Or, that Steve and I are holidaying here too."

"I….have told….. few people – only a few - about your family holiday," Maria struggled for the phrase. "So he might not know. But listen! Be very careful. The smugglers' leader…"

"Rodrigo," Steve supplied, signing for his sister to keep her ear near the mobile.

"Rodrigo," Maria continued, with her voice still low, "- last November he managed to escape from the police."

"Really!" Becky was astonished.

"Even when he was under …I think you say…<u>close</u> custody."

"No! How?" asked Steve.

"I didn't have time to tell you. He was taking the train to his trial, in the main Spanish courts. But he disappeared – and no-one has seen him again."

"So <u>he</u> could be on that yacht too!" said Steve.

"Don't approach <u>anyone</u> you've seen on it," Maria warned.

"We'll look out for him!" murmured Becky, as Steve explained to their friend: "We haven't told our parents yet we've seen Alto, or it might spoil the holiday! We're going to wait until we get some definite evidence."

"Are you sure?" asked Maria, persuasively. "How will you do this?"

"Yes; well, anyway," (Steve was prepared to consider Maria's advice) "the name of the yacht, *'Carisma'*" (and he spelt it out) "would be spelt with an 'h' if it were an English name!" He hadn't discussed this with Becky yet, but his sister was nodding, slowly and surely.

Maria agreed. "That's a Spanish word…..like 'charm', no?" She'd come across it in bilingual tourist guidebooks. "But I didn't know the English word is also….so… similar."

"Whoever owns that yacht may be Spanish," Steve went on. "We think we may be able to track them down and film them." He and his sister exchanged glances in agreement.

Then Maria suggested: "Perhaps Alto is only on holiday here, on his own, or with friends – and he's going back to Spain soon?" Although she suspected already, like the other two, that he was there intending to kill them.

"It's j-u-s-t possible," said Steve, "I didn't recognise the other two men I saw him with on the *Carisma* – they looked Scottish."

"But I think we all really know why he's here," put in Becky.

"Don't approach <u>any</u> of them!" Maria insisted.

"Nor you!" said Steve. "I just don't want to get you into any more trouble – danger this time. Do you understand?"

"Yes, I understand, Steve!"

"But Becky and I have a brilliant clue to help track them down!"

"Clue. Yes?" Maria was very interested.

"If we can't trace them through the local yacht clubs – I'll bet they're not members!"

Becky took her mobile over again and explained earnestly: "We've been bird watching here. And there's a bird, called the Bluethroat. It imitates other birds and other sounds as well. Do you understand: 'imitates'?"

"Yes, '*imitar*', it's the same in Spanish."

"Well it's been staying here for the winter – and it's been singing one of the Majorcan festival tunes!"

Maria found this hard to believe: "You're joking! … You are <u>joking</u> with me!"

"No!" Steve, the expert, took over again, carefully pointing out: "You see them in Majorca, but I don't know what their name is there. They repeat other birds' songs - and imitate other sounds as well. They're small songbirds - with a bright blue throat – neck, and red and white breast – on the front. Called the Bluethroat."

"Oh, OK, I know." Maria was convinced.

Steve continued, slowly: "We think the bird's been imitating Alto whistling the tune. And where the bird's been seen, will give us a clue – about where Alto goes. Do you understand? The bird sings where Alto often comes ashore, where he goes on the land!"

"Yes – the songbird has been near Alto in Scotland - maybe in Majorca also! And it imitates him, singing the fishing festival tune! And Alto's here because he has heard I'm visiting..." she concluded.

"So we're definitely all agreed!" Steve's confidence was on the ascendant. "Now let's discuss our plans for meeting up!"

They'd already made plans by e-mail for meeting up at the Dynamic Earth Centre in Edinburgh for lunch the day after next, after Maria's party had gone to the archaeological dig. They agreed to stay by this, and keep their two mobiles switched on whenever they could, with their tracking systems interacting so they could keep track of each others' movements; and remember they now had to take extra care not to leave them lying around.

When Maria put her mobile down, some of the Majorcan girls were still finishing discussing how haggis was made, while the general conversation was turning from sheep offal to scary local myths and legends. There was a lot of laugher after their teacher had retired to her own intercommunicating room, especially as they knew the evenings were becoming lighter, so they weren't so susceptible to frightening stories - but eventually Maria got a good night's sleep.

CHAPTER SEVENTEEN
Digging Up the Past

The next morning, Maria's school party had been able to look out of the windows of the hostel – which was in a fairly busy street of old, stone-built houses in the Old Town – and see some of Edinburgh clearly for the first time. It was a very cold, bright day; the robust old radiators were turned up fully and everyone was dressed in their warmest, thick woollen jumpers and jeans to sample the substantial Scottish breakfast, trying out porridge, kedgeree, oatcakes and black pudding for the first time. On top of that, they needed their hats, scarves and anoraks for the visit to the archaeological dig.

On the coach trip to the site near Penicuik, just south of Edinburgh, there was a lot of excited banter; Maria sat next to Manolita, and was able to tell her without being overheard, that she suspected she might be being watched.

"Who by?" asked Manolita. Their families had known each other for years and Maria could rely on her integrity.

"One – or more – of the diamond smugglers who weren't caught last year!" Then she told Manolita what her English friends Becky and Steve had just told her yesterday evening. About Steve being sure he'd seen Alto, the tall smuggler, now with a beard. "We didn't catch the other one - Julio, either…the stockily-built one I think must have run a shop in Spain. And both of them might be out here with Rodrigo Gonzalez, for all I know!" Maria was sitting by the window side, and glanced casually out of it again. They were on a fast 'A' road, going towards the countryside; and already starting to pass by fresh green fields with riding stables and sheep.

Manolita already knew the basic facts of Rodrigo's escape, and that his disappearance was under top secret police investigation, being handled by international detectives.

"It's making my blood run cold!" Maria went on: "He's not just a wanted criminal – he's suspected of having international terrorist links! If he's out here as well…..!"

"Have you told your brother?"

"Yes. And he's coming over. Thank heavens - I fear for my life!"

Both girls decided the smugglers wouldn't be interested in harming anyone else in their school party, so there was no point in raising the alarm - for the time being, at least. Manolita promised again not to say anything about them, as she began keeping her eyes open with Maria to see if anyone was following them. Now they were on a slower 'B' road, starting to drive through the beautiful, lush area by the Pentland Hills, with the Glencorse reservoir nearby. They could see there'd been a very light snow-fall overnight, which hadn't settled in the city but had lingered in a few east-facing pockets of the hillsides, as if someone had stroked the landscape with the finest ends of a white paintbrush.

They passed over a bridge, spotting a drift of snowdrops, and soon arrived at the site of the archaeological dig. It was still very cold, but starting to warm up in the sunshine. The Majorcan school party started making its way towards a fenced-off area, with everyone's breath visible in puffs. Maria and Manolita didn't notice anyone suspicious about – or the glint from a high-powered telescope on the edge of a nearby golf course. Mick and Alto were watching their party, standing on a gorse-covered slope on the boundary of a fairway.

Alastair had given instructions to bury the diamonds, once they'd been cut and polished, on the edge of the archaeological site near to the golf course. And to keep a golf caddy in their vehicle to carry about with them. So anyone from the Scottish gang coming to collect the diamonds and drive them to the docks wouldn't attract much attention. The locals didn't expect to recognise everyone turning up at the golf club, and they weren't familiar with the work schedule of the dig, or the international archaeological teams carrying it out. So the crooks - even if they had to wait around the area to be sure their accomplices could move the diamond consignments quickly through the docks and straight out into the Firth of Forth - wouldn't look suspicious. And they could also keep a watch on Maria.

But the archaeologists weren't the only enthusiasts embarking on a new season of their activities. The hardiest female members of the golf club had already started playing a game on the wintry course. Two of them had moved towards the edge of a fairway and the sloping sandy drifts of a difficult bunker. It was on the ridge sweeping down to the archaeological site, where Mick and Alto were lurking. The gorse bushes growing in abundance on the ridge provided ideal coverage for the two crooks, but they now had to wait to resume watching out for Maria in her school party through the telescope. Meanwhile they could hear what the sportswomen were saying to each other.

One of them, unscrewing the cap from a hip-flask, was explaining to the last player, still struggling with a high-numbered golfing iron to get her ball back up the steepest, top part of the bunker slope, that she was having difficulties too. She was having to wheel her own caddie-cart about - her 'caddie' hadn't turned up as he'd suddenly gone down with 'flu. She took a swig from her hip-flask as the last player gave the ball a smart flick, saying: "Well, <u>here</u>'s to the men!" and it finally landed up on the green. "By the way, added the relieved last player, nodding in Mick and Alto's direction, have you seen those two before?" Their heads were just visible from behind, amongst the shoulder-height bushes on the slope.

"No, but there's a spare ball at the bottom of the bunker," the caddy-wheeler pointed out in a loud voice. "I expect they're waiting for us to move on so they can proceed with <u>their</u> round.....without anyone seeing them floundering about!" She lowered her voice tone but it was still intentionally quite audible. "And I'm going to lighten the load of my caddy," she said, determinedly rearranging the assortment of steel-shafted woods and drivers, "by leaving a few irons here until I need them again." She selected three and laid them down side-by-side in the long grass growing round the bunker. Then she added "Did you know the first-ever women's golf tournament was held in 1811 in Musselburgh - on New Year's Day?" as her friend took another hard, accurate swipe at her ball and they walked on after the rest of their group.

Once all the women golfers had moved off into the distance, Mick took the opportunity to go up to the top of the ridge, take one of the golf clubs and bury it in the soft sand of another nearby bunker. He picked a big piece of gorse bush to mark it with as he went off. "It could come in handy later," he explained.

Alto realised that Mick could easily retrieve it – and if he used it as a murder weapon, or planted it at the scene of a murder, it could leave the finger of suspicion pointing at the caddy-wheeling golfer. He took up the telescope again to watch the archaeological teams as Mick was walking back down the ridge, and this time he spotted Maria, who'd thrown back her anorak hood - she'd begun to warm up with the exercise, and the day was getting warmer.

"I'd use it on a man if I absolutely had to," Mick was saying about the golf club, as he passed him the telescope to take a look at Maria: "You mean the one in dark jeans, blue anorak and an olive green jumper? …..But the only way I could get that girl would be with a high-powered rifle. It would have to be clean, you know?"

Alto wondered if Mick really could bring himself to kill Maria, if the opportunity arose and he found her on her own in an isolated place.

A large international archaeological team was being assembled to begin excavations around the site. They all stood huddled together by the area which had been fenced off for later investigation and excavation, right at the end of the project. It was carefully organised. First of all, the Scottish director of the dig, Professor Cameron, spoke to each of the international school parties in turn. A respected archaeologist from Edinburgh University, he was tall with wavy, grey hair, slightly buck teeth and rosy cheeks, looking into peoples' faces from various angles as he spoke, with the teachers translating for their school party.

He gave a friendly welcome to the Majorcan group at the beginning in a mixture of Catalan and Spanish, then advice and briefings in English, with the teachers translating. He told them that archaeological sites were best investigated in winter, when the bracken and most of the vegetation had died right down. After they'd taken a look at, and marked out, the less obvious remains which had been highlighted by the light snowfall overnight, they'd be starting on the side of the hill most sheltered from any biting northerly winds. He delivered an inspiring talk about identifying artefacts and ecofacts, then classifying them by using numbers and making sketches. These projects always took time, and involved patience. If they had any questions later they could ask the leaders on the project.

Maria switched on her mobile again after the introductory talk. They all spread out to work on different areas, wearing heavy plastic excavating gloves over their ordinary ones. Everyone found themselves enjoying it – as they uncovered objects from the past, history seemed more dynamic. Then Pablo phoned her. Maria hastily took off her right-hand muddy excavating glove to take the call. He told her he'd just arrived in Edinburgh; on the first flight in he could take from Palma. He was on his way to the Lothian and Borders Police Headquarters; then he'd set off from there to meet up with her – he wasn't sure when that would be yet.

At around eleven o'clock, with the last of the snow all melted and the nearly invisible lines of the remains traced out, the school parties started sitting down in the site cabin on foldaway chairs around portable stoves, to share snacks and piping hot soup, tea and coffee from thermos flasks. Their breath was no longer visible on the warming air. Maria and Manolita took an early break. Then, as they were beginning to think about leaving the cabin to start work again on the dig, a car turned up at the site.

Pablo was being shown around the area by plain-clothes Detective-Sergeant Jim McCulloch, who was working with the Lothian and Borders Police and had contacted Professor Cameron for permission for them to look about the site. The detective-sergeant was English, from another police force. He had broad shoulders and a square-set face with an earnest expression, dark, greying hair and brown eyes. His accent was easier for Pablo to understand than that of some of the Scottish officers. As Pablo got out, he stayed waiting in the car. He was a very patient, committed man.

Pablo, dressed in a heavy padded anorak over an Arran sweater and thick trousers with walking shoes, greeted his sister in the cabin with a quick hug. They left Manolita finishing a health-food snack and talking with the others for a while, and walked off to a quiet spot to discuss what Steve had said he'd seen. Maria told him that Becky hadn't managed to get a look at the man's face, but both she and Steve said they'd heard him whistling the Majorcan fishing festival tune. (She didn't bother to mention there was a little migrant songbird about giving it out too.) Pablo said that the police in Edinburgh were interested in talking to the

English youngsters, but had decided to let their Majorcan colleague talk about it with them first.

Maria stressed that Steve was convinced the dark, bearded man he'd seen was Alto. "And he said he thought he was wearing mother's old silver brooch, the one we lost in the island cave. It was pinning his duffle-coat together at the top!"

"Rather a funny thing for a man to choose to wear," remarked Pablo, enjoying breathing in the fresh air and looking about him.

"Anyway," Maria went on, "we've arranged – Steve, Becky and I – to meet up at the Dynamic Earth Centre in Edinburgh. It's a science education centre - explaining things like earthquakes and volcanoes, with high-tech models and simulations."

"Great! When?" asked Pablo. "I'll meet you there. Will anyone else you know be there?"

"Tomorrow at one o'clock in the café there. I'll be with the school party. Steve and Becky's parents aren't going – they just have to phone in to them at their hotel at some point."

"Now: they know about this, presumably?"

"That we're going to meet up? – Yes. About Alto? – No, not yet."

"OK!" Pablo reflected. "Well, they'll need to know soon! Tell Becky and Steve I'll be joining you, won't you?" He gave his sister a one-armed hug and returned to the waiting Jim McCulloch.

Mick and Alto had stopped watching through the telescope while Maria and Manolita took their break in the cabin. Mick had now just taken another look and noticed that Maria was outside again, talking with a man. "Who's he?" he asked Alto, handing him the telescope.

"I'm not sure," said Alto. But he thought he'd recognised Pablo Munos, Maria's brother, whose photograph and personal details were in a file in Eulalia's office on board the *Carisma*. The file held details of several detectives involved in the international investigation into the diamond criminals' activities. He decided to tell Mick, then Eulalia.

As soon as Eulalia heard the news, she phoned Alastair to alert him. After he'd perused his copy of the notes on Pablo, he left them lying in the open 'skull and crossbones' file on his desk, and took out a beautiful, princess-cut white diamond, cut to give the fullest refraction of light possible, from the top drawer. As he held it between his spatulate mauvy-pink fingers, the afternoon sunshine coming through his study window threw up lovely, sparkling rainbow colours – rose, lilac, blue, turquoise, yellow and green - glancing around in it, before falling onto Pablo's photograph in distended patterns from the facets.

Meanwhile, Steve had made phone calls to the two nearby yacht clubs to ask if they could tell him anything about a large luxury cruiser called the *Carisma* which he'd seen sailing in the Firth of Forth, and which he wanted to take a picture of. Neither of them gave out the names of members or their boats to members of the public; but the administrator at the main yacht club advised him there weren't many luxury yachts to be seen of the size he was describing. Perhaps though, she said, he'd see it again if he kept his eyes open for it during sailing times, and she wished him luck with this.

He and Becky hadn't really expected the *Carisma* to be owned by someone in the Edinburgh area. It might be – but they couldn't see how they could investigate into this at the moment. They'd received a quick message from Maria letting them know Pablo should be able to join them for lunch at the Dynamic Earth Centre: and they were looking forward to discussing it with him. Right now, they were both determined to look for the male Bluethroat around the Newhaven East lighthouse at Leith. Once their father learned from them it was easily spotted hopping around shopping centres, he decided he was no longer interested in watching for it himself. "That's just a flagrant little attention-seeker!" he remarked, "It's no real challenge."

"At least it's caught Becky's interest, for once!" insisted Steve.

"We want to see if we can record a female one on the mobile," she put in.

They managed to persuade their parents, who wanted to look around the Botanical Gardens the next day, to split up with them for an hour while they investigated the shoreline at Leith. They agreed to meet back up with them at the gardens, and then go on to the Dynamic Earth Centre to meet up with Maria for lunch.

The next day looked as if it was going to be another blue-skied one with a hazy beginning, which would soon be clear. The gardens, off Inverleith Row, weren't far from Leith; and they could see how to walk back there as they all took a taxi north up Inverleith Row, turning right into Ferry Road and left up Craighall Road to a roundabout by the shoreline. Beyond it, the small Newhaven Harbour pier, about as wide as a car, jutted into the Firth of Forth: at the end, built into its right-hand edge, was a small, brilliant white lighthouse. The taxi drove on slowly and stopped at the smartly developed harbour front, where the grand old commercial buildings, the Custom House and the Corn Exchange, stood alongside new business buildings, bars and restaurants. They could just see right out across the Firth of Forth, to the other side. The water was, surprisingly to Steve, quite blue.

"Best stick to this tourist area and keep away from the docks zone, over there," Pat pointed it out, east of where they were.

"OK. Which island is that?" asked Becky, pointing west out to a small, whitish island with a slightly misty appearance, not far off the shoreline. There was another small lighthouse on it.

"I'm not sure," answered Steve. "Granton, probably. The Inchkeith one is right out east, past the docks, on another island out in the middle of the Firth of Forth." Then he asked the taxi driver, pointing to the little octagonal lighthouse at the end of the Newhaven pier, "Is that the Newhaven East lighthouse?"

"It must be," the taxi driver was confused himself. "There are one or two others near here, though."

"OK," said Chris, "we'll call it that to avoid confusion."

"Let's get out here!" Steve's jaw was fixing firmly. "This is where they've seen the Bluethroat."

Before Steve and Becky got out, Chris, who had his own mobile with him, checked Steve's mobile to make sure the tracking system was on. "The navigation system should be working, too! But just in case it fails, here's a note with the directions to get back to the Botanical Gardens. '*At the roundabout go down Craighall Road, turn right onto Ferry Road, then left onto Inverleith Row. Botanical Gardens on right.*' "Take care of your sister," he said, "and don't get separated! We'll see you later!"

Pat turned round and waved to them as the taxi drove back to the Botanical Gardens. She'd just checked her daughter had a map with her too, and was smiling.

"So. The largest enclosed deepwater port in Scotland!" Steve said, as they stood on the waterfront and looked about them. "This must see plenty of action! It's a massive ocean terminal."

"It goes back to the fourteenth century," Becky reminded him. She'd been telling him the later old Scottish folk history of the area, about the sorcery and treason brewed up in sixteenth-century Leith against James VI to stop him landing his boat there. (And the tale about a mysterious Fairy Boy of Leith, aged ten, who would apparently disappear, then reappear overnight, while taking part in international music festivities across the sea in France and Holland. He could even disappear from a room under the noses of people keeping a close watch on him.) Steve, not really interested in pursuing the folk history of the place, just said: "Does it? It doesn't <u>look</u> that old."

They walked up to the approach to the little pier. On one side was a small marina with lots of little yachts and boats moored in it. Next to this a long, low, red warehouse with wide, arched windows had housed a famous fish restaurant which had closed recently.

On the other side there was a concrete slope covered in dark seaweed. Further along on that side there would be another marina - not yet built and still under construction - big enough to take the *Carisma*. "It's a pity they haven't finished the new marina yet," Steve observed. "The *Carisma* might have stopped here. There'll be a few more really large-berth yachts like that around when they do. But it might just sail past anyway – keep a good look out!"

"Anyway, where's the Bluethroat?" demanded Becky.

"He's probably in the Botanic Gardens!"

The pier wasn't very long and they could see from the shore there were no birds flying about near the lighthouse, which stood on the very right-hand edge at the end. "They wouldn't build a nest on the outside of the lighthouse, like a swallow, would they?" wondered Becky.

"No: or at least, they're <u>supposed</u> to make little grassy cup nests in low bushes in the summer! They prefer the coasts - but they <u>probably</u> wouldn't stay around any fishing boats for long - not with competition from the seagulls!"

"Let's go over and have a look!"

On the right as they walked down, was a tiny, dome-roofed building about the size of a garden shed, built like an igloo (only with concrete blocks, not blocks of ice) with no windows and a padlocked, arch-topped metal door. "What's that igloo-thing for?" asked Becky.

"No idea!" said Steve. "Perhaps it's a Second World War bunker."

A metal railing ran all the way around the edge of the pier, a little higher than their waists; it was fenced in with wire meshing except at the far end. They leaned over it for any possible signs of their elusive songbird, but couldn't see anything. There were very few people about at this time of year even though it was a lovely sunny day, and it was quite quiet.

At the right-hand edge at the end of the pier, the metal railing stopped at a point midway on the circumference of the lighthouse base, then continued from its opposite side. So there was an unfenced concrete ledge of pier around half the lighthouse base, dropping straight down to the water.

The white cast-iron octagonal tower of the lighthouse was about twenty metres high; there was an arched metal door to it, which was heavily padlocked with big, rusting metal chains. There was a little decorative octagonal ledge, which small birds could have perched on, running about two-thirds of the way up, and an arched window. The top, which had 360-degree triangular-shaped window-panes for the lantern light to shine out of, had a little gallery around it. It was typical of the small, disused lighthouses all along the coastline. It had been kept well painted and cleaned, which had probably stopped seabirds from nesting on it.

After they'd taken in the view, Steve was beginning to feel they'd missed their last opportunity of seeing the *Carisma* again. But Becky, intrigued by the Bluethroat's new migratory behaviour, rallied her brother's spirits: "He'd more likely have hopped around the shoreline cafes for a while, for the bread and cake crumbs, if he'd had the choice ….like Alto! Let's get back to them!"

As they walked back past the long red warehouse to the waterfront they saw a cluster of four or five house sparrows fluttering about near a cafe's outdoor sign. Steve glanced at them, and then noticed that one wasn't a sparrow. After it had taken a crumb from the pile the others were occupied with, it flew off up into one of a line of trees growing along the shore. Slowly, he went over to take a closer look at it. "Look at this one!" he pointed up gently towards it. "I thought it was a female house sparrow – only look at its beak!"

Becky looked up at the little bird, cocking her head sideways to see. "Yes?"

"It should be chunky and dark if it's a sparrow like the others."

"But it's got a slim, pale one!" she confirmed, straightening her head up again.

"And a very pale stripe, <u>over</u> its eye, not behind it."

"It's not a Bluethroat…." Becky started speculating.

"It <u>is</u> – look at its breast – it's very dark: and see just one or two, <u>tiny</u> bright blue spots?"

"Oh, **yes**!"

"It's a female Bluethroat." Steve was holding his mobile up towards her, filming. Suddenly the little bird started chirruping: *wheet-turrc*, with increasing musical embellishments. "The male's probably about, too, unless he's in the Botanical Gardens!" he whispered.

Becky strolled up and down looking at the other trees. "Well, he isn't in the trees!" She listened, delighted, to the female Bluethroat's song – one or two notes would harmonise nicely with the male's Majorcan tune, she thought.

"She's probably singing a perfect descant to the male!" said Steve. "Anyway, we're probably in the right area!"

Then the bird flew off towards the lighthouse.

Becky decided to follow her back to it. "Maybe she'll attract the male over there, if he can hear her…. Why don't we split up," she suggested, "it's hardly any distance - only for a few minutes. I'll take the mobile – I want to see if I can record them singing together! And then you can stay here for a while and look in the cafes for Alto, without worrying you'll miss seeing the yacht – I'll see it if it passes the harbour! And if you do see him, don't follow him – come and get me! Straightaway! And I'll film him. He wouldn't recognise me."

"We must stay in sight of each other all the time, OK?" agreed Steve. "And let's signal – if you see the *Carisma* or I see Alto – raise your arm, wave, then keep it up with your palm flat to show you've seen something! Like this." And he demonstrated it.

"So we'll have to keep looking back at each other – OK!"

"Here's the mobile!"

"Thanks. Let's meet back at the lighthouse in fifteen minutes' time whatever happens!" said Becky, checking the mobile's clock time and putting it in an anorak pocket. She quickly pulled her thick sweater sleeve back to check her watch, which was keeping pace with the time on the mobile.

"OK." Steve checked his. "I make it half past ten!"

"See you at quarter to eleven!" She set off back up the pier, following the female Bluethroat – which she'd now lost sight of - towards the lighthouse. *It's probably gone to sit up on the ledge, or the little gallery,* she thought.

Steve, meanwhile, wondered what might bring Alto ashore just here. He looked in through the windows of the pubs, delicatessens and cafes to see what sort of people were attracted to them, though they weren't full yet for lunch. The crooks must surely need to go shopping now and then. He decided to ask a few questions at the newsagent's. He walked in and bought a copy of *'The Scotsman'* newspaper and a packet of sweets from the Asian man behind the counter, then asked him if he could remember serving any Spanish people in the last few weeks. The newsagent immediately asked the other shopkeeper - who looked like his brother and was standing arranging the shelves - if he had any recollection of doing so.

Turning away from the shelves towards Steve, this man said: "Yes, I remember a Spanish man coming in here, about a week ago. He had a Spanish accent."

"What did he look like?" asked Steve eagerly.

"Quite tall......he had dark hair and a beard.....blue eyes."

"What was he wearing?"

The man behind the counter, who had suddenly recollected it, now answered: "Yes! I remember him. It was a very cold evening and it had been snowing, I think. He was wearing a dark coat with a dark blue scarf, and a woolly hat – black or blue, I can't really remember....."

"Anything else?" Steve pressed them.

The man behind the counter frowned: "Just jeans;....the coat had toggles with a hood at the back." He couldn't offer any more.

Steve decided that it was Alto. He probably either hadn't been wearing the old brooch then, or it was hidden under his scarf. It was the sort of thing you'd remember if you'd seen it. Remembering Pablo's advice to always search for the slightest details of a criminal, as these could suddenly become vital clues, he asked: "What did he buy?"

The man behind the counter thought for a little while, while the other one resumed shelf-stacking. "He bought <u>two</u> bottles of whisky. I remember: some of the last in stock of an old brand they've discontinued. And I think a newspaper .....some cheese....and yes! a loaf of bread...May I ask why you're so interested in this man?"

The man stacking the shelves stopped again to listen carefully.

Steve blurted hastily: "I'm making investigations for ....it's a sort of marketing project I've got involved with, to help my sister with a school project." It was only a white lie: after all, the smugglers must be trying to market the diamonds they'd stolen. Then, before the shopkeepers could put any more questions to him about it, he asked quickly:

You say the Spanish man bought particular malt?" – hoping his basic knowledge of whisky terminology would persuade them to believe him.

The man behind the counter seemed fairly satisfied with this explanation. "Yes, 'Old Cask'."

This had been the strongest 60% proof whisky to be had on the East Coast of Scotland, blended from several different malt whiskies from various distilleries. It reminded Alex of home. And he'd asked Alto to pick some up from this newsagent's, one of the last places still selling it, along with some bread and cheese. Alex habitually drank too much of the *Carisma*'s stocks of 'Old Cask' (which the rest of the crew left alone because it was dangerously strong); but now Alto was helping him drink less, by sharing it with him – the flavour reminded <u>him</u> a little of Spanish sherry.

Steve noticed there were still a few bottles of 'Old Cask' on the shelves behind the counter. "Has he been in before to buy anything?"

Again the two shopkeepers conferred with each other. Both shook their heads and said: "No, we haven't seen him before."

"Was he with anyone else?"

"No."

"Last question: Can you remember which newspaper he bought?"

"No, sorry: but it was probably '*The Scotsman*', said the second newsagent.

"Thanks so much for your help!" Steve walked out quickly, delighted. He'd got a really good lead on Alto.

There was hardly anyone about, only one or two people he'd never seen before, in the cafes. There weren't any yachtsmen near the little marina and only two small yachts were sailing, far out in the Forth. In the quiet restaurants, one or two waiters and waitresses were tidying up before the lunch hour. Hardly able to contain his excitement, he looked down the pier for Becky, ready to signal to her if she were to turn round – only he couldn't see her. *She must be just behind the lighthouse*, he thought, and made his way over to it.

Steve still couldn't see his sister. His heart started to pound a little. He looked over the rail right round the back of the lighthouse, but she wasn't standing on the ledge. It was so narrow that if a man with very big feet were to stand on it, facing out to the water, he could probably only just avoid his shoes overhanging it. *Oh God*, he thought, *what if she's fallen into the Forth?* He looked down into the water, but it wasn't as clear as he'd expected and it was difficult to tell how deep it was. She could have hit her head badly against the wall and sunk immediately; but that was most unlikely. If she'd just tumbled in, and not had a heart attack from the icy water (which he knew was possible), she'd have swum back – it was only a very few metres to the shoreline. She probably could have waded back.

Still, he didn't think Becky was foolhardy enough in the first place to climb over the railing and try walking round the narrow ledge of pier on the water-side of the lighthouse, just to watch the female Bluethroat again. It was terribly dangerous: she'd have had to cling to the lighthouse wall with her arms outstretched, and then she couldn't possibly have filmed the bird with the mobile - she wouldn't have had a free hand to use.

Even if you just stood there, you'd probably have to lean your back against the lighthouse wall with your arms outstretched, to avoid falling into the water.

He tried the door of the lighthouse, but the padlock was firmly locked and the rusting loops of the chains still in the same position as they were before, obviously undisturbed.

Then he walked back down the pier, wondering if she'd followed the bird back to the trees again. She wasn't there. It was gone quarter to eleven. They'd agreed not to lose sight of each other! Now he suspected she'd given him the slip and was hiding somewhere to fool him. Yes, he decided: she definitely wouldn't have just fallen into the water when there was a meshed-in railing all round the pier. But maybe she wanted him to <u>think</u> she had, for a joke. "Beck-<u>y</u> …." he started calling softly, almost talking to himself, "where <u>are</u> you?" Perhaps she'd gone over to the Maritime Heritage Centre, which was just nearby. But it wouldn't be like her to keep it up and stay in hiding – not when his own disappearance had put her through so much anxiety in Majorca. He'd wait for her to turn up again, and tease her by looking coolly disappointed – not hugely relieved – when she did.

Earlier, while Steve, having looked along the waterfront, squared up his chin and turned and walked into the newsagent's, Rodrigo had slipped unnoticed away from the lighthouse. Dressed in jeans, navy crew-necked sweater and a donkey jacket, his tan had faded and he'd grown a dark blond beard which now concealed most of the scar on his left cheek. He thought he'd just recognised Steve Parker. He decided he'd see for certain when he came out of the newsagents: so he walked down the pier to wait by the little igloo-shaped building, and made a quick mobile call in Spanish to his accomplices: "I think the kid Steve Parker's out here! Guard the girl – she must be his friend! I'll deal with him…."

But luckily, when Steve came out of the newsagent's and started up the approach towards the pier, someone walked out of one of the nearby offices, heading into the town centre. Rodrigo, though he was now positive he'd recognised the young English lad who'd smashed his diamond-smuggling ring, realised he might be witnessed disposing of him. So he sprinted, still unnoticed, back to the end of the pier, hopped lightly up the meshed railing and let himself down carefully onto the narrow ledge, edging round behind the lighthouse. He could get rid of the kid's body in the water fairly easily from there, in broad daylight - provided there was no-one walking about or looking out of a window.

As Steve had walked up and looked round the lighthouse again, Rodrigo flattened himself hard against the wall with his face turned sideways, edging round to the other side as his intended victim peered over each side of the railing. Steve didn't quite see him and had no idea he was there. He instantly headed back down the pier again, giving no time for Rodrigo to jump him unawares. But Rodrigo, determined not to miss this big main chance, leaped back over the railing and started walking silently and quickly up behind him. As he was getting near to him, he started to run.

Hearing strong footsteps coming up from behind, apparently out of nowhere, Steve momentarily remembered the superstitious old folk tales about the area which

Becky had been telling him. The sixteenth-century witchcraft practised on Leith pier against James VI, and the vanishing Fairy Boy of Leith. Surely…. and he shivered. But he didn't believe in that sort of thing - someone must have just moored a boat at the end of the pier, and climbed over the railing to get ashore. He was going to turn round anyway to get another look at the lighthouse.

As he did so, to his terror, he saw the escaped, bearded Rodrigo running up behind him. He recognised him immediately – medium height and very slim, his lean face no longer tanned and the left cheek starting to redden around that pale-pink scar, so nearly hidden by his new dark blond beard. His blue eyes were wildly intent. Steve started to run away, assuming the smuggler's ring leader must have just stepped off a small boat or dinghy. (Surely he hadn't just come out of the lighthouse, which was padlocked from the outside.)

The frantic thought flashed into his mind that the criminals had just caught or killed his sister; then he thought: *no, that's why she's hiding - she suddenly saw them, looking suspicious.* If they hadn't got his sister, he must escape Rodrigo at all costs, not confront him - he probably wouldn't live if he confronted him now anyway. He was worried that if he ran into one of the shops or restaurants along the waterfront to call for help, Rodrigo could easily run away and evade capture. Ideally he needed to head towards a group of people in the street and hope at least one of them would be prepared to try to make a citizen's arrest. And even if they didn't try, it would mean there'd be more people able to witness and identify him.

He was running past the long building of the closed fish restaurant. Would Becky know her way back to the Botanical Gardens? He had the piece of paper with the directions to them. But she had the map, he remembered in exasperation as he turned into the big road running parallel to the shoreline, called Lindsay Road, with Rodrigo closing up on him. He mustn't turn into a dead-end street!

He wondered again desperately: should he run into the nearest shop and call for help? If Rodrigo had already seen Becky without recognising her, he might now have guessed she was about, and run off back to look for her. Yet even if the smugglers knew she was in Edinburgh, they might well not recognise her, now her hair was a bit longer and a little darker; and she'd put on weight over the winter.....As her brother, he felt the strong urge to protect her. He'd play decoy and lead Rodrigo well away from her - but they probably wouldn't bother searching around the area just for her anyway. It was <u>him</u> they wanted. Him and Maria. Witnesses to their crime.

Steve kept running in a straight line down Lindsay Road. He could see the government building of the Scottish Executive ahead on the left, but knew Rodrigo wouldn't follow him towards that if he knew what it was. He wanted this man caught! Lindsay Road continued into Commercial Street, then Bernard Street. Steve was hardly able to read the names as he sped past them with Rodrigo still following him. He wondered if Becky had already phoned the police. Perhaps she'd been watching all this, hiding, then gone into the newsagent's to call for help. Or perhaps she'd just gone straight over to the Maritime Heritage Centre to hide from him for a joke, without even seeing any of the criminals...

He ran past a Youth Centre and a kilt maker's; he wasn't quite confident he could lead Rodrigo into either of those; the huge, grand old Customs Wharf building with its big portico and two-storey-high pillars, then? No, he decided. He ran past a gallery, and a pub: 'The Lighthouse' – but it wasn't open yet, and if he stopped, there might be no-one there to come out and help him. Rodrigo was gaining ground on him fast.

Steve's heart was pounding hard as he turned right into Constitution Street. Extending round the corner each way were the classical wings of the old Corn Exchange building. At its centre was a big dome surmounted by a little clock tower. He didn't know what it was or what went on in there and was just considering running into it, when looking back, he saw Rodrigo suddenly stop on the other side of Bernard Street without turning into Constitution Street. He was taking a call on his mobile. Steve, at first relieved that he might be shaking his pursuer off, then worried that Rodrigo would summon the other thugs to the area to get him cornered. He was so frightened he couldn't stop running.

Constitution Street was quite empty of people: most of the buildings seemed to house offices - he couldn't just rush into one and hope to ask a receptionist to make a citizen's arrest on a dangerous criminal. He ran past the Corn Exchange, the old Assembly Hall and several other newer offices, straight on down to a crossroads with traffic lights. He decided to turn left here into Queen Charlotte Street - not knowing what he was doing but not wanting to run across a busy road again. Looking back to watch out for Rodrigo in case he'd resumed following him, he saw a little sign high up on the wall of the building he'd just run past on this corner - it was a **police station**! But he also saw Rodrigo running up towards him again, fast - he'd started back after him after talking for only a few seconds on his mobile. Infuriatingly, Steve couldn't double back now and try to run into the police station without a very dangerous confrontation with this criminal – if Rodrigo were carrying a knife he might stab him there and then. There was hardly <u>anyone</u> about except car drivers – no policemen; someone had now appeared further up Constitution Street on the other side of the road…and two women were walking up this street with their backs turned to him. He just <u>had</u> to keep on running.

He called out: "Help! Police!" just as the traffic lights were changing to amber: the briefly queuing drivers had all started revving up their engines and one on the other side of the road sounded her horn. And like a nightmare, no-one paid him any attention or ran to his assistance: they hadn't heard what he'd shouted. One of the women walking further up Queen Charlotte Street assumed he was hailing a friend and turned round out of curiosity, to see him waving hard after one of the cars as it drove on. Then she went on talking with her colleague. Steve hoped: He'll veer off when he sees that's a police station.

Yet Rodrigo was still pursuing him. He couldn't believe it. Well, he'd give him a run for his money. Although Steve's face was very cold he was basically warmed up and his adrenalin was flowing. With the traffic lights changed, he decided this was now a quieter road to cross, and turned right into a street he couldn't see the name of. He was now heading south towards the city, down Duncan Place, and the larger office buildings were giving way to a variety of little shops like boutiques, stationers and pet shops. There were one or two more people about. Just as he was deciding whether to run into one of these shops, or stop a passer-by, he came to a roundabout. Bearing right into Easter Road, he kept heading south, instinctively, towards the city, with Rodrigo following.

Steve was suddenly faced with a long run uphill, past small terraced houses. The road levelled up for a while, with lots of little shops along it, but soon started to go uphill again, with terraced houses on either side. Surely Rodrigo would close up on him before he could reach a reasonably large group of people! Steve was a good runner but felt he'd only stayed ahead of him so far by swerving round corners and crossing over the road.

Easter Road was very long. Now it had started to narrow. He had to bear right up a steep bend, with high grey stone walls on either side with ivy trailing over them. Big old deciduous trees behind these kept the sunlight out and it suddenly felt like an old, country road. He completely lost his bearings for a while. Then just as he was starting to feel exhausted, he came to a crossroads with traffic lights. And quite unexpectedly close on the right was the big hump of King Arthur's Mount! He knew where he was now. And it gave him the will to continue.

The road bent round to the left, now called Abbey Mount, and then bent right under a railway bridge. There were still only a few cars about and no-one was walking on the road. Running under the gloomy iron bridge, Steve could hear Rodrigo's running behind him again, echoing all the way around it. He mustn't let him close in on him here! As he raced out of the other side into the sunlight he was relieved to see the way was now downhill, past Holyrood Palace on his left and with the new Scottish Parliament building on his right. He looked behind him and as he'd expected, Rodrigo had slowed his pace to a fast walk: because there'd be more people about here to view a running man with suspicion, not because he'd run out of steam. But this was no time for him to stop running. So, where to?

Up ahead - opposite to, and at a higher level than the Scottish Parliament Building - was the unusual tent-like roof of the Dynamic Earth Structure, where he and Becky were due to meet up with Maria and Pablo. And rising up directly behind it was the two hundred and fifty metres high King Arthur's Mount. Steve turned left into Queen's Drive, where a group of about twenty tourists were following a guide towards Holyrood Palace.

Their guide suddenly stopped to explain something to them; Steve slowed down, getting his breath back a little, and walked up to them. He loitered around the edges of the group with one eye kept on Rodrigo, hoping he'd walk up closer. If he did, he could interrupt the guide and ask someone to phone the police while the others grabbed hold of him. But Rodrigo hung back, and then started to walk away, back round the corner, as the guide frowned at Steve and stopped giving his talk. He was trained to challenge freeloaders who tried to join the group for a free talk on a tourist attraction! Steve realised he was about to be asked who he was: and now that he couldn't point Rodrigo out to anyone, he'd just look foolish. Giving an apologetic smile to the guide, he started off again, running across Queen's Drive and following it halfway round a roundabout as it continued along the base of King Arthur's Mount, on the side known as Salisbury Crags.

Salisbury Crags were completely covered with green grass (he'd thought from the name they'd be rocky.) If he could get some way up them, he'd be able to look down on the roads and see if Rodrigo was still following him from a distance. He ran over the road again and started walking up the main path winding up the crags. Now that the pressure was off him slightly, he could get his breath back more. He'd run more than a couple of miles, he felt sure. He coughed, clearing the lingering presence of a cold he thought he'd already cleared up before the holiday, deep in his chest. Perhaps the run was doing him some good. Apart from a couple further up ahead and one other person off the path, this side of the mount was devoid of people. He wondered if he might be able to persuade one of the walkers to lend him their mobile to phone the police – if they were carrying one.

But looking back down onto Queen's Drive, he noticed Rodrigo had suddenly appeared from another street leading into it. And seen him. He looked as if he was going to follow him up the main path. Steve decided he couldn't catch Rodrigo so easily on this natural terrain. But, holding his nerve and walking slowly, he let him follow him up it some way, then suddenly headed off it, making his way over to a short incline. He ran down it back onto the road, knowing Rodrigo would then look obvious following him.

He wondered whether to summon help at the well-guarded new Scottish Parliament building, but knew Rodrigo wouldn't dare follow him near it: he'd slip away again before he had time to point him out to the security guards. *Though I might be able to persuade them to call more police to the area, to search for him,* he thought: *but then he might leave it altogether!* What was this man likely to do?

Still quite high up the steep slope, Rodrigo was picking his way round the Mount towards the other side, so he wouldn't look suspicious. But Steve was sure he'd soon come after him again. He considered the Dynamic Earth Centre, the nearest structure. It was a big tourist attraction and bound to have several curators and attendants. But he was due to meet Maria there for lunch! He checked his watch. It was 12:30 pm. Ironically, he was in good time. The last thing he'd wanted to do was endanger Maria! And if Pablo were late getting there…her life would be in jeopardy. Yet, he realised, there would probably be enough people about; and if she was there too……if Rodrigo followed him to it, even if Pablo wasn't there yet, they could both point him out as a wanted criminal: and a citizen's arrest would be much more easy. He sped to it.

In front of the Centre was a stylised stone amphitheatre. It had about twelve semicircular tiers of stone seating - several people including youngsters were walking about on them - enclosing a raised circle of bright green turf. Steve leapt up the curve of broad stone steps on the right-hand side, knowing Rodrigo would still be watching him. There was a big white van parked on the fore court right by the entrance – he couldn't see how anyone had managed to get it up there: there was a ramp, but this couldn't have taken such a wide vehicle. Perhaps there was an entrance round the back. He could see through the floor-length windows that the open-plan café was immediately to the right as you entered.

There were a few people sitting down to lunch there but he couldn't see Maria amongst them as he strode in fast through the entrance door. He felt sure Rodrigo would follow him in.

Ahead, a curving staircase led down to the exhibition, which was all one floor below ground level. The staircase was roped off at the top of the stairwell. Perhaps they'd admitted the full quota of people and were waiting for some to come out before they let more in. Apart from the man at the ticket desk over to the left by the exhibition exit staircase, there was a single attendant standing by the big main entrance and two people serving behind the café counter. There would be more curators downstairs. Behind a large, temporarily screened-off area, there were several technicians working on various systems and gadgetry. If Rodrigo walked into the foyer, there'd be enough people to apprehend him.

Steve was playing for high stakes. He speculated that if Rodrigo did approach him here, amongst all these people, it would now be with a bribe or a threat: maybe both. He decided he'd tell the security guard he was expecting a dangerous criminal who was following him to come into the Centre any minute; and that a friend of his, Maria Munos, who could also identify him, was due to join him soon at the cafe. And he'd ask the guard: If they pointed this criminal out, could he please phone the police and help them with an arrest?

But the security guard had just got on his mobile. Steve decided to wait for him to finish. Then he noticed a big sign being displayed by the ticket desk, so he went over to read it: *'We will be closing early at 1pm today for routine technical work. The shop and café will remain open.'* He realised Maria's school party must still be going round the exhibition and decided to wait for her in the café where he could see the exhibition exit staircase - by the shop, also one level below the foyer. They must be coming out soon; then they'd both be together to spot Rodrigo if he came in.

He was very warm by now and decided to bag a strategic table nearest to the exit staircase where he could sit with his back to the main entrance, not easily recognisable to Rodrigo and able to look back every so often to keep an eye out for him. He removed his heavy padded anorak and hung it over the back of his chair, realising his mouth was very dry. He thought that Rodrigo – provided he hadn't given up the chase altogether – would draw attention to himself in this area of Edinburgh if he ran, and felt sure he'd be taking his time making his way across to the Centre. As the security guard was still talking on his mobile and there was only one person passing through the café service area, Steve picked up a layout plan of the foyer and upper level from the ticket desk and decided to go over to the café to make it look convincing. Without bothering to take a tray, he bought a mug of tea and a packet of two shortbread biscuits, keeping a wary eye out for Rodrigo. He strolled back to his table alternately gulping his tea, though he was trying to sip it, and reading the foyer layout plan – which he could just about hold with the biscuit packet in his other hand.

But it had just unexpectedly started to rain briefly, and no-one outside had stopped to watch Rodrigo's behaviour: he'd wasted no time getting over to the Centre in the shower. Although he had no money on him, he recognised the big white van outside as a technical repair van, and saw his opportunity to formulate the perfect excuse to gain admittance to the exhibition. He sprinted casually up the amphitheatre ramp, as if he was just trying to keep warm and dry in the cold damp air, and walked briskly through the foyer entrance.

Steve had noticed him. As Rodrigo looked around for him, he was still walking back to his seat, bending his head down a little to his mug of tea to take just one more sip, so his own face wasn't obvious. His anorak, lined in a different colour and hanging half-skewed round the back of his chair, looked different from when he'd been wearing it and Rodrigo didn't recognise it as his, expecting he'd have kept it on. Then, just as Rodrigo threw another quick look round the foyer for Steve, Steve urgently put his head round the edge of the screen to look at all the technical equipment and see what the technicians were doing. So luckily, he still stayed unrecognisable to Rodrigo.

Rodrigo decided he couldn't be in the foyer, but must have gone down into the exhibition. So he made to go down the entrance stairwell, unhooking the rope which cordoned it off. He was challenged by the security guard, who called out to him that the exhibition was closing for the day, and that anyway he'd need an admission ticket. Steve just managed to see this as he swallowed the gulp of hot tea he'd taken, quickly withdrawing his head from behind the screen. *Now to alert the security guard that this man is a wanted criminal,* he thought. But as he opened his mouth to shout, the tea went down the wrong way into his windpipe!

He could do nothing but choke as silently and quickly as possible while Rodrigo called back to the guard over his shoulder that he was with the technicians, and had just been out to the van to collect a screwdriver. "May I see your identity please?" asked the guard.

Rodrigo stayed at the top of the stairwell, refastening the cordon, to reply: "It's in my overalls – I left them down there!" then hurried down the stairs.

The security guard made a quick mobile call to one of the curators to let them know there was a man entering the exhibition who'd asserted he was a site technician, but who might be bogus, because he'd claimed he'd left his ID with his overalls down there. "If you see him, ask him to stay where he is until he's cleared with security. I'll be down very shortly!" Then he went over to the technicians behind the screen to ask them if there was a man fitting Rodrigo's description working with them. One or two of the technicians had already gone down into the exhibition to deal with the lighting, they said. One of them was fair – but he didn't have a beard the last time they saw him, only a quarter of an hour ago.

Meanwhile, Steve, listening to the chillingly ruthless note in Rodrigo's voice again for the first time since his ordeal in Majorca, was reminded of just how dangerous a person he was up against. He mustn't let him get hold of Maria! Finishing a final, desperately muffled cough as he fought to get his breath back again, he rushed to the entrance stairwell shouting: "That man's a wanted criminal! **Stop him**!" He had no time to explain to the security guard, who was emerging from behind the technician's screen. And no time to consider that he didn't have a plan of the exhibition layout on the lower level. He just put his anorak on again and rushed down after Rodrigo. He'd show him this time!

Scissor-jumping over the cordon, Steve could already hear the heavier, throbbing sounds coming from the first exhibition room at the bottom of the spiralling staircase. As he walked in he realised the 'State of the Earth' room was quite dark – it would take a while for his eyes to adjust to seeing in it. The curators who were normally always there had moved further on, as the exhibition was closing soon and they weren't admitting any more visitors to it that day. (It felt a bit like being thrown into the deep end of the swimming pool on his own.) But the soundtrack was still playing so the technicians could test it out. A commanding woman's voice was giving an introductory narrative which filled the room, coming from unseen speakers. It was describing the universe: the formation of planets, meteors and so on. The atmosphere was instantly overwhelming: entrancing, mesmeric: describing planet earth's position in the universe. Large screens showed awe-inspiring photographs of outer space – with stars, planets, satellites and spacecraft. The soundtrack invited him to start thinking in terms of huge distances in space, light-speed travel and colossal phenomena like the birth of new galaxies, meteorite showers and exploding stars. As he squared his jaw up and looked around, adjusting to the dark, Steve determined that it was here or nowhere that he was going to corner Rodrigo.

There was an earthquake monitor, a seismograph, which Steve had heard about from his friend David: you trod on a plate on the floor to activate it, and it measured how hard you'd hit the plate. The graph on its screen was still settling down, fluctuating with peaks and troughs – Rodrigo had run over it as he'd looked for the door through to the next room. Steve ran through that door into the 'Time Machine' section where a large, square black lift took visitors down ultra-slowly to a slightly lower floor level while the narrator provided a sensation of travelling through time and space. The lift doors were open and it was empty, but descending gradually to the lower level. He guessed Rodrigo must have taken the staircase alternative to the next room, and he burst through the double doors to it, racing down some gloomy stairs leading to another set of double doors. He pushed at these, hoping they wouldn't have been closed. They gave way to another very large, dark theme-room called 'How It All Started'. It showed the Big Bang and the formation of the universe, galaxies and solar systems. Most of the light source was from the glimmering display screens. He was just in time to see Rodrigo slipping through the doors opposite, into the next room, after him!

There was still no sign of any of the curators although the recorded presenter's voice was still penetrating the exhibition: this time it was a man's: less crisp, and more mysterious. Suddenly the very violent sound of a gargantuan explosion filled the room, but Steve realised it was just the soundtrack. He ran after Rodrigo, trying to focus his energy on driving him into a group of people including adults, with curators and teachers. The soundtrack resumed, urging him to conceive of a violently expanding new universe, and imagine black holes sucking in light and matter and gases swirling up to form stars in the Milky Way. With his legs nearly giving way, Steve gritted his teeth and shot through into the next main exhibition, after Rodrigo.

'The Restless Earth' room was narrow and very noisy, suffused with black and red light, and constructed like an elaborate film set to explain the earth's crust and the movement of the tectonic plates. There was something diabolical about the scenery: models of volcanoes simulated spouting molten lava and screens showed real film of raging fires and powerful volcanic eruptions. As Steve ran through, the modelling rock floor lit up to simulate molten rock and the part under his feet shook vigorously to simulate an earthquake. Ridiculously, he regained control of his flagging leg muscles, while volcanic fissures in the floor started emitting strong jets of simulated smoke. He dashed out of the primordial chaos into the next 'chamber'.

The first impression of the 'Shaping the Surface' room was of a contrastingly cooling, soothing atmosphere; it was more spacious and gently brighter: the walls were huge sensurround film screens which filled Steve's whole vision, showing a glacial landscape of snow and ice. The dominating colour was pure, ice-blue-white and there was a large man-sized block of simulated ice standing in the middle to touch. Thankfully there were some people in this room too – at last Steve had caught up with the last visitors admitted to the exhibition. But after the initial relief from the infernal, fiery colours and noise of the previous room, a slight sensation of snow blindness set in; and he realised the screens were simulating a dizzying helicopter flight down through a huge glacial ravine. The angle of the photography swung alarmingly about, giving a sensation of being imminently about to crash, as the helicopter veered dangerously close past sheer rock-face at high speed. Trying to overcome the feeling of vertigo, Steve watched the other people in the room.

There was one exhibition curator: his colleague had just received the security guard's warning, and told him to stay there while he ran right back to the beginning of the exhibition to check for someone resembling Rodrigo's description who'd just entered. There were two school groups with their teachers: one mixed, the other a group of girls aged about twelve - could this be Maria's group?; and three or four other adults in the room. One of these moved slowly out from behind the ice block – it was Rodrigo! He'd suddenly had to slow right down in this room, and pretend to be an ordinary visitor to the Centre, paying attention to the displays. Now standing sideways to Steve, he'd already looked carefully at all the boys his age in the room, and assumed his quarry was still further ahead of him in the exhibition. He was taking the opportunity to cool off while looking at the block of ice....and he hadn't noticed Maria yet.

She was concentrating reading some information with her face turned away from him, and wearing a woolly winter hat so he couldn't identify her so easily. But Steve had recognised her by her profile in her school group the moment after he'd seen Rodrigo. He quickly merged into the other, mixed school group so he wouldn't be noticed. They were all wearing jeans and anoraks and he blended in easily. While Rodrigo decided to reach out and touch the simulated ice block to feel just how cold it was, Steve managed to carefully edge up to Maria and nudge her gently. She turned her head round and recognised him with a sharp gasp: "Steve!"

"Rodrigo's here!" he hissed, holding his finger up to his lips urgently. "Look!" and he pointed him out discreetly, hardly raising his arm from his side. "For God's sake don't show your face!" She drew her scarf up high round her cheekbones. One of the other girls near to them – fortunately not near Rodrigo – was whispering something in what sounded like Mallorqui. If Rodrigo heard this dialect he might recognise Maria more readily! Perhaps he'd already realised it was her school party... but even if not, it probably wouldn't be long before their English-speaking teacher offered to paraphrase the narrative into Mallorqui for them and he'd cotton on. Steve knew he **had** to lead Rodrigo away from Maria – it was even more important than making a citizen's arrest!

The remaining curator was trying to get a look at Rodrigo to see if he fitted the description of the suspect 'technician', although he expected the man would still be at the beginning of the exhibition. (The two genuine lighting technicians already down there taking a casual inspection with their mobiles switched off, had moved further on ahead.) But Rodrigo had been carefully moving round the ice block to avoid being noticed, waiting for his chance to move on out. Even if he couldn't kill Steve here, he might have intimidated him enough by now to dissuade him from ever following his diamond smuggling gang again.

The curator now glanced at Steve, wondering how he'd managed to lag so far behind, and whether he was supposed to be with another school group. Steve ran up to him, pointing out Rodrigo - just as the curator realised he fitted the description of the suspect 'technician' - and shouted: "That's an escaped criminal who's following me because I'm a witness! Please call the police!" Then he dashed out into the next room as two of the girls in Maria's school party gasped in shock, putting their hands over their mouths. Rodrigo followed him out very fast again, and as the doors closed behind him in the face of the curator, who just managed to take a hazy mobile picture of him, Maria confirmed: "That's Rodrigo Gonzalvez, a very dangerous criminal! My friend's right! We've both recognised him!"

"Really?" The curator pulled the doors back open, telling the school parties to all remain where they were and stay calm. He followed Steve and Rodrigo through into the 'Casualties and Survivors' room, radioing the security guard who was already on his way down to help, to phone the police as this man was definitely not one of the technical crew, but a wanted and dangerous criminal. The security guard had been followed down and joined by the senior technician, who'd immediately felt concerned when questioned about a workmate he didn't know of.

Steve, running as fast as he could again, wanted to turn round and face Rodrigo and ask him where Becky was. But ironically, this exhibition room was called 'Casualties and Survivors', and instead he knew he had to keep on running, if possible to the end of the exhibition and back up the exit staircase to the foyer. There was no pre-recorded narrative playing here, it was a quiet room, where there were all kinds of models representing the development of life on earth: fossils and dinosaurs, a very big pouncing sabre-tooth tiger and a little pygmy-sized model of the earliest man. As he ran past it he looked back at Rodrigo, whose face showed full of hate.

Steve didn't give up, knowing there were other people following Rodrigo now. Racing through other rooms depicting the oceans, polar regions and different climatic zones from dry heat to freezing tundra, he realised he was still in a very, very dangerous situation. The sound tracks in each room kept slowing down to a growling drawl as the technicians upstairs switched them off one by one and worked to turn the brighter emergency lighting on. In the high-ceilinged 'Tropical Rainforest' section, he decided to hide behind one of the life-size models of very tall trees with lianas hanging from them, before Rodrigo came in. Steve was very out of breath by now. The room was very dark with green, red and yellow lighting and the sounds of tropical birds and monkeys coming through hidden speakers.

Rodrigo ran through the room and then, as Steve expected, re-entered it when he realised the final room (the Show-dome of special effects) was empty and he couldn't have had time to run through it. He knew Steve must be hiding in here somewhere. He quickly looked around but knew there was no time to find him before the curator, security guard and senior technician arrived. They could just be heard coming through the 'Journey of Contrasts' climatic regions room as one of them opened the doors into the 'Tropical Rainforest' room. As the soundtrack delivered the unnerving sound effects of a sudden tropical thunder storm, and the lighting simulated lightening flashes, Rodrigo ran out of it at the far end.

The others ran in and Steve came out from behind the tropical tree model: "He's gone on ahead! I thought he might stab me if he caught up with me so I hid!"

"The best thing to do!" agreed the curator, and the security guard told him: "We've phoned the police!"

Rodrigo ran out through the rest of the exhibition and out through the foyer of the Centre unapprehended. The two lighting technicians who'd looked through the exhibition earlier had already come out again and were talking about the impostor with their colleagues upstairs, assuming he'd been caught downstairs. No-one had closed the main doors as they were waiting for the police to arrive.

One of the technicians had thought to continue with turning the soundtrack off from the rooms starting at the end of the exhibition, and now it ground to a halt in the 'Tropical Rainforest' room, with a retarded gargling sound, as another technician phoned down on his mobile to ask if everyone was all right: "Sorry - we've just seen him run out through the exit," he said, "very fast! But we're not sure which way he went."

Steve, the other visitors and the school parties (feeling from shaken to intrigued) made it back upstairs to the café. He finally had the time to wave his Special Attractions pass in the general direction of the Reception Desk, while teachers checked and rechecked the roll-call and head-counts of their pupils, and the technicians made careful checks of the equipment.

Pablo, a good time-keeper, was the first policeman to arrive on the scene: because he was already on his way there to meet Steve, Becky and Maria for lunch! He was quite surprised to find he'd just missed Rodrigo, and wondered how he dared menace the youngsters in such a crowded place. He was fairly sure he hadn't just seen him, without recognising him, on his way over. Pablo always carried a mental picture of his police photo about with him, perpetually on the look out for him. He quickly explained to Maria's teacher that Rodrigo was a wanted international criminal, then asked the key witnesses some brief, careful questions. Then he let the Edinburgh police, who turned up shortly afterwards, take over the situation, and sat down with Steve and Maria at a table for some soup.

"I've got something to tell you two," said Steve, before they had time to ask where she was: "Becky's disappeared!" He gave Pablo his mobile number to try reaching her on, saying it had a triangulation system on it but it was still completely switched off.

While the teachers discussed his bravery with their colleagues, Steve explained to Maria and Pablo everything that had happened that morning: how he and his sister had been looking around the Newhaven Harbour area, and he'd suddenly lost her - almost as if she'd just evaporated into thin air with the morning mist! "We'd spotted a female Bluethroat there – you know the bird we were telling you

about, Maria?" She nodded, her eyes wide with concern as he filled Pablo in on this: "Becky heard a male one in our hotel garden, whistling the tune the band was playing at the fishing festival in Majorca – it's one of those birds that imitates other birds' songs – and we decided it might….." he hesitated: "I don't know how much Maria's told you?"

"I hear you think you've seen Alto, who's grown a beard, on a big white yacht, and heard him whistling that tune."

"Yes: so the bird's probably picked it up from him wherever he's been dropping anchor!"

"You mean mooring the yacht? Around the Firth of Forth?"

"Yes. We think it might have been around the Newhaven Harbour area. And anyway, we split up, we parted company," Steve used gestures to explain, "and I went to ask in a newsagent's on the waterfront if anyone had seen a man fitting Alto's description, while Becky went over to the little lighthouse at the end of the pier." He paused to ensure Pablo had understood him so far. "She went following this female Bluethroat, to the lighthouse, to film it with my mobile. We weren't that far apart – we could easily call to each other. I went into the newsagent's – and they said they <u>had</u> seen a Spanish man. They described someone very like Alto. And then, when I came out, Becky had just disappeared! There wasn't <u>anyone</u> else walking about outside – it wasn't exactly crowded! I looked all round the outside of the little lighthouse for her, which was <u>still</u> all padlocked up, you know, with a big heavy lock on a chain?" Pablo nodded. "Exactly like when we first saw it, and then as I was coming back down the pier, Rodrigo suddenly, really suddenly, just appeared out of nowhere –" Steve searched Pablo's eyes for confirmation that he had confidence in what he was telling him. "He just <u>appeared</u> right at the end of the pier, with a beard, following right up behind me: as if he'd just stepped off a boat. Only I couldn't <u>see</u> any boats close enough to the pier for him to get off from…."

"That's odd," commented Pablo, "but I believe you. I wonder what might explain it." He hadn't seen that area. "Maybe he's got a key to the lighthouse and he's locked her in!"

"Yes.....but the way the padlock chains were still all hanging in the same way," Steve indicated this by drawing the twisting shapes in the air, "it looked as if they hadn't been touched!"

"The padlock chains were all still in the same positions," checked Pablo.

"Yes! Anyway, our parents don't know yet we've been separated. And we promised them we wouldn't split up! But that was no distance at all, it was crazy the way she just disappeared and he came out of nowhere. I just ran all the way from there with him following me, all the way here! He nearly caught me, a couple of times!"

Pablo contacted Mr Parker on his mobile at the Botanical Gardens, saying he was over in Edinburgh with Maria and had just met up with Steve, who'd become separated from his sister at Newhaven Harbour. He asked him if Becky was with him, and was told they were still waiting for her to rejoin them there.

"I'm afraid your children may be in danger from the diamond smuggling gang again," said Pablo: "I'd advise you to stay where you are. You could try reaching her on Steve's mobile, which she has with her, but it's switched off at the moment. I'm going to notify the police here now of Becky's disappearance. Then I'll be coming over with Steve in a few minutes once we've finished our lunch." And he gave Mr Parker his mobile number. Then he phoned Police Headquarters and asked them to contact the Lighthouse Authorities to send someone over, preferably with a policeman, to see if anyone had been trespassing in their Newhaven East lighthouse: as Becky Parker had just gone missing from the area in highly suspicious circumstances, which he described. They confirmed they'd keep at least one of their officers in the area. Steve interrupted him to say: "Oh! There's another padlocked building near the lighthouse, a little round one by the beginning of the pier – about as big as a garden shed!" "OK," said Pablo, "We'd better check that out too."

Maria, although she was still feeling nervous, realised with the other two that this time Steve had probably averted trouble for her, rather than getting her into it.

Rodrigo would know now that the police were after him here, too, and leave her and Steve alone.

But what about Becky? They all speculated about whether the criminals, if Rodrigo wasn't the only one in the area, might have mistaken Becky for her, muffled up in a winter anorak, scarf and woolly hat. Or whether Becky might have thought Steve had gone off somewhere else to investigate, when she temporarily lost sight of him, and decided to go back to the Botanical Gardens and wait for him there.

Pablo left a message for Becky at the enquiries desk, in case she turned up at the Dynamic Earth Centre, telling her to make her way straight to her hotel and wait there for Steve and her parents. She should take a taxi if she could, her parents could pay at the other end if necessary. Then he and Steve left Maria to go back with her school party to the hostel, while they went on to the Botanical Gardens by taxi.

CHAPTER TWENTY
Where's Becky?

The taxi dropped Steve and Pablo off at the East entrance to the Botanical Gardens on Inverleith Row. They entered through the large wrought aluminium gates, which were designed in big leaf shapes, sparkling silver in the sunshine. Pablo phoned the Parkers to check where they were waiting for them: it was in the Winter Garden. As they studied the map to find out how to get to it, Steve wondered how his parents would be feeling about him getting involved with the diamond smugglers again. He knew it wasn't exactly his fault this time, but how was he going to explain Becky's sudden disappearance? Pablo was convinced he was telling the truth, anyway.

They walked west along the path leading to the glasshouses and the fossil garden, through carefully trimmed fresh green lawns set with specimen trees, some just beginning to put out tiny new leaves and buds. Steve told Pablo he was very glad he'd come over, and Pablo returned that he felt sure they were nearly onto the rest of the smugglers now - <u>and</u> Rodrigo again: "Thanks to your spotting Alto on the yacht!"

"Listen, Pablo, I just didn't have time to tell you before: when I asked at the waterfront newsagent's if anyone Spanish had been in there, they told me they remembered serving a Spanish man because he'd bought two bottles of a special type of whisky, out of production now – called 'Old Cask'."

"Really?"

"Yes, I don't know if that would help as a lead on him and the others."

"Nothing can be discounted as valuable evidence in this type of investigation, no matter how trivial it seems. Thanks!" And Pablo made a note of the whisky brand in his notebook, still walking along with his bearing very upright. Steve told him that the newsagents had only seen the Spanish man they were talking about once; but he definitely sounded like Alto: tall, with dark hair, blue eyes and a beard, wearing a dark duffel coat with toggles and a hood, jeans, a dark blue or black scarf and a woolly hat. They hadn't mentioned the old brooch which he'd definitely been wearing when <u>he</u> saw him. "And he also bought bread, cheese and a newspaper, they said probably *The Scotsman*."

"OK. Did they say when?" Pablo kept on writing, with a very steady hand as he was walking along.

At first Steve couldn't remember this vital piece of information: it was so soon after the startling appearance of Rodrigo and the ensuing exhausting chase.   He slowed his walk. Was it the day before? Two days…. three days ago? Then he remembered: "A week ago! They definitely said it was about a week ago!"

"This is all going to be very useful to the Police," said Pablo, finishing writing and putting his notebook away again for the time being. "They'll make a recording of what you tell them at their Headquarters, so it's good to get your facts straight now - ready for their questions!" He gave Steve an encouraging smile.

"At Headquarters?"

"Of course." Just then, Pablo received a call on his mobile from the Edinburgh Police. They had someone placed in the Newhaven East lighthouse area on the look-out for clues and anyone suspicious, but it was quiet. He'd knocked on the lighthouse door but it had seemed empty. In the meantime, they were trying to locate someone to open the lighthouse for them but the key holders were on their lunch break and it might take a little while. They'd already liaised with the harbour authorities and gained access to the little round building installation nearby, but there was nothing suspicious there, he told Steve.

Turning left past the big palm houses, they walked past the Alpine House and a courtyard, and came to a massive beech hedge as high as a two-storey house, running for nearly two hundred metres. It was still holding on to all its dry brown leaves. At the end by the glasshouses, there was an archway in it leading into the Winter Garden. They walked through the archway into the garden, which looked truly spring-like with winter-flowering shrubs and bulbs. Chris and Pat Parker were sitting on a bench in the sunshine. Pablo let Steve walk on ahead a little while he took a careful look around.

As soon as Pat caught sight of her son approaching from behind a shrub, she asked him anxiously: "Steve, is Becky not with you any more?"

He laid the bare facts at her disposal immediately: "No, I'm really sorry, we got separated. She's got my mobile – but it's switched off."

His father asked: "Is the tracking system switched on?"

"It was when I gave it to her."

His mother said: "We've tried phoning her too, and couldn't get through…"

"I don't know where she is – she just disappeared!"

Chris, seeing Pablo just behind him, greeted him: "Pablo Munos! So we meet again! I didn't know you were over with Maria as well! Thanks for phoning us and letting us know Becky's gone missing. Perhaps the girls arranged to meet up at a café and leave Steve on his own to do his bird watching?" He always looked on the bright side of things.

"Yes," said Pablo in response to his first remarks, "Good afternoon Pat and Chris!" and he shook hands with him and his wife, with a look which said there was a lot to discuss in relation to his question. "What you suggest is unlikely, because Maria's schedule is organised by her school. We'd all arranged to meet for lunch at the Dynamic Earth Centre café. Becky didn't arrive….."

"turn up," supplied Steve, "we usually say, she didn't 'turn up' there."

"Thanks, Steve. I've left a message at the Information Desk at the Dynamic Earth Centre," Pablo continued, "telling her to please return to the hotel and wait for her family."

Pat couldn't resist asking him another question straightaway: "Are you joining in with the archaeological dig? Or are you here because the diamond smugglers are out here?"

"I'm here in Edinburgh at short notice: my sister Maria as you know is over here on a school geography trip. And Steve phoned her a few days ago because he thought he saw one of the….'still at large', I think you say? Spanish diamond smugglers – Alto, on a yacht here, in the Firth of Forth. So I came over here straight away." Mr Parker's broad face thinned down suddenly as he looked aghast. "Has he not told you this, Mr Parker?"

"First I've heard of it!" he said.

Steve quickly tried to assuage him: "We were waiting to make sure it was Alto, Dad, before we…er…spoiled your holiday! I was hoping I might get a closer sighting of him!" And he described what he'd seen on their fourth day in Edinburgh, through the binoculars on the Forth estuary, and how Becky had also seen the yacht and heard the Majorcan tune being whistled, although the tall dark man's back was turned to them by the time they'd closed in on it. He paused. "Now you know!"

"They're all in danger!" Pat realised.

"And this is going to be another of those holidays!" her husband was rapidly becoming protectively angry.

Pablo said calmly: "We've already tried phoning Becky by mobile, but the one she has is switched off."

"Mine," muttered Steve helpfully.

"We're searching the area and we've asked the Lighthouse Authorities to open up the lighthouse and check it," said Pablo, allowing Steve to start explaining the recent developments more fully.

Steve began again, telling them exactly how he'd lost Becky a few hours ago, and how Rodrigo had just given him the most frightening chase of his life. "Becky and I separated, but only by a few metres, while I went into a newsagent's and she was trying to film this female Bluethroat by the lighthouse on that little pier - but when I came out she'd suddenly disappeared!"

"Did she go inside the lighthouse?" his father asked.

"No – it was heavily padlocked from the outside. With big chains, and they were all still in exactly the same position when I looked again – they'd have moved into slightly different positions if it had just been opened and then padlocked up again. Some of the chain links were rusty so it was easy to tell. And there wasn't anyone about outside... I had a good look up the pier and over the side in case she'd fallen into the water, and then as I was walking back down, Rodrigo, the smuggler who escaped in November, started chasing me!"

As Pat exclaimed "Escaped!! What's going on?" Chris tried phoning their daughter again, but Steve's mobile was still switched off and he couldn't get a reply.

Pablo told them: "It may be important to listen to what Steve has to say about how Becky went suddenly missing when they went bird watching together by the Newhaven Harbour lighthouse. They may have only become temporarily separated. But what you suggested just now, Mr Parker - that Becky and Maria may have arranged to meet somewhere at that time by themselves - is not possible. Because Steve and I have just met with Maria at the Dynamic Earth Centre café, for lunch, as we were all agreed to meet up there, and Maria would have told us of any change in the girls' plans. Her school party came out straight from the hostel: all their excursions are with their teachers and they're not left unsupervised to.... look around the area - explore."

"Now, what's this about Rodrigo?" Chris asked, giving Pablo his full attention. But Steve persisted with his fullest account of events, and Pablo let him continue, knowing he'd soon get round to describing Rodrigo again: "Becky really just disappeared. It really wasn't my fault! We only separated out temporarily, by a hundred metres or so – she went off to the lighthouse following a female Bluethroat. I only gave her my mobile to record it, not because we were going to really split up – it was no distance at all, and we agreed to keep an eye out for each other every minute or so....I came out of the newsagent's; couldn't see her anywhere, with no-one about; so I went up to the lighthouse, looked round behind it, and as I was coming back down the pier, Rodrigo came up behind me and started chasing me! All the way to the Dynamic Earth Centre, and round the exhibition. One reason why I kept on running was to lead him away from the area – I didn't want him to get Becky! And then he escaped, just before Pablo arrived to meet us all there for lunch! There were two or three other people trying to stop him – we nearly made a citizen's arrest - but he's a very fast runner!"

"Are you sure it was Rodrigo?" asked his father, just realising what Steve had been through.

"Sure! With a beard. And I could still just see the scar on his left cheek, underneath it."

Pablo confirmed: "Rodrigo escaped police custody in November. We need to report all the details of Becky's disappearance straightaway at the Police Headquarters."

"She could have just gone shopping," Steve put in: "It's odd the way she gave me the slip – one minute we were so close to each other, there weren't any boats by the shore or people waiting around in cars, and the next moment I'd lost her. Perhaps she was just deliberately hiding from me for a joke, and then tiptoed off to the shops without realising I'd been chased away!" He paused. "She's been telling me the Fairy Boy of Leith story – about a boy who kept disappearing in the 1660s, right from under people's noses."

"That could be what she's done. Let's hope so," said his mother, nearly in tears.

Steve dared play his trump card to console her. "And it was her idea to split up like that –she suggested it: so I could look out for Alto around the waterfront shops and cafes and she could keep an eye out for the *Carisma* in the harbour, just for one or two minutes while she filmed the female Bluethroat."

Pablo explained to Pat and Chris that he'd been expecting to have to speak with them soon anyway. And now he encouraged them to let him go with Steve by taxi to the Police Headquarters, where Steve could confirm Becky's disappearance and describe the suspected criminals he'd seen. "In the meantime, you can straightaway start looking for your daughter yourselves. Let me know, if you find her, immediately! The police here are alerted now, that she's gone missing. They're also keeping a special watch on the hostel Maria's staying at. I suggest you send a message to Becky now, for her to pick up as soon as she switches the mobile on again, if she still has it on her and it hasn't been stolen. Tell her to make her way back to your hotel if she can."

They decided Steve could leave a message for her first. Looking anxiously into the screen of his father's mobile, he said: "Becky, it's Steve. If you <u>are</u> hiding – stop fooling around! Because the police are out looking for you and we're about to confirm you as officially missing. If you've kept my mobile with you, make sure the tracking system's on!" And he described which keypad to press. "I've just been chased by the Spanish diamond smugglers' ring leader – Rodrigo – all the way from the lighthouse to the Dynamic Earth Centre.....then he gave up and escaped! He's blond with a beard. He's grown one, like Alto! He's probably still wearing jeans and a donkey jacket. Don't hang around on your own anywhere, whatever you do! Just come straight back to the hotel and wait for us. I'm going on to the Police Headquarters with Pablo now. Just take care!"

His father now gave his message, urging Becky to get in touch with them fast. "Your brother isn't pulling a hoax on you, Becky. We think he's been spotted by two of the diamond smugglers he ran into in Majorca: they're still at large and over here! And we're <u>very</u> worried about <u>you</u>. Phone us as soon as you can. Keep the tracking system switched on. And DO come back to the hotel, where we'll be expecting you – we're making our way there now from the Botanic Gardens, after we've taken a look round the Newhaven Harbour area for you."

"See you soon, Becky! We love you!" added her mother.

Pablo and Steve went on by taxi to the Edinburgh Headquarters of the Border and Lothians Police. They located Detective-Sergeant Jim McCulloch and followed him into a small quiet office. As they sat down at the desk he told them their discussion would all be recorded. "It's very lucky that you speak such good English, Pablo."

"Yes, thank-you" he said, "My parents run a gift shop in Majorca, so we all speak English!" Taking out the notes he'd already made about the case, he checked them through while Steve confirmed the details of his sister's disappearance by the Newhaven East lighthouse.

Before he asked him about the chase to and through the Dynamic Earth Centre, D-S McCulloch asked Steve about his sighting of the men on the *Carisma* in the Firth of Forth a few days before. Pablo had already briefed him about it, but he wanted to hear from the key witness. "So you didn't have your mobile with you at the time?"

"No. And when we got back in the car, Dad had his mobile but we didn't really get the chance to tell him. We were still just deciding what we could possibly do about it..."

Then Steve described how he'd seen Alto, now with a beard, on the yacht.

"Are you sure it was him?" DS McCulloch asked, patiently.

"Positive: the tall dark one," replied Steve. "I was watching him through our very high-powered binoculars. I started to realise who it was when I thought I recognised the old silver brooch Maria's mother gave her to wear at the fishing festival in Majorca. We lost it in the cave when I was using it to cut our hands free from the ropes they'd tied us up with. He was using it to fasten up his duffel-coat, I think because the top toggle was missing." Then he explained how, as he and Becky had approached the big yacht, Alto whistled the Majorcan fishing festival tune, which they both recognised. But that unfortunately, Becky hadn't had a chance to get a good look at him as his back was turned to them by then. He described the two other men on board: one with cropped fair hair, the other fairly burly and red-headed with a beard; and wearing jeans, Arran sweaters, anoraks and knitted hats.

"British, would you say?" asked Jim McCulloch.

"I should think so, but we couldn't quite hear what one of them was saying when he spoke."

"Now, can you describe this yacht?"

Steve had been discussing it with Pablo. "Well, I'm not that knowledgeable about boats, but it was <u>very</u> big and it looked really expensive: one of those big white luxury cruisers, with a sundeck and a big control room on top. Called the *Carisma*."

"How was the name painted on?"

"In black letters."

"Capitals?"

"No. Ordinary script."

"And not spelt with an 'h', you said!" reminded Pablo.

"Yes, I was going to say that!"

"That's the Spanish spelling – C-a-r-i-s-m-a," Pablo confirmed. "We can look through some pictures from yachting brochures to find one of a yacht like that, Steve."

"Really? OK."

"And search through the international yacht registry databases to see who owns one called the *Carisma*," said the Detective-Sergeant. "Now, the blond bearded man who chased you from the lighthouse and through the Dynamic Earth Centre. Would you say that was definitely Rodrigo? Or could it have been the fair-haired man you saw on the *Carisma* cruiser yacht?"

"It was Rodrigo – <u>definitely</u> Rodrigo, because of the scar on his left cheek….<u>and</u> his voice when he spoke to the Dynamic Earth curator…everything: definitely him. But when he stopped in the street during the chase to take a call on his mobile, I wondered if he was going to call the others out to follow me too."

"The museum curator managed to film him running through the Dynamic Earth exhibition with his mobile: but as you know it's quite dark down there. It wasn't a very clear picture, but we've taken a copy of it anyway for our records. Did he say anything to you or threaten you with a weapon at all?"

"No but he was after me all right."

"You had quite a lucky escape. Would you like a cup of tea?"

"Please! Yes I'd love one."

Over a cup of tea, Pablo explained how, owing to his police duty shifts, he'd never seen Rodrigo face-to-face, and had just missed him at the Dynamic Earth Centre as he turned up hoping to meet all three youngsters for lunch. "I would have gone straight out after him - but I wanted to make sure my sister was quite safe, and all the others as well: in case one of the other smugglers turned up there for some reason. And I'm not sure I'd be able to identify him just from his photograph anyway."

Jim McCulloch told him: "We've got some very clever technology now to match digital images of people to our database of criminals' photographs. An individual's bone structure has unique marks which can all be cross-referenced."

"That's very interesting," said Steve.

"But for Alto," Pablo said, "we have no criminal record, and there might well not be any for these other two men you were describing, either."

"I was hoping if I saw the yacht again I could take some photos, but I haven't seen it again – it might stop off in the Leith area, though, if that newsagents still has some stocks of 'Old Cask' going!"

Pablo explained to the Detective-Sergeant, who was pulling a quizzical expression: "Steve told me of another clue just now in the Botanic Gardens." He let Steve go on.

"I went into the newsagent's on the waterfront by the pier, just before Becky and I were separated. And I asked the newsagent – actually I spoke to <u>two</u> shopkeepers, both Asian men. I asked them if they'd served any Spanish people in there recently. And they both remembered a tall, dark, bearded Spanish man with blue eyes, wearing jeans, a dark jumper, dark duffel coat, scarf and a dark woolly hat. All his clothes were navy or black – Pablo, you took notes down of everything while I was telling you the first time, didn't you?"

"Yes, I'll give you a copy, Jim."

At that point, another detective who'd just joined them on the case, came in. "Give them to Andrew," said D-S McCulloch. "I think it's quite possible that if Rodrigo's still working with the diamond smugglers, he's seeing some of the Spanish gang – here. They must have a connection here." He stopped the recording for a while. "Have you got any leads, yet, Andrew?" he asked the other detective.

"Not yet, but we're working on it."

Steve realised that some of their investigations were what were often called 'highly sensitive'; in other words, top secret.

DS McCulloch switched the recorder on again and asked Steve when the Spanish man had visited the newsagent's.

"They said about a week ago," Steve resumed. "Anyway, he bought some bread and cheese, a newspaper, and two bottles of a particular brand of whisky from a big selection they had – called 'Old Cask'. It's out of production now…"

"So maybe he'll try stocking up on it before it disappears off the shelves forever," Jim McCulloch concluded. "Thank you, Steve, I'd wondered what you were referring to at first. Being English, I've never heard of that particular one myself!"

"Yes, he might even dare to go back to that newsagent if he really had a taste for it," his Edinburgh colleague agreed. "I'll get someone onto it. Perhaps ask the newsagents if they could put a poster advertising it in the window, at a discount, and keep watch on the area in plain clothes!"

DS McCulloch then asked Steve to give as full a description of all the Spanish diamond smugglers, and the men he'd seen crewing the *Carisma*, as he could - with the exception of Manuel and Antonio, who were now behind bars. Steve knew he was testing his memory power, and enjoyed giving him accurate descriptions. Then he asked Steve if there was anything else the Lothian and Borders police should know in connection with the case. Steve considered telling them about the Bluethroat. He'd already told Pablo.

But, he decided: if they didn't get to hear from Pablo about why he and Becky had gone to Newhaven Harbour to look for one of these little birds, he'd better leave telling them himself. He felt he'd look rather foolish trying to explain this particularly unusual evidence at the moment. It was just too amazing and would sound far-fetched. He thanked the detectives for all their help, and they advised him to return straight to the Parkers' hotel with Pablo.

CHAPTER TWENTY-ONE
Door Within a Door

While Becky had been walking round the fenced side of the disused old lighthouse, playing her recording of the male Bluethroat's rendition of the Majorcan tune on Steve's mobile, she realised the female had flown off somewhere else. She hoped the tune would attract her back: if she heard it, she might even adapt her own song to accompany it! But no - she seemed to have completely left the area now. Becky decided to wait for a few minutes. Looking out across the Firth of Forth at the lovely scenery, she leaned, relaxing, against the padlocked lighthouse door for what she thought was going to be a while. But she fell through it.

She'd discovered a very frightening new feature installed recently by the diamond smugglers, posing as workers with the lighthouse company. The company, still responsible for the upkeep of the property, had it inspected occasionally. A slightly smaller trap door had been inserted into the main part of the lighthouse door. Its steel edges were barely visible, as the ordinary door panelling had been replaced over it. When the trap-door opened, it didn't trigger off the alarm which would sound if the main door was opened by intruders. And it could only be opened by a voice recognition system. The male Bluethroat had been imitating Alto's whistling tone very accurately, and as Becky played the recording back, the trap-door unlocked, prompted by a particularly melodious trill – even though the password hadn't actually been spoken. Because a few weeks ago, the recognition software had recorded Alto whistling in the background while it recorded Alex saying the correct password to install in the memory.

As Becky fell back into the cold cast iron interior of the lighthouse, she just managed to stop falling over, but not to stop herself from saying "Bloody hell!" with fright; she'd dropped Steve's mobile onto the concrete floor and stepped back on it as she regained her balance. Turning round she saw, not a spiral staircase, which she'd expected, but three men sitting on crates, and one on a chair up on a platform reached by a ladder, where he could look out of the little arched window. The three sitting on crates were sorting through some packages, and stopped when they heard her. One, a burly man with longish thick wavy red hair and a beard, wearing jeans and an Arran sweater, was just taking out a small shiny object from a packet to examine it: he replaced it very fast when he saw her. Realising immediately this wasn't Maria Munos, he decided the girl must be a curious youngster who couldn't possibly tell they were handling diamonds. He wondered how she'd managed to get in.

But, as the trapdoor swung shut again and locked tight, Becky realised it was the diamond smuggling gang. She'd seen the tiny object glinting between Alex's thick fingers, and knew it was a diamond catching the sunlight coming in from the window. She thought she recognised him as one of the men she'd seen on the deck of the *Carisma*. The man on the platform – slim, with blond hair and a beard, wearing a donkey jacket and jeans - seemed to be instructing him and the other two, who were both dark and dressed in jeans and anoraks. The blond man got to his feet as soon as she fell through the trapdoor and started climbing down the ladder. One of the dark men hissed in Spanish to the other: "A kid's got the door password!" She noticed he was wearing a navy yachting cap over his curly hair. He had a slight beard and a small gold earring in one ear.

"Hang on, how did <u>this</u> happen?" Alex demanded in English, his strong Scottish voice reverberating around the lighthouse column. "We didn't leave it open, did we?" Then he stood up to challenge her. He was tall as well as burly. He thought that to an ordinary youngster, the four men could be passed off as employees of the company maintaining the lighthouse, so he asked in a slightly gentler tone: "Hello, <u>you're</u> not an employee of the lighthouse, are you? Are you all right?" He knew she hadn't hurt herself, unless she'd twisted an ankle.

Becky kept her wits about her. He'd probably have no idea who she was. "Yes, thanks…I was leaning against the door and the inner part of it just swung open…." She faltered, picking up the mobile, which she'd dropped on the floor, and putting it back in her anorak pocket. "Sorry!"

The stockier Spanish man, Julio, said one of the very few English phrases he knew as professionally as he could: "It's our new security door" and got up, offering to let her out. He would have to use the exit password for the voice recognition system.

But Rodrigo snapped furtively in Spanish: "Take a look to see if anyone else is out there! Take a look!" (Which Becky half understood.) Then he impatiently got to the trap-door first himself, and through it, using the Spanish password. While he looked outside, which only took a few seconds, he kept it held open: if he'd stayed like that for too long, Becky could have squeezed out past him and run away. But he closed it again fast before she could follow him out, and stayed outside.

"Will you let me out, please?" she asked Julio nervously, and went to phone her parents on the mobile – but she couldn't get the ON/OFF switch to work – it had got jammed OFF, with several other switches, when she'd stepped on the keypad struggling to regain her balance on the concrete floor of the lighthouse. Which the men could see.

Alex asked her: "Look, do you realise you're trespassing?" while Jaime took a call on his mobile. Determined not to show she'd realised who they were, she replied: "I do apologise, I wasn't trying to get in, I just leaned against the door and it gave way!" She wondered whether to start banging on it and calling for help if they didn't open it again immediately.

The mobile call to Jaime was from Rodrigo, outside, saying he thought he'd recognised Steve Parker walking away from the lighthouse back to the waterfront, and that this girl could well be his friend. As Becky was insisting: "Look, I'm not deliberately trespassing!" Julio and Alex quickly gagged her, and tied her hands behind her back and her ankles together, using a coil of rope lying on the floor under a little table. On the table were a torch, some maps and other equipment used for measuring and weighing diamonds. She nearly kicked it over as she resisted. Then they made her sit on a crate. All three men agreed, in a mixture of Spanish and English, that she definitely wasn't Maria, but could have been spying on them with Steve, if it really was him outside.

"If he's over here too," said Jaime quickly in Spanish then hesitant English as he continued thinking, "we'd better act fast!" And he phoned Eulalia on the *Carisma*, which had sailed back out to sea from the Firth of Forth. When he told her, in Spanish, they thought they'd caught an English friend of Steve Parker, and that he was probably still snooping around the lighthouse area, she instructed him:

"All of you except Julio: get over here now! And bring the girl. Be extra careful who's watching."

Jaime handed Eulalia over on the phone to Julio, then gave her orders in English to Alex. Alex was to phone the Scottish skipper of a small cabin boat immediately, to come and collect all of them except Julio, who would walk back with the rest of the diamond packages in a haversack and check into the Bed & Breakfast accommodation the gang used in the harbour area.

Eulalia told Julio to stay in the B&B, and phone Rodrigo to let him know it wasn't safe to return to the lighthouse anymore; and also to keep watch over the lighthouse to see who else might come round there, reporting everything suspicious back to her. "And do what you can to change your appearance – grow a moustache, cut your hair."

When he'd finished talking to her, Julio said to Jaime, still in Spanish: "I know they need <u>you</u> on board, but why not let Alex do this? Steve Parker wouldn't recognise <u>him</u> at all."

"In case the police get onto the yacht," Jaime replied. "It's got a Spanish name. If they keep it under surveillance, he doesn't look Spanish, and <u>he</u> hasn't got a criminal record! The sort of person they need on board. We don't want it to look as if the *Carisma* has a Spanish crew as well. Or they'll swoop down on all of us."

"Any reason for this sudden evacuation?" the Scottish skipper of the small cabin boat was asking Alex over the phone, after he'd agreed to come and collect him, Jaime and a very heavy crate from the lighthouse. The smugglers usually slipped onto the *Carisma* one at a time to avoid attracting attention to their activities.

"Yes," replied Alex: "we suspect that English troublemaker Steve Parker, who stopped us operating in Puerto Pollensa, is up here snooping around. And we seem to have just caught the friend he was with!"

Becky realised frantically that she'd just fallen into the same sort of dangerous situation which Steve and Maria had got into in Majorca. But she assumed the crooks were going to leave her bound and gagged in the lighthouse for the real lighthouse workers to discover when they next inspected it. She started thinking how she could get rid of the gag over her mouth and call for help when they left. Then suddenly, Julio and Alex put her, struggling hard again, into the crate she'd been sitting on. They packed a few of the diamond packages around her. "For your comfort!" said Julio in his mocking, 'May I be of assistance to you?' style before replacing the lid - fortunately made of loose-fitting slats which allowed her to breathe.

Then, while Jaime kept a look out for the cabin boat from the window, everyone except Becky kept very quiet in case anyone was about outside. During this time Rodrigo had sprinted back up to the lighthouse ledge overhanging the water to wait for Steve as he came out of the newsagent's and walked back up the pier to look for his sister. When Steve tried the lighthouse door, Becky tried to call out and bang against the sides of the crate with her shoulder and a knee, but the gag over her mouth and the cushioning diamonds packages muffled her and prevented her from being audible to anyone but her captors.

Soon after Steve had turned and run away from Rodrigo, the old cabin boat turned up with its skipper, an older weather-beaten man with grey hair and a beard. He was part of a long-established web of corruption extending to Scotland; he regularly visited this disused lighthouse and another one on the west coast, where the cut, polished diamonds were usually stored for collection. His boat had been associated with the ferry crossings for a long time and didn't attract much suspicion. After Alex, Julio and Jaime manoeuvred the crate with Becky in it out through the lighthouse door, he helped them quickly tie ropes around it and lower it down onto the cabin boat, which he'd moored at the end of the pier. Once Alex and Jaime had climbed over the pier rails and joined him on board, the skipper started the engine, leaving Julio waiting in the lighthouse to make his own departure - for the B&B - after they'd left the area. Although there was no-one else walking around the waterfront, for all they knew they could already be attracting attention to themselves, and they couldn't be too careful...

Inside the crate, Becky was terrified. These men, two of them fitting her brother's description of Rodrigo and Julio, were associating her with 'that trouble-maker

Steve Parker', though they didn't know she was his sister. They were probably abducting her so they could silence her for good! This was no ferry trip, that was certain. She wished now she and Steve had come to the harbour in the afternoon, while they were operating visitor trips to the islands from there: then the smugglers wouldn't have dared do this in broad daylight. But surely, she thought on, they'd try to ascertain her identity before taking the decision to murder her. And they'd want to be certain she knew what they were up to. After all, she might only have happened to have been walking about out on the pier near Steve, without knowing him; or have only just met him on holiday. Surely they wouldn't kill her on the off-chance she knew all about their activities: they must realise that the trap-door mechanism was faulty – and her insistence that she'd fallen through into the lighthouse by accident could easily be believed. Perhaps they'd leave her trussed up somewhere, and hit her over the head to make her forget what she'd seen. Wasn't that what often happened to witnesses of crime scenes when they were hit over the head? They got concussion, then couldn't remember what had happened... "Let me out of here!" she tried screaming through the gag again, more throatily this time, but still too indistinct to be heard over the noise of the engine as the cabin boat made away from the lighthouse. She suspected from the motion, as if they were going into deeper water, that they were sailing away out of the Firth of Forth, towards the sea.

Worrying they might shoot her in the crate, she decided to try dragging the gag down off her mouth with the hard edge of a diamond that was sticking out at the side of one of the packets. After a while she succeeded, then managed to pull the mobile out of her anorak pocket with her teeth and balance it on her knees, to give the ON/OFF switch another try: after all she'd only tried hurriedly pressing it for a few seconds back in the lighthouse. Perhaps she could unjam it this time. Luckily, as these keypads tended to, the rubbery switch suddenly sprang unexpectedly back into position when she pushed it hard with the tip of her nose. She quickly pushed it in again to 'ON' with her nose, then, in the same way, started dialling her parents' mobile number - which Steve had in fact, though she didn't know, stored in the memory. She didn't know how to operate the tracking system, either, which had got switched off earlier when she'd stepped back on the dropped mobile.

But half-way through her dialling, the little cabin boat hit a bigger wave with a bump, and the mobile dropped onto the bottom of the crate. Cramped and tied up as she was, Becky just couldn't quite reach it again, unless she used a foot! And she knew she wasn't quite going to be able to use her big toe to dial her parents, or the police, even if she managed to remove her sock. Not from that angle, with her legs bound at the ankles. Activating any of the stored numbers, she thought, if there were any, <u>might</u> have been slightly easier: only she wasn't sure how to do this and she knew she couldn't do it with her toes anyway. So slipping off her left trekker shoe, she very carefully pushed the slimline mobile into it, using both feet. Luckily there wasn't another big wave for a while, and she could just squeeze the trekker back awkwardly onto her left foot with the mobile inside, carefully avoiding putting pressure on the most important switches. If she pretended to limp when they let her out of the crate – <u>if</u> they let her out - as though she'd twisted her ankle falling through the lighthouse trapdoor, she wouldn't crush the switches down into the keypad, and maybe she'd be able to use it later on.

They hadn't searched her anorak pockets yet, but they probably would. She wondered how much longer it would be before the crooks lifted the lid off the crate. She was expecting them to talk to her again before deciding what to do with her. Becky decided not to rush things by calling out now and demanding they untie her, in case they panicked and shot her. She'd at least wait until she was out of the crate. They must be taking her somewhere. To think <u>this</u> had suddenly happened! She could hardly believe it, when she'd been so careful trying to keep her distance from these people.

After a few more minutes, the cabin boat reached the *Carisma*, sailing some way off the East Coast. The skipper cut the engine out. Jaime, lifting the crate lid off, noticed she'd worked her gag down from her mouth. But he knew she couldn't have extracted the mobile from her pocket with her mouth because of the way her hands were tied behind her back. And anyway, it had been jammed when she'd put it back in her pocket.

"Let me go, will you?" she just managed to ask as collectedly as she could before he quickly pulled it up again, making sure it was tight.

"Not yet," he replied, then untied her ankles so she could get out of the crate and walk, still with her hands tied behind her back. Then he untied her hands, just to let her climb up the ladder behind him on board the big yacht. She decided not to refuse to move: she had no choice. Alex followed her, while the skipper of the little cabin boat steered his boat back for the East Coast to head back West. Once she'd climbed on board the *Carisma* Jaime retied her hands behind her back and she was frog-marched, limping on her left foot so as not to put any weight on the mobile's key-pad, and protesting in a furious mumble through her gag, into Eulalia's office.

Eulalia was standing in a black trouser suit and pink T-shirt, with a gold necklace round her neck, her hands on her hips. "Search her pockets to check her ID and see if we need to confiscate anything – anything at all!" she commanded in Spanish, walking round Becky and studying her face carefully. Then she apologised to her in English: "I'm sorry if they hurt you, and to have to keep you in this discomfort - for just a little while longer." Becky kept quiet and still, hoping she might get some easier treatment from this woman. If she played along with them they might untie her and leave her on her own long enough to call the police on the mobile.

Jaime unzipped her anorak and checked the pockets, quickly looking for any extra ones on her jumper. Fortunately, Becky wasn't carrying her shoulder bag with her pocket diary and all the names and contact details in it: just, in her pockets:- a handkerchief, the map of the area, her purse and a notebook with a brief jotting about the Bluethroat's markings on it. These were all brought out and set down on a coffee table, while Jaime asked in Spanish: "Where's her mobile? The keypad got all stuck in when she dropped it and nearly fell over... she trod on it getting up....so it's OK, it probably isn't tracking us while it's jammed, switched off..."

Alex had understood her mobile was missing: "It must have fallen out of her pocket onto the floor of the crate when we hit that big wave. Don't worry, I'll check with the cabin boat skipper..." He phoned him from his mobile: "John:

when you get back, can you check inside the crate? We think the girl's mobile dropped out of her anorak pocket into the bottom of it. When you find it, can you make sure it's <u>deactivated</u>? We don't want it springing back into action and getting us tracked down by the authorities…"

"OK," was the reply. "But I'm heading back to pick up this new Spanish member of your crew, Alto, on Eulalia's orders. It'll be a wee while before I can show up and go take a look: it'd be a bit dangerous here – give me a few minutes!" "But hurry up!"

Then Jaime confirmed to Eulalia in Spanish that Rodrigo was sure he'd seen Steve Parker, and had gone running after him. "We've left Julio to go back to the B&B and phone him from there. He'll tell him not to return to the lighthouse and to phone us as soon as he can." Eulalia nodded her approval, then still talking in Spanish and swiftly indicating Becky with an arching eyebrow, asked: "What have you said to <u>her</u>?"

Alex gave in his newly acquired second language, with a grin: "We just challenged her and let her think we were working for the lighthouse authorities."

"Well she won't believe that now. You were lucky to get away from there without being seen. <u>Very</u> lucky. Who is she?"

Alex only understood her last question.

"We don't know," both men said.

Eulalia sat Becky down on one of the big cream sofas, and went to her desk. She'd already decided to call Alto out to the *Carisma*, leaving Mick to stay watching Pablo and the Edinburgh police from as far away as possible. She'd told them, speaking to Alto in Spanish, to leave Maria alone if they saw her again, now that her brother had flown over and she had police protection. But Mick was to keep a look out around the gang's rendezvous points in case the police were picking up any clues about them. And like Julio, who was also going to be staying on shore, Mick was told to change his appearance.

It wasn't long before Alto rejoined them, picked up and dropped off by the old cabin boat. The old skipper still hadn't had the opportunity to check if the mobile the girl had been carrying had been left in the crate because of all the traffic on the Firth of Forth. And because Alto had told him the international police were investigating the area around the archaeological site, and he wanted to get back to the West Coast as soon as he could. "We <u>need</u> to know where it went!" Eulalia told him, before the *Carisma* sailed further out to sea with Miguel in command of the control room.

Becky was taken by Eulalia, followed by Jaime and Alto, to a little semi-soundproofed room on the yacht. It was air conditioned, with no window, padded with dark red leather all the way up the walls and over the ceiling, with leather benches round it. Leaving Alto outside, Jaime whispered to him in Spanish: "This room's like a padded cell. Where the <u>real</u> boss – the man who owns the *Carisma* – speaks in privacy to people. And where I can practice my guitar without getting on peoples' nerves." Then he followed Eulalia and Becky in.

Alto had been asked to take the *Carisma*'s main mobile phone up onto the top deck with Alex, and keep an eye out for any vessels in the area which might be being navigated by undercover police. As they were going up there, he took a message from Rodrigo in Spanish: "I'm still following Steve Parker – it's definitely him - now in the King's Mount area of Edinburgh. "If I can corner him safely I'll do it, but there are a few tourists about … not to mention the police around the Parliament building – and the kid's quite a sprinter!"

Up on the main deck they could look out around the North Sea. It was virtually a cloudless blue sky and there were no ships approaching them for miles on the dark, grey-blue swell of the sea.

Meanwhile, in the little semi-soundproofed room, Jaime ungagged Becky and he and Eulalia started cross-questioning her. "Who are you?" Eulalia demanded quietly. She was sitting opposite her on a padded bench, recording the interrogation on her own mobile. Becky realised they definitely didn't know; and that she mustn't let them connect her in any way with Steve, because of what he knew about them: if they thought there was any chance he'd told her about them, they'd kill her. She'd give her interrogators a false ID. "My name's Carol Saunders," she declared, choosing the name of one of her classmates in Surrey. "I'm on a school trip out here and you'd better let me go now, please." Eulalia was in a quandary. Becky continued: "And I wasn't trespassing in your lighthouse. The trapdoor just opened while I was leaning against it. Who are you, anyway?" If she could possibly reach the 'Record' switch on the mobile inside her left trekker shoe, she'd record this conversation as proof of her abduction to the police – *If I ever get out of here alive,* she thought. She felt for it with a clenched-up toe. But she couldn't manage to locate it – the mobile had slipped too far down towards the heel of the trekker-shoe.

Eulalia had to decide whether she'd been given the truth from this girl – who might be Steve's sister, on holiday with him; or a school-mate of his. How much did she know? She lied herself. "My name's Mrs Corvato. I own the Newhaven East lighthouse. I suppose you didn't know that."

"No, I didn't."

"It's no longer used by the lighthouse company, we bought it from them recently. You've been trespassing on private property."

"I'm sorry," Becky said spiritedly, "but don't you think you're taking this citizens' arrest business too far?" (Her father had always maintained he'd 'Have a go' at anyone he found breaking and entering the family home, so she remembered to pretend to show Eulalia some sort of sympathy.) "I wasn't breaking and entering – I leaned on the door and the centre of it just opened like a cat-flap - I didn't know it would – the main door was padlocked!"

"Look," Eulalia replied, "you're not the first young person we've had trespassing around our property - which we're going to convert into a gift shop. Do you know someone called Steve Parker?"

"No," Becky bluffed, and instinctively pulled a gazing expression she'd seen her father use in family card games.

Eulalia looked at her sharply. She'd formulated a cunning response in case this girl turned out not to know him. (And she didn't <u>look</u> as though she was lying.)

"Well he's been creating a lot of trouble for us, that's why we decided to take this action. To teach you youngsters you can't get away with trespassing just because you're under-age – legal 'minors'." She had to ask one more question to ensure she could get away with releasing this girl: "What were you doing: studying the lighthouse as part of your field trip?" *In which case,* Eulalia realised, *I shouldn't have pretended to be the owner because more students might come round, asking questions.*

Becky thought fast. So this member of the diamond smuggling gang was pretending to be an indignant vigilante resident: Mrs Corvato. She wondered if that was her real name – probably not, but she'd remember it. And <u>she'd</u> keep up saying she was in Edinburgh on a school trip; but she'd have to stall Mrs Corvato if she tried asking for a phone number to contact her teachers on, to verify that she was 'Carol Saunders'! "No, I wasn't supposed to be studying your property for a survey. Actually, we had some free time to look around. My friends had gone with our teacher to try to reserve a café table for lunch and I just went up to the lighthouse to see if it was open to the general public. My school party'll be expecting me back this afternoon. And you've no right to keep me here – you could be put in prison for this!" Becky stopped herself from going on any more. She knew she could probably call the police now if they left her alone, at least ungagged; and this helped her keep her nerve, and her temper.

Eulalia was becoming convinced. "Well, I'm the owner of the lighthouse. It's up to me to decide whether I'm going to complain to the police about you...I thought I'd question you here on board the yacht, rather than risk having you scream my property down, and get <u>us</u> arrested as child abductors. You have to see things from <u>my</u> point of view. Just what were you going to do? Vandalise it? Or use it as a smoking den with your school friends? Don't tell me you weren't trying to get in there!"

"Look, I leaned on the door and it just opened! You've let these men tie me up and take me off in a crate!" "The only way my builders could bring a trespasser to me for cautioning – without being accused of some terrible crime themselves," Eulalia insisted, beginning to feel sorry for Becky and believe her story. "You see, if they'd

187

kept you ungagged in the lighthouse and called the police, you might have started yelling, then it could have been said you were screaming for help – then they, even I – might be accused of God knows what….and suddenly the crime victim's accused of being the criminal! I'm recording this conversation, you know, because it really is very frightening being accused of the crimes a trespasser's committed, whether you're a builder or the owner."

She was considering letting Becky (or 'Carol' as she thought she was called) go free with a caution not to trespass in 'her' lighthouse again, pretending to be acting in a kind, forgiving way. She'd even get her mobile back for her from the old cabin boat skipper if only he'd phone to confirm he had it with him in the crate…) This girl would feel too foolish trying to explain any more than that she'd inadvertently trespassed on some private waterfront property and been told off for it: she'd probably mention, by some woman on her yacht. Becky was staying silent.

"Now you know what it's like being locked away for breaking the law," Eulalia said. "But this is just to caution you, we won't try to prosecute your family. I hope your experience has been a short, sharp shock to you and stopped you from becoming just another young offender – I'm not ashamed to take the law into my own hands."

What a clever actress, thought Becky.

"Apologise and I'll let you go."

"I'm really sorry." But as she gave her apology Becky still didn't trust 'Mrs Corvato' at all. A lot of thoughts were going through her mind. The diamond smugglers must be thinking about letting her go. But what would they do? Drop her off at the harbour in their small cabin boat? If so, they must be confident of making a quick getaway somewhere abroad, because she'd got a good look at all of them. They'd probably have to change their appearance. She could see that 'Mrs Corvato', who was saying: "OK, we'll let you go now!" was a dyed blonde: so she could easily look different for a start; and she couldn't quite imagine what Jaime, who was now untying her hands and feet, would look like without his light beard. Becky was determined to tell the police everything immediately as soon as, if, she got any time to herself here to phone them; or if she could only get back to Leith safely. She'd underestimated how infinitely tricky these people were, just as she'd underestimated the Scottish weather. She rubbed the circulation back into her aching legs and sat watching the purple marks on her wrists where Jaime had removed the ropes: they'd disappear after a while.

But just as Eulalia was offering this reprieve, seriously about to let Becky go, and then start arranging to return to the Mediterranean as soon as possible, Steve blew his sister's cover – inadvertently. Becky had been fumbling around for the recording switch on his mobile again with her big toe, hampered by her sock, and now she accidentally touched the switch for playing back messages. Her brother's muffled tones now started coming out of her left trekker shoe: *"Becky, it's Steve. If you are hiding – stop fooling around! Because the police are out looking for you and we're about to confirm you as officially missing...."*

It sounded quite menacing at first to Eulalia, as her eyes opened wide and startled.

"She's got the mobile!" Jaime cried in Spanish, wresting the trekker shoe off her foot, as Steve's voice went on: "If you've kept my mobile with you, make sure the tracking system's switched on!" and describing which switch to press. Grabbing the mobile he made sure the tracking system was still switched off, watching the picture of Steve's anxious face as his message was replayed: *"I've just been chased by the diamond smugglers' ring leader Rodrigo – all the way from the lighthouse to the Dynamic Earth Centre...then he gave up and escaped! Don't hang around on your own anywhere, whatever you do! Just come straight back to the hotel and wait for us. I'm going on to the Police Headquarters with Pablo now. Just take care!"*

Eulalia, trying to constrain a furious look, asked for the mobile so she could start to play the message back from the beginning when it finished. She let it play out, afraid of losing it by touching the wrong switch. Chris Parker's voice came on: *"Your brother isn't pulling a hoax on you, Becky. We think he's been spotted by two of the diamond smugglers he ran into in Majorca: they're still at large and over here! And we're very worried about you. Phone us as soon as you can. Keep the tracking system switched on. And DO come back to the hotel, where we'll be waiting for you – we're making our way there now from the Botanic Gardens, after we've taken a look around the Newhaven Harbour area for you."* Finally her mother's message came: *"See you soon, Becky! We love you!"*

Becky was reassured by the sound of her family's voices, and very relieved to hear that Steve had just escaped with <u>his</u> life - even though their protective action had ironically just increased the danger she was now in.

"So, **Becky**, your family's left quite an important message for you on your mobile!" Eulalia called her by her real name, triumphantly. "It seems they're missing you!"

"<u>I'm</u> not Becky," she insisted desperately, "I've borrowed her mobile! I'm Carol!"

"And why were you keeping it in your shoe?" Jaime asked cynically, as he helped Eulalia replay the message from the beginning again: *"Becky, it's Steve! If you <u>are</u> hiding – stop fooling around! Because we're about to report you as officially missing to the police."* Eulalia stopped the message at that point and demanded: "Well?"

"I was just replacing my ordinary shoes with my trekkers to walk around the lighthouse area, and forgot I'd left Becky's mobile in one of them! I'd only just put them on when I fell through the door!"

"You don't expect us to believe that, surely?"

"That's why I was leaning on the door – I was keeping my balance changing my shoes. That message was left for Becky, not me!" Becky bluffed bravely. "I left my rucksack outside the lighthouse door."

"Do you know who Steve is?" Jaime asked her coolly.

"Her brother, I guess....sounds like he's in trouble again!" This time her response was feebly delivered. She could tell they'd seen through her.

Eulalia and Jaime were laughing at her. "It seems your friend Becky's in quite a spot of trouble!" Eulalia said sarcastically. "And now, I'm just going to phone the police....on her behalf."

Becky knew this was a lie. After discussing something in Spanish with Jaime which she didn't understand, Eulalia got up and strolled back to her office with Steve's mobile.

"You've no right to keep me here against my will!" Becky shouted after her, then to Jaime: "Just let me go!"

Jaime suddenly walked quickly out of the semi-soundproofed room, without locking it, and down the very short corridor following Eulalia. Becky rushed out after him as he exited through a heavy, padded door which he locked and bolted from the other side. She thumped on it hard with her fist then stopped and turned back to look at the luxurious accommodation she'd been left in. Next to the little padded room there was a neat bathroom with no porthole. She walked back into the padded room. A polished mahogany shelf set into a wall held a few books, mostly about ocean voyages, including the Bible. She felt that at least for the time being she wasn't going to experience any more rough handling from these people. But for how long? She selected a book and pretended to read it while she racked her brains as to what to do.

Eulalia was video conferencing in her office with Alastair's Spanish boss, the very cool and elusive character known only to these members of the diamond smuggling cartel as 'Senor C'. She couldn't see his face on the screen properly, though: it was sinisterly pixelled out, with only the basic outline of his head defined, and little black and white chequers indicating where his features were, and the shadows around them. It was for security reasons – so he couldn't be identified by anyone hacking into their computer, or recorded. His voice was digitally altered, and electronically enhanced too, so that it couldn't be identified.

Eulalia was saying: "The international archaeological dig at Edinburgh must have interested Steve Parker, the English boy who escaped from our cave rendezvous at Puerto Pollensa…" Then she could tell him that Pablo had also flown out.

"I know of him," came the reply, in a digitalised voice to match the mysterious silhouette on the screen; an underworld voice which sounded as if he was speaking through the dangerous elements of very stormy weather. "Yes, he ruined our operations there. The kid who discovered the diamond packets in the cliff face."

"I've never seen him, only the note in the file," continued Eulalia, "but Rodrigo's seen him in Edinburgh and he's following him…"

"With a view to accomplishing what they botched up in the cave, I assume."

"The kid's here with his family, and we've taken his sister on board."

"Where are you?" Senor C quickly demanded.

"Don't worry, quite far off the East Coast. No-one can hear us." And Eulalia explained how Becky had fallen into the Newhaven East lighthouse through the trapdoor, and damaged the keypad on her brother's mobile, "Which I've just confiscated. It's not giving out any tracking signals. I've checked it with Jaime, don't worry!"

Senor C reflected for a few moments then said: "I want Steve - <u>and</u> the Majorcan

192

girl! But Becky – don't kill her – yet…" he ordered. Then he enquired coolly: "Rodrigo – he's not back yet?"

"No, I've told him not to go back to the lighthouse again. Alto thinks he's seen Pablo Munos…."

"<u>Or</u> back to the *Carisma*, it's too risky," interrupted Senor C.

"I've advised the crew to try to change their appearance. And I've just kept Julio on at the B&B to watch for police activity in the Leith area," Eulalia then confirmed, "but everyone else is back on board."

He resumed for her: "Alto thinks he's seen Pablo Munos. Maria's policeman brother?"

"That's right. At the archaeological dig. Alto's only seen our file photo of Pablo, but we've played a message back left by Steve Parker on his mobile his sister was carrying, saying he's going with Pablo to Police Headquarters – so he <u>must</u> be around here! I've told Alastair – he's already got a note on him."

"Maria's brother Pablo over here in Edinburgh….tut, tut. We've got to move pretty smartly. I want you to transfer from Alastair's yacht…"

"The *Carisma*?"

"Yes, the one you're sailing in. Take the *Carisma* to be completely refitted at a little boatyard I know, called the Bosun's Boatyard. I'll give you the phone number…I want it completely refitted – as a catamaran if necessary – and given a new name. I want it to take some time. Then you can all go on a luxury cruise, on a big liner." He could see every expression on her face but she couldn't see his. "Don't worry, I'll have some passports and all the necessary paperwork prepared."

"Why can't Alastair just sink this yacht and claim on the insurance, if you don't want it recognised?" she asked.

"Too risky, it might be noticed. Tell him for me, will you? I haven't got the time myself. It'll be given full-scale cosmetic surgery at the little boatyard. Here's the number…"

Eulalia, when their conversation had ended, was left flustered. The Majorcan police were pursuing them here on the coastline of Eastern Scotland, with the British police! Where she thought they'd never get onto her crew. And now Alastair's magnificent yacht was going to be changed beyond recognition at a little boatyard! He'd be furious. He was always telling her it was his only means of relaxation in his disappointing early retirement from the lighthouse company.

She found Jaime and asked him: "Jaime, can you book us into a boatyard please? I'll give you the name and number of the one we've got to use – as soon as possible, for a complete refitting. We've got to leave this yacht now because the police are onto us. I'll discuss it with you all later." Then she went straight to the *Carisma*'s control room to give Miguel the instructions she'd just received from Senor C., and to confirm they definitely had on board Becky, the sister of the English boy who discovered the diamonds with Maria Munos. "She's not to be harmed. Her parents are holidaying in Edinburgh, would you believe it?"

"Really?" Miguel responded coolly, turning round some more in his seat. He hadn't heard this yet, he'd been too busy navigating. Next to Senor C, he was the most level-headed member of the cartel she knew. He looked up at her again with his large unfathomable brown eyes.

"Perhaps she and her brother are on the same archaeological dig as the Majorcan girl, Maria Munos. Alto's seen her policeman brother, Pablo Munos, at the dig too."

"Yes, I know that," replied Miguel, as he checked some more of the computerised controls. "Well don't worry, we can handle all this," he said, finally finishing what he'd been setting. "And I've just about had enough of the British weather, too. I'd be quite happy to get back to the Mediterranean. It's too cold for me up here except when I'm sitting in the control room with the sunshine coming through the windows!"

Eulalia went up onto the deck in her padded anorak with a fur hood, to talk with Alto and Alex. She asked them if any other vessels had approached them, and they told her it had been all fairly clear for a good mile around. The sea was calm. "I've had some very important instructions from Senor C.," she said: "which we'll all have to discuss a bit later. He's told us to keep the girl safe for the time being. She's definitely Becky Parker, the sister of that confounded Steve Parker. Alex, could you get some sandwiches brought to her? She'll talk more easily if we keep her relatively comfortable." Eulalia went back to her office.

Alto needed to make a phone call to one of the diamond cutters, who was setting some diamonds into Maria's mother's antique brooch for him. He'd vowed to give it as a present to his wife when he got home – or if she came over to Northern Europe with their daughter. The *Carisma*'s crew needed their main mobile line free; so Alex suggested to him he could go and make the sandwiches in the kitchen and use the mobile phone there, while <u>he</u> stayed on deck to answer any calls on the main line – he was after all wearing the warmest clothing, suitable for offshore Scotland in February – not the Spaniard.

"Thanks," said Alto.

"Yes, there's a 'company' mobile in the kitchen with a black sticker with a skull and crossbones logo on it. Use that. Could you keep an eye on the 'Old Cask' for me, too, and make sure our supplies aren't going down? I don't like the sound of this – I wonder what Eulalia's going to tell us."

Alex had explained to Alto that all their 'company' phones, except the main one, bore these distinctive stickers, in various colours. But once down in the little galley kitchen, Alto couldn't see a mobile anywhere anyway – someone had borrowed it.

Meanwhile, back in her office, Eulalia took out Steve's mobile which she'd confiscated from Becky. She'd decided it might be holding information which would make it worth keeping for the time being; but she wasn't sure exactly how to use it and didn't want to lose any data by misusing the complex network of its functions. She needed to check out the manual for her own very similar mobile. And before that, she had to phone Alastair. So for the time being she just made a note of all three names and numbers - including Steve's parents' mobile number – which were stored in his mobile. Her own mobile was an almost identical model to Steve's, lacking only one or two tiny updates in the design features which were hardly noticeable, even at second glance; but she didn't want to make any mistakes.   She put a navy blue 'company' skull and crossbones sticker on the back of her own, which she'd so far avoided doing, to distinguish it from Steve's. Her throat was feeling rather dry and as her office drinks cabinet had run out of mineral water, she decided to go along to the kitchen and get a drink of mineral water and a ham sandwich for herself and Miguel before she phoned Alastair. If she was the one who had to let him know of the facelift being arranged for the *Carisma* at the Bosun's Boatyard, she'd better appear presentable and not tired out, or he'd probably lose his temper with her.

Taking her own mobile, with its new navy blue sticker on the back, to the kitchen, she found Alto there. Eulalia didn't usually spend much time there herself. The men could usually be trusted to keep it spick and span. Realising that Alex had delegated the task of sandwich-making to Alto, she took a ham one for Miguel and poured herself a glass of mineral water out in the sparkling sunshine which came through the porthole, noticing the level of 'Old Cask' whisky was going down in the bottle. She chatted to him, not mentioning Alastair's boss. Then just as he was about to ask where the kitchen mobile was, she suddenly checked her watch and announced she had to get back to make a phone call. Tired and needing refreshment, and with important things on her mind, she glanced at her mobile lying on the work surface as she left, but forgot that she'd brought it with her, thinking it must be the one that belonged in the kitchens. Alto assumed this too.

Shortly after Eulalia left – first for the control room to take Miguel his sandwich – Alto picked up the mobile she'd left behind and looked for a sticker. It had a navy blue skull and cross-bones sticker on the back. *Oh*, he thought, *this must be the one that belongs in the kitchen: Alex said it had a black sticker on it when he probably meant a navy blue one. Perhaps she'd borrowed it and she's deliberately left it back here.* Then he had second thoughts, wondering whether it might be Eulalia's own, which she'd left behind, and he ran after her with it. But she wasn't in her office when he looked in. So he left it on her desk. Then he noticed Steve's mobile, confiscated from Becky, on her desk. He picked it up and looked for a sticker on it. There wasn't one. He decided to take the mobile with the navy blue sticker on up into the control room to see if Eulalia was there, and sort out which mobile belonged where. But Eulalia had already given Miguel his sandwich and just left the control room for the nearest bathroom to powder her face, so she wouldn't blush if Alastair lost his temper with her while she told him, videoconferencing, that he was to lose his beautiful yacht – at least lose the appearance of the *Carisma* as he'd come to know her.

Alex had also just gone into the control room to ask Miguel if he knew anything about what Senor C. was planning. Alto told them both that Eulalia seemed to have been using the kitchen mobile phone outside the kitchen. "This one with a dark blue sticker on the back," he said in Spanish, holding it out. "Is it OK if I keep this one in the kitchen now?" he asked. Miguel translated this quickly into English for Alex, who hadn't had anything to eat yet and was dying for a glass of 'Old Cask', especially now that he'd been ticked off by Eulalia for delegating the sandwich-making to Alto. "Sure," he said casually in his newly learned Spanish, "take that one!" Then he added in English: "One belongs there! But the kitchen mobile has a <u>black</u> sticker, on the front, and it's a different make from that one, as well."

Alto understood the first part of what Alex said. He didn't stay too long as Miguel had turned his piscine profile round, so that he was looking straight ahead out of the control room windows again and obviously concentrating on navigating.

Alto returned to Eulalia's office to leave a note on her desk for her in Spanish:

'Is it OK to keep a mobile for the kitchen? Alex says that "one belongs there"' (he gave the English phrase) *'and it should have a black sticker on it.'*

Then he went back to the kitchen with Eulalia's mobile to make his phone call to the diamond cutter regarding the old brooch that was now in his possession.

When Eulalia returned to her office desk, primped and powdered, to videoconference with Alastair, she felt ready to face him and to cope with all his reactions. She looked out of the nearest porthole. A lovely sunset was just beginning its gentle, ultra-slow-motion explosion in the sky and to extend its glistering reflection over the sea. Then she read Alto's note and immediately became flustered again, wondering if *'one belongs there'* may have been Alex sarcastically referring to <u>her</u>. She'd caught him before, imitating her – and Alastair – in a formal, 'posh' style of speech. But she mustn't delay phoning Alastair any longer. She decided that Steve's mobile must be hers, and that someone had probably peeled the navy blue sticker off the back fidgeting while they were talking on it, and had now borrowed Steve's. These men needed telling that she was back now, and they couldn't just borrow her mobile without her permission to make phone calls. She didn't like people taking things from her desk without her permission either, and just leaving her a note. Alex or Miguel had probably started it, by taking the mobile actually belonging to the kitchen out of there. Too much strong whisky was being drunk, too.

Anyway, she could always get Steve's back later – she'd already taken down all the phone numbers stored on it. Alto probably had it.

Thinking she was dialling Alastair, she pressed the first memory switch on Steve's mobile under the impression it was her own. She couldn't even remember Alastair's number off the top of her head any more, she'd used the memory facility so many times. But she'd never heard his voicemail message. A standard, pre-recorded message from the phone company now came through, giving the number, and she assumed it was his. As she held the mobile in her hand she wavered, wondering for a split second whether she really had her own mobile; but decided that if this <u>were</u> Steve's mobile, his parents' number was bound to be stored on the first memory switch and they'd probably have a personalised 'sorry we're not here' recorded message of their own voices on their number for him by now, if they hadn't already got one: anyway, if they cared about their daughter's whereabouts, right now they'd be answering the phone directly, on call. Or, if the first memory switch was for a friend of Steve's, they'd probably have their own personalised pre-recorded answer message too. No, Eulalia decided again, *This <u>is</u> my mobile.* She left a recorded message:

'Alastair,' (she knew he'd recognise her voice) *'we have to get the* Carisma *docked at the Bosun's Boatyard along the Firth of Forth. As soon as possible. And keep it there having a re-fit. The police are onto us. Then I have to transfer with the others*

to a cruise liner. On Senor C.'s orders. We've got Steve Parker's sister on board – the sister of the kid who scuppered our Puerto Pollensa operation. Let me know as soon as you get this message.'

She left Steve's mobile switched on, ready to take any incoming calls. Unfortunately it was during a lull in the attempts by Pablo and the Parkers to contact Becky on it. Eulalia didn't bother to check for messages on it as she'd just spoken with her two main bosses, and now had to speak to her crew. She would check for any more messages later, with Miguel.

CHAPTER TWENTY-THREE
Breakthrough!

Rodrigo had taken the phone call from Julio warning him not to return to the little lighthouse while he was pursuing Steve through Edinburgh to the Dynamic Earth Centre. On his slow walk back to the B & B in the harbour area, he felt exhausted and frustrated at having missed his opportunity to dispatch the English kid who'd given him so much trouble. While he was still on the outskirts of the city, he bought a black ink cartridge from a stationery shop and stopped to have something to eat in a busy café. He kept his head down reading a newspaper and decided that at least he could make a reconnaissance of the waterfront area along the final part of his way back, looking out for any police on duty. He would only finally return to the B & B when he was satisfied there was no sign of a plain-clothes police presence, either, to discover this bolt-hole used by the gang.

He paid for his sandwiches, then in the café toilets he carefully applied the black ink to his hair and beard and combed it through with a wet comb, until his hair appeared very dark brown. Then he dried it a little under the hand drier. Leaving the café while the people at the serving counter were too busy to notice his changed appearance, he walked back up via the Newhaven Harbour waterfront area to one of the Leith B & B districts by the docks. He saw one uniformed policeman by the lighthouse, and quickly went down another street to avoid being noticed.

By the time he walked in through the front door of the little terraced cottage, it was nearly evening. The landlady was out but Julio was there, with a 'five o'clock shadow' of stubble around his mouth and jaw-line. He usually shaved at that time but was now growing a beard and moustache in accordance with Eulalia's advice. Julio held out a can of lager to him: "Rodrigo! You look as if you've been out in a marathon! And you've dyed your hair! I preferred you blonde!"

"Thanks, but I have to stay very sober to make a few phone calls. And watch the news in a while…..What a chase! I nearly caught Steve Parker. A lot of people saw me. I chased him right up King Arthur's Mount and all round the Dynamic Earth

Centre. I <u>nearly</u> got him. But they were getting onto <u>me</u> and I ran out as fast as I could. I'd have run all the way back here too, only I'd have been stopped! I've put some black ink on my hair but it's not safe out there right now. They're onto us!"

While Rodrigo went into the bathroom to rewet his hair and combe the dye into it more evenly, then into the kitchen to make himself a cup of tea, Julio took a phone call from Eulalia. She told him they had Steve Parker's older sister Becky on board the *Carisma*, and that Alto had seen a man looking like Pablo Munos visiting Maria at the archaeological dig. They'd also picked up a recorded message from Steve left on his mobile, which his sister had had with her, saying he was going to Police Headquarters with Pablo.

Julio put the phone down and asked Rodrigo when he walked back into the room: "Did you know Pablo Munos, Maria's brother in the police, is over here too? I've just been speaking with Eulalia. At least Steve Parker couldn't get a mobile picture of us – his sister was borrowing his mobile…"

"I'm staying out of diamonds for the time being – it's too dangerous right now!" Rodrigo stayed very edgy. He made a phone call to Senor C and told him about his nearly catching up with the English boy. Senor C advised him to recover from all his exertions, and meanwhile not to return to the disused lighthouse or the *Carisma*. "It's too risky now. I'll let you know how we're going to proceed soon. And I'll phone you when we're ready."

"Senor C.'s got some plans coming up for us," Rodrigo told his accomplice. Then he suggested: "Why don't you shave your head, then you can wear a woolly hat when you go out of doors and you won't be so recognisable later on, especially bearded!"

"Good idea!" Julio agreed. "Nothing like the present, either!" he added on his way to the bathroom, worrying that the police might turn up to arrest them at any moment.

Left to himself for a few minutes, Rodrigo made a mobile call to the international terrorist cell he operated in. "You're having a rough time," his contact sympathised. "Can you take a train down to London and fly back to Madrid?"

Rodrigo agreed and said that he could. He didn't want to co-ordinate the diamond-smuggling gang anymore – he was too easily recognised in connection with the others. But he told his contact he'd wait several days before moving down to London. In the meantime he'd keep a low profile – he'd hung around the bed and breakfast place too long. And with both he and Julio changing their appearance at the same time, their landlady might start to get suspicious - even if she didn't watch the local news bulletin on television. All she knew was that they worked part-time in a yachting crew; she assumed there was a lull in sailing activity at the moment during the colder months. They'd shown her photographs, of themselves in warmer weather on the deck of the *Carisma*, in which you couldn't see the whole yacht or its name. They'd told her it was called the 'Southern Belle'.

Julio re-entered the sitting room, as bald as a coot but still growing his 'five o'clock shadow'. "What shall we tell our landlady?" he asked, with one eyebrow raised expectantly.

Rodrigo thought. "Why don't we say we're going to a Heart of Midlothian football match and we're going to get ourselves up in our team's colours from head to toe?"

"That's a good idea!"

"Say you're going with a black and yellow pattern on your hair stubble, and I'm going to wear a yellow bandana round my head."

"The only trouble is, Hearts colours are dark red and white, Alex told me."

"Well then that's not our team!" Rodrigo said. "We'll support one of the Scottish teams which has a black and yellow kit. I know I've seen at least one." Then he told Julio he'd have to part from the smuggling gang for a while, but would be back when the time was right. "Look sharp, Julio! And of course, don't actually put yellow paint on your hair, will you? You'll stick out like a sore thumb! I'll keep in touch."

Before their landlady returned, they both watched the local evening news bulletin which showed the brief, grainy mobile phone footage taken by the Dynamic Earth Centre security guard, of Rodrigo running out through the doors of the 'Shaping the Surface' room. He was virtually unrecognisable in it, but the identikit picture of his face coming up on the screen afterwards was enough to shake his nerve.

Tomorrow, or the next day, he decided, he'd make for the local nature reserve. All he needed in his ruck-sack were some blankets and the two brand new hot-water bottles from the spare bedroom in the B&B, a few snack bars and his battery-operated shaver. He could trim his newly-dark hair very short and shave his beard off as soon as he parted company with the landlady. If he filled the hot-water bottles with boiling water before he left, and covered himself with leaves, he could just about last out in the bitter cold overnight, as long as he didn't burn or scald himself! He could stay hidden there from the police for a few days – it would probably be safer than having the two of them both remaining at the B&B. He told Julio he'd leave in the next couple of days, letting the landlady think he was coming back in a week or so and paying the rent in advance. They'd better think of ways of distracting her attention away from the next few news bulletins, if she watched them.

*   *   *

At dawn the next day Professor Cameron and two colleagues were already at the archaeological site. The very light fall of powdery snow at the beginning of the international dig had highlighted some of the less obvious lines of the remains of a settlement, and now they were looking to see if the low early sunlight revealed any more.

After only a few minutes, one of them noticed two men who'd appeared on the edge of the golf-course. They'd been moving quickly and purposefully, but once aware of the archaeologists' presence, had abruptly slowed their walk and started skulking about. Professor Cameron had warned his colleagues there might be international thugs operating in the area: they now wondered what anyone could possibly be doing at such an early hour up there -   unless they were keen ornithologists. But these two men weren't holding binoculars as would be expected of genuine enthusiasts, so the professor phoned the police while his colleagues resumed their work. From the descriptions of them, the police believed that one of them could be

Mick Hamilton. The other man they weren't sure of, but in fact it was the lightly moustachioed, bearded Julio, now wearing a green woolly hat over his shaven head. Eulalia had told them to pick up any diamonds recently delivered to their temporary cache and then leave it for good, digging it over with the spades which had been left down there.

Mick and Julio had just picked up the last of the diamonds in their haversacks. They hadn't expected the archaeologists to be about quite that early. Now they'd been spotted, they didn't want to attract any more suspicion by running away. Mick quickly took out the telescope from his rucksack, but they couldn't rescue the first impression they'd given, that they were up to no good. Their car was parked by the golf-course car park and they gradually, awkwardly, started walking away in that direction.

Meanwhile, the archaeologists had been warned by the police not to approach them, so they continued working from where they could best keep a watch on them, hoping the police would arrive soon. They weren't disappointed when within a few minutes Pablo turned up with his red-headed counterpart in the Midlothian and Borders police, Fergus Dalgleish, in his uniform.

As the two officers got out of their unmarked car, Mick took a look at them through the telescope and recognised the man who'd been to the archaeological site before, whom Alto had pointed out while he was talking with Maria. It was her brother, Pablo Munos, now wearing a blue Fair Isle sweater, jeans and anorak. Eulalia had sent a photo of him by mobile phone, confirming that the smuggling gang should particularly beware of this Majorcan police officer: he'd been onto them for quite some time. Mick broke into a run, shouting to Julio to follow him back across a corner of the golf-course to open fields and countryside. He made off in the direction of their car which was parked on the other side of a small hillside by the golf-course car-park. The terrain was bordered by trees and hedges and there was plenty of cover for them, if they could get to it.

The two police officers didn't know whether Julio and Mick had a car or not. PC Fergus Dalgleish quickly radioed for reinforcements with tracker dogs before he and Pablo started off running after them on foot. If they'd had time to pick up the force's two fastest Alsatian dogs, Prince and Simba, on their way over, they could probably have caught them very easily.

As the criminals approached a large field full of steers, Julio suddenly swerved away from Mick and ran into a copse with old oak trees, while Mick jumped down into a deep dyke behind a hedge which ran around another field. They'd try to shake off their pursuers before meeting back up at the car – they had a good chance because they knew the area better.

Fergus followed Julio into the copse. Pablo managed to find the break in the hedge he'd seen Mick disappear through, and stopped, looking out across the dyke, which only had a few puddles of water in it, across into the next field of emerald green grass. It was full of sheep, calmly grazing as if no-one had disturbed them. Pablo realised Mick had probably run along the dyke and round one of the sides of the field. Just as he was about to jump down into it and follow him, Steve phoned him on his mobile, using the text code he'd been given to indicate it was an emergency. Pablo took the call.

Steve was also up early: he'd been recharging his father's mobile from the special socket in his own hotel room – the socket in his parents' room wasn't working for some reason, and needed rewiring. As soon as it had recharged, it gave out the voice message left by Eulalia, thinking she was leaving it on Alastair's number.

"I think I know where Becky is!" he now told Pablo excitedly. He explained how his sister's captors had somehow mistakenly left a message for another member of their gang on his parents' mobile number. "They must have been dialling it out from my mobile, which I gave to Becky! Listen to this!" and he played it back.

'Alastair, we have to get the Carisma *docked at the Bosun's Boatyard along the Firth of Forth. As soon as possible. And keep it there having a re-fit. The police are onto us. Then I have to transfer with the others to a cruise liner. On Senor C.'s orders. We've got Steve Parker's sister on board – the sister of the kid who scuppered our Puerto Pollensa operation. Let me know as soon as you get this message.'*

Pablo, getting it recorded, listened to Eulalia's message to the end; breathing in the still, fresh cold air strongly and deeply, which, like the sheep grazing the sunlit dewy grass, he could see in front of him in steamy puffs as he exhaled. Then he told Steve he was out by the Pentland Hills with a colleague trying to catch two of the crooks: "But don't worry! Finding Becky's even more important!"

Steve made sure Pablo had definitely understood the message, then said: "It definitely doesn't sound like Becky playing a hoax!" He was certain of that. "But do you think it's a trap for the police? Or a decoy?" he asked, worried. He'd watched a movie with his friend David in which a criminal gang lured detectives into a dangerous trap.

Pablo looked around the landscape, as, gently jingle-jangling with bird whistling, it was gradually becoming suffused with dawn light. "No....I don't believe it is. Thanks, Steve! We'd better get someone over to the Bosun's Boatyard, and make a check on all the cruise liners. Can you phone Police Headquarters straight away and replay this message to them?" and he gave him the number.

"Sure! Good luck with the chase, Pablo!"

Both realised there was no time to lose. Pablo phoned D-S Jim McCulloch, who wasn't normally on duty at that time but had asked to be kept informed at all hours of any important developments, and had just arrived at Headquarters. He told him that he and Fergus Dalgleish were out by the Pentland Hills following two men believed to be Mick Hamilton and Julio, and to expect a phone call from Steve at any minute. "He's received an important recorded message from Becky's kidnappers – definitely the same people involved in the diamond smuggling. They seem to have dialled the Parkers' number by mistake, and left a message intended for their boss on <u>their</u> phone. They've got Becky on board the *Carisma* but they're going to take it to be ...rebuilt...refitted at a boatyard called 'The Bosun's Boatyard'. And then they all plan to leave on a cruise liner. We don't know which one, or when. And we don't know what they want to do with Becky. But they know she's Steve's sister."

As Pablo was speaking, Headquarters switchboard took the message as it came in from Steve. D-S McCulloch made some swift phone calls to organize a twenty-four-hour surveillance of the Bosun's Boatyard and a check on all the cruise liners docking in the Firth of Forth.

Reinforcements soon arrived at the archaeological site in two police cars, led by the Edinburgh-based Detective Sergeant now helping with the case, Andrew Morrison. But Mick and Julio had managed to give Pablo and Fergus the slip and escape in their car on a minor road, back to their B&B houses (Mick was staying in another one near to Julio's).

The archaeologists helped the police investigate the entire area for any clues as to what these two men might have been getting up to. But no-one noticed the dug-over hide, which Mick and Julio had carefully covered over with dead twigs and bracken and dug-up turves of rough grass, without treading on them. Although the two Alsatian dogs Prince and Simba detected their scent around it, the crooks' scent trails criss-crossed over the area anyway, stopping at the spot where their vehicle had been parked. The police officers found wide-based tyre tracks running for a few metres in some damp dirt along the edge of the roadside, which might help them trace it. And half a footprint.

CHAPTER TWENTY-FOUR
Stormy Stow Away

Jaime had managed to book the *Carisma* for a complete overhaul of her structure at the Bosun's Boatyard later that evening, when all the law-abiding boat-builders had gone home. A snow-storm was brewing as the big white yacht docked in at the little shingle harbour along the Firth of Forth. It wasn't very accessible in rough weather conditions, because of a rocky approach. The sky was a deep, menacing grey colour and there was a lilac tinge to everything in the twilight. There were only a few fishing boats bobbing about on the choppy water and most people had gone home for the evening, or were in the pubs.

Julio and Mick were already waiting in the covered boatyard - where there were several small yachts and one or two larger ones - in two black jeeps, one of them hired, ready to pick up the rest of the gang and drive them to the docks. While Eulalia went to the office cabin to see the man who was to organize the complete refitting, the others got into them. The back seats had been taken out of the hired jeep, the larger of the two, to make room for crates. Miguel took the driver's seat and Alex sat next to him, waiting for Eulalia to return. The smaller jeep, being driven by Mick, had been fitted with new tyres with different treads after the police had followed him in the Pentland Hills area. Alto sat behind him between Jaime and Julio, with his long legs drawn in uncomfortably.

They were all even more nervous now, because Eulalia had just confessed that she'd got the mobile phones confused, and left the message for Alastair on one of the memory numbers of Steve's mobile. She'd only recently switched Steve's off again because she'd noticed that Alto was carrying her own mobile, which she'd put a navy blue skull and crossbones sticker on. He'd decided to borrow it while the *Carisma* was going in for a re-fit. "So where's <u>that</u> message gone?" Miguel had asked. "I don't know," she'd replied, "probably to some friend of hers in England, who might not check her messages for a while anyway. Let's hope so." And she'd quickly phoned Alastair again, dialling his number fully this time, which Miguel gave her.

"Perhaps if a kid gets Eulalia's message for Alastair, he'll just think it's some kind of computer game they're playing," Julio was saying, as one of the boat builders came up to the smaller jeep and asked which one of the *Carisma*'s crew was Alto. "Here," the boat builder said, handing him a small package through the window, "they asked me to forward this to you: they said you might as well have it now – to save on the postage!"

Alto unwrapped the package while he asked Mick to describe what had been going on around their diamond drop-off point by the archaeological dig. While Mick told him, he wondered what he could be opening. Inside a cardboard box was the old silver brooch, still with its leaves slightly bent round, and now set with some of the newly-cut and polished diamonds which gently gleamed in the twilight as he picked it up to examine it. Surely it was now unrecognisable as the old brooch which Maria Munos had lost in the rising tide in the cave at Puerto Pollensa. He put it back into his pocket, hoping his good luck would continue. It had helped her escape from the cave, after all. And he hadn't been caught yet. Once he got home, it would make a very attractive present for his wife. He hoped she'd like it. Julio remarked that diamonds were more than <u>his</u> wife deserved:

"I work all night at this business and when I come home she complains I never do an honest day's work!"

Alex came over to ask Julio and Jaime to help him offload two crates, one with Becky in it, from the *Carisma* and into the back of the big hired jeep. They'd laced her sandwiches and drink with powdered sleeping tablets on her second day on the yacht, so it had been easy to put her back in the crate – otherwise she'd have put up a terrible fight.

"What's in the other one?" asked Jaime, looking at the other crate.

"I don't know," said Alex. "Something Rodrigo wants looking after."

Meanwhile, Mick turned the radio on in his jeep to listen to the football results on the sports programme, then the news bulletin. He and Alto, who could now stretch his legs out more easily in the back, listened intently as it was announced:

'Police are trying to trace a large white luxury cabin cruiser called the Carisma, *last seen in the Firth of Forth. It may have on board English schoolgirl Becky Parker, aged 12, believed to have been abducted by a gang involved in international diamond smuggling…'*

Then their own physical descriptions were given out. They heaved a sigh of relief on Rodrigo's behalf when they heard him still being described as blond and bearded. They knew that wherever he was, his hair was now short and dark and he'd be clean-shaven.

Dusk was swiftly overtaking the twilight, but the outside lights were still not switched on at the Bosun's Boatyard. Becky's crate was loaded into the back of the big hired jeep while Miguel waited in the driving seat. The jolting began to rouse her, with a heavy head, from her drugged sleep. Alex got back into the smaller jeep to drive it.

Miguel was saying "Hurry up, Eulalia!" under his breath, as she finally emerged from the office cabin with the boat builder. She'd struck a deal with him to rebuild the *Carisma* until it was unrecognisable as Alastair's cabin cruiser. They'd phoned Alastair to get his consent to the work, although really he had no choice in the matter: they were just letting him know how it would be done. Eulalia got into the passenger seat of the hired jeep and they all drove off.

Night had fallen by the time they reached Leith docks, and big, heavy snow clouds kept passing over the half-moon.   After a while, Becky had regained sufficient consciousness to hear Eulalia talking to Miguel in Spanish. "I understand from the boat builders there's a cargo-loading service. One of their men has all the necessary passes, documents and devices to get us through the security systems. He'll get them to us, then we have to make our way to one of the warehouses. I'll direct you."

"He'd better have them ready," said Miguel. "How long do we have to wait there for?"

"I don't know yet." Eulalia phoned the men in the other jeep to let them know they were about to stop and wait for their contact to bring them their security passes.

She was speaking in English now, and Becky realised they were arriving at the docks. Then Eulalia spoke briefly again with Senor C. by mobile in Spanish. It was the first time she'd heard his voice without it being electronically disguised – it was quite deep but she couldn't tell which part of Spain he was from. Again, she relayed his instructions to the others in English.

Becky tried to ascertain what their plans for her were. Her crate was to be lifted into the hold of a major passenger cruise liner headed for the Baltic Sea, from what she could make out. "<u>More</u> cold weather!" Miguel was opining. She of course didn't hear Senor C. tell Eulalia: "If a convenient moment arises at sea, we can dispose of her if necessary! Or we can hold her to ransom at any north European capital we choose. I haven't decided yet..." Eulalia was waiting for a signal. There was a petrol station nearby and a car pulled up, turned its lights off and then flashed them on, once, twice. A man got out of the car and pulled out a newspaper from a stand outside the shop. It contained several insertions. Then he put it back, and as he did so he quickly slipped a slim, polythene-wrapped sheaf of papers inside the newspaper alongside the insertions. Then he selected another newspaper and took it into the shop to pay for it. Eulalia got out of the jeep and went over to the newsstand. Taking the newspaper he'd put back, she went into the garage shop to pay for it. When she came out she had all the documentation – security passes and passports – they needed. She sorted through and distributed them.

Becky, listening in, didn't feel that her time was up yet. *Or I'd have read something about it in my horoscope*, she thought optimistically. *And if Steve managed to escape from that cave, I should certainly be able to get out of <u>this</u> situation*.....She envisaged being able to make enough noise inside the crate by thumping against it, to attract the attention of anyone in the docks - or one of the cruise liner's crew, if they boarded it. They couldn't <u>all</u> be in league with the diamond smugglers. She'd just have to wait.

They drove off, through the automated security barrier, towards a very large warehouse. It was sleeting heavily by now, and the cold wind had picked up from the sea. They had to stop at another check-point, this time with a security man inside a little booth. Miguel and Alex showed him the required passes through the hatch in the booth window, saying they had some last-minute goods – crates of whisky - to deliver, which had been delayed. Alex added: "We have to make a painstaking check through the crates already in the warehouse too, to make sure they packed the right quantities for each different malt. There may have been a mistake on the computer's stock-keeping system. It'll take a while. Here's what should be inside." And he showed him a print-out of a goods list which had been slightly changed from the original print-out for the stored goods.

"OK," said the security man, waving them through, " just press the exit button from the inside when you're ready to leave and I'll let you out again. I have to close the doors while you're in, for security reasons. And to keep the place dry." They already knew this. He opened the doors of the warehouse for them automatically and they drove in.

The lights were on. Then the doors closed again.

"It's hardly a dry place," Alex remarked, punning on all the bottles of whisky stored there. Then Becky heard something which nearly destroyed all her hope. Eulalia put her window down in the hired jeep to speak, rather reluctantly, to him. "Senor C. says there may be time to get the kid's crate filled with unset concrete before it's lifted into the ship's hold. So it just looks as if it contains a sculpture if anyone opens it up searching for her. Can you arrange it?"

Alex made two phone calls while Becky strained to listen to his responses, her heart thumping in her mouth with terror. She didn't want to be turned into a work of art displayed in some cold North European country! Then he told Eulalia: "We can't do it – there's just no time to arrange it, no-one here who'll do it at the moment."

Becky started to breathe several sighs of relief, each deeper than the last as she realised the full horror of what she'd just missed.

"OK," said Eulalia. "I'll tell Senor C. Is the '*Empress*' still due to depart tomorrow afternoon?"

Miguel put in: "I should think so. This storm's not likely to last into tomorrow."

A few minutes later, Miguel received a phone call from their North European crane operator, who'd arrived at the docks for his duplicitous night-shift. "What do we say to the security official?" he asked him.

The crane operator spoke fluent English with a Scandinavian accent. "That you've discovered the main mistake, and are having to transfer the two crates you brought in onto a cruise liner heading for the Baltic, for a special customer. And that you'll still have to check through all the rest in the warehouse. Say you've driven a long way down from the Highlands with your boss Mrs Corvato: she doesn't want any more mistakes made with this important order, so she's down to check through the consignment personally. If they're suspicious, say she has a Spanish sherry business as well. Tell them you'd appreciate a rest in the docks area before doing any more driving - all the way back up to the Highlands. He'll think we'll be putting those two crates for the Baltic into another warehouse to wait for the connecting ferry early in the morning. The construction work isn't supposed to be finished yet for the *'Empress'* to berth at Leith, she's a big liner. But our friends in the crew can take the opportunity of this storm to adjust the mooring closer up to the new part of the harbour. I can operate the crane from there, and get those two crates into the hold now - when they won't be checked in so 'conscientiously', as they say!" Miguel agreed this was a good suggestion.

As the sleet storm continued, with the salt air preventing it from becoming snow, the two jeeps drove out of the warehouse to the far edge of the newest docks, still under construction. The huge 'Empress' cruise liner was now moored very near them. The crane operator stuck special labels on the two crates, saying 'FRAGILE' in green lettering to identify them later, then got into the cabin of a very tall crane. It took Becky's crate first, swinging in the high wind, while one of the crew opened the ship's hold. Alex took out a bottle of 'Old Cask' from the little jeep's glove compartment and took the cap off. There was a small measure of whisky still in it, which he held up respectfully towards the manoeuvring crane. "I declare these docks officially open!" he declared, and swiftly drank it.

With each minor adjustment the operator made to the angle of the crane's swing, Becky felt, swaying inside her crate, as if he was going to let her go and drop her from a great height. But it was gradually lowered into the hold of the cruise liner, and the second crate put down alongside it.

Meanwhile, the smugglers swopped jeeps. Miguel drove back with Eulalia to the warehouse, to wait in their little jeep until early the next morning to board the ferry to the *'Empress'* from another part of the docks complex, which was vast. By then they'd be posing as new recruits to the big liner's crew, with more false documentation. Mick, Alex, Jaime, Julio and Alto were to board it later in the morning: all separately, among the many hundreds of other passengers, as Alastair had insisted; meanwhile they returned to Mick's B&B accommodation in the hired jeep. Exchanging jeeps made it more difficult for the police to keep track of them if they were noticed. They arranged to leave the keys of the hired jeep hidden under a stone at the dockyard, for the crane driver, so he could return the jeep to the hire centre once they'd all boarded the *'Empress'*.

Creeping about back in the kitchen of Mick's Bed and Breakfast accommodation late at night, trying to make a pot of tea without disturbing the landlady, Alto vowed to himself he would never, ever get involved in crime again after the anxieties he'd experienced smuggling diamonds. He'd realised what a vast, dangerous network the gang was operating in, and that it was time to untangle himself. He could see Mick becoming more ruthless working in it: he'd just brought a golf-club back in from the caddy they always left in their jeep. "I'm packing it for the Baltic trip," he'd said significantly: "it might come in useful." Alto remembered what he'd said to him about the golf club he'd buried on the golf course: *"I'd use this on a man if I absolutely had to..."* He felt perhaps now, Mick might even be prepared to use one on a defenceless girl. He just didn't know. And it frightened him.

*   *   *

From seven that morning the Bosun's Boatyard had been under surveillance by an undercover police officer posing as a fisherman. In the evening, when the *Carisma* had arrived for a re-fit, two armed Scottish officers, newly arrived on duty, were called in to help arrest the smugglers. But by the time they arrived, the birds, including 'Mrs Corvato', had already flown. They'd just missed them.

However, the police caught three boat builders in the act of hastily re-spraying over the name *Carisma* on the side of the yacht, in the covered yard. And though, as soon as the boat builders had started work on her, they'd stripped out and burned everything which could provide clues to the owner's and crew's identities, they hadn't as yet had time to remove fingerprints or, of course, any DNA particles. They were questioned, while police headquarters sent in forensics experts to examine the yacht. And, after the careful check which had already been started on the British and International yachting associations databases came to an end, it was found that there was no 'Mrs Corvato' registered on any of them.

CHAPTER TWENTY-FIVE
Pursuing Rodrigo

E
arly that morning when Steve had replayed to his parents the message Eulalia wanted Alastair to receive, they'd felt like making their way straight to the Bosun's Boatyard. But Chris soon received a phone call from D-S Jim McCulloch requesting them not to approach it. He said he was acting on the information given out by the message, assuming it wasn't a hoax. "It's very likely that the woman who left it has Steve's mobile he lent Becky, and she pressed the wrong button on it to send the message through to her accomplice. And she must be with Becky. Do please let the police deal with this – these are all <u>very</u> dangerous criminals! The boatyard's going under twenty-four-hour undercover police surveillance: there's a danger that if you go there, the crooks might realise you're Steve and Becky's parents and leave the area before they can be apprehended."

"OK, I see," Chris was saying.

"Of course Chris," he reassured him, "we're also checking the cruise liners due to dock and depart from the Firth of Forth in the next few days. There's every hope your daughter will be returned to you safe and sound: keep optimistic! We believe it's possible the criminals kidnapped Becky believing she was Maria, and they'll free her when they realise their mistake."

Chris quickly relayed all this to Pat, who asked if she could speak with the Detective-Sergeant. "But they <u>must</u> have seen or heard the news, Mr McCulloch," she said, "we heard it this morning - so they must already be sure they've got someone called Becky Parker: so why haven't they released her yet?"

"Not necessarily," Jim replied, "they might not be up-to-date with the news; and if they are, perhaps they're organizing how to release her without being caught, or setting up a ransom demand. It might take a little time yet," he advised. "I'd stay where you are, in your hotel, and keep your mobile switched on so I can contact you with any developments."

There was little point in alerting the Parkers to the possibility their daughter might be held hostage in the name of international terrorism, if Rodrigo decided to seize this opportunity for that purpose. There was no need to cause them further alarm at this stage.

Chris thanked him for all his help so far and decided to buy a new mobile phone as his old one couldn't receive good video images taken in the dark. If their daughter's abductors contacted them he'd want as much information about them as he could get, including what they looked like. He anticipated they might just send him a gloomy, half-lit picture of their daughter and themselves, so he needed a mobile with excellent picture resolution. As soon as the shops opened he went out and bought one. When he came back, he gave the police his new number, stored all the numbers from his old mobile on it and showed Steve how to use it. He told him what D-S Jim McCulloch had said, and that of course it was all confidential: "If you tell anyone else about the police operations, Becky's life will be in even more danger. But just so you know, they're doing all they can to get her back."

"Do you mind if I make a call to David on this?" Steve asked, holding up the new mobile.

"Sure, do!" replied Mr Parker. "But don't tell him too much yet about the smugglers. Anything!" He corrected himself quickly, "– don't tell him anything about them, though I expect you're dying to. You never know who gets to hear all your chat these days. I know David's a good friend – but wait till we've got Becky back before you tell him all the details. OK? Just say she's gone off to do some shopping on her own if he asks after her…"

"OK!"

"The phone'll flash an indicator if someone else is trying to get through to our number – for God's sake answer it right away if it does, and put them over to us - straightaway!"

"Don't worry!"

"I'm just going to get on the internet with your mother to take a look at the travel routes operating around the Firth of Forth. If you get any news coming through, come to see us straight away!"

"OK, I will!" Steve assured him firmly, then went down into the lounge to make the phone call.

There were one or two other people in the lounge, talking in subdued voices. They could be talking about the Parkers for all he knew. He couldn't really mistrust anyone he'd seen around the hotel so far; but he also knew he shouldn't underestimate the crooks' potential for operating in broad daylight. He was dying to talk to David fully about it, but the will to protect Becky was stronger. It would be reassuring just to be able to talk with his friend, even if he couldn't discuss everything with him right now.

Disappointingly, David's mobile message-answering service was on. But Steve waited compliantly for the tone and then spoke as relaxed as he could: "Hi, David. It's Steve. Up in Edinburgh. How are you?....Listen, I'm having an amazing time here. You know you said you trusted Becky about horoscopes turning out to be true? Well," he referred to the back of his natural history notebook, "on 3 February I wrote down what she said was forecast for me for the whole of this month: 'You unexpectedly run up against someone from your past you thought you wouldn't see again, in unfamiliar territory. They could land you in deep water if you allow yourself to get involved.' And guess what? It's all happening! I am getting into deep water – if you see what I mean - like the last time I was on holiday! I can't wait to tell you about this one. See you soon! By the way, you won't get me if you try to phone me back on my usual number, Becky's taken my mobile off with her – somewhere. I'll explain later.... So try this number instead:...it's for my father's new mobile. Then after about 2pm today I should be on his old mobile number...." He gave him the numbers. Steve knew David probably wouldn't bother to phone his sister – he usually only saw her when they were all together - and if he did, and managed to get through, the crooks would just tell him he'd got the wrong number.

Becky had told her brother what it had felt like waiting in their hotel in Majorca, wondering where he was and only wishing she'd agreed to go to see the black vultures with their parents. Now it was <u>his</u> turn to feel guilty. This time, it was definitely <u>his</u> fault that <u>she</u>'d gone missing. They'd already known about the diamond smugglers when he'd led her into this. He wished he hadn't gone to look for the Bluethroat with her in the harbour area! And he resolved never to lead her into trouble again. But, he realised, it was no use wishing that he hadn't done what he'd done. He must think positively.

Knowing his sister, she'd probably be able to persuade them to let her go. Where, he wondered, were they likely to drop her back if they returned her? His parents had already asked around the shopkeepers and sailing people in the Leith area for any clues as to their daughter's whereabouts, and drawn a complete blank. Not there, surely. It was far too dangerous for the smugglers now. Reluctantly, he considered what Becky had said about <u>her</u> horoscope. She'd hinted at the old stereotype of a tall dark stranger. Well, even if he was right to be cynical about these things: maybe it <u>was</u> the tall, dark Alto who'd abducted her! And it would probably be him who'd deliver her back safely. After all, too many people had got a good look at Rodrigo. Yes: perhaps Alto would dare sail back with her in a small boat and leave her unharmed somewhere in the Edinburgh area, before escaping himself. How could anyone want to kill Becky?

There was no-one else in the computer room when Steve met back up with his parents to return his father's new mobile in exchange for his old one, which he was now taking over. "Have you installed a tracking system on your old one, then?" he asked.

Chris said he hadn't had time yet: "But you're not going off on your own <u>now</u>, <u>are</u> you?"

"No!"

The three Parkers were able to discuss, without being overheard, all the possibilities of where the crooks might take Becky: anywhere in Ireland - there were cruise stops at Belfast and Dublin; or somewhere around the North Sea like Amsterdam, or Oslo. Or the Baltic Sea: Stockholm perhaps...... or back to Spain. But they finally decided that, as the men had probably thought she was Maria when they abducted her, they'd probably just return her to the Edinburgh area and let her go, very soon. They discussed this till they were exhausted, and needed lunch.

There wasn't very much to be said over the table; but Chris reminded his son of his brave escape in Majorca, and encouraged his wife to bear in mind how resilient Becky could be in difficult situations.

Afterwards, while his parents went back to the hotel bar, Steve took his tweed jacket to put on over his heavy sweater, intending to go out later to the nearby newsagent's to buy the early evening newspapers. Keeping onto his father's old mobile, he went into the lounge again to look at the newspapers and magazines. While he was looking through 'The Scotsman', he suddenly realised he hadn't given Maria the new phone numbers, so he phoned her. This time he had more luck getting through. Maria had just finished lunch at the youth hostel and was waiting for the coach to pick up her school party to start work again on the archaeological dig. "How's it progressing?" he asked her.

"Very interesting! Full of surprises!" she told him. "Archaeological ones. But have you heard any news of Becky yet?" she asked intently.

Steve told her about the police response: the surveillance of the boatyard, and the investigations into all the cruise liners operating around the Firth of Forth. He knew she was used to maintaining integrity in these matters. Maria wouldn't tell anyone else, and her family would keep this information to themselves. If Pablo had already told them, she didn't say. She encouraged him to stay hopeful that he would get Becky back safe and sound. "The police are getting so close to the criminals now, that they probably won't risk killing your sister in case they're caught and given the maximum prison sentences."

"Yes," agreed Steve, "they were sure they were going to get away with it when they tried to kill <u>us</u>....now their priority must be to get out of the country as fast as they can!"

Maria wanted to tell Steve that Rodrigo was a suspected international terrorist. After all, she'd already told her friend Manolita; but then, she knew Manolita was used to keeping very important secrets – her family had long been friends of the Munos'. And she had to remember, that if the Parkers didn't know that Rodrigo was probably a terrorist, it would help them keep a cool head when they were talking and negotiating with their daughter's abductors. So she still didn't divulge what she knew about Rodrigo to Steve. Though inadvertently, she gave him a clue, when she asked: "How good do you think Becky would be in a hostage....I'm sorry, I mean... in this sort of... <u>crisis</u> situation?"

"A crisis situation?" Steve repeated, beginning to think about the implications of the first word she'd used. "Well..... not bad. She's a bit stubborn, but she doesn't sulk too badly for long, like some girls. She's quite good at talking herself out of trouble, and she can sometimes stay in a good temper even when she's under pressure. And she knows some Spanish. But probably not well enough to understand the criminals when they're talking fast..."

"She's got a good sense of humour," Maria suggested.

"Oh yes!" said Steve. "I think she'll bear up. And I hope they'll give her up soon. They can't take it out on her, just for being with me because she's my sister," he said optimistically.

"I know. I think they could have mistaken her for me," said Maria, reaffirming what they'd said was possible when they met with Pablo at the Dynamic Earth Centre.

"They're just trying to scare us off from tracking them down. They want to intimidate everyone by taking her captive for a while - as they couldn't get <u>us</u>."

So will you be staying in Edinburgh until she's released?" Maria asked, sure that he would.

"Of course, I expect so. Yes, sure! And they'll probably let her go any day now. Anyway, I'll phone you as soon as I get to hear any news about her," he said. "Do you think Pablo will stay on here after you go back to Majorca?"

"I don't know."

"I'll phone you before you go back, anyway. Like I say, I've got my Dad's old mobile phone to use now and there isn't a tracking system on it. But if he puts one onto it, I'll incorporate your mobile onto the network... Then you'd better not lose yours! Just take care!"

Steve decided to spend the rest of the afternoon reading through the papers. He reflected on what he'd talked about with Maria. The diamond smugglers wouldn't dare kill Becky, he thought, squaring up his jaw. But he vowed anyway that if they did, and the police couldn't find them for some reason, he'd spend the rest of his life hunting them down in disguise. As it was, if they weren't going to kill her - and they couldn't possibly be - they'd be giving her up soon.

While he looked through the national newspapers, he kept telling himself how important it was to stay calm in a crisis situation. One article described the taking of hostages by a terrorist group in the Middle East. He recalled Maria had unintentionally used the word 'hostage' when they'd spoken just now on their mobiles. And he began wondering whether the diamond smugglers might possibly have anything to do with this type of organization. He shuddered. Just what sort of trouble had he got his sister into? Terrorists often held onto their hostages for a long time, while they negotiated the release of all kinds of prisoners. But then, he thought, if this Spanish gang had any terrorist connections, they'd soon declare which cause they were representing and issue an ultimatum. And so far, anyway, these men hadn't demanded anything in return for Becky, not even ransom money.

As Steve went on looking through the newspapers, he made a mental list of all his sister's good qualities. As Maria knew, Becky had a good sense of humour, and got on with other girls (she didn't sulk for as long as David's sister). She was careful when playing her music, which usually got on his nerves, to keep it down on low volume if he was nearby. And she stood up for him: she'd even told a white lie to their parents recently when he'd stayed on at David's house for a ham and chip supper. (He'd known their own mother was cooking a vegetarian supper, which sounded unappetising to him, so he'd asked Becky to tell her he was helping repair David's bike!) Recently she'd generously conceded that bird watching could be interesting – and had even got involved in following the Bluethroat: unfortunately!

He pressed on, gazing out of the large deep bay window of the hotel's front lounge. She helped him with his school projects sometimes….. ….he wondered whether he'd got her good points in order of priority so far.

The early February dusk was just starting to fall, and a dull metallic tinge seeping into the whole sky was foretelling imminent snow. Watching a bus full of people stopping to take on more passengers at the bus-stop over the road, he speculated on how many of them were tourists. Suddenly he thought he recognised a face staring out of one of the windows. Wasn't that Rodrigo, though his hair was now short and dyed black? He'd shaved his beard off…..and Steve thought he could just make out the long pale pink scar running down his lean left cheek!

He raced outside as the bus started off along the road, to read the number on the back. He could see it was the Number 3 as it gained speed. Quickly he phoned Pablo at Police HQ on his father's old mobile to let him know what he thought he'd just seen, giving the number of the bus and the name of the road it had just turned up. "He's dyed his hair dark and shaved his beard off again, but it's definitely him!"

"I'll get a police car to follow it right away!" said Pablo.

"OK! I'll keep my mobile switched on!" said Steve, wishing he could either get onto the bus at the next stop, or follow it with Pablo in the police car. But he'd promised Pablo and his parents not to get himself into any more danger and to let the police do all the pursuing of the crooks.

As he reluctantly turned back to face the hotel and climb the steps up to the entrance, wanting so much to run after Rodrigo, Steve suddenly couldn't believe his luck. There, leaning against the front wall of the hotel, was a bicycle. It looked like one of the Edinburgh hire bikes he'd seen used for sightseeing. Someone must have left it there – maybe while they'd gone to look at one of the city sights - because they couldn't find a proper safe place to park it where it wouldn't be in the way, and perhaps forgotten where it was. Either that, or it was being hired by a hotel guest who probably wasn't going to need it again until the morning.

This was too tempting. He could borrow it to follow the bus. (And later justify borrowing a hire bike to help catch such a dangerous criminal, he believed.) Now that the police were on their way, he could phone his parents later to tell them exactly where he was. He'd say he'd borrowed the bike just to ride to the main local newsagents and pick up a copy of the evening newspapers, to test it out, assuming it was for the hotel guests' use; and that he just happened to notice Rodrigo. He'd tell them he'd phoned Pablo, and was waiting for the police to arrive.

And right now, he thought, *I can follow Rodrigo as far as I can until the police close in – which surely won't be long....*

Steve knew it was dangerous. He knew he'd undertaken not to follow the criminals any more on his own, to his parents and the police. But he decided he <u>couldn't</u> just sit around the hotel while these crooks were keeping his sister somewhere! There was no time now to phone his parents to let them know what he was doing or where he was going. And he didn't even know the answer to the second question!

He nearly flew back into the lounge and seized his tweed jacket from the sofa where he'd left it, putting it on as he ran back out. He needed the pockets to hold the old mobile in, as he already had handkerchiefs, pens and a notepad in his jeans pockets. He whipped his gloves out of his jacket pockets and thrust them on, as well as the cycle helmet that was hanging from the bike's handlebars. It was getting distinctly colder again after warming up gently for a little while in the afternoon, and a fresh breeze was starting to blow. He jumped onto the bike, checked its lights were on and raced along the road the number 3 bus had turned up. It was probably heading south. He couldn't see it anymore so he turned up the next road he expected it to go up, and luckily caught sight of it again. While it stopped at the next bus stop, he hung back and stopped to see if Rodrigo got off. But he didn't.

Steve followed the bus along its route, as the streetlights and the lights in the houses began to come on, and each time, at the stops, only one or two passengers smartly got off, most of them going home from work. The bus always started off again quite fast. He realised he didn't quite have enough time for a convincing conversation on his father's old mobile with his parents to say he'd gone on a short bike ride in the area to pick up a newspaper on 'one of the hotel bikes'. He was closing in on Rodrigo again.

225

He also soon realised the bus was heading out of the city. After it had gone down a few roads of older, grey-stone terraced houses with gardens, it suddenly came to a very large roundabout, with only big, busy A-roads leading off it. It started going round the roundabout. Did he dare follow it? This would be totally against the law, of course, and highly dangerous. A few rabbits had somehow made their way across onto the roundabout, and were hopping about and nibbling the grass. He decided that as it was an ordinary bus, it would surely soon turn off one of the fast A-roads onto a minor road leading to one of the outlying towns and villages. The police hadn't turned up yet; at least he couldn't see a marked police car anywhere, though they could well be following in plain clothes, in an unmarked vehicle. So he steeled himself and kept following the Number 3, racing as fast as he could and hoping he wouldn't have a terrible accident.

Luckily the wind was behind him. He probably wouldn't be stopped by plain clothes police if they were following the bus knowing Rodrigo was in it, but they'd probably radio for a marked police car if they saw anyone on a bike on such a fast road. His leg muscles were starting to ache.

Thankfully the bus kept in the slow lane, and as he'd guessed, was soon out of the main Edinburgh suburbs: just as he was nearly losing sight of it in the distance, it turned off at a sign saying 'Dalkeith Country Park'.

It was easier again following the bus through Dalkeith village. At the end of the High Street it stopped and Rodrigo, one of the last passengers left on it, got out on his own. He was wearing jeans and a black sweater under a navy blue padded anorak, and carrying a large grey rucksack. The bus drove off. By now it was getting quite dark, and cold. Steve was following very cautiously some way down the street, glad he wasn't wearing his anorak or Rodrigo might recognise him more easily if he turned round and saw him. He knew that wearing his thickest jumper under the tweed jacket gave him a different appearance. But it was quite still at this end of the High Street now, so he'd look more conspicuous anyway.

Rodrigo was walking towards the very large, wide-set entrance pillars of the country park. It wasn't officially open to visitors until April, but the public in

Scotland had year-round right-of-way to walk around open spaces, and there were no closed gates. Rodrigo walked through the entrance, past the closed ticket office and up sloping ground to the right where several huge bare chestnut trees were just beginning to put out tiny little dark buds. Underneath them lay lots of crisp, beige-coloured leaves. It hadn't rained there recently. It was very quiet, apart from the gentle stirring of the wind in the tree tops. And now, it suddenly started snowing again, very lightly.

Steve wondered where Pablo was. He leaned the hire bike against the big left-hand entrance pillar and phoned him. "I've managed to follow the Number 3 bus with Rodrigo in it, on a hire bike from the hotel all the way to the entrance of Dalkeith Country Park. He's gone in among the big trees to the right of the entrance. Where <u>are</u> you?" he asked.

Pablo passed his mobile over to Fergus Dalgleish.

"Steve, its PC Fergus Dalgleish here. <u>Don't</u> follow him into the park! We're in an unmarked white van. At the moment we're parked by the old church ruin a few metres back from the park entrance. Don't blow our cover by coming back over to us yet, either, in case he's watching you. But don't follow him into the park. Do you think he's seen you?"

"No, he hasn't!"

"We've been tailing the bus, and we noticed you as we caught up with it on the A-road: we saw you turning off after us. You shouldn't have come out here; this man's very dangerous and probably armed."

"I know. But I <u>had</u> to!" said Steve.

"Stay well back from him! Don't follow him into the park. Wait until you can't see him and he's walked far enough away not to be able to see you – and then make back for our van, please!"

"Then we're going out for him!" said Jim McCulloch to Andrew Morrison. They were sitting in the front of the van, both armed, with shoulder-holsters under their jackets.

Just before reaching the park entrance, Steve had passed the blackened ruins of the old church, still standing by the new one, with its partially bricked-up arched windows and thick buttresses topped with gargoyles, where the white unmarked police van was. He asked to speak to Pablo again, getting on his bike and turning back to face the policemen. "Look, Pablo, he's already gone into the park. And I'm going in after him! They've got my sister!" he insisted. "And it's a very big country park - you might lose track of him! Why don't you just keep following me, and then you won't! Over and out!"

He decided to start cycling slowly, casually through the entrance and along the wide tarmacadam driveway. It was all he could manage for a while anyway. He hoped Rodrigo wouldn't recognise him from a distance, and would just assume he was a cyclist out for a short evening ride and about to go home now it was starting to snow. Steve expected to be able to see him soon, making his way through the trees, as he could already just hear the dead leaves crackling. It was feeling like winter again: he could feel the deep cold biting into his bones as the wind kept picking up, and whispering around the tiny snowflakes as if it were reminding him of how it had been wafting thistledown around in the summer, then promising to propel the next summer's airborne seed heads to their destination, when next summer came.

In fact, the broad driveway soon swept round to the right, with the old Dalkeith House standing a long way back across a field on the left; and the raised ground with horse chestnut trees didn't extend as far as he'd thought. Rodrigo had briefly stopped to put a black woollen hat on then run down the slope on the other side of it, and joined the driveway before it turned left further ahead to continue through very dense, mixed woodland on either side. Now he was walking along it very fast, and was nearly into the woods. Steve hung back on his bike, for a while, nearly back-pedalling. There was no-one else ahead in the failing light; he knew the police wouldn't be far behind now, so he continued, very slowly.

Rodrigo couldn't have heard Steve on his bike, but something made him turn round. (He was wary anyway in case he might be being followed, and it was quite a natural precaution to take before entering a forest.) He could just make out the boy's pale face and dark hair in the dwindling twilight: he was bicycling up behind him suspiciously slowly. When the young cyclist quickly turned his face away, pretending to look back towards Dalkeith House, and inadvertently showed a distinctive square jaw, it was obvious it was Steve, following him. Rodrigo suddenly pulled out a revolver with a silencer attached to it (so there was no noise of an explosion from the gun, just a mild 'pop' followed by the zinging sound of the bullet going through the air) and took a couple of carefully aimed shots at him. Then he started running.

Steve had to do a double swerve on his bike to miss them: both bullets went past him on either side with less than a metre to spare. It unnerved him; but he knew Rodrigo would now concentrate on running away from him without firing at him anymore for the time being, confident this would scare him off. Steve didn't know Dalkeith Country Park at all, though he knew it had a lot of mixed woodland as well as fields and rivers: Rodrigo would probably have studied the map, he thought.

Rodrigo ran left into the woodland, among trees including sycamore, spruce and pine: some trunks were much thicker than others, and Steve realised he'd have to discard the bike to follow him in. He stopped where he was, to take the lamp off the front, which he needed with darkness rapidly encroaching; and looking back, saw with relief that the police were now driving slowly up the driveway. They stopped their van right behind him, switched its lights off and the four plain clothes officers got out, expecting him to get in. But Steve, obstinate, ran rapidly over to where Rodrigo had just disappeared into the freshly-scented woods – and realised he'd had to go through an adventure playground area. "This is where he went in!" he called back to the police in a voice as low as necessary for them to hear. Pablo and Fergus were carrying large torches with long beams, which picked up the little snowflakes as they fell disintegrating into the cold ground. They were waving him back towards them hard, while the two detective-sergeants had taken out their small firearms in readiness, though they hadn't heard Rodrigo's first two shots.

Steve took his father's old mobile out of his left jacket pocket and transferred it to the little pocket on the top right, which just held it, and switched it on. He hoped it might be able to video something of what was going on, though it hadn't been designed to take night-time pictures and the gentle snowfall didn't help. Before he could tell Jim McCulloch and Andrew Morrison - who were running into the tree-surrounded adventure area up in front of Pablo and Fergus - that Rodrigo had just taken two shots at him with a very quiet gun, Rodrigo aimed another at him. It whizzed past him, again narrowly missing him. "He's got a silencer!" said Jim McCulloch, who'd been trained in recognising one from the sound it made.

There was an extensive wooden tree-walk in the playground, about 5 metres high and wide enough to allow two people to walk past each other, entered at either end through a heavy palisade with very sloping wooden rutted steps up to the walkway. It gently zigzagged through the area with bends, resting points and solid, filled-in fences on either side which looked to Steve about as high as his own chest. It was wide enough to allow two people to walk past each other. Rodrigo had made for it as soon as he'd seen the plain clothes police approaching. He was now running along it nearly bent double with his head just below the line of the fence, to avoid being shot back at by them.

As the two detective-sergeants ran on ahead, Fergus caught up with Steve, who was only now prepared to hang back from the chase as the police had definitely caught up with Rodrigo Gonzalvez. "You're very stubborn, aren't you?" he said, propelling him by the arm and pointing to a very thick tree trunk. "Just get behind that tree and let us go after him now! If you're shot and we have to attend to you, we'll never catch him! And we **don't** want you shot!"

The police had decided to split up: with each of the armed detectives, accompanied by one of the other officers, moving in on Rodrigo from either side of the tree walkway.

"OK!" Steve replied, "I really promise this time! He's already taken two shots at me! That was the third!" and he positioned himself behind the big tree. Fergus ran on ahead into the palisade on that side, following D-S Morrison and shouting to him what Steve had just told him.

A half-moon had risen amongst the heavy dark snow clouds, and Steve decided to concentrate on filming the action as well as he could with the old mobile. Taking it out of his top pocket, he popped his head out from round the tree trunk and panned around the adventure area with it. He realised the park was normally too busy during the day to be a regular rendezvous for the crooks: plenty of people still used it for dog-walking and conservation activities during the winter. Rodrigo had come out here now because he was on the run and desperate (though he could well have been going to meet up with someone else on this night). Steve couldn't see him, but he must still be somewhere on the walkway. The police had just got onto it from either end and were slowly walking along towards the middle, calling to him to give himself up.

Just then a forest ranger, completing his evening patrol of the park, heard the disturbance and drew up in his jeep to investigate. Steve told him what was going on, saying he'd helped lead plain clothes police there after a wanted criminal named Rodrigo Gonzalvez. He was still filming what was going on in the adventure area with the mobile. Again, he didn't have time to say that Rodrigo was armed, before he rapidly fired three more shots at the police. It seemed Rodrigo had run out of ammunition after this, at least for a while; and Andrew Morrison and Jim McCulloch closed in on him. Rodrigo gave himself up, with his hands raised above his head.

One of the shots had grazed Fergus Dalgleish's arm. The forest ranger quickly ran back to bring out the First Aid kit from his jeep to him. He bandaged the young officer's arm and then drove him to the nearest hospital, while Rodrigo was escorted handcuffed back to the police van. Rodrigo was questioned on the spot as to the whereabouts of the rest of the gang, insisting that there were no other members of it in the country park and that he didn't know where any of them were heading; or who or where Becky was. Although his English was very good he pretended he wasn't very fluent.

Meanwhile, another marked police car with three more armed officers turned up. One of them, a woman, stayed in the car with Steve, taking a statement from him about what had just happened, while the other two immediately started searching the area. Once it was apparent there were no other crooks in the vicinity, Andrew Morrison, Jim McCulloch and Pablo drove back with Rodrigo to the main police station in the unmarked van.

Steve was taken back to the hotel in the police car. On the way back, he offered to send them the video he'd taken with his father's old mobile, if it turned out to be clear enough. And he gave an apology for worrying the police who were on the case by risking his own life. "I know I shouldn't have followed him out there. But it was so frustrating; he was so close to escaping again! And we caught him!"

His parents were waiting for him in the hotel's front lounge. They'd already been notified that their son would shortly be returning safe and sound after following Rodrigo - against all advice - to Dalkeith Country Park, where he'd finally been arrested. They thanked the police, who soon returned to the police station, then listened to Steve as he described what had happened. He gave his pre-prepared white lie that he was already out on a hotel hire bike to buy an evening newspaper, when he saw Rodrigo. It made following the bus seem less foolhardy: he'd tell them the whole truth later when Becky was back. Fortunately, they'd also just received some good news from one of the police officers who'd investigated the Bosun's Boatyard. "We're doing all we can to trace the owner of the yacht," he'd told them, "It may well have been registered under a false name. The woman who brought it in called herself Mrs Corvato. That's a Spanish name. We'll try to keep you up with all the information regarding your daughter as it comes in…"

Steve could see by his parents' exhausted, worried faces that it would be easier for them, and him, if they didn't know how close he'd just been to losing his life that evening – quite apart from the dangerous cycle ride on the main road. So he didn't tell them how nearly Rodrigo's revolver shots had missed him. "Don't worry, Dad!" he said. "There's a cycle path to the country park. We can easily get the hire bike back!" But Mr Parker stayed frowning, as the heavy sleet of the gathering snowstorm started dropping down the window panes.

Alex and Mick boarded the *'Empress'* as passengers, not too far apart from each other, but scarcely exchanging glances, in the middle of the next morning after Miguel and Eulalia were already on board and had changed into the basic uniform worn by the cleaning staff. Jaime, Alto and Julio boarded a little later, all completely separate from each other among the hundreds of other passengers, as Senor C. had insisted. All the smugglers were travelling under false passports.

Alex and Mick started settling into their cabins, which were quite luxurious, on the port side; but Mick became annoyed when Eulalia advised them not to get too used to all the elegant comfort. She said they'd soon be moved into two other cabins on a less busy corridor on the lower deck, where two individual passengers on the starboard side were complaining they weren't satisfied with their own facilities. "I let them and the steward know there were some other passengers who'd rather be on the starboard side," she said.

"What for?" asked Alex. "We could get recognised anywhere on the ship!"

"Because you're going to confuse whoever might be after you as much as possible. I'll let you know when it's been confirmed you can swop cabins. And you're going to dye your hair," she said firmly, giving them some dark hair dye which she'd bought from the chemist's on the *'Empress'*. They were both reluctant to try this, but Eulalia insisted: Alex and Mick's hair was lighter than it appeared on their false passport photographs, which had been specially adapted for this escape.

It was agreed with their international accomplices in the crew that the three Spanish men would take over three sick-bay cabins, usually kept locked and reserved as spare sick bays for passengers who fell ill. The police were already on the look out for Alto and Julio, and Jaime also was of Spanish appearance. No-one would even know they were in there if they kept quiet, because the only person to check them occasionally was one of the assistant carers, to see if they needed cleaning. She had had extra spare sick-bay keys cut for the smugglers; and the cleaner allocated to that corridor was Eulalia. This way, they wouldn't have to speak much and could spend a lot of time in their cabins - even if they were noticed, and the assistant carer had to explain that these three men were under observation with sea-sickness. But it was unlikely anyone would find out they were there. This woman could soon alert them if she thought any of the medical staff were coming to check up on the spare sick-bays, or put other passengers in them; so they could go upstairs to one of the bars or saloons while she explained they'd got better and had been checked out.

Meanwhile, Eulalia gave Alto some blond hair dye. The police knew what he looked like and he hadn't changed his appearance yet like the others. Although his fake passport used his usual photo, he needn't show it again if they escaped into one of the Baltic countries before the cruise was over.

The criminals kept in contact with each other by mobile. Eulalia told them she and Miguel were now pretending to be Portuguese with poor English, so not to be surprised by this if they bumped into them at any time. (Miguel was teaching her a few Portuguese phrases as he was in fact originally from Portugal.) Half an hour later, she phoned Mick and Alex to say she'd managed to get their cabins swopped for the two standard ones on the starboard side.

Once the two Scotsmen entered their new cabins, careful not to be observed by anyone, they used the hair dye, carefully removing the stains from the more basic bathroom fittings before they had time to set in. Now both dark, they were confident they were no longer recognisable to the police. Mick was also growing a moustache, which naturally came through fairly dark as his hair was originally a mousey blond, and Alex had already shaved off his beard and cut his thick red hair shorter. He had a big, chunky chin.

"I don't mind my new dark hair – but I was just getting used to marble surrounds and gold-plated taps," Mick pretended rather sarcastically. "I preferred the other cabin."

"Don't worry," said Alex, "Eulalia's having to clean the ship. It'll do her ego lots of good!" They decided to venture into the main bar for a drink before too many passengers came in at lunchtime, which was when the liner was due to embark for the Baltic.

The police strongly suspected, after making some enquiries about the crew, that the criminals were planning to make their escape on the *'Empress'*. Just before the liner was due to depart from the Firth of Forth, they boarded her to investigate. They'd already asked the Captain to send a copy of the passenger list to Police Headquarters, and they intended to begin by questioning a few people with Spanish names. They'd also be asking other passengers randomly if they'd seen anyone on board resembling their photo fit pictures of the criminals. The *'Empress'* was a huge cruise liner, with very big public rooms.

In the main bar, as Mick was making up his mind what to drink, Alex ordered a measure of 'Old Cask' whisky for himself, delighted that they stocked his favourite brand. He sent a text message down to Alto in his sick-bay cabin to let him know: *"They've got some 'Old Cask' at the main bar. Provided one is a bleached blond, do join us! Alex."* As Mick was ordering a beer, Julio phoned him from his sick-bay room to say that Rodrigo had been arrested. He'd heard it on the radio. (Julio, now that he'd been spotted with Mick near the archaeological dig by Pablo and Fergus, was reluctant to join up with him again in case it made them both more easily recognisable.)

The English barman had just heard from one of the barmaids that the police had boarded and were looking for a gang of Spanish diamond smugglers travelling under false passports. Though he couldn't hear what Julio was saying to Mick over the mobile, he thought he'd heard a foreign accent. There were plenty of people from various countries on board, but this voice sounded Spanish – or was it Italian? He hesitated for a moment as he sorted out Mick's change, trying to listen closer. But Mick had now finished speaking with Julio. As the barman turned his back to him at the till, Mick signalled to Alex that something significant had cropped up: "Big news!" he murmured. Careful to avoid a conversation with any of the other passengers, they both moved off with their whiskies away from the bar towards some comfortable chairs with views out to the ship's port side.

Alto came in with his hair and eyebrows bleached blond, and his beard shaved off, looking quite different. He was wearing a pale blue shirt, black jeans and a Fair Isle sweater. He ordered a tot of 'Old Cask' and decided to sit down and talk to the two Scotsmen as if they'd all only just met, in low voices, so they wouldn't be likely to be approached by anyone else. He didn't even recognise them at first, but they were still wearing the same clothes - Alex was in his favourite cream Arran sweater and jeans, Mick in jeans and a green sweatshirt. Just then, they heard the nearest set of double doors swinging back after Detective-Inspector Jim McCulloch, who'd walked into the bar in plain clothes.

As the Detective–Inspector strolled up to the barman, he glanced round the vast bar room and noticed two old ladies having a sherry and two or three other groups of people sitting talking. The bar had only just opened. Not far away by the sliding doors with a view out to port, two dark-haired Scotsmen were sitting talking to a blond man with a Spanish accent. So far as he knew, Rodrigo hadn't escaped from the police again, and anyway this blond man bore no further resemblance to him, appearing to be much taller than him for a start. One of the dark-haired men, Alex, was looking straight at him. D-S McCulloch cheerfully asked the barman, who was replacing the cap on the whisky bottle: "May I ask what brand of whisky that is?

"Of course sir, it's 'Old Cask'." The barman held the bottle with the label facing towards him.

"That's quite old malt," said D-S McCulloch. "It's quite a dark brown colour <u>now</u>, isn't it? It <u>was</u> a golden colour, if I remember…." he said pointedly and loud enough to be heard by the three men including the blond Spaniard, and watching to see if they reacted. He'd decided they were probably members of the gang who'd changed their appearance. The big dark-haired Scotsman had just given a very slight start and curtailed what he was saying; and he now turned round slightly, watching him rather furtively out of the corner of one eye.

Mick had just warned Alex and Alto that Rodrigo had been arrested. And there was something about the man who'd just walked in that made Alex wary. He didn't look like an ordinary cruise passenger: he was wearing a heavy dark suit with a mac over it, and looked somehow as if he was on business – although all the other passengers who were on the deck to enjoy the scenery were also wearing coats. "Come on," he suggested to the other two, gesturing over to him with a scowl and quickly draining his glass, "let's get out onto the deck!"

"I see what you mean!" muttered Mick, as Alto also came to the same conclusion. The man who'd just told the barman that it was a little too early for such a strong whisky, and that he'd have an orange juice instead, was a detective.

Jim McCulloch was contacting D-S Andrew Morrison on his mobile with a coded message to bring another colleague and join him in the main bar as soon as possible. Then, as the three suspect men went out through the glass doors onto the deck, he showed his ID to the barman, who told him: "The smaller dark man who's just gone out onto the deck sounded like he was talking to someone with a Spanish accent on his mobile just now: I mean, the man he was speaking with – over his mobile - had what sounded like a Spanish accent ."

"Thanks," said D-S McCulloch, "that's very helpful."

Once out on deck, Alex, Mick and Alto, standing among several passengers, soon noticed that a police patrol car was parked on the shore by the gangway to the ferry serving the *Empress*.

"We'd better get off this ship," murmured Alex.

"What about Julio and Jaime?" asked Mick. "What are we going to do?"

"Let's get in a lifeboat – most of the passengers are bound to start going in for lunch soon - and see if we can let it down when the ship's moved out."

Alto made a quick very quiet call to Julio and Jaime in Spanish to say that the police were probably searching the liner. "We're going to try to get into a lifeboat," he said. "Meet me on the starboard side of the ship straightaway, on the middle deck."

The three men started walking towards a less crowded part of the deck towards one of the lifeboats. "I hope it's obvious how to let them down," said Alex, "I only know how to use the one on the…ruddy…*Southern Belle*." (He nearly said *'Carisma'*, but used their code name for Alex's yacht, in case they were being overheard.) They started hurrying along, pretending it was because of the cold breeze.

"I'm going round to the other side to get into another lifeboat with Jaime and Julio," said Alto, just able to remember his English. "If we split up, the police might not be able to follow both of them! Like we did with the jeeps…"

"OK," the two Scotsmen agreed, and were about to say something else, when they just heard the big glass doors from the main bar saloon slide open again behind them. They'd already moved quite a way down the deck and Alto turned back to see who was coming through them.

D-S McCulloch stepped out onto the deck with D-S Morrison and another secretly-armed detective. At first they couldn't see the three suspects. But as they moved about questioning the passengers, Alto was in no doubt he'd be caught if he didn't move fast. Pushing past a couple of passengers saying 'Excuse me!" in as British an accent as he could manage, he walked very fast round the deck until he was out of sight of the detectives again at the front of the ship. Then he broke into a run to get to the starboard side, and dived overboard.

Jim McCulloch just heard the splash as he was moving fast to catch up with the other two suspects he'd just caught another glimpse of. Mick and Alex leaped into one of the lifeboats and managed to let it down the side of the ship. D-S McCulloch radioed to the police sea patrol boat to follow them as he dashed round the deck to follow Alto, with gasping passengers making way for him; using his mobile he warned his colleagues in the patrol car by the ferry gangway to stay on standby.

Alto had remembered to take the old silver brooch out of his pocket and pin it onto his Fair Isle jumper just before he dived overboard. He was swimming off now in an easterly direction out towards the sea, in very, very cold water. Fortunately for him, and rather unusually for that time of year – but not unknown – a warm sea current was beginning to circulate around the area. Or he might have suffered a heart attack from the shock of really icy-cold water. As it was, it was still just bearable.

The police sea patrol boat pulled alongside Mick and Alex as they made for the far side of the Firth of Forth in the lifeboat, and they gave themselves up. They were taken ashore to a large police van which had arrived and was waiting by the patrol car. But Alto, a strong swimmer as well as a good runner, had nearly reached Musselburgh further down the Firth of Forth before he was hauled out of the nearly-freezing water into the patrol boat, manacled and told: "You're under arrest!"

When he was asked: "Do you have anything to say?" he couldn't speak anyway as he was having to take deep breaths and his teeth were chattering uncontrollably as well.

"He looks like one of those Mediterranean sunfish that're replacing the herring stocks!" one police officer said, wondering if Alto understood his English as he got him to sit up. Then, noticing the starfish-shaped silver brooch glittering on his jumper, he asked him: "What's that, a conversation piece?"

Alto managed to nod, indicating that he was interested in talking.

When the sea patrol boat got back to the shore, Alto was taken, wrapped in a blanket, into the police car to warm up in the passenger seat. The driver turned the front heater on fully for him and he gradually became less numb with cold. A little later, the two armed police officers who were in the back of the patrol car got into the big police van with Jaime and Julio, who'd been arrested by Jim McCulloch and his colleagues on the 'Empress' before they could get into another lifeboat. Now Jim McCulloch got into the patrol car with D-S Morrison and questioned Alto as to Becky's whereabouts, while the other crooks, who were remaining resolutely stony to all questioning, were taken off in the van under armed guard. A few press photographers had arrived at the scene to take photos for their newspapers.

"You could have died in that freezing cold water, Alto," Andrew Morrison was saying.

Alto was just about ready, mentally and physically, to talk. With his teeth still chattering a little, he revealed that Becky was in a crate marked 'FRAGILE' in green lettering, in the hold of the *'Empress'*.

The detectives' colleague Gavin MacDonald was still questioning the crew on the big liner. Jim radioed him with the news and got the police sea patrol to take him back to the *'Empress'*, leaving Andrew Morrison with Alto.

Jim and Gavin raced down to the ships hold with a trusted member of the crew and started looking along the rows and stacks of crates. "Here it is!" cried Gavin, as he came across a very large crate with a 'FRAGILE' label on it in green lettering. They started opening it up, using a jemmy. A lot of nails had been hammered into it to seal it. As they worked, they became rather disturbed that they couldn't hear any noise from it. And it was <u>very</u> heavy. At last they managed to get it open – it was full of automatic weapons.

Then they heard the drumming and pounding of Becky's feet against her crate, which was on the other side of the hold. They rushed over to it, realising that there were two crates with a green 'FRAGILE' label down there. Reassuring her as they were opening up her crate - "It's all right, Becky, it's the police!" – they freed her.

Jim McCulloch sighed heavily with relief when he saw that she was all right, still asking her: "Becky! Are you OK?"

"Yes thanks!" She could see she was no longer at the mercy of the diamond smugglers. Then she assured them that she was fine, except for terrible cramp in her legs and pins and needles in both hands.

The two detectives and the member of the crew knew they'd had a stroke of luck trying the other crate first, because they'd discovered an arms cache, as well as the abducted girl. It had been organised independently of the diamond smuggling, by Rodrigo, for the terrorist cell he was operating in.

Jim McCulloch phoned the Parkers immediately to advise them their daughter had been found alive and well, in the hold of the *'Empress'*. The wonderful news was broken to them just as they were reiterating to Steve that he shouldn't have followed the police to the country park on his bike. And he was emphasizing that, actually, they followed him.

"Anyway", Mr Parker was saying as he answered the call on his mobile, "it doesn't matter who followed whom, because………Chris Parker? Hello? Becky's…..SAFE AND SOUND! They've FOUND her!!" He thanked Jim McCulloch profusely, while Steve, overjoyed, attended on the rest of the phone conversation with his mother.

Pablo realised that he was now going to be busy for several days helping the Lothian and Borders Police question the men they'd caught trying to escape from the *'Empress'*, and investigating their false passports and ID. Maria and Steve had already confirmed from photographs he'd shown them of the Spanish men now under arrest, that they were the ones who'd abducted them in Majorca. But though several suspects had now been flushed out, he was still needed on board the liner to continue questioning passengers and the crew before it embarked for the Baltic. He was particularly interested in the cleaning staff, as two of them, he'd been told, were new arrivals and claimed to be Portuguese: a man and a woman. The description given by Personnel staff of the woman was similar to the one which Becky had just given of 'Mrs Corvato' to D-S Gavin MacDonald, which he'd sent on to him. Pablo wasn't familiar with Portuguese himself, although it was a language very similar to Spanish and the two countries were right next door to each other. But he <u>could</u> identify a Portuguese accent.

First he questioned the man calling himself Marcos Chavez, speaking in Spanish and English, in one of the ship's small administration offices. Wearing a dark green short-sleeved shirt under his regulation cruise company cleaning overalls, he was medium height and had a faded deep tan. His large, rather hang-dog looking brown eyes held Pablo's quite steadily, and his full mouth stayed turned down at the corners as he spoke. He said he didn't know either language very well, he was Portuguese. He certainly had a Portuguese accent. He said he'd always worked at sea, and at the moment it was as a cleaner on this vessel. Pablo noticed perspiration breaking out on his forehead as he spoke, and that his hands were also getting clammy when he went to push his wavy brown hair off his forehead. But this could easily be because he'd only just stopped his cleaning for the interview.

Then Pablo called in the woman calling herself Izabel Silva. She was wearing jeans and a white short-sleeved blouse under her cleaning overalls, and a fine gold necklace. She definitely fitted the description Becky had given of the woman on board the *'Carisma'* who'd called herself Mrs Corvato. She was small to average height, trim, with blonded hair, brown eyes and a Mediterranean tan, and wearing make-up; about the same age as the man: in her early thirties – as indicated on her passport. She gave brief, pert responses to his questions in English, with a more dubious Portuguese accent. (Miguel had reminded Eulalia to try speaking with a slightly Russian accent, and make her voice sound rather nasal, in order to make herself sound Portuguese to this policeman.) Pablo wasn't quite sure if she <u>was</u> Portuguese. "Have you always lived in Portugal?" he asked her. Sensing that her accent wasn't very convincing, she replied that she'd also lived for a while in Spain – "but I haven't been back there for years," she gave quickly, "and I hardly learned any Spanish…" She was anticipating him asking which part of Spain she'd lived in and realised that this might give her away. Pablo noticed this and asked her: "Where abouts was that?"

"Galicia," she responded. This north-western part of Spain was where the Spanish language was a little more similar to Portuguese, and where she may have picked up a Spanish accent without speaking much Spanish, if she were Portuguese.

"Oh," he replied, suspecting more now that the woman was really Spanish, just from the way she pronounced it. "Well, I mustn't delay your 'bazar', or whatever the word is, any longer…" he said to both of them, using the Portuguese word for 'to make a hasty getaway', one of the few he knew. 'Izabel' looked blank, then across at 'Marcos' for help, who continued to look at him, though the constant expression in his eyes changed to a momentary flicker of irritation; then he finished: "Thank you both for your time."

Both of these people had denied any knowledge of the diamond smuggling, the arms cache or Becky's abduction, but there was no need at the moment to fetch Becky back to the *'Empress'* to identify them. Pablo was recording the interviews on his mobile, and he also photocopied their ID and passports so that he could run a check on them later. If they turned out to be Miguel and Eulalia – and he believed they <u>were</u> the last two crooks from the *Carisma* - they could be apprehended at the *'Empress'*'s first port of call if necessary.

For now, he had to get back to the police station to start questioning the men who'd been arrested. With the discovery of the arms cache, the police were convinced that the diamond smugglers were part of a larger operation than was originally supposed. While the forensics department would be checking the two crates with green 'FRAGILE' labels for DNA and fingerprints, Rodrigo, suspected of providing material support to terrorists, was being taken straightaway to London for interrogation, this time under top security.

*   *   *

Back at the main police station, the sodden Alto had been given some dry clothes and was waiting in the interview room to be questioned in Spanish. Pablo was going to start with him as he seemed to be the one most inclined to talk; but before he went into the interview room, one of the officers showed him the diamond brooch which he'd taken off Alto's sea-soaked jumper for safe-keeping. Although it was a little misshapen at the ends and now set with diamonds, Pablo recognised it as his mother's. The old silver made it distinctive, and there was no mistaking the design of three fan-shaped leaves, tied with a ribbon.

He went into the interview room with PC Fergus Dalgleish. After the official preliminaries, and being introduced to Alto as PC Pablo Munos, he told him that he was wanted in connection with diamond smuggling activities. Alto said nothing at first, but just looked at him expectantly, so he showed the brooch to him and asked him, in Spanish, where he'd acquired it. Alto, knowing who Pablo was and that Steve Parker was available to identify him, immediately confessed that he'd just recently started working for the smuggling operation but he didn't know much about it. He seemed genuinely contrite about his involvement in it, and invited Pablo to have the brooch back: "We know it belongs to your kid sister! I was contacted and told to go back to the cave to collect anything they'd left behind there….and found it. I wouldn't enjoy seeing my wife wearing it now, anyway: not now the kids have stirred up trouble for us again! But perhaps Maria will appreciate the diamonds I've had set in it," he offered, a little tongue-in-cheek, but nevertheless still somehow sounding glad that she hadn't drowned in the cave.

"She won't if they're stolen property!" insisted Pablo. But he believed Alto to be one of the more sensitive, less ruthless members of the criminal gang.

The next morning, after he'd interviewed Jaime and Julio, and helped question the other arrested men (none of whom were prepared to give much information away), Pablo went to see Becky and her parents at the Garden Hotel. Becky welcomed him with a broad smile. She'd made a quick recovery from the mental and physical stress of her abduction, and had given the police all the details she could about her ordeal. Now she was happy to just hang around the hotel, and be on hand in case they came up with any more questions.

They all went into the computer room for some privacy and he showed her the mobile recording of the two new cleaners on board the 'Empress'. She carefully studied the pictures and listened to their voices. "I've only heard Miguel, I haven't seen him – he was usually in the control room of the 'Carisma'. But that sounds like him. And the woman's definitely Mrs Corvato! Or Eulalia, which they were calling her…"

Pablo was now certain that these two people were the last of the crew of the 'Carisma'.

The man seemed to have been Portuguese, but had looked extremely nervous. And the woman's Portuguese accent, when she'd been speaking to him in English, had never quite convinced him. He remembered how she'd flinched when he'd tested her out by saying something quite complicated in Spanish, about diamond smuggling, which she was pretending not to understand. "OK, Becky, thanks for all your help, you're really helping us to catch these people," he said.

By now, the 'Empress' had disembarked for her cruise around the Baltic Sea, so it was in the hands of the Copenhagen police to arrest Miguel and Eulalia when she next docked.

Pablo told the Parkers the cruise ship had already departed, but that these crooks should be apprehended by the police at the next port of call. He requested them to keep this utterly to themselves, or it might jeopardise the operation. Then he asked them where Steve was, and they told him that he'd gone to the hotel pool for a swim. "OK. I'll wait for him in the lounge."

As Pablo was making for the lounge to wait for Steve, he was lucky enough to see him come through the lobby, returning from the swimming pool. "Steve!" he greeted him. "I'm glad to see your sister's OK. I've just been to see her and your parents. And I could do with you, to confirm something...." As the two or three other hotel guests in the lounge had just got up from their seats, he took him there to show him the mobile pictures he'd taken of the two new cleaners on board the 'Empress'. "Do you recognise either of these people?"

As he'd guessed, Steve had never seen them before: "Who are they?"

"We think they're two more people who were on the *Carisma*, involved in Becky's abduction. They're still on board the *'Empress'*, which is sailing on the North Sea now, out to the Baltic. But we'll be arresting them soon. We do need your complete silence about it until then."

"That's great! Of course, Pablo!"

"Did you enjoy your swim?"

"Yes. The water was rather cool, though."

"Not as cold as the Firth of Forth. We caught one of the crooks trying to swim away."

"Really? Which one?"

"Alto."

"The tall one......he should have attracted a shark! By the way, I've phoned Maria and I've told her I'd like to join in with the archaeological dig tomorrow – I haven't discussed it with my parents yet."

"That's a good idea. In fact, I'd rather like to see the Pentland Hills area again myself – and I've got a day off. Why don't I suggest to them that I go along with you, if we can get permission from the people who organise the dig?"

"That'd be great! OK!" and Steve went off to dry his hair while Pablo went back to see his parents, who were still in the computer room.

*   *   *

"Hmm... uncovering the past sounds safe enough," remarked Chris, "especially if you're going too, off duty." He and Pat had been discussing how to get Steve interested in something equally absorbing as international crime-busting, but less dangerous.

Pat agreed. "And archaeology's usually more organised than nature-watching, there's less wandering about all over the place! Good idea!"

"Let me just find out if they'd mind us joining in....." Pablo made a quick phone call to Professor Cameron, who said that they'd both be welcome to come along and participate. Pablo added that if it was OK by him, "As I'll be coming along off duty, after all the excitement of the last few days, I'll probably just prefer to spectate for most of the time! Though I'm sure Steve will want to get involved with all the digging....."

"Of course. We'll see you there tomorrow!"

Chris asked Pablo to relay his thanks to the professor, and when Steve came in, he briefed his son to stay with the international teams at the excavation site, and return to the hotel with Pablo at an agreed time.

Pablo, taking an early lunch break as he'd agreed with his colleagues, went on to see his sister at the hostel. They met in the empty dining room, as lunch at the hostel was always at 1.00 pm. The old radiators were giving off a comfortable amount of heat, and Maria's cheeks were a healthy pink. They spoke in Mallorqui. First of all, he told her just how much progress the police had made in catching the diamond smugglers. "We think we may have all of them within a couple of days....they're quite likely to be linked to international terrorists – but possibly just through Rodrigo. And there's plenty of evidence being collected against them. Don't talk about it anymore with anyone. And don't worry – you'll be quite safe continuing with your field studies now! If there <u>are</u> any of these criminals remaining around Edinburgh, they're bound to stay away from the area around the dig – where we nearly caught up with Mick Hamilton and Julio earlier. And just to be on the safe side, we're asking an undercover officer to keep an eye on it."

"It's all good news, then!" said Maria.

"Yes. And there's some more. I've a surprise waiting for you…"

"Oh? What's that?"

Pablo told her that he'd got their mother's old silver brooch back from Alto. "The Palma police believed Rodrigo's story about there being a rip-tide around the cave off Puerto Pollensa, although Jose said he didn't believe it for a moment. Anyway, they were busy on other jobs, so they waited before they went in there to search for evidence – just long enough for Alto to get back there first to get rid of anything incriminating; he found it wedged in a rock." He told her that it was now a little misshapen, and set with cut and polished smuggled diamonds.

"Oh!" said Maria. "May I see it? Where is it?"

"Well, before our family heirloom goes back to Majorca, they'll need to examine it forensically, because some of it's now stolen property. So I've given it to a jeweller here in Edinburgh to take the diamonds out (he might not be able to get the settings off they put on). And maybe he'll be able to offer the police some suggestions on where they're being cut. I'm taking a few of them back for the Spanish police, as well – they might have a better idea in Spain as to where they were originally mined."

"Perhaps they can return them to whoever they've been stolen from, if they ever find out!" Maria speculated. She was heartened that she was going to get her mother's brooch back more or less in the shape that it had originally been in.

Then she mentioned that Steve had phoned to say that Becky had recovered from her ordeal. "I already knew, because I've phoned her for a chat, and she sounds fine. He said he wants to join in with the archaeological dig tomorrow. He hasn't discussed it yet with his parents…"

"Yes, why not?" Pablo encouraged. "Actually, we've just all been talking about it: I'd like to come along too, and I've cleared it all with Professor Cameron, so provided I can get the time off, which I think I can, Steve and I will both be there tomorrow. We probably won't see any more suspicious activity out there, but if we do, it'll just be me who follows them this time! And the undercover officer, if he's out there by then…"

*   *   *

The next morning a fresh, blue early spring sky spread across the Pentland Hills area as Steve and Pablo took the bus to the archaeological dig. Pablo knew Fergus Dalgleish was being posted to the area to work undercover, but wasn't due to turn up yet. All the international teams had already started work when they arrived. Everyone involved with the dig had heard about the diamond smuggling, and people were keeping their eyes open for any more suspicious-looking types on the edge of the golf course.

Professor Cameron greeted them and showed them the area they were currently excavating. Then he took them into the site cabin to show them the computer graphics of the entire site: the geology, the vegetation, and the underground ruins of the Bronze Age Celtic settlement to be excavated. He and Pablo stayed talking for a while, and Steve went out to see Maria's school party on their patch. "Hi Maria!" he called as soon as he spotted her. When she looked up and smiled, he could see she'd been very absorbed in what she was doing and he'd just broken a profound concentration.

"Steve! Are you going to join in with me and Manolita?" Her friend was working next to her. They were both kneeling on mats, carefully digging dirt away from what looked like an ancient pavement with their trowels. Manolita waved at him with hers: "Hello, Steve!" she said in her best English.

The supervisor on their part of the grid, called Tim, showed him what they were doing, and then asked if he'd like to see a demonstration of the resistivity equipment they were using, first.

249

"Oh, OK, what's that for?"

"It detects all the underground features we're going to excavate."

"Sure. Thanks!"

"Here, would you like to try?" Tim gave him the twin-probe meter to take readings, while he held the cables out behind him. The whole of the area had been marked out into a grid to carefully translate the readings from the meter onto the computer, which produced an accurate map of all the underground remains. They took it right out to the edge of the site, over towards the next area which had just been fenced off. Tim explained to Steve that although they'd already done this once, doing it again after rain produced different results; and sometimes gave an even more accurate picture of what was waiting to be discovered underground. As he took the readings, Steve realised they were following a particular line, a wall of an ancient Celtic settlement.

When they'd finished taking the meter readings, his supervisor was impressed. Leaving the resistivity equipment where it was so he could keep an eye on it, Tim asked him if he'd like to help him and a few others finish setting up a grid on the next excavation site, fenced off nearby. "It won't take long, and then you can go and help the others with the digging!"

They used bamboo canes with coloured tape, lining them up carefully and making sure the poles were straight. After a while, Tim told him: "Actually, did you know we've already used the theodolite measurer to do this: it uses a laser to measure distances, very accurately. We've already made a grid with Professor Cameron and taken the meter readings from it."

"Then why are we doing it all over again like this?" asked Steve, stopping with his hands on his hips.

"We're going to compare the two methods, to see how accurate we can be with this simpler way!"

After ten minutes or so, as the last two bamboo canes and coloured tapes were being set up as straight and accurately as possible, Tim strolled over to report the completion of the new grid to Professor Cameron, who'd just come out of the cabin with Pablo. Just then, Manolita called one of the other supervisors over to identify an object she'd just started uncovering. She was very excited about it. The professor went over too while Maria, after she'd peered down at the intriguing object which was being unearthed, got up off her knees, which were beginning to get a bit sore, to allow the other supervisor some room to kneel down and take a look. He took over whisking away the dirt and dust, with a delicate little brush, from what appeared to be a Bronze Age artefact.

Once it was safe to dislodge it from the soil without damaging it in the slightest, he held it up and examined it: a long, elegant comb with curvy designs along both sides. Then he gave it to Professor Cameron, saying: "What do you think? A little weaving-comb?"   "Yes, it looks like it. It's distinctly Celtic." Professor Cameron described how the ancient Celtic peoples who lived here would have used it for making cloth, and how they decorated even their everyday implements with designs inspired by nature and the curving hills. "They might have traded their cloth for things made out of bronze – like weapons - further south…. Now it needs washing carefully," he gave it back to the supervisor, "then we can pass it round for everyone to take a look at."

Manolita was invited to follow the supervisor to watch him wash the artefact using special equipment in the cabin. Maria went off to tell some of the others what it was, and Steve followed her. A little group of students, including Tim, soon gathered around to look at where it had been found. Then Steve suggested to Maria: "Let's take the twin-probe meter further afield, to see if we can find anything there which they might have missed!" And he explained how rainfall could suddenly throw up changes in the readings thrown up from under the soil. "They're going to show us the results on the cabin computer in a bit, when they sort out all the data that's been logged in from my readings. Come on!" He took her over to the resistivity equipment Tim had left on the edge of the main excavation site.

Switching the meter on, he asked Maria to hold the cables out behind him, then he ducked under the rope which sectioned off the new excavation site.

"Are you sure they don't want you to do this with a supervisor?" she asked, having to take up the cables for him in case they got tangled.

"It's all right, I'm making a note of where these new readings start," he said, jotting the first one down in his natural history notebook. "They've just invited me onto this new site to help mark out the grid: and they've already let me take the meter over the site everyone's working on now....so they won't mind if I log in some more data for <u>this</u> site – we won't be in anyone's way, and like I said, as it's been raining recently it'll be useful to them. They can get another angle on what's underneath. And they're all busy at the moment. Then we can start digging again on your patch!"

Steve took the resistivity equipment right to the far side of the new site, with Maria assisting him. It was close to the sloping, gorse-covered ridge on the edge of the golf course, where the crooks had been spotted. Then Tim his supervisor noticed what they were doing and came over to see them. "I see your enthusiasm's running away with you!" he said, just as Pablo came over too.

"I hope it's all right," said Steve. "only there were so many people coming over to look around where Maria and Manolita were digging, and we've already seen the artefact – so we thought we'd make some room for them and come over here and do something useful for a while…..have you seen these new readings?" he quickly handed the meter over to Tim before he could find a reply.

They were rather surprising, indicating quite a large, square cavity beginning under the soil where they were and extending under the slope of the ridge. Steve had briefly beenshown how to identify underground cavities as well as other features using the meter readings, although Tim hadn't been expecting him to actually come across one when he'd taken him along the line of the wall on the other site. Professor Cameron was coming over now, too, his tall figure with the wavy grey hair moving very fast. Fortunately, as he came up to them they could see he was smiling. "Actually, we've already taken the resistivity equipment over this site: but let's see how your readings compare with ours, they vary according to how the weather's been, you know!" He was intrigued when they told him they'd discovered a large underground cavity extending under the grid, and went back directly to the cabin computer to take a look at the graphics with them. He took the resistivity equipment back there too.

Manolita and the supervisor who'd just finished washing the artefact had been joined in the cabin by some more of the students, who were learning how to proceed with this stage of an archaeological find. Professor Cameron, Pablo, Tim, Maria and Steve gathered round the computer to look at the graphics which had just been produced on it. They showed a wide, deep cavity as big as a small room, which seemed to be approached by a short tunnel, going into the ridge. Professor Cameron looked perplexed as he studied them on the screen. "I can't understand this: we went over the grid meticulously a few months ago, back in October, using the most accurate methods – and this didn't show up at all! Look, here are the graphics from the readings we made then...." And he brought them up on the screen for comparison. Everyone could see they were nothing like these most recent ones.

"Could it be subsidence?" asked Tim.

"Very unlikely given these geological strata, the soils and the weather we've had," Professor Cameron responded calmly and quickly. "And we're nowhere near the main part of the old settlement.....it just <u>could</u> be a burial chamber."

What Steve had found so interested Professor Cameron that he immediately started excavating around the ground above the short tunnel leading to the cavity, with Tim? Steve, Maria and Pablo watched them. They soon found that the tunnel began right at the surface of the soil: Mick and Julio had hastily crossed the entrance over with gorse twigs and spread dug-up turves and bracken over it to disguise it. The professor looked down into it, remarking: "Someone's already started excavating this chamber, if it <u>is</u> ancient. It's only a very recently-made little tunnel..." It sloped down gently into the earth and he could see the cavity at the end, made in the ridge. "And it looks like a newly-made bunker." He lowered himself a little way down into the tunnel with a torch and shouted up immediately: "No, this isn't an ancient chamber! It's just a modern bunker someone's dug out! I'm just going in to take a look!"

The professor could see the sides of the tunnel and bunker weren't going to collapse easily, or he wouldn't have gone in: there were crate planks put up against the earth walls to strengthen them. The bunker was obviously used for something of a covert nature, and he guessed it was connected with the criminal activity which had been going on in the area recently. In fact the smugglers had made it at night, to store their sacks of cut and polished diamonds, before taking them to the lighthouse. There were no sacks left in there of course: but the strong pool of his torchlight showed up a few tobaccos papers on the dank earth floor, and a couple of empty whisky bottles lying about. He picked up samples of these in his gloved hand; put them in an unused polythene bag he carried in the pocket of his waterproof jacket and brought them back up to the surface. "There's nothing much down there. But these are for the police forensics department," he said as he emerged from the tunnel entrance and laid them on the ground. "Don't touch them!"

"Old Cask!" cried Steve, the first to notice the label on the whisky bottle through the polythene. "Alto's favourite whisky!"

Pablo confirmed: "It looks like this was the thugs' hide-out: they might have used it to hide their stolen goods….and we might be able to get DNA samples from the bottles and cigarette papers." He called HQ.

Fergus Dalgleish soon arrived at the dig site, in his uniform. The police knew it wouldn't now be worth waiting undercover to see if any more crooks turned up there: the smuggling organization wouldn't dare send anyone back to the area. "It still looks as though I'm going to have to wear some different clothes on duty later, though," he said. "My uniform's going to be soiled once I get out of this bunker!" He listened to Professor Cameron as he explained just how they'd found it, and then went down to take a look inside. Mick and Julio thought they'd dug it well away from the archaeologists' excavation area, and when they'd last left it, clearly hadn't expected the police to discover it, or they'd have tidied up their litter. "There are one or two footprints on the bunker floor which might be worth photographing, or taking a cast of," he said when he came out; brushing what dirt he could off his sleeves.

Then Fergus told Pablo the police had now gained access to the disused lighthouse and found a makeshift platform and a portable flashlight at the top. This had presumably been used to give the all-clear to the smugglers' boats. "And do you know what? A rumour's been circulating around the area that the lighthouse is haunted."

"What does 'haunted' mean?" asked Pablo.

Maria, who'd been listening with Steve, didn't know either, so Steve supplied: "You know, the spirit of a dead person returning – a ghost coming back."

"Oh, *si, si*!" said Pablo. "*Un aparecido*."

"An apparition. Yes!" Steve confirmed.

"That's right," went on Fergus. "We suspect the rumour was started by the smugglers – to stop the locals getting suspicious about any reports of a light being seen coming from it. They'd think it was just people telling ghost stories. And it would keep people away from it, too. Anyway, I'm going to phone Jim McConnell now. We're very grateful to you, Professor Cameron. Thanks. You too, Steve!"

Steve looked at his feet, grinning with great satisfaction. He knew he'd helped complete the picture of the smuggling operation for the police.

While he was on the phone, Jim McConnell asked to have a word with Pablo. He said that now his day off had been interrupted by more unexpected investigation work, he was entitled to another day off before he returned to Majorca. "And while we're in touch, you might be interested to know the Edinburgh investigation team's just discovered that the *'Carisma'* might be owned by someone with the Christian names Alastair Hamish."

"Oh?"

"The full name it's registered under: 'Alastair Hamish Fielding' is false: there's no-one of that name listed in the Scottish records. But we checked on who was in charge of lighthouse security when the crooks changed the interior of the lighthouse. The director responsible was one Alastair Hamish Stevenson. It could just be a coincidence, but he's now a prime suspect in all of this. I'll explain the details to Fergus when he gets back in......see you later Pablo – thanks!"

*   *   *

Fergus returned to Police Headquarters leaving Pablo, Maria and Steve to enjoy the rest of their day on the archaeological site. Jim McConnell explained to him that Alastair Hamish Stevenson was on the board of the company managing the lighthouses. And at about the time the *'Carisma'* was registered, local witnesses remembered the lighthouse being repaired by what they thought were workmen with the lighthouse authorities. It was just possible that Stevenson; or an accomplice of his; or just someone familiar with him, used his two fairly common Christian names to register the yacht – and only bothered to use a different surname. Or: it could be a complete coincidence. "Now," said D-S McConnell, "Alastair Stevenson's basically retired these days, and only attends board meetings about once a year. But we have a search warrant to search his house...."

That evening, Andy Morrison and Fergus took away a file from Alastair's study for their investigations. It was the one with the 'company' sticker of skull and crossbones on it, relating to the *'Carisma'*. And it would soon expose a large, delicate network of bribery and corruption, including people working for the lighthouse authorities and extending to some of the most dangerous international terrorists operating in Western and Northern Europe.

"Here's to you, Steve and Becky, for probably saving me from being kidnapped!" said Maria, raising her glass of sparkling fruit juice up to theirs. The Parkers were hosting a celebratory lunch for her and Pablo on her last day in Edinburgh, at the Garden Hotel's bar restaurant.

Pablo joined in the toast, with a glass of white wine with Chris and Pat: "Yes, you could well have averted my sister's abduction – and even her murder!"

"And to Maria!" said Pat……

"Cheers!" added Chris.

"Now you can't claim bird watching's boring!" Steve insisted to his sister, taking another, challenging sip from his drink.

"Well, OK then;" Becky rose to the bait. "Now I suppose I'd describe songbird-watching as a fairly risky activity. Like watching your action replay of chasing Rodrigo through the country park in the dark……." and she leaned over to advise Maria, who was peering at the screen of her father's old mobile: "it gives you eyestrain after a while!" Steve had just given it to Maria to watch the video action of Rodrigo's arrest. (There hadn't been time to show her at the archaeological dig.) "You can't see Steve in <u>any</u> of that," Becky continued, in case Maria hadn't understood: "he was hiding behind a tree during the shoot-out!"

"Well actually," he rejoined, "the police have made a copy of it, so it can't be <u>that</u> useless! And that mobile wasn't designed to film in the dark. Anyway, that was the climax – he <u>did</u> shoot at me earlier on, but I hadn't started filming it." (Becky pulled a 'Really? You surprise me,' face.) "And at least <u>I</u> didn't have to be <u>rescued</u> …from a crate!"

Maria changed the subject. Her flight back to Majorca was scheduled for late that afternoon. "What are you doing for the rest of your holidays?" she asked them.

"We're letting Dad choose what to do," replied Steve, "except don't forget I want to

257

see Deep Sea World again!" he insisted to him.

"We've hardly had time to think," said Chris, "but I suppose we'll be visiting Dalkeith Country Park first, to retrieve the hire bike…we'd better leave it back where Steve found it and offer to pay the person who had it however much a day's hire costs!"

"And how about going to see the Edinburgh Parliament?" suggested Pat. "It's got a very interesting history, and you can sit and watch the debates."

After a thoroughly enjoyable meal, with mutual taking of photographs and talk of staying in touch and perhaps meeting again, they knew they eventually all had to say goodbye. But before they did, Pablo produced a small leather box and opened it, to show everyone the old silver brooch. It was no longer set with cut, polished smuggled diamonds – but was still misshapen. Maria was delighted to see it again, even in its changed form.

"I've just got a jeweller to remove the diamonds they had set in it. Now we've got it back – don't lose it again, will you?" he said to her.

"No, I won't!" promised Maria. "I'm dying to give it back to Mother! Thanks, Pablo!"

"It's great you've got it back from Alto!" said Steve. "I recognised it as soon as I saw it on his duffel-coat through the binoculars! In fact, it made me realise it was him, when he'd grown a small beard……But I don't think I'd have recognised it once it was set with diamonds." As he looked at it, he vividly remembered the ordeal he and Maria went through, escaping from the flooding cave.

They all agreed it now looked like a starfish – an *estrella de mar*. Steve, who was still considering working as a marine biologist one day, remarked that the diamonds must have looked like the little raised bubbly bits on the skin of a starfish, which help it breathe. As everyone was still looking at the brooch, he mentioned: "Did you know there's a species of starfish called the 'Crown of Thorns', with lots of legs – up to twenty! -? Every so often, it starts overpopulating disastrously and destroys really large areas of coral reef.…"

"Really?" asked Pablo, understanding most of his English as all the words sounded so similar to the Spanish.

"It eats coral."

"<u>Which</u> species?" pursued Maria.

"The 'Crown of Thorns' Steve repeated.

"I know 'crown'", said Maria: "'*corona*'…of <u>thorns</u>, what are these?"

"Oh," Steve searched for a synonym. "Spines, barbs….like a bull's horns – but on a <u>plant</u>…"

"Oh, *si*, *si*, *epinas*!" said Maria, as Mrs Parker was supplying: "A rose, you know, *rosa*, flower, when you pick it, be careful because of <u>thorns</u>!", and miming pricking her finger on a thorn. "Like Christ's crown of thorns. Jesus's," she said.

"That species destroys the coral?" asked Pablo almost disbelievingly.

"Yes: it destroyed 100 square metres of Australia's Great Barrier Reef, in fewer than 10 years!"

"I didn't know that!"

"And it's poisonous!"

"*Venenoso*!… T*oxico* - *si*, *si*," followed Pablo.

"So we can rule <u>Australia</u> out as a holiday destination," remarked Chris, who was by now recovering his old buoyant style.

"That's incredibly silly!" said Becky.

"It's poisonous, <u>and</u> predatory!" said Steve, trying to avoid a note of triumph in his voice.

Maria laughed: "Now, probably, this brooch will remind me of the Portuguese man-of-war in the flooding cave too!"

"Don't worry, the 'Crown of Thorns' starfish has got some predators of its own…..",

Steve added, mainly for his father's benefit: "it gets eaten by species like giant snails and puffer fish!"

They knew they'd all soon be in touch again; probably not while Pablo stayed in Edinburgh to help the police investigation team, as Steve and Maria had told them all the information they needed to know about the criminals they'd encountered in Majorca, and Becky had filled them in on the details of the people she'd seen in the lighthouse and on board the '*Carisma*'. But it was only a question of time before the Danish police caught up with Miguel and Eulalia, as soon as the '*Empress*' docked at her first port of call, Copenhagen. Making sure no-one except those at their table could hear, Maria promised to let Becky and Steve know when they did. By that time, most of the smugglers would have been caught and it would be Becky's turn to participate in the international videoconferencing during any court proceedings, to help verify that the right people had been caught.

"It will take some more time to bring to justice <u>all</u> the people involved in the bribery and corruption," said Pablo. He reminded Steve and Becky to let the police take care of <u>any</u> investigations the next time they ever uncovered <u>any</u> criminal activity, whether it was to do with the smugglers or not . "Say, Becky," he said hushed and earnestly, " ….for example: if you think you recognise the Scottish skipper of the small boat – we haven't caught up with <u>him</u> yet…: tell <u>us</u> immediately!" He raised his voice a little: "And Steve, you might make a good detective yourself one day, so in the meantime – take <u>care</u>! You've been very lucky…"

*   *   *

After all the goodbyes had been said, the Parkers decided to visit Dalkeith Country Park in the afternoon. It was promising to be dry again, and even a little warmer; and as they arrived, it looked different to Steve from how it had seemed when he'd first entered it – as night was falling, following Rodrigo. Now, it was fresh and bright. Although the leaves hadn't appeared on the deciduous trees yet, the ends of the twigs stirred vigorously against the blue sky, and the growing grass sprang rich and lush under their feet. They called in at the visitor's information centre as arranged, where they'd been holding the hire bike for him to collect. They took it back to their car and put it on the roof rack, then Becky asked him to retrace his steps from the night he followed Rodrigo. So he did, and she followed him, enjoying the gentle exercise. "This place is very different from the mobile pictures! They make it look so grim!"

"What do you expect?" he asked. "It's a country park, for people to enjoy themselves in!"

By the time they'd all looked around and had lunch at the café, and he'd taken a photo of his sister standing on the tree walk, Steve had some sunnier, less sinister memories of it to take home with him.

*   *   *

The next day, they visited Deep Sea World again, which Steve especially enjoyed.

"I can't quite warm to the sharks," Becky commented as they were passing through the underwater tunnel. Steve, who'd just stopped staring up through the glass ceiling, raised his eyes up to it once more, in mock despair - indicating impatience that she'd just said something silly again. And as he did so, he was lucky enough to spot a rare one, swimming directly above them.

The day after that, they visited the new Scottish Parliament building. It was an interesting building, quite angular from the outside. "Designed by a Spaniard!" noted Steve from the guidebook. Security was very tight. They were all frisked at the entrance and their personal belongings examined by passing them through special detecting equipment on a conveyor belt.

Chris led them up the stairs to the public gallery which curved around the chamber, to watch the MPs debating from the floor. CCTV screens were suspended on poles along the gallery from the ceiling, to ensure the public had a good view. The ceiling of the chamber was designed like the old hammer-beam roof of the Old Parliament Hall: it was constructed along the lines of early boat-building techniques, with polished, narrow wooden boarding giving the effect of the curving hull of a boat. The semi-circular rows of MPs' seats down below gave yet more curves to the interior of the new building.

As Steve and Becky listened quietly to the MPs, they realised they were in the middle of debating about the lighthouse authorities. One MP described them as very old-fashioned and badly organized: he received approval from several more MPs, who were nodding and saying 'Hear, hear!' and "Aye!"

Steve recognised that all the fuddle and muddle of the management, which was being taken over by a new company, had allowed the diamond smugglers to get away with operating the disused lighthouse for their own purposes. Pablo had told him the smugglers might be using another one on the West coast of Scotland, too. The Parkers were glad to hear that something was being done about the situation.

At a suitable pause, when the vigorous debate had run its course, several visitors started to leave the gallery. Becky leaned over and whispered to her father: "They've probably just heard about the diamond smuggling ring!"

"Yes, and demanded a debate!" he replied. "If everyone's ready, we can go back down now and look round the shop."

Steve and Becky bought a few postcards, including some of Edinburgh Castle and King Arthur's Mount. "I'm going to send one of these to David," said Steve. Their parents bought some to send to their friends too. "Do you know, I think I must finally, really be on holiday now," said Chris.

From there they went to take in the huge sweeping views of Edinburgh from the top of Calton Hill, formed by volcanic rock about 100 metres high. It was very exhilarating, with a climb of some steep steps to start with. There were several old monuments up there, including the Nelson Monument: you could see the Firth of Forth from the top of that, but Becky wasn't sure she wanted to go up it. While their parents went to check if the Old Observatory building was open, she and Steve gazed into the distance to see how far across and beyond the city they could already see.

"I wonder if I <u>would</u> ever make a good detective, like Pablo said I might," Steve said, focussing on the hills to the North West.

"<u>Maria</u> might!" Becky was impressed with her interest in becoming a forensics expert. "<u>You</u> might make a good MP – they're very argumentative!" she said, examining his profile.

Steve rose to the bait. "Why don't <u>you</u> have a go at being an MP?" he turned round and replied. "They work long hours – so when you got home, you'd be too tired to do any <u>more</u> arguing…!" he said teasingly.

"OK – I might!" Becky challenged. To her mild annoyance, he didn't seem very interested in pursuing that as a serious possibility, but looked back out towards the horizon.

"Anyway, I'd still like to be a marine biologist; I think…who knows what the future holds?" Then he took a few photos of the views, out towards Newhaven Harbour and Salisbury Crags, to remind him of the long chase through the city.

*   *   *

A couple of days later, Maria phoned Steve and Becky – talking with both of them on their father's old mobile - to tell them that the Copenhagen police had boarded the *'Empress'* and arrested the two cleaners her brother had questioned at Leith. They'd soon admitted their true identities: it was Miguel and Eulalia. They'd got Steve's mobile phone back from Eulalia, who' d even saved some of the film she'd taken of Becky with it when she'd held and questioned her on the *'Carisma'*. "They'll be sending it back to you via the Edinburgh police, by recorded post when they've finished with it. You'll have to wait for a few weeks, though."

Maria described how Miguel had written the mobile phone number of the Scottish skipper who'd taken Becky out to the *'Carisma'* in his pocket diary, next to a sketch of the islands around a particular area of the West coast of Scotland, with a note of the tide times. "The police identified the area from the drawing, and they've just arrested someone there who regularly sails his small boat round to the East coast. They discovered a bag of uncut diamonds in his cottage!"

"So that must be the last diamond smuggler arrested! Thanks, that's good news, Maria!" said Steve.

"No, actually!" she said. "Well, it's good news! But that wasn't the last diamond smuggler! The last person we definitely know about is someone known as 'Senor

C.'. They found a message from him, dated last October, in the Scottish skipper's cottage, telling him they were going to start dropping the uncut diamonds off at the Firth of Forth on the East Coast, instead of the West Coast of Scotland. Which the skipper kept – he said he usually burns his printed instructions…."

"In the fireplace probably!" put in Steve.

"Yes, they were lucky. Perhaps it wasn't cold enough yet for him to need a fire as well as central heating…..the Spanish police traced Senor C. through a phone number for him found in the skipper's address book: and they've just arrested him. He's Rodrigo's boss!"

Steve and Becky both exclaimed: "Well done, oh <u>well done</u>!" and "That's great news!" "And the international police are still investigating the crew on the 'Empress', especially one or two people who have recently…not yet…. nearly stopped doing their job," Maria didn't know the English phrase.

"They've given their notice in?" suggested Becky.

"Yes, I think so: they haven't stopped work yet but they say they are going to."

"That's it," Becky confirmed.

"And Pablo told me the Edinburgh police are still investigating some people who're working at the docks…"

"Great work by the police!" said Steve. "Listen, Maria, we'll send you some nice photographs on when we get back home!" he promised. He was sure the ones he'd taken of her and Pablo, and Manolita holding the Celtic comb, on the archaeological site would come out well; as well as the ones they'd taken over lunch.

"And we'll have some for <u>you</u>, soon."

"I can really relax now," Becky said.

Steve said goodbye to Maria first, then after she'd chatted briefly with Becky again, those two said goodbye again.

*   *   *

When the time came, Steve found it hard to leave Edinburgh to go back home. Both he and Becky reluctantly pretended to conclude, with their parents, that this had been another 'ruined' holiday; but secretly they felt the memories of it would sustain them through any boring times in the future. "At least you know it's hardly likely to happen again," Steve reassured them.

Whilst they were waiting for their parents to finish packing their suitcases, he and Becky went out into the hotel garden – the 'sprinter garden' as they called it, to stretch their legs before the journey back to Surrey. Since the beginning of their holiday, one or two more winter pansies and snowdrops had come out, under the winter-flowering japonica. They kept an eye out for the Bluethroat, but they couldn't see him. "Perhaps he's left for an even more sheltered spot," suggested Steve.

"Or there aren't enough guests at this time of year to watch him!" said Becky.

Before they all finally left their hotel rooms, Becky took a long last look out through her windows down onto the 'sprinter garden', mildly disappointed at not seeing the little songbird again.

"Come on!" Steve put his head round the door. "What's the matter, Becky?"

"I was just wondering where the Bluethroat went to. Isn't the sprinter garden boring without him?"

"Well," Steve obliged, "when I get my own mobile back from the Edinburgh police, I'll play back the recording of the male singing the Majorcan tune for you. We can copy it onto your computer as a holiday souvenir. OK? Now hurry up! Let's go!"

They were soon out of the hotel front door, scrunching over the gravel drive in their winter anoraks, carrying their bulging suitcases towards the waiting taxi. Their parents had already got into it. As with most of the mornings there at that time, they could still just see their breath on the air. Suddenly, a male Bluethroat flitted down from a tree onto a shrub just a little way in front of Steve, as if to attract their attention. It teetered its tail up and down for a while, then stood erect and sang a new tune from its repertoire.

"Look!" cried Steve, "Practically with its wings akimbo!"

Then it flew diagonally across their path, and away, fast – like an individual little 'Red Arrow' jet display.

"The Bluethroat!" Becky called after him.